PERŪN'S HAMMER

IAN HELLER

MENL○
PARK♀
PRESS⨟

Perūn's Hammer

Published by Menlo Park Press
Longmont, CO

ISBN: 979-8-218-61159-0
FICTION / Science Fiction / Time Travel
FICTION / Science Fiction / Hard Science Fiction

MENLO
PARK
PRESS

Perun's Hammer is dedicated to two women who, more than anyone else, made the book possible:

My wife, Penny Heller. You are my rock, my inspiration, my true love. Thank you for being a wonderful mother to our boys and the perfect wife for me.

My sister, Rosalind Fassett. You are a brilliant collaborator and I'll always be grateful for your incredible editing, insights and suggestions.

PROLOGUE: PERSISTENCE

Ding!

I pulled my phone from my jacket to see the message: *A friend would like to share a video.* I glanced around at the other passengers, bemused, wondering who had accidentally sent the file. I clicked *Decline* and settled back in my seat.

Ding!

Before I could decline it again, the video was automatically added to my photo library, which was odd. I knew I wasn't the intended recipient, but I couldn't resist watching it. The video was nothing special—just a steady, wide, drone shot of Chicago as seen from Lake Michigan. After 30 seconds, I stopped the playback, deleted the file, and turned off Bluetooth so it wouldn't happen again.

Ding!

Holy shit, you've got the wrong person, I thought, as I reached for my phone. Then I stopped. With Bluetooth off, my phone should not have been able to receive any files at all, so it was either malfunc-

1

tioning or someone was overriding the settings. I'm an investigative journalist, the lead anchor on a weekly television news show called *RECON*, and people like me are frequently targeted by cyber attackers. But hackers *take* information; they don't *add* it.

A little exasperated but now curious, I opened the file, fast-forwarded through the part I'd seen, and hit *Play*. To my surprise, a missile streaked down from the east, hurtled straight into the ground north of the Loop, and detonated. The devastation was incredible: Chicago's skyline was wrecked—the few proud skyscrapers still standing were shattered or bent, and a dark cloud covered the city. The CGI was amazing, so I decided the most likely explanation was that a nearby passenger worked for a film production company and had transferred the file to my phone by mistake.

We arrived at the station, and I walked into our building at 20 E Marshall, where I've worked for more than three decades. Since I'm a public figure, I wear a Cubs ballcap and sunglasses to disappear into the crowd. I took the elevator to the 43rd floor, dropped my phone off with Warren Del Rio, our Director of IT, and asked him to check if the security settings had been compromised.

I went up to the 47th floor and stopped at my assistant's desk to tell her about my phone problem and the weird video. Rosalie Jemison had transferred from our Washington, D.C., office just a few months earlier, after my longtime admin retired abruptly. An African American in her late 30's, Rosalie is blessed with an abundance of intellect, an ability to be formidable when necessary, and an apparent addiction to CrossFit. She's the perfect assistant for me—ruthless about protecting my time.

From my office windows, I admired the glorious, sunny panorama of the lakefront, stretching from Navy Pier to the north to Adler Planetarium to the south. Chicago is magnificent (for many miles), majestic, and energizing. There's an old song by Rodgers & Hart called *I'll Take Manhattan*. They can have it—I'll take the Loop.

I sat down at my desk, logged into my computer, and saw a notification: I'd received a new video. Strangely, it was the same damn missile-hitting-Chicago footage that kept showing up on my phone. I called Warren, who told me he'd log into my computer remotely and check it out.

Twenty minutes later, he bounded into my office with his ever-present smile and placed my phone on the desk. "Hey, Rich; I checked out your files. They're definitely just videos—no malware. They're both the same file and they're really bizarro!" Warren was a living contradiction: big, muscular, and handsome, but in some ways, a complete nerd. Scratch the surface, and you'd find a sixteen-year-old gamer underneath. He was also a genius with technology

"What's 'bizarro' about it—well besides the whole missile-destroying-Chicago thing?"

"It's at least 16K. It's the best resolution I've ever seen. You can zoom in super close, and the details are amazing!"

"That's interesting, but what I'm worried about is who put the files on my phone and computer."

"I'm working on that now." He frowned. "Nothing wrong with your phone. As for your computer, I'm looking through log files, backups, firewall software, and a bunch of other stuff. Might take a while, but I'll find it."

He deleted the videos from my devices, and I thought that was the end of it.

Instead, it was the beginning. A few minutes later, the file showed up on my computer again, and I quickly learned it was impossible to delete it permanently. Every time I tried, it came back. I thought I was just being harassed by some rogue hacker, but I was wrong. The mysterious video was going to change history. And since we wound up calling that "missile" *Perun's Hammer*, that's what I'm calling this story, too.

At lunch, Rosalie walked out of the *RECON* building, crossed Michigan Avenue, and found an empty bench in Millennium Park, on the sidewalk surrounding the Great Lawn. She reached into her purse and pulled out a Silent Circle Silent Phone. The Silent Phone looks like an iPhone but is designed for secure communications, including automatic message redaction. Texts are deleted on both the sending and receiving devices after a preset "burn time," which she had set to one minute. She texted:

Subject received object video. Threat: 1

When she received confirmation that her message had been read and burned, she replaced her phone and walked back to work.

1

LIFE IS LOVE, LIFE IS PAIN

March 31st: 198 Days Before Arrival (Cont'd)

Most nights when I leave the office, I take the El north to Lincoln Park, where I share a condo with my girlfriend Eliza, who's a theoretical physicist at Northwestern University. But some nights, I take the METRA North line to Highland Park, to spend time with my wife Angela.

I know what you're thinking, but you're wrong—I'm no philanderer. Eight years ago, Angela was cursed with early-onset Alzheimer's. Desperate to hold on to her, I took her to specialists, research centers, and alternative treatment providers, trying to stave off the disease that slowly but relentlessly stole the mind of my beautiful wife. None of it worked. In the fourth year of her disease, when our live-in nurse was on vacation, I took a month off to care for Angela full-time. She had treated me as a stranger for almost a year, which was heartbreaking and lonely. One evening, as we strolled along the lakefront, she stopped abruptly. I glanced at her curiously and felt a flood of emotion and desperate hope when her eyes filled with warmth, love, and—that greatest gift of all—recognition.

"Richard," she said, using my full name, as she did when she had something important to tell me. She paused and looked away, confused, as though trying to figure out where she was. I thought I'd lost her again after a fleeting moment, but when her eyes met mine, she still knew me. "You look so sad, my love."

"I miss you, Angela."

"I'm so sorry I left." She kissed me softly and placed the palm of her hand against my cheek. "I don't think I'm coming back again, Richard." She smiled bravely through her grief. "Be at peace and find happiness."

I shook my head, choking back tears, and pulled her into my arms. "No Angela, I only want you! Please don't leave me..."

She stiffened and pushed me away. "Get off me!" she yelled, her eyes empty now, except for fear.

Getting Angela back for those few precious moments ripped the scars from my grief. But as I attended support groups for families of Alzheimer patients, I learned how fortunate I was to receive Angela's blessing to keep living. So many others agonize over conflicting emotions, torn between the faithfulness they'd pledged their partners and their own unmet needs for love, companionship, and affection. I finally made the agonizing choice to find a memory care facility equipped to provide the round-the-clock care she needed. I went back to work and returned each evening to an empty apartment that I could only fill with despair.

The following year, I emceed a charity event for Northwestern University's Lurie Children's Hospital. My problems paled in comparison to those of children afflicted with life-threatening diseases, so I always helped at fundraisers, no matter my personal struggles. However, I wasn't looking forward to it, and I really had to work to be a passable host for the evening.

When the event was over, I was putting on my coat, my mind adrift, when a woman in her mid-50's approached me in the hallway. She was pretty, with a light complexion, perceptive blue eyes, and thin, blonde hair that was going gray. She seemed a little forlorn. Like me.

"Mr. Penton?"

"Yes?"

Our eyes met, and I sensed a friend.

"I'm Eliza Sage; I volunteer here sometimes. I wanted to say thank you for supporting us. There are children receiving treatment here who wouldn't be able to afford it if not for your contributions."

"Thank you," I replied, touched. "But people like you are the real heroes. It's easy to give money. It takes so much more commitment to give time."

"You gave time tonight," she countered. Her smile couldn't hide her sadness. There was an awkward silence for a moment.

Finally, I stammered, "Are you okay?"

"I was going to ask you the same thing," she confided. The tension broke and we laughed together like two friends sharing a joke, though we didn't know what it was. She studied me, as though deciding what to reveal, and then plunged on. "I lost my husband two years ago and it's been difficult."

I touched her arm to comfort her. "I'm so sorry. In a way, I've lost my wife, too."

"I know." Her voice quivered. "I know about that. I'm so sorry for you, too."

A lot of people knew about Angela. During the early days of her affliction, we had agreed to do a segment on *RECON* about our fight against the disease. Eliza must have seen it and guessed that Angela was forever lost to me by now.

I asked her to coffee, and from that awkward but tender beginning, we began the long, slow process of building a relationship in challenging circumstances. It wasn't easy for her to resolve the conflict of loving a man who'd lost his wife's mind and soul, but not her body. It wasn't easy for me to move past my guilt. As the years passed, we both just accepted that this was a part of our relationship and came to peace with it.

It's unusual for a national news program to be based anywhere except New York, LA, or DC. When we started in the 1990s, we were a regional investigative news show called *Chicago Reconnaissance*, which came to be known as *Chicago Recon*. Over time, the show grew in influence, audience size, and prestige as we poured our hearts and souls into producing the best damn television journalism in the US. By 2000, we were a national television show, so we dropped *Chicago* from the name and became *RECON*, one of the most famous news programs in the world.

While I thrived in big cities, I grew up in the tiny mountain town of Del Norte, Colorado. My first news job was at a small station in Laramie, Wyoming, where I met a girl who became my first wife. Two years later, I was in Denver, doing special features. Like most reporters, I wanted to move upmarket, and I eventually made it to news nirvana: New York City, working as an investigative reporter for a network affiliate.

I came home to our tiny apartment one day to find my wife had left me, which was bad, but she had taken our dog with her, which was somehow worse. I spent much of my time in New York lonely and heartsick; I was so miserable that I couldn't wait to leave. I wanted to be in another major market, so I applied for a job at a regional investigative news magazine that our Chicago affiliate was starting up. Less than a year after moving to Chicago, I met Angela, and we'd had a happy marriage until she became sick.

On the day the strange video showed up, I was scheduled to visit Angela and her primary caregiver, Molly, after work. When I arrived, they were sitting on Angela's fourth-floor balcony. She was dressed in one of her favorite outfits—a sundress we'd bought in Costa Rica years ago—and tennis shoes. The memory of that vacation was vivid and drew conflicting emotions, but I set them aside to speak with Molly.

"How's Angela?"

Molly smiled. "She's doing pretty well, Mr. Penton. She's been watching the boats on the lake."

At this, Angela looked over at us, but there was no glint of recognition. "I saw a big ship today," she announced, holding up the binoculars I'd bought her years ago. She loved boats of all kinds; our Costa Rica visit had been one of several cruise vacations.

Molly patted her hand. "That's good, Angela. What was it called?"

"The *Tillbeck*," Angela announced. "It was a great big ship called the *Tillbeck*. My husband's going to tell the story."

"Which story?" I asked her.

"About the *Tillbeck*, of course," she responded as though it were obvious. "And I'll ask Heloisa to help him!"

Molly spoke softly. "She stares out on the lake with her binoculars for hours. I can't keep up with everything she reports about the boats on Chicago's North Shore!" She furrowed her brow. "Do you know who Heloisa is? She's talked about her before, but she mentions the name more often now."

"Yes. Heloisa was a little girl from Ethiopia. She lived in a home for refugees in New York that Angela and I supported. In 1992, we paid for a procedure to repair Heloisa's heart valve—a potentially fatal genetic defect that could only be corrected with surgery. I never met the girl, but Angela visited her until Heloisa was adopted at age five, and the new parents cut off contact. That was really hard on Angela. I guess those memories still haunt her."

I didn't tell Molly the rest of the story. We'd spent nearly every dime we had to pay for the surgery and later decided to adopt Heloisa ourselves. But when we tried, we learned another couple had already started the process. Angela grieved over that lost connection for months.

Molly and I chatted for a while; then she went home, and I kept Angela company. We walked on the grounds for a little while, and occasionally she held my hand for comfort—not because she recognized me. Sometimes she chattered away; other times, she fell silent. Twice, she delightedly told me about her husband, Rich Penton, who was a famous reporter on television.

Eventually, I took a car to the station, got back on the train, and made my way into the city. When I walked into the condo, Eliza came to me wordlessly, held me in her arms, and I cried to my girlfriend about losing my wife.

2

WORTHY OF AN OSCAR

April 1st: 197 Days Before Arrival

The next morning, Warren appeared in my office door, a puckish smile spread across his still-youthful face. Warren had been an Eagle Scout and an All-American defensive end at Michigan State University. He'd played in the NFL until injuries cut his career short. Eliza's nickname for him was "Clark Kent," because he was earnest, 6'4", still built like an athlete—he'd taken up jujitsu to stay in shape —and was blessed with a full head of dark hair. Various women in the office thought Warren belonged in the movies, not hidden away in the server room.

"What's up, Warren?"

"I have a theory about why someone made that video and put it on your devices."

"You have my attention. But I'm honestly more concerned about *how* they got it on my devices. And why I can't delete them without them showing up again."

Warren looked perplexed. "I don't know that, yet. But my theory explains the motive, which may lead us to the perp."

I suppressed a smile.

He announced, "I think a special effects guy made it!"

I raised my eyebrows, amused, and waited. Warren's a smart guy and it only took him a second to realize he'd said the obvious.

"I mean," he clarified, "I think a special effects guy made it specifically to impress *you*."

"Why do you think that?"

"Because you're famous, you're on television, and you have connections in Hollywood. A special effects guy trying to make his mark would assume that if he put videos on your devices, you'd watch them. Maybe he thinks this video is so good, you'll send it to a director. Also, special effects creators are hardcore tech geeks. People like that have friends who are world-class hackers."

It seemed unlikely, but it was a better explanation than anything I'd come up with on my own.

"Even if you're right, it's not going to do the, uh—perp—any good. I'd never help someone who hacked into my devices. Hell, if we catch them, I'll prosecute 'em."

After Warren left, I was working on emails when I heard a chime, and then a notification popped up on my screen: *One video has been added to your computer.* I opened a Finder window and checked my downloads. The four-minute video was still there—but now there was another file, and it was much larger.

I clicked on the file, and it began to play. The movie had no titles. The video didn't fade in, and there was no establishing shot to set the scene. Instead, it opened with an interior shot of a tepee—like the ones Native Americans lived in during the 19th century. The director had found Native American actors to play a family: a father, a mother, a baby, and a little girl. They appeared completely authentic. Their makeup was invisible, and their costumes were nicely worn-in, not fresh from the wardrobe department like in old westerns. If the scene was any more vivid, you could have smelled the smoke from the small fire in the center.

The adults ate from a small pot; the mother was breastfeeding the infant and the little girl sat to one side, playing with a homemade doll. After a few seconds of this, the actors stopped talking and started listening to noises coming from outside of the tepee. People were shouting urgently in a Native American language—it was obvious they were raising an alarm.

The parents reacted quickly with practiced movements. The mother pulled the baby off her breast and gathered the daughter in her arms. Her husband sprang to his feet in one fluid motion and walked towards the camera. He pushed aside the flap of the tepee and stepped outside.

As he moved to his left, the point of view rose higher, revealing an enormous prairie covered with tepees; men, women, children, and horses moved among them. The CGI was dazzling; men on horseback raced around the village, rousing everyone. The scene felt real. It was gritty and dusty, with tension in the air.

Without the coordinated movements of a military organization, several hundred warriors mounted their horses and headed towards the hills.

I paused the movie. This film was much more intriguing than the missile video. Perplexed, I got up and walked out of my office, lost in thought.

Rosalie studied me. "You okay?"

"Yeah. I think so. I have a bit of a mystery on my hands. Can you ask Beth, Monalisa, Carl, and Warren to come to my office? You might want to sit in on this, too."

Beth, as befits a producer, showed up first, holding a notebook, a laptop, and a mug of peppermint tea. In her mid-50s, with dark hair perfectly coiffed and in a stylish dress and heels, Beth was always put together, even though she had raised four kids as a single mom. The news business is hard on marriages.

Carl, our top director, in his early 60s, arrived next, looking too pale and too skinny. He wore a wrinkled gray sweatshirt over a polo shirt and jeans, carrying nothing but his mobile phone. His bushy gray hair was unkempt; his glasses were stylish for the 1980s, and his tennis shoes were falling apart. Carl was a mess. But then, he was always a mess. He smiled at me, and I smiled back.

How are you today?

I'm fine, you?

Me too.

All said without a word.

Warren loped in happily. Given his encyclopedic knowledge of all things related to computers, I had a hunch he might be able to help us understand the technical aspects of the video.

Maura Lisa McPeek, whom everyone called "Monalisa," was our senior editor, cutting stories and creating animations and special effects. In her late 20s, she was irreverent, tiny, tattooed, and an unapologetic smoker, despite the harsh condemnation of the entire team. We heard Monalisa before we saw her because she was outside the office flirting with Rosalie, who clearly didn't return her interest. When she walked in, Beth asked, "Making any progress with Rosalie?" and we laughed as Monalisa scowled back.

"Fuck off, all of you," she hissed. "Just look at her; she's abso-frickin'-lutely gorgeous!"

"Thank you, Monalisa," Rosalie said, as she pulled the office door closed behind her. We laughed again as Monalisa sank lower into her seat, dying of embarrassment.

Monalisa managed to get away with blurting out things no one else would dare say, which is quite an accomplishment in a news-room. But she also tended to share—machine-gun like and with no filter—whatever thoughts popped into her quick mind. This often generated riotous laughter, giving us all wonderful, *You have to hear what Monalisa said today!* stories to take home.

Rosalie had been with us the briefest amount of time, and I knew the least about her. She'd come highly recommended by our corpo-rate HR department. She held a biology degree from American

University and had previously taught at a high school in DC. She was extremely private about her personal life, but she was enormously competent, and that was all that mattered to me.

With everyone seated at the large conference table in my office, I told them about the videos appearing on my phone and computer, explaining that I didn't know where they were coming from, and if I deleted them, they reappeared.

"Whoa," Monalisa said, shaking her head. "That's fucked up."

"Yeah," I agreed. "It's a pretty strange situation, so I want you to watch them so you can help me figure out what's going on."

First, I showed them the film of the missile destroying Chicago. It wasn't much different than a typical Hollywood disaster film, so no one was impressed.

Then I queued up the second video. After the scene in the teepee, the camera followed the warriors as they rode towards the hills. Soon we could make out U.S. Cavalry troops approaching, and the two groups began exchanging rifle fire. The Native Americans significantly outnumbered the soldiers, so the Cavalry stopped advancing. The digital effects artist was proving to be a poor director: there was no plot development, no music, and even the dialogue that was in English wasn't clear enough to understand most of the time. This video reminded me of some of the footage my photographers shot when we were embedded with the Marines in Fallujah. Terrifying, but clinical.

A mounted officer in the background was shouting unintelligible commands; next to him was a Native American—a scout from some U.S. Army-friendly tribe, I guessed. A crimson cloud popped out just above the scout's eyes, and he slid to the ground, dead.

Due to my time with combat troops, I'd unfortunately seen people killed instantly, and the filmmaker portrayed it correctly—they just go limp and collapse. I found this to be disturbingly accurate.

The officer was rattled to his boots by this, because he yelled loudly, whirled his horse around, and took off towards the woods as his soldiers followed close behind. There was a river behind the trees, and the soldiers retreated across it and began climbing the bluffs we'd seen in the distance as the Native Americans pursued them. There were casualties on both sides, but the troopers got the worst of it. When the Cavalry reached the top of the bluff, they worked madly to get into defensive positions, piling up saddles, leather satchels, food tins, rocks, and even dead horses between them and the Native Americans. But despite the modicum of cover they'd established, the two hundred or so soldiers seemed doomed.

Then the shot jumped higher and zoomed to a wider angle. From the southeast, other troops furiously drove their horses towards their brothers-in-arms on top of the hill.

The new group of soldiers numbered about the same as those trapped on the summit, and they enjoyed the advantages of surprise, momentum and—crucially—covering fire from the entrenched troopers. They were soon followed by a pack train—mules carrying supplies—escorted by another large group of soldiers, and the battle became a stalemate.

Abruptly, the camera turned away from the scene and rapidly flew north, following the steep bluffs that tapered to a long grassy hill along the river. We saw yet another group of mounted soldiers surrounded by a growing number of warriors.

Now, I'm no military expert, but I couldn't imagine why the Cavalry commander had split his men into at least four groups when attacking a much larger enemy. Hadn't he ever heard the term "divide and conquer"? Well, he'd done the dividing, and the Native Americans were doing the conquering.

This group of troopers was cut off from the rest of the soldiers— they appeared desperate and doomed.

I was looking at one officer who was wearing a buckskin coat, a tan hat, and short blonde hair when Carl called out, "I think that's

General George Armstrong Custer! This is the Battle of the Little Bighorn!"

I paused the video, and we studied the officer. Unlike other depictions I'd seen, Custer wasn't defiantly pointing his guns at his attackers. Instead, he looked small, terrified, and panic-stricken.

Warren pulled out his phone to look up the battle on Wikipedia. After a minute, he said, "Well, that guy sure looks like Custer. About two hundred and sixty of the six hundred men in the 7th Cavalry were wiped out, but that was mostly the group with Custer. He had two brothers, a brother-in-law, and a nephew with him at the time— his family really took a hit! He was a crappy general—he graduated last in his class at West Point."

He paused. "Those soldiers on the cliff were saved by General Terry's army—"

"The Cavalry rescued the Cavalry?" Carl asked.

"—yeah, but they won twenty-four Medals of Honor," Warren continued.

"For attacking Indians for being Indians?" Carl objected.

"Looks like it," Warren conceded.

"Carl, I think the preferred term is 'Native Americans' now," Beth interjected.

"They probably don't care, as long as you're not shooting at them," Carl grumbled.

"Well," I said, "at least we know what we're watching now. Ready to see the rest?"

I started the video, and from a high angle, we watched as a large group of warriors gathered on horseback below the hill where Custer and his men had formed a defensive circle and were firing madly. But they were quickly overrun when the Native Americans swarmed through them in a coordinated attack. One warrior rode directly at Custer, who wheeled his mount around to point his pistol at the attacker, but he was too slow—the warrior clubbed him off his horse, and he disappeared in the chaos. Soon, all the soldiers were either dead or wounded.

The film went dark for several seconds. At first, I thought it was over, but then I saw stars and could just make out the grassy hills in the moonlight. Daylight broke, revealing dead and mutilated Cavalry troopers lying in the grass. The valley where thousands of Native Americans had encamped was now empty, and we could see why. Off in the distance, thousands of mounted soldiers, with banners and flags, marched towards us, followed by dozens of wagons.

The film ended abruptly.

No one spoke for a minute as we pondered what we'd just seen. The direction—a generous term for this disaggregated group of shots —was miserable. The sound was authentic, but dull. There was plenty of noise, but zero attempt to use audio to enhance the film. The digital effects, however, were a whole other story. They were worthy of an Oscar.

"Fuckin' brutal," Monalisa said, matter-of-factly. "The missile-hitting-Chicago film looked like someone CGI'd a shot for a disaster movie. I mean, it's well done and all, but the second one was just an hour of brutality."

I turned to Beth. "Let's focus on the Custer video."

She thought for a moment. "I can't imagine why anyone made this movie. I agree with Monalisa that the CGI was amazing. Maybe it was made by one of those newfangled AI video generators? In any case, the video is a stark contrast to the awful editing and audio. Who would direct a movie so well in one area and so incompetently in another?"

"Carl?"

I could see Carl's eyes glisten a bit; the violence had gotten to him. He shook his head. "Well, I kept thinking, 'Okay, Carl, this is CGI, and these are pixels dying, not people.' It was just so damn graphic and, well, realistic. But it's not made like a commercial film or a documentary, so what's the point?"

"Any other thoughts?" I asked.

"Why would someone put this on your computer? And why are you all so certain this is special effects and not real actors?" Rosalie asked.

"Money, honey," Monalisa answered, drawing a frown from Rosalie. "The bigger the scene, the more money you save using the amazing skills of people like yours truly, instead of actors and sets. Also, it takes CGI of some kind to make violence that looks authentic. You can't bash in some dude's head for real, which is why violence in old movies seems so fake."

I agreed. "I can't see any other way you could shoot this. But we need to decide what to do."

Beth spoke up. "Someone in Hollywood may know who did this. It's a strange film, but again, the CGI is impressive."

Carl agreed. "I can make some calls to my friends in the Directors' Guild."

"Wait!" Monalisa said, sitting upright, making her diminutive stature even more obvious, since the top of her head was still a good six inches lower than anyone else's.

"Yes?"

"I want that damn video. I want to figure out how the special effects were done."

"I was thinking the same thing," Warren said to Monalisa. "Want some help?"

Monalisa shrugged with faux condescension. "Sure, Warren. But try to keep up, okay?"

Warren laughed. They were so different that it was easy to forget that the big, easygoing, jock and the feisty dynamo with blue hair were close friends. But they had a lot in common, too. They were both highly technical, brilliant, nerdy, and entirely forthright, albeit in different ways.

I thought about the next steps. "Carl, go ahead and see if you can find out anything about this film. There can't be that many Custer movies, TV shows, and documentaries made in the last ten years, and this certainly can't be any older than that. Monalisa, you take the lead in evaluating the video to see if you can figure out what tools were used for the CGI. I don't really know the capabilities of these new AI video systems, so take a close look at those. Warren, if you have time to help Monalisa, that's great, but our network security comes first."

"Let's not spend too much time on this," Beth cautioned. "We have a lot going on, and it's not like we can take this to the Pentagon to help them finish their investigation into the Custer debacle."

We all laughed.

"Okay then," I said, "that's the plan. Thanks for your help."

Our efforts to track down the origins of the Battle of the Little Bighorn video yielded no results. Carl found no one who could identify the filmmaker. Monalisa kept putting off my questions about the CGI. Warren finally admitted that he had absolutely no idea how someone had penetrated our security. He then provided a bewildering description of all the additional network security protocols, patches, and software he had added to prevent future intrusions.

As investigative journalists, we double down when a problem becomes more difficult to solve. But the harder we tried to figure out the origin and meaning of the videos, the more mysterious they became.

The evening after the team watched the Battle of the Little Bighorn video, Rosalie stood alone in her kitchen. Using her Silent Phone, she texted:

Subject received BLB asset. Viewed/discussed in group. Threat:1.5

Once she received the confirmation and the message was burned, she shoved the phone into her bag and went to bed.

A few years earlier, the Russian space agency, Roscosmos, launched two satellites seven months apart. The Leonid Kulik *carried a powerful, infrared, deep space telescope and embarked on the long journey to the far side of the Sun, where it gathered detailed images impossible to capture from any other vantage point. Notably, the telescope not only searched along the horizontal plane of the planets, but it also scanned the vertical or Z-axis, which helped it spot interstellar objects. The* Nikolay Federov *was a relatively simple communications relay satellite, positioned to receive data from* Kulik *and transmit it to earth stations operated by Roscosmos. This data was encrypted.*

The Russians kept the reasons for these missions a secret from the rest of the world. NASA was frustrated that Roscosmos was encrypting data transmissions from a scientific mission. However, given the state of relations between the two nations since Russia invaded Ukraine, that wasn't much of a surprise. Various U.S. intelligence agencies decided the satellites were not a threat, and other than noting their locations in space, made no attempt to gather more information about them.

3

TO REALITY AND BACK AGAIN

That night, I showed Eliza the missile video on my phone as we sat on our terrace, thirty-five floors above the city. When I told her about the Custer video, she was even more intrigued. We moved to the kitchen, I fetched my laptop, and we spent hours researching the event.

Finally, she stretched and yawned. "Your next step isn't about finding a filmmaker. You need to find an historian." I laughed, but she was serious. "You have a lot of assumptions about the motivation of whomever made this video, but you're just guessing. What if this isn't about entertainment? If the filmmaker's goal is to answer historical questions, he wouldn't worry about production values like editing and a soundtrack."

I tried to be open-minded about it, but it didn't make sense to me. "I don't see it. Why go to all this effort to produce a hyper-detailed movie about a battle from a hundred and fifty years ago, just to make a historical argument? I mean, who cares? *Cui bono?*"

Eliza rolled her eyes. "That's what's wrong with businesspeople and journalists. You think everyone is motivated solely by their own self-interest."

I surrendered the point, and we went to bed. We lay under the covers, and I held her close, wondering at her instincts and her brilliant mind. She was a physicist at one of the world's leading educational institutions but retained the open mind some scientists lose over time. She didn't scorn or dismiss me when I talked about hunches and intuition.

I don't really understand Eliza's work (I tell her, "I don't speak math"), but investigative journalists believe in hunches—ours and other people's—and her suggestion resonated with me. I decided to find an historian who specialized in the Battle of the Little Bighorn so I could get an expert's opinion on the strange video that had appeared on my desktop that morning.

Well, technically, the previous morning? Had it only been eighteen hours? I pondered the strange concept of time and how it goes by so fast some days, so slow on others. *How sad that it only goes in one direction.*

A few days later, I flew to Grand Junction, Colorado, to meet with Dr. Samuel Whitlock, one of the leading authorities on the Battle of the Little Bighorn. After landing, I grabbed my luggage, switched on my phone, and it buzzed with incoming text messages as I walked off the plane. I flipped through several of them and then read one from Monalisa that said: *I don't think it's CGI.* As soon as I started the rental car, I called her.

"I know it's crazy," she answered instead of saying hello. "But I can't find any evidence of CGI in your fucking movie!" Monalisa's use of the f-word increased in proportion to her level of excitement.

"Wait, Mona—"

"I started with the basics," she interrupted, with an impressive, rapid-fire delivery. "You know, like mismatched lighting. Amateurs get this wrong, so the angles of shadows aren't consistent and shit like that, but I knew this guy was a professional, so I checked, and I wasn't surprised he got something basic like that right. He's doesn't shoot for shit, but he's no fuckup for accuracy."

"Well, do you think—"

She ignored me again. "Same thing with focus mismatch. I didn't find any evidence of that either."

Focus mismatch is a common way to spot videos with poor CGI. If you combine elements from two video files, it's extremely difficult to ensure that all objects and people that are supposed to be at the same distance from the camera move in and out of focus together.

"You're saying there was no focus mismatch?" I asked quickly, trying to participate in the conversation.

"NO, RICH!" Monalisa yelled, "because EVERYTHING is in focus! Do you know how fucking weird it is for EVERYTHING at EVERY DISTANCE in EVERY FRAME in an HOUR-LONG video to be IN FOCUS?"

"Very weird?"

"ABSO-FRICKIN'-LUTELY WEIRD! And there's no color mismatch, either." She slowed down, talking to me like she was explaining this to a child. "That's when colors aren't consistent across the frame because the effects and real elements weren't rendered to the same light temperature. 'Light temperature' is when—"

"I know what light temperature is! And focus and color mismatch too, for that matter. For God's sake, I've been in television for forty years."

"Yeah," she replied, dismissively, "but most of that was when there was ancient technology. Today's editing systems are all younger than I am, so I can't assume anything. Were your early shows even in color?"

"Yes, they were in color! Please stay on topic."

"Sorry," she conceded. "There aren't any hidden pixels in this video, either. And I checked every AI generator on the market right now. I even researched emerging capabilities and then I ran multiple AI detection algorithms and forensic software. There's nothing artificial in the film. The audio-video synchronization is perfect, there aren't any odd audio artifacts, no inconsistent elements like mismatched backgrounds, weird facial expressions, unnatural movements, biometric inconsistencies—nothing.

"And there's more. I used an app called SunCalc, which can plot the angle, direction, and movement of the Sun for any geo coordinates, for any date and time. So, I uploaded the coordinates for the battlefield and, guess what?"

"What?"

"The fucking Sun is in exactly the right fucking place for the whole fucking battle!" she yelled.

"I agree; that *is* weird. But whoever made the film could have used SunCalc the way you did—maybe he's just detail-oriented."

"Oh, yeah?" she challenged. "Try this out for detail-oriented. I had a friend run every distinct face through Clearview AI."

I felt my pulse speed up. "How'd you get access to that?" I was nervous that our determined young editor was going to get in trouble. Clearview AI can only be used by law enforcement agencies and can identify a person from a photograph with 99 percent accuracy.

"Dude, I wish I could tell you, but I can't," she replied, savoring the secret. "But not one face matched to any living person."

"Monalisa, that doesn't help your case that this isn't CGI. In fact, it practically proves the film *is* CGI. A real film would have actors, and Clearview would have found a match somewhere!"

I could feel her relishing the moment—her *case closed* argument had arrived.

"I said any *living* person. Clearview identified Custer and several other U.S. Cavalry officers! Explain that!"

My head was spinning. "Wait, wait, wait. You're saying someone rendered likenesses of those individuals into the video?"

"I don't know how they got in there. I can't find one fucking bit of evidence that there is any fucking CGI in this fucking cowboys and Native Americans movie!"

We were both silent for a second, but I was unable to resist correcting her. "Um, actually, it's a *soldiers* and Native Americans movie."

"Really?" she replied, disgusted. "I just told you one of the most amazing things you'll ever hear in your whole goddamn life, and you're correcting my word choice? Jesus *Christ!*"

I laughed—at her wild enthusiasm, the preposterousness of the situation, and the completely unexpected news she'd dumped on me during my ten-minute drive. "Sorry. I couldn't help myself. But what are you saying? No one videotaped the Battle of the Little Bighorn!"

"I know that; I'm not stupid," Monalisa protested. "There's not one frame in this video where any of the cowboys—sorry—SOLDIERS or Native Americans shows any recognition they're being filmed. It's obviously a production film and not archival footage, because even if you could travel back in time to videotape the scene, someone would sure as hell be staring at the crazy film people. And probably shooting at them, too!"

I pulled into one of the guest parking spaces at Colorado Mesa University. I glanced at my phone: ten minutes before my meeting. Time to get some coffee and find the professor's office.

"Okay, then. What's your opinion about the source of the video?"

She paused for a few moments before answering. "Two alternatives. One is that it's a scene from an expensive movie filmed with some breakthrough cameras that have infinite depth of field, made by a director who has an unbelievable devotion to historical accuracy but a poor fucking grasp of cinematography, audio engineering, or editing—and who found actors who look exactly like Custer and some of his officers..."

"And the second alternative?"

"Someone's created a whole new type of special effects that no one has ever used before. It's decades beyond even our best CGI and AI tools. And don't tell me that maybe it's something new that I haven't heard of yet, Rich, or I swear I will fuckin' kill you, because I am all over this stuff—from Google to the dark web—nobody knows more about what's cutting edge than *me!*"

I caught up with her words and understood that between the bravado, swearing, and threats, she was saying that the second alternative was a new form of CGI. Got it. "I believe you," I reassured her, knowing that anything less than full agreement might lead to my imminent death. "So, of the two alternatives, which one do you think it is?"

"It had to be created digitally, but not the way we do it today," she concluded. "That's why I said it's *not* CGI or AI—at least, not the way we know it. The perfect focus at every depth of field is only possible with computers. And that's just one of the problems. I'm going to find out who made this video and how, Rich. I abso-frickin'-lutely have to know."

"Wait," I said sharply. "I want to know, too. But I don't want to share this with anyone until we have more information."

"I won't bring anyone new into the loop," she protested. "And, FYI, I haven't!"

Except for your Clearview friend, I thought, but decided not to say it out loud. "I have to go," I said, as I climbed out of the car.

"Call us when you're done. Everyone in the office wants to know what the professor says." Then she hung up.

Were phone greetings going out of style? I wondered as I walked across the campus.

After a stop at a coffee shop, I found Professor Samuel Whitlock's office. The door was open, and I could see a man sitting at a desk inside, but I politely knocked on the metal frame. The man looked up.

"Professor Whitlock?" I asked, recognizing him from photos I'd seen.

"Call me Sam, please." He shook my hand and waved me into a seat. "To what do I owe this honor? I have to say that when Rich Penton wants to see you but won't tell you why, you begin to wonder what scandal you've gotten involved in. In my case, without even knowing it!"

I immediately liked the Professor. About my age, he was a little taller than I was, with silver hair, glasses, and a thick mustache. "There's no scandal here, Professor," I reassured him. "But I recently received some information about the Battle of the Little Bighorn, and I'd like to get your expert opinion." I realized I was still calling him Professor instead of Sam, but that's how Eliza and I had referred to him after I told her about my trip. I gestured towards the door. "Okay if I close that?"

Whitlock smiled and wiggled his bushy eyebrows. "The mystery deepens."

I chuckled as I pulled out my laptop. "I want to show you a video. It's forty-four minutes long."

Whitlock frowned slightly. "Couldn't you have just emailed it to me? Or sent a Dropbox link or something?"

"I'm afraid not. I need to show it to you myself, and I'm sorry that I can't leave you a copy either."

Whitlock was unimpressed. "I don't even know what it is yet. So, I'm not sure if that's a loss."

"Fair enough," I laughed. "Me neither."

I set my laptop on his desk, opened the screen, and pulled my chair next to his. I clicked on the file and the video started.

I had to play the video over and over again because Whitlock was astounded at its accuracy. At 12:30 a.m., I protested that we absolutely had to stop for the night. I checked into a local hotel and slept soundly—until 7:10 a.m., when the phone in my room began ringing. I woke up in a daze and floundered around until I could find the receiver.

"Hello?" I grumbled.

"Rich, it's Sam Whitlock. Time to get up. I'm in the lobby, and I've got a cup of coffee for you. We're going to Billings, Montana, on an 8:45 flight."

I yawned and shook my head, waiting for my brain to function again. Then I realized what he meant.

"The Little Bighorn?"

"Yep," he confirmed. "The Little Bighorn."

Monalisa and Warren's friendship began five years earlier when they realized they were both playing *World of Warcraft* online. They started teaming up in the game from their respective apartments and enjoyed it so much, they kept playing as new expansion packs were released. Ever since, they'd spent several nights a month chatting over gaming headsets as they played deep into the night.

They started having lunch together and this turned into drinks after work, and then Monalisa invited him to meet up with her friends on a Friday evening. Warren had always been part of the jock crowd, and Monalisa's friends were very different. They included gays, trans, crossdressers, and other free spirits who were accepting, friendly and fun. Over time Warren became part of the group—despite his Clark Kent appearance.

He'd walked Monalisa home on many occasions; twice he had to hold her up because she'd partied too hard, and at other times, he comforted her for hours because a girl had broken her heart. His friendship with Monalisa brought joy, laughter, entertainment, and a wonderful group of people into his life.

Eventually, he realized he had fallen in love with her, which was a strange situation for Warren. He was always pursued, never the pursuer, and here was a woman he adored but could never have.

One Friday night after they'd had a little too much to drink, they went back to her apartment, and he poured out his emotions.

Monalisa smiled affectionately at him. She took him in her arms and held him tightly. Then she used both hands to pull his face close to hers, kissed him once on the lips, and said softly, "I love you too, you gorgeous bastard. But I don't want to sleep with you."

The walk home that night had been lonely and sad for Warren. When he woke up the next morning, he was horrified by what he'd done. Hung over and worried he'd ruined their friendship, he collapsed on his couch in his Michigan State Football pajamas, flipped on the television and scrolled through the channels, wallowing in misery.

There was a knock at the door. Warren opened it to find Monalisa there, dressed up, hair styled, wearing sunglasses, and holding a smoldering cigarette. She looked Warren up and down for a moment and shook her head.

"Cool jams. Now get dressed; we're going to Tiztal for chilaquiles."

Warren stared at her, amazed and grateful that she wasn't there to end the friendship after his outburst.

Monalisa sighed. "Warren, I'm hung over, and I need coffee and breakfast, or I'm going to be *impossible* to be around. Get moving!"

Although they teased each other about almost everything, in the years since this incident, Monalisa never mentioned it.

The day after Monalisa's call with Rich, she glared at Warren as they stood in her editing room, arguing about the mysterious videos. He was frustrated that she insisted there was no CGI or AI, and she was mad at him for disagreeing with her when he'd hardly looked at the file.

"I don't have to analyze it," Warren protested. "It *has* to be CGI. Or maybe some new AI tool you don't know about. We know the filmmaker didn't have a bunch of actors actually kill each other, and no one was shooting video during the Battle of the Little Bighorn."

"Oh yeah?" Monalisa objected. She waved towards the computer that had the file open in Adobe Premiere Pro. "Then show me any evidence this isn't actual footage, Warren!"

"So, you're saying this is a real film of the battle?"

"NO! I'm saying it's some whole new way of manipulating video images. I've searched everywhere, and there's NOTHING that remotely approaches what this technology can do!"

Warren shook his head. "And so, someone invented an entirely new kind of software that would absolutely *revolutionize* filmmaking around the world but instead of—hmmm...I don't know...issuing a press release, they decided to hack into our network and load a movie onto Rich Penton's computer?"

"I don't know why the fuck they did that," Monalisa snapped. "It was my responsibility to evaluate the video, and I'm telling you it's not CGI or AI the way you and I understand them. Study the fucking file before you tell me I'm wrong about something that is—by the way—my fucking job!"

They continued to argue in circles and finally agreed that Warren would scrutinize the video himself to see if he could figure out where Monalisa went wrong (which is how he thought of it), or how he was going to make it up to her for questioning her expertise (which is how she thought of it).

Warren studied the strange file all night. The next day, Monalisa suggested a nice way for him to make things right would be to take her to the Art Institute on Saturday.

They had a great time. Warren paid for everything.

4

BATTLE STATIONS

April 8th: 190 Days Before Arrival

Rosalie

Rosalie dressed for work in the primary bath of her greystone while her family slept. She was sore from the previous night's Krav Maga workout—the Israeli martial arts method that emphasizes real street fighting techniques. No one at *RECON* knew she was one of the top practitioners in Chicagoland.

She and her husband, Michael, had adopted two children five years earlier—a brother and sister, now ten and twelve years old. After making bag lunches for them, she enjoyed a quick breakfast, pausing to hug and kiss her husband as he lumbered into the kitchen in his bathrobe.

"Morning meeting?" he asked, yawning.

"Yes. Six o'clock downtown, then at *RECON* by seven."

She went to the kids' bedrooms, kissed them gently, then switched on her professional demeanor as she walked briskly down the broad steps to the sidewalk and into the chilly air of a Chicago spring day

Beth

"Got it, Rich," Beth said into her office phone. "See you ASAP." She cradled the receiver, checked the time, and brought up commercial flight schedules from Chicago to Billings, Montana. She frowned, then called the Transportation Department for *RECON*'s network. "Hi, this is Beth Robileski with *RECON*. I have an emergency requisition for either a G280 or a Legacy."

"Who's the news signoff?" the coordinator asked.

"Rich Penton," Beth lied. Rich's plane had just taken off from Grand Junction to Denver en route to Billings, and she wouldn't be able to reach him until it landed. This proved to be unnecessary when she called Rosalie to tell her that a requisition for the use of a corporate jet had been sent to Rich.

"Where are you going?"

"Billings. Rich is headed to the Battle of the Little Bighorn site with the professor."

Rosalie opened Rich's email account, found the requisition, and clicked on it. "He just approved it."

Beth smiled into the receiver. "Thanks, Rosalie, it's amazing how much more productive Rich has become since you arrived." She made a few more calls and then headed to Carl Swinton's office. She had thirty minutes before they needed to leave for the airport.

No sweat.

Carl

Carl didn't know he was going to Montana until Beth texted him as he rode in on the BNSF Metra line from Naperville. But, like everyone on the production team, he had a go bag at the office with enough supplies to last him a week. Beth was waiting in his office when he arrived, and she smiled at her longtime friend and colleague. It was widely held in the news community that Carl was one of the best directors in the business; the shelf full of Emmys in his office attested to that.

"Let's go make history," she said.

Carl beamed. He wasn't prone to long spells of happiness, but chasing down and directing stories brightened his whole world. He loved thinking about their work as *making history*. They took the elevator to the lobby and jumped into a waiting SUV.

Warren

Warren sat in the IT office in the server room on the 43rd floor. The muted lights matched his mood. He had made absolutely no progress in discovering how the mysterious videos appeared on Rich's computer. So, he'd added every kind of security software he could find, making it harder for everyone on the *RECON* team to access the Internet. The running joke was that the network was about to announce a new show called *Access Denied* because those words seemed to appear whenever someone opened a web browser.

Warren was also depressed thanks to an incident in the employee breakroom that morning. He was getting coffee when he ran into Jessica, a production assistant. Jessica was nice, pretty, and apparently entirely unaffected by his good looks and muscular build. She was the first woman to interest him since his infatuation with Monalisa years ago, and he sensed a connection, but she showed no signs she viewed him romantically.

When Jessica started to leave the breakroom, he decided to take a chance. "Hey Jessica, want to get lunch sometime?"

As he spoke, he suddenly recalled a dream he'd had the previous night—he'd asked Jessica for a date and his mind evoked his greatest professional frustration when she answered: *Access denied.*

But in real life, Jessica looked at him like she was seeing him for the first time. After a moment, she said, "I'm sorry, Warren. I've only been divorced for a year or so. You seem like a great guy, but I'm not quite ready to date yet."

Warren could not hide his disappointment; he hadn't experienced much rejection.

"Warren? I'm not saying no; just not yet. I need a little more time."

He nodded, and they parted. He wasn't sure if her encouragement was sincere or if she was just letting him down gently. So, he focused on work, grateful for the distraction, and remotely logged onto Rich's computer. "Darn it!" he yelled—Warren didn't swear much because he thought it was rude. But he came close in that moment: Rich's desktop displayed a new video file.

Angrily and impulsively, Warren clicked on it and deleted it.

Monalisa

Monalisa decided she needed some dedicated time to research Rich's videos, so she called in sick and stayed home. She sat at her desk—a huge piece from Goodwill that Warren had lugged up the stairs, not some Ikea shit he would have had to assemble for her—and opened Tor, the browser used to search the dark web. Then she went to Grams, the best search engine for the job, and began exploring the hidden world for clues.

One of the traits about the dark web that Monalisa appreciated was its anonymity. Tor routes users through a series of proxy servers, run around the world by volunteers. The disadvantage of this architecture is that it's impossible to index the dark web in the manner Google organizes data about the World Wide Web. Monalisa waited on searches that timed out or followed long paths to dead ends. But she doggedly kept searching for information on any new forms of CGI that she might have missed in her earlier search. If there was something that would allow people to create more footage like the Little Bighorn film, she had to know about it, in case bad actors tried to pass off deep fake video as real. *RECON* relied on her to know the difference.

After all, I'm the senior video editor for America's leading television news magazine...Jesus Christ, I sound like Rich Penton.

After a few hours, she found a discussion thread on the Hidden Wiki, where deep fake editors shared clips they'd created to get feedback. Posting under the name FUtrollboy, she uploaded thirty seconds of the Little Bighorn video and explained that several of the historical characters' faces matched on Clearview AI.

Over the next several hours, Monalisa read with fascination as deep fake editors evaluated the video. No one had seen it or could figure out how the CGI worked. That made her feel better, because it confirmed she wasn't behind the technology curve. But it was maddening, too, because it meant there weren't going to be any easy answers about the origin of the video.

"Not a great return for a whole sick day," she sighed. Glumly, she studied the monitors that covered her desk when something caught her eye. "Ho-leeeee fuck!" she whispered sharply. Someone had just added a message to the wiki:

I know everything about this. How it was made, who made it and why. Let's talk.

Elated, she replied, *OK, let's set it up* to a user identified only as BlackSpider150. For a moment, she wondered if she should tell someone at *RECON* what she was doing but decided against it. First, they would make her stop. Second, she might get in trouble because she'd shared a small portion of the video on the dark web.

Monalisa was confident she could navigate through this, and she sent the mysterious poster her confidential email address.

Exactly 591 miles away, BlackSpider150 was excited, too. His job was to find out if anyone else had a copy of the Little Bighorn video—or some other bizarre historical movies—and he'd found no evidence until now. He knew virtually nothing about CGI, AI, video editing, or the Battle of the Little Bighorn. But he was supported by a large team of experts who constantly scanned the web and the dark web, and one of them had alerted him to the video FUtrollboy had posted.

He knew his bosses would be anxious—they did not want any of the videos to get out, for reasons he didn't understand. But it was good news for him because it might get him from behind the desk and into an operational role. Just when he was about to give up, FUtrollboy had given him the break he needed.

BlackSpider150 headed upstairs to get instructions on what to do next.

Beth and Carl made it to Billings before Rich and the professor because they flew a corporate jet on a direct flight. Thanks to the Flight Aware database, a group of people gathered at the airport, hoping for a chance to see who was on board. Beth knew that if she let Rich into the terminal, they'd lose at least half an hour as he shook every hand and granted every request for a selfie—he couldn't say no. So, she arranged with TSA for the local affiliate to meet them on the tarmac in two vehicles: a production truck with a crew and a passenger van. The agents pulled Rich and the professor aside as they took the stairs down to the tarmac and diverted them to the waiting vehicles.

Rich

When we got off the plane in Billings, I was surprised to see Beth standing with two TSA officers. I took a selfie with them at their request, then introduced Professor Whitlock to Beth.

"Nice to meet you, Professor," Beth said, shaking his hand. "Ready to go to the Little Bighorn site?"

"You bet," Whitlock grinned. "One of my favorite places on earth. I can't wait to share it with you and help you figure out this mysterious video you've received. And please, call me Sam."

"Got it, Professor," Beth replied. We climbed into the rental van, and Beth turned to the driver. "Let's roll." He steered down the steep road towards the interstate heading south out of town.

My cell phone rang, and I glanced at the screen.

"Hi, Warren."

"Hi, Rich. Hey, I don't know if this is good news or bad news." He sounded distressed.

I was alarmed. "What's up?"

"There's a new video on your computer, and I don't know how it got there." Warren later admitted that he had at first deleted the file, then retrieved it from the Trash folder, although it didn't matter since they always came back anyway.

I glanced around the van and cupped my hand around the microphone while pressing the phone speaker to my ear so no one could hear Warren. This, of course, had the effect of ending all other conversation as everyone strained to listen. "What's it about?"

"It's Amelia Earhart. It shows the whole last leg of their trip when they disappeared, including what happened to them."

5

ORDER OF BATTLE

I thought through the electrifying implications of what Warren was saying. While there was a lot of historical information and a large trove of archeological data about the Battle of the Little Bighorn, Amelia Earhart's fate remained one of history's greatest mysteries. "What happened to them?" I whispered, as the others in the van leaned in closer.

"It was terrible," Warren said, the horror evident in his voice. "They landed on a beach on some desert island. Amelia—"

"Did they starve?" I interjected impatiently.

"Someone starved?" the professor asked, genuine concern on his face.

Warren continued in my ear. "Oh my God, Rich; it was so much worse than that. She was ripped apart."

"Ripped apart?" I repeated, louder than I intended.

"Who was ripped apart?" Carl asked.

I looked up from the phone. "I'll explain everything later. Let's focus on the Little Bighorn story for now." I thanked Warren, disconnected, and smiled at the other passengers but offered no explanation. I needed everyone—including myself—to focus on the task at hand.

"Little Bighorn, here we come!" I yelled. That drew a few grins, but everyone was obviously curious about my conversation.

I wish I could tell you, but I have no idea what Warren is talking about! But I wondered about the subjects of the two videos. Was there a connection between the Battle of the Little Bighorn and Amelia Earhart?

As we drove, the professor gave us a synopsis of the battle while he pointed out details of the video that coincided with little-known facts of the event. He eventually gave up trying to get everyone to call him "Sam" and, an hour later, we arrived at the Little Bighorn Battlefield National Monument.

Soon after, we were joined by Nadine Harlow, an historian for the Cheyenne tribe. Professor Whitlock had called her while we were in transit and invited her to participate. He explained that while the official account of the event came from U.S. Army combatants, Native Americans had their own oral histories that differed in significant ways.

We stood around a large map of the park as Nadine, the professor and the NPS staff gave us an overview of the battle, which was entirely consistent with the video. Next came an extensive battlefield tour. As we drove along the narrow asphalt road atop the grassy ridge, stopping at historical markers along the way, we had a great view of the valley where the Native Americans had camped. The Little Bighorn River wound along the base of the bluffs below us.

Then we gathered in a meeting room at the visitors' center that offered a panoramic view of Last Stand Hill, through floor-to-ceiling windows. I sat down next to Beth and noticed a large television in one corner. I leaned over to her. "Shall we show it to them?" We'd been treating the video like it was a state secret, but we had no idea of its origin. She wrinkled her brow for a moment, then nodded.

Nadine and the NPS group reacted to the film with stunned disbelief. They gasped, asked me to pause and replay key scenes, and pointed out countless obscure but accurate details. Joined by the professor, they held an intense, expert discussion.

When it was over, the lead ranger, Barb Halloran, asked, "Okay, the eight-hundred-pound gorilla in the room is: who made this movie and when? We've seen every single depiction of the battle ever made, and none is this accurate." When I didn't respond, she continued, "I assume this is in the public domain?"

"I don't really know," I replied. "Why do you ask?"

She paused for a moment, trying to fit the pieces together. "Well...logically, it must have been made decades ago. About when they first invented color film."

"Why is that?"

"Because this movie was obviously shot here on the battlefield. But not recently. The battlefield hasn't looked like that in several decades."

"What do you mean?"

"For one thing, this visitors' center and the monuments aren't there, and neither are the roads. I don't know how they hid the headstones marking where the soldiers fell but consider the erosion. The ravines are a heck of a lot deeper in the movie than they are today."

I sighed. "The truth is that we don't know who shot this film, when it was made, or why." I let that sink in. "Some of you have been wondering why we're here. As Beth said when we first watched this film, it's not like there's a need for an exposé on the truth behind the Custer battle."

"Actually, Rich," Nadine Harlow countered, "few battles are as misunderstood as this one. If your video is proven accurate, it supports the oral histories handed down for one hundred and fifty years by Native Americans."

I leaned in. "Go on."

"Did you notice anything special about the warrior who knocked General Custer off his horse?" she asked.

I thought for a moment and then shook my head. "I saw a warrior knock Custer off his horse during the final charge, but I didn't notice anything special about him."

She grinned, knowingly. "Would you mind playing that sequence again?"

"Sure."

I cued up the scene, and we watched as a man Nadine identified as Chief Comes in Sight led the charge that finished Custer. One of his warriors raced towards the General.

"Is that the guy you're referring to?" I asked.

Nadine smiled. "That's the *warrior* I was referring to. But look closer."

I played the scene in slow motion. Custer turned his mount and brought his pistol around to face an attacking warrior. Before he could level his gun, the warrior swung a club with perfect timing and knocked the General out of the saddle. I paused the video and, for the first time, noticed the warrior was significantly smaller than the others.

"That's a woman!" Beth exclaimed.

Barb Halloran shook her head. "Good eye, Nadine. I always thought it was a Native American legend that a woman knocked Custer off his horse."

"Native American oral traditions are very detailed," Nadine replied. "That is Buffalo Calf Road Woman. If it wasn't for her, the U.S. Army almost certainly would have won the Battle of the Little Bighorn—or the Battle of the Greasy Grass, as the Plains Indians call it. This video illustrates a little-known fact of the battle that was never widely accepted by historians. I'm glad to see the story told accurately, even if you don't know the source of this video."

"Nadine," Beth asked. "Why was her role so important—besides knocking Custer off his horse?"

"Buffalo Calf Road Woman's primary influence on the battle actually took place a week earlier—during a different fight."

Professor Whitlock grinned and put his hands behind his head. "The Battle of the Rosebud!"

Nadine nodded. "Or 'The Fight Where the Girl Saved Her Brother,' as we know it. In that battle, General Crook's armies and his allies, the Shoshoni and Crow, were close to defeating the Lakota Sioux and the Cheyenne. Chief Comes in Sight was Buffalo Calf Road Woman's brother, and he had been wounded as the warriors began to withdraw. Buffalo Calf Road Woman rode through bullets and arrows to scoop her brother off the field of battle, saving his life."

I thought about that. "So, you're saying if she hadn't saved Chief Comes in Sight, he wouldn't have been at the Little Bighorn to lead the charge that overwhelmed Custer?"

"Yes. But more importantly, her bravery inspired the warriors to reengage in the battle. They attacked General Crook's forces so fiercely, and inflicted so many causalities, that he withdrew to Sheridan, Wyoming, and didn't move for seven weeks as he waited for reinforcements."

"I get it," I replied. "You're saying if Crook hadn't lost that battle, he would have been at the Little Bighorn supporting Custer!"

Nadine and Professor Whitlock both nodded.

Barb Halloran spoke up, almost apologetically. "Buffalo Calf Road Woman's involvement is such a little-known and recently discovered part of the history of the battle, we don't even discuss it here."

"Why so recent?" Carl asked Nadine.

"The chiefs declared that no one was to speak of the battle outside the tribes for one hundred years. In 2005, the oral history was shared publicly, at an event in Billings, for the first time. That's when Buffalo Calf Road Woman's role was revealed."

"Wait," Barb exclaimed. "That means this video isn't that old after all! It's incredibly unlikely that this filmmaker would have known such a secret prior to 2005."

"That makes sense," I agreed.

Barb continued. "Then what about the uncanny accuracy of the geography? Is it all CGI?"

I shrugged my shoulders. "We can't find any evidence of CGI. We're here because this video appeared on my computer at work last week, and we don't know why or how it got there. No one at *RECON* had ever heard of Buffalo Calf Road Woman until now."

"What about those new AI systems that generate video?" Barb continued. "Could those systems have created this footage?"

I explained to her that we'd researched that angle too. Then the conversation turned into speculation, friendly arguments, and a general agreement that none of us could fathom how the film was made, or when.

As the late afternoon sun painted the grassy battlefield with golden light, I took the group outside and handed the reins to Carl, who had been badgering me about capturing footage before dark. So authorized, Carl took command. For the next few hours, we shot as much video as possible, including interviews and B-roll shots of the monuments, the visitors' center, the battlefield, the river, and the valley. It was a rushed, fun, and energizing day in the field, but we'd travelled to the Battle of the Little Bighorn National Monument to solve the mystery of the strange video I'd received. Instead, the enigma became even stranger, despite—or perhaps thanks to—the experts we met.

We stayed the night in Billings at the Northern Hotel, where each room has a mural painted above the headboard. Mine showed Custer standing bravely among his fallen men, firing both guns at a warrior racing towards him. A male warrior.

There's a lot of history we have to rewrite, I thought as I went to sleep.

Rosalie and Michael took their children to Northstar Restaurant on North Western Avenue for a late pizza dinner. Trouble entered the restaurant in the form of a tall, heavyset, inebriated man dressed in a rumpled suit. He talked too loudly, walked unsteadily, and ogled their daughter Olivia as though they couldn't see him.

Michael stiffened. Rosalie heard him take a breath and saw him put his palms on the table, ready to get up to confront the creep.

She put a hand over his. "Don't. He's just a drunk. He's not worth it."

Michael's eyes, full of fire, caught hers. She was right, of course, but it was infuriating to see this jackass leering at his daughter.

The drunk walked up to the counter to order food and began barking commands like he owned the place. A young man walked smartly from the back and—unlike the drunk—really did own the place. He wasn't about to let some asshole abuse his employees, so he ordered the man to leave. An argument ensued and became louder until the restaurant owner threatened to call the cops. That broke through the man's drunken veil, and he stumbled towards the door.

But he stopped again to look Olivia up and down. "You're going to make a fine piece of ass someday," he sneered, his eyes hungry with lust.

Michael leapt to his feet, followed quickly by Rosalie, who stepped in front of him. "Michael, no!" she insisted, putting her hands on his chest. "Listen to me! He's not worth it!"

They argued while the man left the restaurant. Rosalie finally persuaded Michael to sit down. He was seething with fury, but she looked calm and thoughtful. When his eyes met hers, he suddenly understood. "Rosalie, don't—"

But before he could finish, she whispered, "Watch the kids," and darted out the door.

Michael started to scramble after her but then stopped—he couldn't leave the children alone.

"Goddamn it!" he yelled.

"You said a bad word!" his son accused.

Rosalie looked up and down Western Avenue and saw the man disappear into a parking lot just north of her. Closing the distance quickly, she peered around the corner of a building to see him fumbling with his key fob in the dark. She slipped off her high heels and approached him silently.

"Hey," she said from a few feet away.

The man spun around, squinted into the darkness, and began to laugh. He towered over her, a strong smell of alcohol on his breath; when he spoke, his voice was nasty and threatening.

"You're a little old for my tastes. You should've brought your daughter."

"She's twelve years old," Rosalie said, evenly.

"Old enough to bleed, old enough to breed."

Rosalie brought her arms together so quickly the man had no time to react. The heels of her shoes punched holes in both of his cheeks and knocked out some of his teeth, a couple of which burst from between his lips. As he stood frozen with pain and shock, she whipped up her right leg, putting the bony part of her shin deep into his groin. He screamed and fell to his knees while Rosalie tore her shoe heels from the bloody holes in his face. The man grabbed his groin and fell on his chest; Rosalie used her bare foot to force him onto his back. She knelt next to him and calmly used his tie to wipe the blood off the heels of her shoes.

"She's twelve years old," she repeated matter-of-factly. The man, writhing in pain, stared at her, terrified, blood trickling down both sides of his face. She looked directly at him, calm and in control. "I'm trying to decide whether or not to kill you."

The man's eyes widened, one hand feeling around his bleeding cheeks, the other covering his groin. "Please don't kill me. I'm sorry. I'm so sorry!"

Rosalie cupped her shoes in her hands, placed the heels against his temples, and squeezed until the man cried out in pain. A voice in the back of her head said, *That's enough*. She released the pressure. "Stay out of this neighborhood. I won't be this nice next time. Do you understand?"

The man choked out a *yes* and then turned to his side and vomited. Rosalie slipped on her shoes and walked to the front of the restaurant, where Michael stood, holding their children tightly to him.

"What the hell?" he demanded. "I thought you said he wasn't worth it! And I should have been the one to confront him—not you!"

The kids were scared; Olivia looked wonderingly at her mother, trying to piece together what had happened. Rosalie took Michael's hands and then brought him close to her, trying to calm him down. They embraced for a minute until he whispered in her ear, so low the kids couldn't hear. "Did you kill him?"

She shook her head.

"That's good," he said, softly. A minute later, he added, "But a part of me wishes you did." Rosalie laughed under her breath and the tension broke. He held her tightly, and then they walked off as a family, holding hands to help each other heal from the trauma.

Michael is a good man, Rosalie thought as they went home. *A wonderful father and husband and no doubt a great accountant.* She loved that he was naturally protective of her and their children.

But he was no killer. That was *her* job.

6

EAST INTO OBLIVION

April 21st: 177 Days Before Arrival

"Rich, this is Marc Thibodeaux."*

Rosalie escorted the man into my office. In his mid-seventies, Thibodeaux looked as rugged and competent as you'd expect of a man who had spent forty years searching for lost airplanes and ships in some of the most remote parts of the world—from the cold tundra of Newfoundland to uninhabited islands in the Pacific. Thibodeaux had founded the Society of Archaeologists for the Recovery of Technological Artifacts (SARTA) in 1987. Among his many adventures, he'd led fourteen missions to determine the fate of Amelia Earhart. According to Beth, his theory about Earhart's disappearance closely matched with the video we'd received.

I invited Marc to sit down at my conference table, and we were soon joined by Beth, Monalisa, Warren, Carl, and Rosalie. As I was

---

* This account of Amelia Earhart's disappearance is derived from Finding Amelia: The True Story of the Earhart Disappearance by Ric Gillespie, who is the basis for the character Marc Thibodeaux. His organization, TIGHAR, inspired the fictional SARTA group. Any errors belong to the author.

thinking of the right way to introduce the video, Monalisa jumped in impatiently.

"Rich is trying to figure out how to tell you we have video of Amelia Earhart's final flight, including the ending, which is as fucked up as you thought."

I glanced at her, annoyed. "Monalisa—"

"Well, you were having a hard time getting the words out, Rich. I'm just trying to help." As usual, she was unapologetic.

Thibodeaux looked confused. "What do you mean, 'video?' I've seen every documentary; hell, I've participated in most of them."

I glowered at Monalisa. "How about we just show you what we found, Marc?" He nodded, and I started the video.

A twin-engine aircraft rolled across a grassy field. The pilot paused at the end of the dirt runway, turned into the wind, and stood on the brakes while winding up the engines. The pilot released the brakes, and the plane leapt forward, rushing from right to left on the screen. It hit a bump and dipped up and down; a puff of dust appeared behind it.

I heard Thibodeaux draw in his breath. "Stop the video!" he yelled, then jumped up excitedly and ran around the table to gesture at the monitor. "Rewind it a bit! I want to look at the aircraft right before and after that puff of dust!"

As I did, Thibodeaux pointed at the bottom of the plane's fuselage. "See this? Whoever made this video knew what they were doing. Not only does this shot look *exactly* like archival footage of the event, but Earhart had a long-range antenna under the body of the plane supported by two posts. SARTA believes this puff of dust was caused by one of the posts striking the ground, which ripped off the antenna. That was a key factor in Earhart's inability to communicate with the *Itasca* later."

I knew from my research that the United States Coast Guard Cutter *Itasca* was the ship assigned to use radio signals to guide Earhart and her navigator, Fred Noonan, to Howland Island, where they planned to refuel. The ship was never able to establish contact with the lost aviators, and the missing antenna could have been the primary culprit.

"We only have one, grainy, black and white movie and a few old photos of the takeoff from Lae, New Guinea," Thibodeaux continued. "In that film, we can see the puff of dust when something hits the ground on takeoff, but the antenna is difficult to make out." He gestured at the screen. "Whoever made this knew about our theory, because you can clearly see the post and the antenna being torn off!" He paused, looking mystified. "Where did you get this? Usually, SARTA is asked to consult on Earhart documentaries—especially if the filmmaker shares our theories."

Monalisa answered before I could. "We don't know who made it. This is the second video that popped up on Rich's computer. One second, it's not there and then—poof—there it is. We've also looked into every CGI and AI possibility, and it's not that. We don't know what these videos are, but since the last one was abso-frickin'-lutely perfect, we had to ask you about this one."

"'The last one?'" Thibodeaux repeated. "How many are there?"

"Well," I explained, "two other videos have appeared on my computer. One shows a missile strike on Chicago, but since that didn't happen, we can't investigate it. The second one is a forty-four-minute video of the Battle of the Little Bighorn." I filled him in on the details of our investigation and watched his face darken as he listened.

"Rich...is this some kind of practical joke? A hidden camera stunt? If you're trying to—"

Monalisa interrupted him. "For fuck's sake, just watch the video already! You really think we'd go to all this trouble just to yank your chain?"

Thibodeaux, who had obviously sized up Monalisa quickly, smiled at her, bemused, but trying not to show it. "By all means, continue. Consider me fascinated to see the rest of the video."

I hit the play button, and the camera followed alongside the plane as it took off. As in the Custer video, there were no fades or transitions: one moment we were outside the plane; the next moment, we were in the cockpit watching and listening to Earhart and Noonan. Earhart was dressed in light khaki pants and a drab green blouse adorned with a silk scarf tied around her neck. Noonan was rail thin, wearing a denim, button down shirt with the sleeves rolled up, black slacks and a black tie. They looked lean, confident, and competent.

Earhart keyed the mic. "Position 4.33 South, 159.7 East. Height 8,000 feet over cumulus clouds. Wind 23 knots." She waited expectantly for a few moments, but there was no reply. "What do you think, Freddy? Too far away?"

"I think so, AE. But we should be able to pick them up soon."

"Can you pause the video?" Thibodeaux asked, baffled. "I've been researching Amelia Earhart and Fred Noonan for most of forty years. These actors look and sound exactly like them. *Exactly*. This must be CGI, with their appearances and audio simulated from archival footage, right?"

Carl spoke up before Monalisa uncorked more profanity. "It's not CGI, well, at least the way we understand it. This video is... *realer* than real. It's, um, *flawless*. Everything at every distance is in focus, which isn't possible with real cameras, because they have depth of field limitations." His eyes were owlish behind his glasses. "Does that make sense?"

Thibodeaux nodded. "We shoot a lot of video and photography. I understand what you're saying, but I wouldn't say it 'makes sense.'"

Carl grinned. "Fair enough."

I restarted the video and the plane flew on. What must have been hours was condensed into about ten minutes, as the flyers became increasingly agitated and fearful when they couldn't raise anyone on the radio. Earhart spoke into the mic. "KHAQQ calling *Itasca*. I will listen on the hour and half hour on 3105 kilocycles." She turned to

Noonan. "Fred, why aren't they answering us?" The tension radiated through the decades and off the screen.

Marc commented without taking his eyes off the screen. "If they had known the long-range antenna was gone, they could have switched to the short-range antenna. As they approached the *Itasca*, they would have heard the ship's transmissions clearly. But neither of them was a professional communicator, and I guess it never occurred to them."

Almost perfunctorily, Earhart picked up the mic again. "Partly cloudy." There was no reply. She tried again. "*Itasca*, this is KHAQQ. Please take a bearing on us on 3105 kilocycles on the hour."

Thibodeaux provided historical interpretation. "She's listening on 3105 kilocycles for a radio beacon to guide her in, but the *Itasca* can only broadcast on 270 to 550 kilocycles. She was supposedly informed of that before takeoff, but apparently she wasn't."

Earhart keyed the mic. "KHAQQ calling *Itasca*. Please take bearing on us and report in half hour—about one hundred miles out." A few minutes later, she tried again. "KHAQQ calling *Itasca;* we must be on you but cannot see you... but gas is running low. Been unable to reach you by radio; we are flying at one hundred feet."

Marc spoke up, emotion filling his voice. "They heard this," he lamented, shaking his head. "The *Itasca* and other radio stations could *hear* them, but they couldn't *talk* to them."

Now the two aviators looked out the windows with binoculars, desperately straining to see any sign of Howland Island as Amelia Earhart banked the plane to the left and held it there.

"KHAQQ calling *Itasca*. We are circling but cannot hear you. Go ahead on 7500 with a long count, either now or on the scheduled time on the half hour."

"We'll be in the water in a half hour, Amelia!" Noonan yelled, fear in his voice.

Earhart heard something through her headphones and then

shook her head. "*Itasca*, we received your signals, but unable to get a minimum. Please take bearing on us and answer on 3105 with voice."

Thibodeaux shook his head. "Assuming she's hearing anything but static, it wouldn't matter. *Itasca*'s broadcasting in Morse code. Earhart was a good pilot, and Noonan was a world class navigator, but neither of them knew Morse. Hardly anyone uses it now, but Morse was an essential part of radio communication back then."

"I had to learn Morse code to get my Signaling Merit Badge," Warren announced.

Monalisa rolled her eyes at her friend. "God, you're such a nerd."

On the screen, Amelia checked her instruments and picked up the mic again. "We are on the line 157 337. We will repeat this message on 6210 kilocycles." Earhart dropped the mic and pointed out the window. "I see an island!" she exclaimed; her voice full of relief. She banked to the right and swung around so Noonan could study the tiny speck in the ocean with binoculars.

"It's not Howland," he concluded after a minute. "But it's got a flat beach. I think we can land on it!"

Only a narrow strip of sand lay between the waves and the vegetation; we could see an old, wrecked, freighter abandoned at the northwest edge of the island.

Amelia let out a deep breath. "Thank God!" They flew over the island and then circled it. "I have to land now," she called out. "We're almost out of gas!"

The natural landing strip was an extremely tight fit, but Amelia Earhart was up to the challenge. She put the Lockheed Electra 10E smoothly and perfectly down on the center of the beach. There was hardly a bump as the wheels touched the sand and she cut the power and began to apply the brakes. Still carrying a lot of speed, the plane's left wheel—the one closest to the water—plunged into the sand. The landing gear collapsed, and the aircraft came to a violent stop. The left propeller twisted itself into scrap metal as it struck the ground, and the right engine spun wildly for several seconds before Earhart feathered it off.

The video switched to the inside of the aircraft; Earhart was in obvious pain and Noonan was unconscious. He had a nasty gash on his forehead from smacking his head against the co-pilot's wheel, which had bent from the force. Amelia leaned over, trying to rouse Noonan.

"Freddy! Freddy!"

She released her harness and then his; he slumped forward, and she held him up. Amelia's headphones had been ripped off on impact; she put them on and then called out on the radio, changing frequencies, and talking frantically. Finally, she dropped the mic onto her lap, pulled Noonan's limp torso into her arms, telling him everything would be okay.

The shot went dark.

Thibodeaux glanced over at me, his face white. "Is it over?"

I shook my head. "Nighttime."

A minute later, it was daytime again. The video played on, showing scenes that appeared to cover a couple of days as Amelia Earhart split her time between various tasks. Sometimes, she took care of Noonan, who was too injured to climb out of the plane. Other times, she ran the right engine for a few minutes and called for help on the radio, or wrestled luggage out of the top hatch of the plane.

"Running the right engine charged the batteries on a Lockheed Electra," Thibodeaux explained. "And if they're using the top hatch, the fuselage door must have been jammed shut by the accident."

Noonan had revived, but was in serious pain from his head wound, as well as his right ankle, which we couldn't see but must have been broken. He seemed groggy, as though suffering from a concussion, and was sweating profusely.

"It's probably 120 degrees in that metal airplane in the South Pacific sun," Marc noted.

They had landed about a week before the month's tidal max; now the rising tides had reached the bottom of the aircraft. The left wing floated a few inches above the sand and was beginning to pull the damaged landing gear out of the hole it had made during the crash. The right engine was still above the water and running, but it coughed and sputtered and died as the fuel ran dry.

"You have to get through now," Noonan groaned, his voice ragged with pain. "We can't charge the batteries anymore. This is it." He tried to push himself out of his seat. "I've got to get out of this damn plane!"

Amelia keyed the mic. "WPA Howland—help me. Water's high." She removed the headphones and pushed them onto Noonan's lap. "Here, put your ear to it." It seemed to me she was trying to keep him alert.

Noonan dropped back into his seat and put on the phones while she spoke into the mic.

"This is Amelia Putnam; this is Amelia Putnam. SOS."

Thibodeaux muttered, "Putnam was her married name. She hardly ever used it."

Noonan, who was almost delirious by now, grabbed the mic from her. "Stop. Amelia...speak. Ankle...oh, God." He handed the mic and phones back to Amelia and she called out on the radio.

"Help. Help us quick." The body of the plane rocked as the water began to lift the fuselage.

"I'm too hot," Noonan complained. "I have to get out." He struggled to stand, barely able to hold himself up in the narrow space between the two seats.

Marc shook his head. "He'll have to climb out the top of the cockpit. Not an easy task with a broken ankle."

The flyers talked back and forth, breathing hard in the heat, and then Noonan slipped and collapsed on the wet floor of the fuselage, landing behind Amelia's seat. Water was slowly leaking into the aircraft. Amelia picked up the mic, closed her eyes to focus and then spoke very deliberately. "George...get the suitcase out of my closet in California!" Then she said something that sounded almost but not quite like, "Howland; New York City, New York City, New York City!"

I paused the video and looked over at Thibodeaux. "At first, we thought she was saying, 'New York City.' But that doesn't make any sense, and it doesn't sound quite right."

Marc shook his head. "She's saying, '*Norwich City*.' That's the name of that wrecked freighter you saw earlier. It came ashore on Gardner Island, now called Nikumaroro Island, in a storm, in 1929." A thoughtful look came into his eyes. "Have you ever heard of Betty Klenck?"

None of us had.

"Betty was a fifteen-year-old girl in 1937. She lived in St. Petersburg, Florida, and her father had a state-of-the-art shortwave radio. He built an enormous antenna that gave the Klenck household astonishing reception from all over the world. On July 4th, three days after Amelia and Fred disappeared, Betty claimed to have heard their radio transmissions."

"Wait," I protested. "She heard transmissions from the South Pacific all the way in *Florida*?"

Warren interjected. "That's not uncommon. Transmissions like that 'skip' off the atmosphere."

Thibodeaux agreed. "I interviewed Betty while she was still alive and spent hours evaluating her notes. In fact, I have her original note-book. Many of the lines these actors are delivering are exactly as written by Betty."

I thought about that. "Could anyone get access to that notebook to write those lines into a script?"

"Sure. The notebook's been online for a long time." He furrowed his brow. "But this video is...well, really weird. I mean, it doesn't feel like a film or even a documentary. It feels like someone was right there, videotaping Amelia Earhart and Fred Noonan in their last hours." He shrugged his shoulders self-consciously. "Sorry. That probably sounds crazy. Maybe I'm just too emotionally invested in the story."

Beth reassured him. "Actually, the Little Bighorn video had the same feel to us and was just as accurate."

I agreed. "Let's play it to the end and see what you think, then. But I have to warn you, it's extremely gruesome."

He shook his head, knowingly. "The crabs got her, didn't they?"

I nodded.

"Shit. I can't imagine why any filmmaker would depict that. Why not just end it before that happens and imply the rest?"

"I don't know," I admitted. "We don't have to show it if you don't want to see it."

Thibodeaux waved off my offer. "I came here to give you an assessment based on decades of research. I need to see the whole thing."

We rejoined the castaways; Amelia was still in the pilot's seat, intermittently calling out to Noonan while trying to raise someone on the radio. She glanced out the window. "The water's coming up!" she yelled to the navigator, who was sitting behind her. His reply was unintelligible.

"This is Amelia Earhart! Amelia Earhart!" she yelled into the mic, and then turned to look at Noonan as he slipped on the wet, metal deck. "Come back here, Fred!"

"I can't make it!" he cried and collapsed in exhaustion.

"Damn it...damn it...damn it!" She keyed the mic one last time. "*Norwich City*!" she cried. "We're by the *Norwich City*!" Noonan was lying on his back, struggling weakly, and then seemed to lose consciousness. Amelia jumped out of her seat, scrambled towards him, and tried to force open the jammed cargo door. She pushed and pounded on it and then sat in the water and kicked at it with both feet, but it wouldn't budge.

The plane began to float off the beach. Earhart gave up on the cargo door, wrapped both arms around Noonan, and tried to drag him to the front seats in an effort to lift him through the roof hatch. The plane was pitching violently with the wave action, throwing them around the fuselage, but Amelia Earhart fought desperately. Several times, she was able to get him to the front of the plane and strain to lift him off the deck, only for the sea to toss the plane around, slamming them both to the back of the aircraft.

Long after it was obviously hopeless, Amelia Earhart, exhausted, gave up and stumbled and crawled towards the cockpit. She climbed up and stood on the pilot's seat, steadying herself by grabbing onto the opening of the top hatch, and gazed at Noonan's limp form, her face streaming with tears.

"I'm so sorry, Freddy," she cried. "Goodbye, my dear friend." Then she climbed out of the roof hatch and was rocked off the plane into the water.

She plunged deep beneath the waves and came up sputtering and struggling. Earhart swam towards the beach, fighting hard against the tide that sought to take her into deep water. I was convinced that had she waited any longer, she never would have made it to shore.

Amelia Earhart dragged herself onto the beach and rolled onto her back, gasping for air. The water kept rising, so she crawled farther up the slope by the leather bags she'd removed from the plane and collapsed, crying. Then she sat up and watched as the ocean stole her beloved Lockheed Electra 10E away from the island. Amelia pulled herself to her feet, picked up the bags, and carried them into the brush. She lay down next to them and fell asleep; the video became dark again as night fell.

Daylight returned and Amelia was asleep in the same spot. She stirred and sat up, glanced around as though confused, and then scrambled to her feet and ran to the edge of the beach. Seeing nothing, she found the highest point of the island and looked out to sea. The camera followed her gaze and we could just make out the Lockheed, still floating, now miles away. A couple of minutes later, the aircraft slipped beneath the waves, taking Fred Noonan's body with it.

"Oh, my God!" Marc shouted. I scrambled to stop the video.

"What is it?" Beth asked.

"If this video is right—" he caught himself. "I can't imagine how anyone could know, but if this is right, the Electra floated much farther than we thought. That would explain why we haven't found it!"

"But how could it float that far?" Carl asked. "It was filling with water."

Marc shook his head. "It could have taken hours for seawater to fill up the fuselage and the fuel tanks were like buoys. When they're empty, a Lockheed Electra 10E can float for hours. But if Amelia's plane is that far from the island, it's in very deep water. I don't think anyone will ever locate it."

He caught himself. "I mean, it's all just conjecture, right? Someone just made up this version. But damn, everything about this video is authentic to the last detail—from the bags we know they carried to the instrument panel, to the clothes they wore to how they looked and sounded." Thibodeaux's face was grim. "Please, Rich, I don't *want* to see the gruesome ending, but I have to."

We watched as Amelia dragged the bags under some trees above the beach. "She's on the leeward side, where she's less exposed to the wind and elements," Thibodeaux told us. Earhart knelt in the sand and took stock of her meager possessions, removing some clothing and various containers. When she pulled out a roundish, glass bottle, Marc exclaimed, "We found that jar—it's freckle cream!"

Amelia began exploring the island. "She's searching for fresh water," Thibodeaux explained. "But there's very little of it on Nikumaroro—and usually none."

As Earhart walked among the Pisonia trees southeast of where she landed, the camera suddenly tilted up to track a small, silver, float plane that appeared out of nowhere and roared over at low altitude.

We could see the star-in-a-circle insignia of the U.S. Navy near the tail. Earhart sprinted for the beach. She removed her scarf and jumped up and down trying to signal to the plane as it flew away, but the aircraft disappeared into the distance.

"Oh, my God!" Thibodeaux was now wrapped up in the video as though it were real. "It was that close. All Lambrecht had to do was go around one more time!"

"Lambrecht?" I asked.

"He was the pilot. That floatplane was from the battleship USS *Colorado*. He took one pass over Gardner Island before moving on."

Amelia made her way back to her small camp, sat down among her luggage and cried. The screen went dark. When it was light again, it was apparent that a few days had passed. Amelia Earhart lay prone, and as the sun climbed higher in the sky, we heard her ragged breathing. She was obviously dying of thirst. She'd managed to start a fire, which smoldered now, and the bones of a few fish lay about, as well as the smashed carcasses of several enormous crabs that had apparently moved in too soon to feast on the castaway.

"Coconut crabs," Thibodeaux noted. "The largest land crustacean on earth."

A monstrous-looking crab darted out from the underbrush; it must have been three feet long and it used one of its gigantic claws to pull on Amelia Earhart's neck. She lifted a hand weakly and tried to push it away, but its claw closed around her skin and ripped away a chunk of flesh. She tried to scream, but it was a dry hack.

"Oh, my God!" Thibodeaux cried out, tears in his eyes.

We watched in horror as Amelia Earhart was killed and devoured by the large crabs, which were soon joined by dozens of smaller strawberry crabs. It must have taken hours in real time, as her blood turned the sand red and the creatures disassembled her skeleton, using their claws to drag her bones back to their nests.

When the video ended, Thibodeaux was quiet for several

seconds. Finally, he said, "Whoever made this is either a fanatic or a monster. But he got every single detail right, as far as I can tell."

We took a break to recover from the tragic and ghastly video. When we reconvened, Thibodeaux had dozens of questions. He wanted to know how we had gotten the video, our views on its provenance, the technical aspects that Monalisa and Warren had documented, and more. We told him everything we knew, including a rundown on our investigation of the Little Bighorn video.

But we had questions for him, too. The most pressing one was why he believed Betty Klenck's claims that she'd heard Amelia Earhart's radio transmissions all the way from Florida.

"Well, there are many reasons. She and her father tried to tell the authorities about it at the time, and no one listened. She stuck to her story for seventy years, even though there was nothing in it for her. Her notebook sat in a drawer for most of that time."

"I understand that," I replied. "But isn't it more likely that even if she was telling the truth, she was really hearing some hoaxer who was broadcasting from nearby?"

Thibodeaux shook his head. "No, I don't think so. There are too many details that match up with the facts. Simple things, like mentioning the *Norwich City*, or using the name, 'WPA Howland.' The airport there was a Works Progress Administration project, which wasn't widely known. But there's one thing Betty documented that literally no one in the world would have known except Amelia Earhart and her husband, George Putnam."

"What was that?" I asked, fascinated.

"Did you hear her say over the radio, 'George...get the suitcase out of my closet in California?' It was revealed years later, by her husband, that Amelia kept some secrets in a suitcase—letters, documents; we'll never know for sure—that she didn't want anyone to see in the event of her death. That suitcase was kept in a closet in their house in California. Amelia told George that if anything happened to her, he was to get that suitcase from her closet and destroy the contents. There is no way anyone could have known that, and yet Betty wrote it in her notebook."

Thibodeaux had confirmed the accuracy of the third video in the same way other experts had corroborated the second one. What we didn't know yet was that the first video—the one showing a missile hitting Chicago—held its own surprises.

Rosalie took her Silent Phone into a stall in the women's restroom. She texted:

AE asset received/viewed/analyzed w/expert Marc Thibodeaux. BLB asset vetted by experts and field research. Threat: 2.5

After the message was confirmed and burned, she returned to work.

7

THE MYSTERY OF MONALISA

April 22nd: 176 Days Before Arrival

Monalisa was delighted when BlackSpider150 told her that he lived in Chicago and could meet for coffee the next morning. She woke up early, watched the Little Bighorn video again, and left her condo at 8 a.m. to make her way to a coffee shop. As she entered, she held up a piece of paper with the name "FUtrollboy" in large letters. Sitting at a corner table, a tall, broad, blonde, light-skinned man in his 50s waved to her, a smile on his face. She walked over and sat across from him, eyeing him warily.

"FU, troll boy," Monalisa said. If the man caught the joke, he didn't show it.

"It's a pleasure to meet you," he said in a deep, accented voice, holding his hand out formally. Viktor Dyavol had flown in from Washington, DC, the previous evening. People tend to trust locals more than out-of-towners, so whenever possible, he claimed to live in the same city as a target.

Monalisa was startled when her tiny hand disappeared into his – it was gigantic. She'd been around a lot of hackers, programmers, and gamers, and they weren't usually vigorous physical specimens. This man was enormous: tall, with heavy shoulders, a thick neck, and fore-arms the size of her legs. He was even bigger than Warren. She frowned at him. "You don't look like any hacker I've ever met."

"I'm not a hacker," Viktor replied, "I'm an editor. But is it a crime to be good with computers and weights?"

He was trying to be disarming, but Monalisa wasn't buying it. Still, she'd put in too much effort to run at the first sign of danger.

"Where did you get your video?" she demanded. "And what do you know about it?"

Viktor smiled. "Someone sent it to my client, but he didn't have the expertise to analyze it, so he called me."

Warning bells went off in Monalisa's head. Whatever this guy did for a living, she didn't believe it involved hours sitting at a keyboard.

"How long is your file?"

Viktor recognized it as a test question. "Seventy-three minutes."

"And what do you know about it, since you're such an expert and all?"

Viktor had been thoroughly briefed in preparation for this conversation. "It's mysterious. Infinite depth of field, the lighting is right; even when we inspect it pixel by pixel, everything is in place."

"Who's 'we?'" Monalisa probed.

Viktor shook his head. "I can't specify, I'm sorry to say. And what about you? Who's your 'we?'"

"I can't specify, I'm sorry to say," Monalisa parroted. She pressed on. "You said you know everything about the film: who made it, why it was made, and how it was done. Are you going to tell me?"

Viktor paused. "Sure. But it's only fair we trade information. You want to know how the film was made. I want to know where you got your copy."

Monalisa wasn't going to reveal her connection to *RECON*, espe-cially since she doubted he had any new information about the video, and she wondered why he'd even suggested a meeting. She'd ask one more test question, and if he failed, she'd take off. She was sure she could lose him; he wasn't built for speed.

"I have another question about the video."

"Go ahead," he nodded.

"The shot comp on the video jumps around all over the place. Why do you think the director used so many J-cuts?"

Viktor had memorized some common editing language, including the term, *jump cuts*. "No idea," he answered, confidently. "The film is full of J-cuts. Perhaps when we share our information, we can figure out why the director chopped it up so much."

Monalisa stood up. "You're lying, you son of a bitch. 'J cuts' and 'jump cuts' are completely different things. I don't think you know shit about this video. I can't figure it out, and I can already tell I know about a million times more about this shit than you do."

Viktor swiftly changed tactics. "I *know*," he whispered, gesturing with his hands for her to calm down. "The last thing we want to do is reveal our findings to someone who can't help us in return. Got it?"

Monalisa appeared unconvinced, so Viktor continued. "I really think we can help each other. Please sit down."

Monalisa glanced around the coffee shop to reassure herself she wasn't alone with this man she increasingly sensed as dangerous. Reluctantly, she sat down again.

Viktor leaned across the table and spoke in a low voice. "I know who made the video and why. We're still guessing on the how. But I can't go into that in public. Do you have a place we can talk in private?"

Monalisa stared at him stone-faced for a moment and then burst into laughter. "Seriously? You think I'm going anywhere with you, alone? For fuck's sake, why don't you just kill me here?" She stood up again and stepped away from the table. "I'm leaving now. And I've got friends watching this coffee shop. If you follow me, I'll call the cops."

Viktor sighed. He knew she had no lookouts, because his

employer, the SVR – the Russian Foreign Intelligence service – owned the coffee shop through a shell company, and it was under constant surveillance. "I'm sorry you feel that way. If you change your mind about sharing information, please contact me. You know how to get in touch." He held his coffee up as a salute.

"*F you*, troll boy," Monalisa replied, and this time there no doubt how she meant it. She backed away from the table, ducked out the door, and disappeared down an alley.

Viktor felt his phone vibrate in his pocket. His boss had been listening to the conversation. The text said: *Clean up time*. He texted back: *Address?*

Like many people, Monalisa kept a business card tag on her backpack. One of Viktor's associates had read it from a surveillance camera and quickly figured out where she lived. Seconds later, he was on his way to the home of Maura Lisa McPeek.

Two of Viktor's associates were following McPeek and texted him that she was not heading straight home. She was taking a circuitous route, probably to ensure she wasn't followed, and was more than ten blocks away from her condo when Viktor reached her front door. He slipped the lock and turned over every nook and cranny of her apartment as his associates made it to her building and watched the entrances.

A text told Viktor she was approaching, so he retreated into a hallway a few feet from the front door. He looked hungrily at her bed; he planned to spend a lot of time with her there—then he'd force her to tell him where she got the videos and kill her.

Monalisa stepped inside and locked the door. When she turned back to the room, Viktor was standing a few feet in front of her. He grinned and gazed up and down at her body; both of them knew she could never escape before he would be on her.

Monalisa's eyes lit up with fire and fury. This caught Viktor by surprise—he loved trapping a woman and seeing her realize her helplessness, and he was aroused at the thought of using this bitch mercilessly. But this reaction was unexpected; she showed no fear at all. Instead, Monalisa screamed as loud as she could and attacked him with all her might, throwing her hundred pounds against him, wrapping her legs around his torso, and nearly knocking him off his feet. She scratched at his face with her nails, and he panicked as they came dangerously close his eyes.

"Get off me, cunt!" he yelled, balling his fist, and slamming it into her torso. He felt ribs break and Monalisa shrieked with pain. Then he launched a brutal blow against her skull, rocking her head sideways; her small body went slack, and she slumped to the floor. For a moment, Viktor thought she was dead—too soon for his tastes. He knelt next to her to see if she was still alive and was relieved to hear painful, raspy breathing.

A minute later, Monalisa woke up in agony, and it took a few moments for the fog to clear before she understood what was happening. In horror, she realized that the monster—the thing she hated more than she had ever hated anything—was on top of her. She felt her nakedness below her waist, and she could tell by his motions that the monster was unbuckling his jeans.

Monalisa screamed with rage. She couldn't reach his face, so she slid her hands under his shirt and used all her strength to drive her long fingernails into his back. Powered by adrenaline, she pulled downward, cutting deep, bloody gouges into his skin.

Viktor felt searing pain as his back was sliced open; he roared in fury and wrapped his enormous hands around Monalisa's throat, her eyes bulging as he cut off her breath. He squeezed harder and felt her small neck snap in his grip, and she went limp underneath him. He scrambled off her, blood dripping down his back, and forced himself to resist the urge to run. Others might have heard the commotion, and he could not afford to draw to more attention to himself.

After a minute, he regained his composure and checked her pulse. Dead. Good. But he was frustrated. This little bitch made him kill her before he could use her. Worse, he'd learned nothing from her. He hoped her computers might hold some secrets—if his colleagues could hack them.

He jerked with a start at the sharp sound of a knock at the door. "Viktor?" a voice called urgently, but softly. Viktor fastened his belt and went to the door. One of his associates slipped inside. "We heard screaming." He glanced at the girl's body on the bed. "You killed her already?"

Viktor nodded. "She didn't know anything, and she was screaming, as you pointed out."

The associate didn't dare question Viktor. He had no interest in getting on the wrong side of a professional assassin—and sadist.

"Of course. She was alone?"

"Yes. Any reaction to the screams?"

"No. We think the units around hers are empty right now."

"Then take your time cleaning up," Viktor ordered. "Leave the bitch on the bed. There's no way to remove the body without making things worse."

When Viktor walked to the bathroom, the associate stared at the blood soaking through the killer's shirt. Dyavol wrapped a beach towel around his torso, cinching it in the front, and walked back into the room, his wounds searing in pain.

"Give me your jacket," Viktor ordered. The associate quickly obeyed, and the assassin pulled it on, stretching the fabric tightly—it was far too small for him and his huge hands stuck out several inches from the sleeves. He stared angrily at the bloodstains on the floor. The little whore had drawn more blood than he'd lost since the war. He yanked the cords from Monalisa's gaming computer, stuffed it in her backpack, slung it over his shoulder and left.

A few minutes later, the second associate joined the first, and together they wiped down the room with practiced hands. They heard an electronic chirp several times and finally figured out it was coming from a phone in the victim's slacks. Removing it carefully, they saw text messages from "Rosalie" checking in on the girl and soon a phone call came in from the same person. It was time to go. They stuffed bloody rags into a dark plastic bag, wiped down the cell phone, and dropped it on the bed; it was tempting to keep it but that was too risky. The authorities might locate it before they could turn off its tracking features. Checking the hallway carefully, they walked out of the apartment.

Thirteen minutes later, Chicago cops knocked on the door. The dispatcher reported that the woman's employer had cause to suspect a crime in progress, so the cops kicked in the door to find the broken, half-naked body of a small young woman with blue hair lying on the bed. They called for an ambulance, because that was the required procedure, but the girl was clearly dead.

Minutes later, Rosalie hung up her phone at work and stared blankly into her computer screen. She was numb to the sounds around her: phones rang, televisions blared, and people talked, laughed, and argued as she sat motionless. Finally, she brought one hand to her face to wipe away the lone tear that ran down her cheek.

Crippling, oppressive, grief washed over me as a Chicago Police Department detective told us about the murder. While he talked, my mind searched for a motive. Monalisa wasn't a journalist, so she didn't make enemies through her work. But I knew that in her drive to find answers to the mysterious videos, she had confided in someone who had Clearview access, and she'd searched the dark web. A nagging hunch formed that this had somehow led to her death.

Then I got angry. If the police didn't find out who killed Monalisa, I would. After all, *RECON* did investigations, too.

After the meeting, I walked in a daze to my office and was intercepted by Rosalie. "I'm very sorry, Rich," she said gently, studying my eyes. To my surprise, she put her arms around me and held me close for several seconds. Then she stepped back. "Let me know how I can help." I mumbled thanks and scooted into my office as quickly as I could, before she saw me blubbering like a baby.

Warren was devastated by Monalisa's death. He wanted revenge, and his large frame trembled with rage. He had no evidence that Monalisa had encountered her killer because of the videos, but he sensed it was true. The videos seemed like a curse to him. Everything about them was odd and impossible to explain, and not just their incredible authenticity. He'd practically cut the *RECON* team off from the outside world with security measures and despite this, videos kept showing up on Rich's computer. And that was virtually impossible, because he had put in place one extra layer of protection that only Rosalie knew about: he'd arranged to have Rich's computer turned off most of the time. Every morning, Rosalie turned on Rich's desktop and logged him into the network with credentials Warren gave her. Warren turned off the computer at night. Yet the Earhart video had appeared on Rich's computer *less than three minutes* after Rosalie had turned it on one morning.

Knowing Monalisa as he did, he was sure she would have sought answers on the dark web. Warren avoided the nether regions of the Internet, but he knew someone who was an expert in that domain: Heath Cobb, a professional hacker and one of the eclectic members of "Monalisa's Posse." When Warren called him, Heath was distraught about Monalisa's murder, but the two quickly worked out how they might identify the killer—the first step towards bringing him to justice.

After Viktor returned to his hotel from the girl's apartment, he received cryptic, urgent instructions from his boss not to leave his room. Then a messenger arrived with word about the girl's *RECON* connection and informed him that the organization feared it had been set up on a sting operation. Perhaps the television people had arranged the meeting, and hadn't anticipated the girl would be killed when she returned home.

Viktor was furious at the insinuation that he was at fault. In advance, they'd established that if his contact wasn't cooperative, he'd back away. But if she seemed like a security risk—for example, if she might call law enforcement, as Monalisa had threatened—then Viktor was to eliminate the target. And that's what he'd done, at the direction of his boss who had texted him the order personally! In Viktor's opinion, if anyone was to blame, it was the idiot who had read the woman's backpack tag and failed to warn them of her connection to *RECON*.

After a few days, with no unusual activity from either the intelligence community or the news people, the organization speculated that the girl hadn't told her employer about the meeting. But the *RECON* connection remained a problem. They were highly intelligent people, with lots of resources, and were not likely to accept losing one of their own to a crime that might be related to their work. Worse, the SVR was now certain that *RECON* had a copy of the video. As a result, Viktor was told to remain in Chicago. His services might be needed again because, for reasons he didn't yet understand, *RECON* could not be allowed to broadcast the video. Viktor was ordered to prevent that, no matter what it took.

Warren told Beth Robileski about his plan to track down the killer and she knew just who to ask for help: her boyfriend Hubert

Gossich, who owned North Shore Data Analytics, one of the world's leading artificial intelligence firms. He was the nerdiest man she'd ever dated, but probably the kindest—and most definitely the smartest. That night, she studied him as he lay on his back in her bed, his bright red, curly hair splashed across the pillow.

"Hubert?" she called softly.

"Mmm?" The covers came up to his exposed, freckled chest, and he looked absolutely content. Hubert often told her she was the most beautiful woman he'd ever dated, and while Beth knew that couldn't be true, she sensed that Hubert saw her that way.

"Hubert," she said urgently. "I want to catch a killer."

Hubert opened his pale blue eyes and got up on one elbow. "The police are working on it, sweetheart."

"I know. But the Chicago Police Department doesn't have anyone like you on the force."

As he always did when she complimented him, Hubert blushed, his skin turning crimson.

"I'm sorry; I didn't mean to make you uncomfortable." Beth smiled. "But you really are brilliant."

He blushed again, then reached out to comb his hand through her hair. "I'd love to help, but what do you want me to do? I don't know anything about law enforcement."

"But you know how to find someone," she countered. "Remember those stories you told me, about people who were identified based on their Internet breadcrumbs, even though they never used their real names?"

"Sure," Hubert nodded. "It happens all the time, but it takes a lot of data. I'd love to help track down Monalisa's killer, but I can't go on nothing. Do you have any information about the person who did it?"

"Not yet. But I think Monalisa's death was related to a story we're working on. Rich told me she'd mentioned something about the dark web, so we're starting there."

"The dark web's very sketchy. Does anyone at *RECON* know how to navigate it?"

Beth shook her head. "But Warren stopped by to see me today. He's already got someone looking for evidence there. With your help, we might be able to track down the identity of the killer—if it's related to Monalisa's work."

Hubert thought it over. "Well...get me some data and I'll see what I can do."

8

BLACK AND WHITE RIOTS IN COLOR

Several of us attended Monalisa's funeral in her Iowa hometown. It was intensely sad, and there was a pall over the *RECON* offices when we returned to work. So, the next Monday morning, when I logged onto my computer to find another video had arrived, we were ready for the distraction. After I summoned the team, and we sat down at my conference table, I glanced over at the empty chair: Monalisa's absence felt like a punch to the gut. It would be strange and painful to watch the video without her profane commentary and boundless energy.

We were surprised to see that this video started in space. Earth was a small, blue dot; we could see the Sun in the distance, and the background was dotted with stars. That was unusual but not unprecedented. I'd seen a couple of Hollywood films that opened the same way. Then the camera flew towards the central United States; it only took a moment to determine that the location of this film was Tulsa, Oklahoma.

Without a cut, the camera swept through the streets of Tulsa and then stopped abruptly as it pulled up to a crowd of several hundred white men in front of a squarish, four-story building that appeared to be a courthouse or town hall. Most wore hats and skinny ties; they were carrying guns and seemed agitated. We later figured out we were watching the first day of the Tulsa Race Massacre, dating the scene to May 31st, 1921. Oddly, I felt less bewildered than I had when watching the previous videos. This one was just as mysterious as the others, but our minds were normalizing these strange movies of past events.

We heard a noise in the background, and the men turned to their right, checking their guns, and bracing for trouble. The camera panned to reveal a group of about two dozen ancient-looking cars and trucks arriving, carrying close to one hundred armed African American men. A white man with a badge, gun belt, and a large mustache strode off the steps of the government building, the crowd grudgingly parting for him. He must have been the chief of police or sheriff, but he moved with uncertainty, like he was in over his head. The Black men got out of their vehicles, and the sheriff walked up to them as the white men closed ranks behind him. There were twenty or so uniformed cops in the crowd—far too few to prevent trouble; the only Black cop in the scene joined the sheriff, and the camera moved in close to them.

"I need you men to go back home," the sheriff said.

"We're here to offer our services, Sheriff," the leader of the Black men replied. He gestured towards the crowd. "Seems like you could use some reinforcements, and most of us are veterans."

"Everything's under control," the sheriff countered, his voice revealing his stress.

The Black cop tried to placate the man. "I appreciate what you're doing, but the sheriff's right. It's better if you men go home."

The Black men began talking about protecting a boy named Rowland. When this name came up, anger rippled through the group of white men. I learned later that the Black men were trying to prevent the lynching of Dick Rowland, a 19-year-old African American man. The sheriff insisted he didn't need any help, and the whites were getting fed up with the whole exchange.

Unable to persuade the sheriff to accept their help, the Black man finally told the group they'd have to go back to "Greenwood." Reluctantly, the Black men turned to leave, picking their way between some of the white men who had gotten close. The scene was a tinderbox, needing nothing but a small spark to explode into violence. Most of the Greenwood men were back in their vehicles when a white man approached a tall Black man who was carrying a large revolver. "Nigger, what are you doing with that pistol?"

"I'm going to use it, if I need to," the man answered, putting his hand on the butt of the revolver.

"No, you ain't," the white man sneered. "You give it to me."

"Like hell I will."

The white man lunged forward, they struggled for a moment, and then the gun went off, and the war was on. The Black men were greatly outnumbered, but they'd already started their cars and trucks, so they were able to drive away before most of the white men could start shooting because they were standing behind others. Gunfire rang out, and men on both sides fell, but the Black men were soon gone, and things died down quickly.

One Black man hadn't made it to the vehicles in time. He lay screaming on the ground, blood pouring from a bullet wound in his stomach. An ancient-looking ambulance pulled up, and the driver and a helper jumped out—and ran straight into the cocked rifles and pistols of the white men, reveling in sadistic pleasure while the cops did nothing. For the next minute, we watched in horror as the victim writhed in pain and died, while many of the white men cheered.

The film laid bare the depth, ugliness, and tragedy of race hatred. Most of the scenes appeared to be in the Black part of town, because white people were in the streets, shooting into buildings where Black people shot back. Many structures were set ablaze by whites, but when fire trucks showed up, they were turned away by the mob. Cars full of white men drove down the streets, their occupants firing indiscriminately. We saw men, women and children killed as they fled. A white man climbed through the window of a neat clapboard frame home and trotted out a minute later carrying a jewelry box and a fur coat. Flames appeared behind him—he had set the house on fire after robbing it.

Night fell, and the point of view rose several hundred feet, panning to reveal a large neighborhood in flames, but without electricity—unlike the brightly lit areas of the city surrounding it. A minute later, it was daytime again, and the camera hovered next to a train station. On the left, we could see hundreds of white men inside and around the station. On the right were a few dozen Black men, trying to keep the white men at bay, taking cover behind cars, piles of railroad ties, telephone poles, and stacks of freight.

A train appeared and began slowing down to pull into the station, the engineer apparently unaware of the trouble he was about to roll through in Tulsa. Pulling a few passenger cars, the steam engine's brakes squealed, and men on both sides—for no visible reason—began shooting at the train as it approached. The engineer ducked below a window; the passengers quickly did the same. A second later, the engine belched an enormous cloud of smoke and lurched forward. As it became apparent that the train held no combatants—it appeared to be entirely empty, with everyone out of sight—the men stopped shooting as it huffed and rattled off into the distance. A moment later, the men started firing at each other again.

The Sun was climbing in the sky when the stalemate ended. Some of the white men laid down a covering fire, and the rest charged forward as a group, screaming and shooting as they ran across the tracks, trampling the Black men into the ground as they stormed past. The violence was gut-wrenching. All these people lived in America—the home of democracy. Many of the men, white and Black, had fought in World War I. Now, for something as thin and meaningless as skin color, white men were attacking and murdering Black men, women, and children.

The camera flew up from the street and darted between several open-cockpit biplanes flying low over the Greenwood District. These were two-seaters, and in most of them, men sat behind the pilots and shot down into the streets with rifles. A couple were armed with machine guns and sprayed bullets everywhere. We saw men in two planes lighting incendiary devices which they dropped onto rooftops, quickly turning buildings into conflagrations. This was the first incendiary bombing in history, and it wasn't part of an overseas conflict. It involved white men attacking an affluent district in Tulsa, simply because its residents were Black. The people of Greenwood were so busy fighting for their lives that they had no time to fight the fires and would have been shot dead if they'd tried.

The brutality continued, and I wondered for a moment why it seemed even worse than the other films. Part of it was that the event was a much larger tragedy. Also, unlike Custer and his men, the victims in this film were not the aggressors. But there was something else, too. I was beginning to believe that we were watching real footage of these events. I couldn't shake the feeling that we were witnessing the actual Tulsa race massacre of 1921. I remembered my phone call with Monalisa when she excitedly told me she couldn't find any evidence of CGI.

The film moved on to the second day of the massacre. We watched as cops, military personnel, and bands of armed white civilians rounded up Black people. The camera narrowed in to focus on a group of five white men leading a well-dressed Black man along a sidewalk. He maintained his dignity and bearing as they taunted him, refusing to respond as they yelled, "You sure do think you're one important nigger, don't you?" The group pushed the man down an alley and shot him dead in cold blood; he collapsed onto the dusty ground as the white men celebrated.

The camera flew up from the street, traveled across several blocks, and hovered over a fairground, where armed white men surrounded thousands of Black people of all ages. Whole families, homeless and held captive, for nothing more than their skin color. Then the shot cut to an overhead view of a field next to a river, where dozens of Black people lay dead or dying on the ground as a bulldozer dug a deep trench, and white men tossed bodies into it. It was mass murder and a mass grave, American style.

Abruptly, the film stopped. Carl was a mess of tears, holding back sobs. Beth and Warren were crying quietly, and Rosalie's fury was obvious. I realized with horror that this example of the fruits of racism was almost lost to America's consciousness, even as hatred was making a roaring comeback in our country.

My team and I thought we'd seen it all, but it took everyone around the table a couple of minutes to regain their composure. I tried to find words that would help. "Well," I started, and then cleared my throat. "To paraphrase someone we all wish was here to help us: 'Let's figure out who the fuck made this, why the fuck they showed it to us, and what the fuck we're going to do about it.'"

As people do when they're emotional, they laughed a little bit. Carl gave me a thumbs up.

"Hey Rich," Warren said tentatively, "Shouldn't we find out how they put it on your—uh—frickin' computer, too?"

I shook my head. "No, I don't think you're going to figure that out, Warren, and I don't think anyone else could, either. So, I appreciate the security measures you've put in place, but let's back off a little, okay? This mystery keeps getting deeper, and it's time the *RECON* team gets back to communicating with the world like normal people, okay?"

Warren nodded somberly. Then Carl, recovering from the film's gore, announced, "ACCESS GRANTED!"

We laughed through our tears, as our network guru grinned sheepishly.

After everyone had left for the day, Rosalie retrieved her Silent Phone, and texted:

TRM Asset received/viewed/evaluated. Predict vetting next w/TGCC. Prep for IC inquiry. Threat: 3.5.

The message was confirmed and burned, and Rosalie went home.

9

THE ENEMY OF MY ENEMY

Heath Cobb knocked on Warren's apartment door.

"Thanks for coming," Warren said, swinging the door open.

Heath was one of Monalisa's gaming friends. Medium height, wiry, dressed fashionably, and sporting stylish blonde hair, Heath looked like he belonged in a boy band. He was also exactly the kind of person Warren spent his professional life working to defeat—a hacker who stole data and destroyed the careers of technology professionals. They'd partied together several times before Warren learned what Heath did for a living. Monalisa told him casually at Revival Food Hall after work one evening.

Warren was stunned. "He's a *hacker*?"

Monalisa nodded enthusiastically. "Oh yeah. And a great one, too!" She seemed proud.

"Holy moly. You *do* understand what I do for a living, right?"

Monalisa rolled her eyes. "For God's sake, Heath knows *RECON* is off limits. I told him to stay out of our network."

"He couldn't get *into* our network in the first place," Warren objected, following Monalisa right off the main topic, as usual.

"What's your problem?" Monalisa demanded, miffed. "Heath's a friend of mine and he's not a threat to you or *RECON*, so let it go!"

After Monalisa's murder, Warren decided Heath's skills could come in handy. The two met in person so Warren could show him the Little Big Horn video and explain the challenges in understanding how it was made. Heath, eager to help, spent most of the next thirty-six hours on the dark web and was ready to report what he'd found.

Heath sat at the kitchen counter, his back to the small living room. Warren leaned his big shoulders against the refrigerator, his head towering over it, and tipped his bottle of beer at Heath. "Thanks for coming over; I can't wait to see what you found."

"Happy to help. I've got some pretty good stuff for you." Heath opened his laptop. "I spent hours on dark web forums about video editing and found nada. I mean, there's a lot of interesting shit down there, but nothing specific to this film. And then I started searching for info on 'deep fakes' and found this." He spun his computer around and showed Warren an exchange of messages between users named FUtrollboy and BlackSpider150.

"FUtrollboy?" Warren read. "Is there a screen name more like Monalisa than that?"

Heath chuckled. "I know, right? That's our girl. Check out the video she attached." He clicked on the screen and played thirty seconds of the Little Bighorn video.

Warren read the whole exchange twice. "Heath, you're a miracle worker, man. I can't believe you found this. BlackSpider150 is our man. I wonder who he is."

"No idea. What other information do you need to track him down?"

Warren gestured towards Heath's laptop. "What I need you to do next is see if BlackSpider150 has posted anywhere else on the dark web. What words and phrases does he use, what topics does he ask about? Does he reveal any other identifying information through his online actions?"

Heath broke into a smile. "Good news, my man. I already did that." He reached into his pocket and flipped a USB drive to Warren. Warren caught it and grinned back at him.

Heath continued. "I've got more than two hundred posts by BlackSpider150. After he connected with Monalisa, he reposted her video clip to see if anyone else knew about it. He also engaged in a lot of dialogue around emerging CGI techniques—and he asked questions about who might be developing next-gen technology. You know, stuff more advanced than the AI video generators available to the public."

"Did he get any answers?"

Heath shook his head. "No one had any idea how that video was shot, but it generated some dialogue with this 'Black Spider' character. There's a lot of information in there."

Warren held onto the drive as if it was delicate and precious and smiled. "This is fantastic, Heath. Thank you. I have a hunch this is going to be very helpful."

Heath grinned appreciatively. "It took me nearly thirty hours to find this, my friend. You can't search on the dark web the way you do with Google, but I don't think there's much more out there. I hope it's enough." He stood up and stuck out his hand. "Nail the fucker, will you?"

Warren grinned, shaking Heath's hand a little too enthusiastically for the hacker's taste. For such an attractive man, Heath decided, Warren was the opposite of cool.

"I'll try really hard," Warren replied. Then his face grew dark and serious. "And if I get my hands on him, I'll kill him myself."

Heath was startled, not just by the words, but because he sensed Warren meant them. It dawned on him that Warren's apparent lack of guile was misleading. *This man is easy to underestimate*, he thought as he walked out of the apartment.

I took a rideshare to see Angela for the first time in a month. She was on her balcony holding her binoculars in her lap when I arrived. An orderly sat by the door.

"Hi Angela," I said, sitting down on the bench that lined the railing.

"I can't see when you sit there," Angela replied irritably.

I slid over. "How's this?"

She nodded, put the binoculars to her eyes and scanned the lake. The Sun was setting, casting a golden glow on the water. I missed the days when Angela and I could share these scenes in a meaningful way.

"I saw a big ship today," she announced.

"Did you? Was it the *Tillbeck*?" After my last visit, I had searched for the *Tillbeck* on the Internet, only to find that there was no evidence a ship of that name ever existed.

She shook her head. "No, this was the *Deutschland*. I have to know about it for my husband's story," she said matter-of-factly.

The *Deutschland* didn't sound like the name of a yacht or a lake freighter to me, so I searched for it on my phone; this time, I got a hit. The SS *Deutschland* was a passenger liner that had been scrapped in 1925. Definitely not the ship Angela had seen—assuming she'd seen a ship.

I tried to engage my wife in conversation, but it was fruitless. A couple of hours later, I told her I had to leave. For decades, every parting meant a kiss and a hug; now our goodbyes were meaningless to her. As I stood up, Angela lowered the binoculars and said, "Heloisa is going to help you."

I wondered what chemical processes in her brain were bringing back memories of that little girl from long ago. I went downstairs, climbed into a rideshare a few minutes later, and we drove away from despair towards a city of hope.

RECON's next security lapse occurred less than a week later, but this one didn't come through the Internet; it walked in the front door. Like many administrative assistants who support powerful people, Rosalie enjoyed quite a bit of freedom and deference. The effect was especially profound on people like Larry, the security guard stationed in the lobby of the *RECON* building. It was his job to make sure no one got in who didn't have permission. *RECON* had tight rules around visitor access, which was only granted in advance of a visit, and was absolutely noted in the computer.

So, when Larry saw Rosalie Jemison walking towards him with a tall, rugged-looking man, he turned to the computer on the security desk. A quick double-check confirmed the schedule was empty, and he studied the approaching pair, trying hard to remember if he'd seen the guy before. He decided he was sure he hadn't.

"Good afternoon, Ms. Jemison," Larry nodded. "It's rare that I get to see you here on a Saturday."

Rosalie looked at him slyly. "Are you saying I'm not working enough weekends, Larry?"

He was immediately rattled. "Oh—ah—no; I mean, of course not, Ms. Jemison. I was just sayin' it's really nice to see you. I didn't mean no offense."

When Rosalie smiled broadly, it occurred to Larry that he'd never seen her smile at all. He felt relieved that she wasn't *really* angry at him.

"Larry," Rosalie said in a low, conspiratorial voice. "No one here knows about my boyfriend, John..." She gestured towards the tall man. The guy was handsome and athletic; he seemed like a match for Rosalie.

"Nice to meet you, John," Larry said. A moment later he extended his hand.

"Thanks Larry," the man replied, shaking it.

Rosalie continued. "I want to give John a quick tour so he can see where I work. I tell him about it, but I can't bring him to the office during working hours. We're private people and we keep our personal lives...well...to ourselves."

Larry was conflicted. He wanted to give Rosalie whatever she wanted, but breaking the rules was a big deal. He'd been warned about it during team meetings: no exceptions, ever.

But then he remembered that Rich Penton himself—who was the whole reason *RECON* even existed, for Chrissakes—had brought his girlfriend in a year and a half ago. Mr. Penton had also asked Larry to break the rules, because he hadn't scheduled the visit. Obviously, Larry wasn't going to say no to Rich Penton, so he'd obliged him and nothing bad had happened.

Rosalie was waiting patiently. *What the hell.* Larry winked at them. "I don't think it's going to hurt anything if you two have a quick look around. But don't get my ass in a sling over it, okay?"

Rosalie smiled broadly and gushed. "Thank you, Larry. I won't tell anyone, I promise!" They rode up the elevator in silence and Rosalie used her badge to access Rich's office. She logged in to his computer using the credentials she'd gotten from Warren and stepped aside. "John," whose real name was Gary, pulled a USB drive out of his pocket, slid into the desk chair, and went to work. Rosalie sat down in one of Rich's conference room chairs.

"How does this work?" she asked. Gone were all traces of the chattiness she'd shown around Larry.

"You said he synchs his phone and his computer with a cable every day, right?"

"Yes."

"Next time he does that, this app will be added to his phone. It'll run in the background; he won't know it's there unless he's good with technology—"

"He's terrible."

"Or he gives his phone to someone in IT Security for some reason."

"I'll make sure that doesn't happen."

"In that case," Gary said, finishing up his work, "pretty soon, you'll get copies of all his emails and text messages."

"On the new phone you gave me," she confirmed.

"Yep."

"I get his emails when I'm at work, but not when I'm out of the office," she thought aloud. "Now I'll have them 24x7, and his text messages, too."

Gary studied her. "I damn well hope you're right about the need to do this. We just tapped the email and text messages of one of the world's best-known journalists," he stressed, as though she wasn't getting the seriousness of the situation. "If *RECON* finds out and identifies us, we're going to be in deep shit."

She stood up and Gary reflexively stood up, too. "I have it under control," she said and then walked out the door, waiting for Gary so she could lock it behind him.

A few minutes later, they stepped out of the elevator holding hands, chatting in soft, excited tones, like couples do during an adventure. Rosalie thanked Larry profusely for his assistance and discretion and he shook their hands again. When they were a block away, she dropped Gary's hand and walked away without looking back. Gary watched her go. He had a lot of respect for and a little bit of fear of Rosalie, but the stunt they'd just pulled could land them both in jail.

He hoped she really did have it under control.

10

THE PURITY OF EVIL AND GOOD

May 12th: 156 Days Before Arrival

Viktor Stolypin Dyavol was born in 1966, in the Soviet city of
Mezhdurechensk, the home of the enormous Raspadskaya coal mine.
His father, Vilen, began working at the mine when it opened in
1973. The dangerous and demanding work eventually wrecked his
health, the decline exacerbated by the enormous amounts of vodka
he drank each night. He raged back at the world while Viktor's
mother cowered and hid as her husband took out his frustrations on
his only child. By the time Viktor turned seventeen, he had grown
large and strong. One day, his father slapped him for some petty
offense, and Viktor knocked the drunk unconscious, as his mother
pleaded with him to show compassion. *Where were your pleas for
mercy when the monster beat me?* he had wondered contemptuously.

In order to avoid trouble with the police, Viktor never struck his
father again. Their relationship was reduced to the mumbles required
to survive in the same household. He couldn't wait to get away from
Mezhdurechensk and test himself as a man, and he decided the best

way to accomplish these goals was to join the Soviet Army. When he turned eighteen, he packed a few possessions and walked out of his parents' house forever.

The Soviet Union and Afghanistan were engaged in a long and protracted war at the time, and Viktor soon found himself in combat. Built for strength and endurance and blessed with the ability to think and act despite being surrounded by terror, Viktor was invited to join the Spetsnaz—the Soviet special forces—where he found a father figure of sorts. Captain Alexander Kotlyarevski recognized Viktor's potential and gave him something he'd starved for his whole life: praise. Viktor became so devoted to the captain that everyone knew not to criticize the officer in the presence of the formidable young corporal.

One day, during a firefight, a little Afghan girl came running towards them, screaming in fear, tears streaming down her face. Viktor drew a bead with his weapon, but Kotlyarevski waved for him to lower his rifle. The captain scooped up the terrified little girl and pulled her out of the raging battle.

"It's okay, little one," he soothed.

And then the bomb strapped to the girl exploded, vaporizing her and the captain simultaneously. A half dozen other soldiers were wounded, and Viktor was covered in flesh and blood—most of it from the only man he'd ever truly admired. Viktor never again took mercy on any insurgents—even children. And if the girls were of a certain age, he'd extract revenge in other ways, too.

Viktor left every engagement and mission under his own power, at worst suffering minor injuries. His strength didn't fade as he grew older, but his professional prospects dissolved entirely. First, the Soviet Union fell, then the Russians got out of Afghanistan, and by 2005, Viktor was reduced to jobs in Moscow as a bouncer and occasional enforcer for a local organized crime gang. This generated enough income for a small apartment, vodka, and the prostitutes he used to release his sexual energy and anger.

Everything changed when a major from his old unit walked into his bar one evening. They drank and shared war stories, laughing at some of them while Viktor was reminded of his grief and rage about Captain Kotlyarevski. When they were good and drunk, the major glanced around the bar, leaned in conspiratorially, and offered Viktor a job doing what he did better than anyone: killing. The SVR needed his services, the major told him. In the years since, Viktor had become fluent in English, and he had traveled the globe providing security, intimidation, and assassinations, as his bosses needed.

Now that he was working on the *RECON* case, his boss told him there were other videos besides the one with soldiers and Indians. Some of them were documentary-style depictions of historical events, which struck Viktor as very odd, but the SVR was most concerned about a brief film showing something blowing up the city of Chicago. It was especially important that the Americans didn't pay attention to *that* one.

The SVR's strategy was to discredit the videos by persuading the United States government that the Russians had produced them. So far, this seemed to be working. US intelligence agencies had concluded the videos were part of an SVR disinformation campaign. The irony was delicious, even though Viktor didn't fully understand the situation. *Why were the videos so important, and if Russia didn't make them, who did?*

Viktor was told to find out which videos *RECON* had received, if they had figured out the truth behind them, and if they planned to do a broadcast explaining the meaning to their audience. He and his boss discussed the situation and came up with a clever way to get this information. It would take some work, and they'd have to find the right targets, but they ran their idea up the chain of command. After the debacle with the girl, Viktor's bosses knew he was motivated to ensure he was back in their good graces. He was competent, and he was already in Chicago, so they approved the plan.

Eliza and I live on the 35th floor of 2550 North Lakeview Avenue. One of the benefits of this location is our proximity to North Pond Restaurant, situated within Lincoln Park. We can see North Pond (the restaurant and the small body of water) and stroll there in less than ten minutes. Sometimes we talk about work, but as a theoretical physicist at a great university, Eliza can understand nearly everything about my job, while I can grasp little to nothing about hers. Nevertheless, we have great conversations, and she often manages to break down complex scientific theories so I can comprehend them—at least a little.

One night, when were at dinner at North Pond, Eliza tried to help me understand a physics concept, not just to satisfy my curiosity but to help me in my job. Thanks to the mysterious videos, that concept was time travel. I kicked off the conversation by demonstrating my nuanced and sophisticated understanding of the subject.

"Time travel is science fiction bullshit."

Eliza's blue eyes filled with humor as she shook her head and sighed. Her hair was gathered into a ponytail behind her slim neck, and she wore a simple cocktail dress and low heels. She directed her bright blue eyes to mine. "We have time travelers among us, Rich."

I raised my eyebrows and then studied the people in the restaurant with faux suspicion. "Hmm... No nineteenth century suits. No dinosaurs." I peered out the window. "No DeLoreans." I turned back to Eliza. "You got me. Who's the time traveler among us?"

She gave me a withering stare. "God, you really did grow up in a cabin, didn't you?"

I laughed. "Not quite. But explain to me how it is that we have time travelers among us."

"Well, my child," she began, as I grinned and picked up my wine glass. "Isaac Newton—of whom you may have heard—even atop the mountain in Colorado from which you wandered..."

"Is he here? Isaac Newton is our time traveler?"

"No. This explanation is a bit more involved than that. Among Newton's correct discoveries and accomplishments were a few ideas that were later proven entirely wrong."

"Such as?"

"Such as claiming that space is absolute, and time is absolute. He thought they were fixed. In other words, he assumed distances are measured the same in all cases and places, and so is time. A meter is a meter, a minute is a minute, and these never vary under any circumstances throughout the universe."

"That's not the case?" I was surprised.

Eliza shook her head. "For two hundred years, these claims went unchallenged in the scientific community. Indeed, experiments that produced data inconsistent with these principles were deemed faulty. Science has a nasty habit of developing its own rigid belief systems that reject contradictory data. Then along came a genius named Albert Einstein. You've heard of him, perhaps?"

"Yes. Crazy-haired fellow who used to leave his house without his pants on, as I recall."

"Urban legend," Eliza replied. "Anyway, you are no doubt aware that Einstein posited both the general theory of relativity and the special theory of relativity."

Until this very moment, I'd had no idea there were two theories of relativity. I decided not to admit my relative ignorance and nodded.

"In his *special* theory of relativity—which he developed in 1905, if you can imagine—Einstein determined that neither time nor space are absolute. Instead, they are relative to each other—thus, '*relativity*.'"

"What does that mean?"

"The best example is the speed of light," she explained. "We know that light travels 186,000 miles per second in a vacuum like space, right?"

"Right." I'd heard that before.

"And you've heard that nothing can travel faster than light?"

I nodded again.

"Well, that's only part of the story. Note that the definition of 'speed' includes two components: distance—186,000 miles in this case—and a unit of time: one second. All speed measurements include both components, right? Distance and the time it takes to cover it."

"Makes sense. If I say my car does the quarter mile in twenty seconds—"

"Then you'd have a slow car," she interjected. "But yes, that's the idea. One of Einstein's breakthroughs in the theory of special relativity was that the speed of light was absolute to all observers, regardless of their speed."

"Okay... can you give me an example?"

"Sure." She thought for a moment. "Let's say you're wearing a spacesuit and standing on the moon. Meanwhile, I'm in a rocket speeding away from you as fast as I can go, which we'll arbitrarily set at half the speed of light."

"Got it. I'm lonely already. Please come back."

"Okay, I will. If you can answer one question correctly."

"I'll try."

"Well, we can't ask for more than that, I suppose," she sighed, winking at me. "Right after I take off, a beam of light is shot from earth towards me, but it first must pass by you as you stand on the moon. Light moves at 186,000 miles per second. You're standing still, so when the light beam goes by you, that's the speed it's going in the vacuum of space."

"Makes sense."

"Remember, I'm moving at half the speed of light. When the

beam of light passes me, how fast is it going relative to me and my rocket?"

"That's the question? If I don't answer this correctly, I'll be all alone on the moon?"

"Well, you won't be lonely for very long. You'll run out of air quickly."

"You're so comforting." I laughed and then did the math in my head. "Okay, I think I've got this. If the speed of light is 186,000 miles per second and you're flying at half the speed of light, that means relative to your rocket, the light beam is passing you at a rate of 93,000 miles per second. 186,000 divided by two is 93,000. Now, turn your rocket around and pick me up for dinner."

Eliza shook her head. "I'm going to fly back and pick you up because I miss you. But your answer is incorrect."

I did the math again and got the same answer. "What am I missing?"

"Remember what I said at the beginning. Einstein proved that light travels at the same speed in a vacuum, *regardless of the speed of the observer.* That means that no matter how fast I'm traveling, when light goes by me, it's moving 186,000 miles per second faster than I am."

"Wait...what?" I was completely confused. "If it's traveling 186,000 miles per second relative to your speed, wouldn't that mean it's traveling at one and a half times that rate relative to me?"

Eliza shook her head. "No. Light can't travel faster than 186,000 miles per second. The answer isn't in the speed of light—it never changes for any observer. The answer is in how fast *time* moves— time has slowed down for me compared to you. To both of us, every- thing would be happening in 'normal' time. But if we could see each other as this happened, it would appear to you as though I'm moving very, very slowly and it would look to me as though you were moving very, very quickly."

I sighed. "Okay, I am an idiot. I don't understand this at all. I'm just a talking head, remember?"

She shook her head. "Don't be discouraged; none of this fits with our lifelong experiences of time and space because at the speeds of everything we do, the differences are too small to detect. That's why it took one of history's greatest geniuses to figure out, after two hundred years, that Newton was wrong. Thanks to Einstein, we understand that as we move faster, time slows down."

I pondered that for a moment. "So, if you were going half the speed of light when the beam passed you, then your second was much longer than mine?"

"Relative to yours, yes. It would seem like a normal second to me because everything in my frame of reference would slow down, including my physiological processes and my perception of time. But when I got back to the moon to pick you up, much more time would have passed for you than for me."

I thought for a minute. "But how does this relate to time travel?"

"Well, remember, the speed of light is constant, but time slows down the faster you move. If you took off on a spaceship that flew at 87% of the speed of light, time would pass at half the rate it does on earth. If you flew at 99.5% the speed of light and came back after ten years, one hundred years would have passed on earth."

"Wow, now we're getting somewhere. But who are the time travelers among us?"

"All of us," Eliza said. "We're all traveling into the future, but we're doing it at a rate we understand. One second equals one second. Astronauts on rockets or space stations travel into the future by a few microseconds—not enough to notice. But if we can go from the Wright brothers' first flight in 1903, to thousands of satellites traveling at speeds of 17,000 miles per hour in space in a little more than 120 years, it's not hard to imagine a civilization a billion years ahead of us traveling at near-light speeds. That's one way to make interstellar travel possible, but wherever you went, you'd be moving forward in time by thousands of years on every trip."

"That doesn't seem very useful. Are there other mechanisms to enable time travel?" I asked.

"Goodness, yes!" she exclaimed. The conversation obviously excited her. Who knew time travel could be so sexy?

"Let's discuss general relativity. Einstein spent ten years working on that theory, which he released in 1915. In GR, he proved that time slows down when you are near a massive object, even one the size of Earth, which is quite small in celestial terms. Consider special and general relativity when it comes to satellites. Thanks to their great speed, special relativity causes them to fall behind earth clocks by about seven microseconds per day. But since they're farther from earth, they're less affected by gravity, which causes them to *gain* forty-five microseconds per day compared to ground clocks. The net effect is that satellites move about thirty-eight microseconds into the future each day."

"That sounds like virtually nothing. Does it really matter?"

"Oh yes," Eliza said, brightly. "If satellites weren't equipped with clocks that ran slightly slower than earth clocks, GPS coordinates would be off by more than six miles in a single day."

I absorbed what she'd said. "Okay, I think I understand. Special relativity makes satellites move slower than earth time, but general relativity has an even greater effect that causes them to move a little more quickly into the future. I can understand how some advanced civilization might build rockets to go some fraction of the speed of light that causes them to move into the future. Or maybe use gravity in a way we don't understand."

"Excellent!"

"But what exactly is gravity?"

Eliza threw up her hands. "Nobody knows!"

"Wait," I protested. "Newton discovered gravity back in..." I waited for her to complete my sentence. I had absolutely no idea.

"1687," she offered.

"Right," I replied, like it had slipped my mind. "Are you telling me that more than three hundred years later, we don't know what causes gravity?"

"Not really. Some physicists think particles called 'gravitons' generate gravitational force, but we've never observed or even detected them. Einstein theorized that gravity results from the curvature of spacetime around objects. No one knows which is correct—and both might be wrong."

My head was spinning. "So, neither of these has been proven? We really don't know where gravity comes from?"

"We don't. Think about it, Rich. You can stand on the beach at night and watch the waves crash while the tides rise and fall. From 240,000 miles away, the moon causes all of Earth's oceans to move as they do, but we don't actually understand the force that connects them. We call it 'gravity,' but what it is remains a mystery. And we know that gravity dilates time like speed does, but we don't understand how. But we do know that if you could manipulate gravity, you could theoretically control your movement through time."

"Is there any evidence you can manipulate gravity?" I asked.

"Evidence? Not really. But if we knew how, our fundamental relationship with space and time would be transformed. Some physicists propose a theoretical spacecraft with a propulsion system that creates its own geodesics by curving spacetime around it. Such a craft would experience no acceleration effects like G forces but could instantly achieve effective velocities of hundreds of thousands of miles per hour."

I stared at her blankly. "Is that even possible in theory?"

"It is if you can control gravity—which might be child's play for a civilization that developed millions of years before we did. For all we know, they use gravity, time dilation from speed, or some other mechanism to travel here today."

"Ah yes," I said, lightly. "Extraterrestrials." I glanced around the restaurant. "Much better odds of those in the restaurant than time travelers."

Eliza wasn't laughing. "Maybe not extraterrestrials, Rich. They could be something else entirely. Some people use the term *interdimensionals*, but that really has no specific meaning."

I was surprised. Eliza was a world-class scientist and had never mentioned *extraterrestrials* or *interdimensionals*—whatever that meant—before now. "I defer to your expertise," I said, mystified, "but one more question."

"Mmmm?" She raised her eyebrows.

"Does the satellite example mean science has proven that time travel to the future *and* the past is possible? We're obviously on the subject of time travel because of these videos I've been getting. And they're from the past."

"Good question," she began. "And the answer is no. Great speed will slow down time but that's far different than actually going backwards in time. Mathematically, these and other theories work equally well in either direction. However, experimentally, we can only prove that traveling forward in time is real."

"So, we don't know if there's any way to travel back in time?"

"No, but there's a logical argument that it should be possible."

"What is it?"

"Well," she continued. "You know how time is sometimes called, 'the fourth dimension?' It's different because it's not spatial, but it's like another dimension."

"Sure."

"So, the other three can be described as left and right, forward and back, up and down, right? We all have the ability and the choice to move in these directions."

"Yes."

"Then why would we only be able to move one direction in this *fourth dimension* we call time?"

"That makes sense." The logic was hard to dispute.

I signaled for the check. As the waiter headed towards us, I asked, "Are there many physicists actually working on traveling back in time?"

"Sure, lots of them. I'll introduce you to one of the leading thinkers in the field. He's at MIT."

"Thanks!" I exclaimed. "What's his name?"

"Chandra Ramanujan."

Something about the name seemed familiar, and then I remembered a segment *RECON* produced on a Nobel Prize winning physicist, who told me his work was based on an early 20th century Indian mathematician with the same last name. "Is he related to—" I couldn't come up with the full name...

"Srinivasa Ramanujan?" she suggested as we stood up and headed for the door.

"That's the guy. Is Chandra Ramanujan related to Srinivasa?"

"No one knows. One of the great tragedies of science is that Srinivasa Ramanujan died at thirty-two years old, and his lineage is unknown. He lives on through his work; mathematicians are still finding insights in his journals, and some of his breakthroughs weren't understood until they could be analyzed with modern computers."

"Wow! Well, if Chandra Ramanujan is anything like Srinivasa, he must be a real genius."

"He is," Eliza nodded. "He grew up in poverty in India like Srinivasa did, and now he's a physicist at MIT. His latest work on the topography of the universe implies the possibility of *superluminal signal propagation*—" she paused and looked over at me. "Sending signals faster than light," she clarified.

"'Superluminal signal propagation,'" I echoed, slowly. "I love when you talk dirty."

She laughed, slid her arm through mine, and laid her head on my shoulder as we walked.

"You're one smart cookie," I told her. "Not to mention sexy."

"Mmm hmm. You're a lucky man, Rich Penton."

I laughed and held her a little tighter. When we walked into our condo, I took Eliza's hand and led her to the bedroom where we made love with the veranda doors open, a pure breeze coming off Lake Michigan. I fell asleep with her curled up in my arms.

11

A TRAIL OF BREADCRUMBS
AND THE BIG, BAD, WOLF

May 13th: 155 Days Before Arrival

When Viktor received the intelligence report on Maura Mcpeek's coworkers at *RECON*, he determined that his first target would be the director, Carl Swinton. Viktor's paradigm of directors was that they were screaming, controlling assholes, so he was surprised when he read the psychographic profile of Swinton: soft spoken, married to the same woman for thirty-five years, and as reliable as a wolfhound. He couldn't imagine how Swinton had managed to succeed in the world of television news with its cutthroat reputation, but there's an exception to every rule and Viktor would take the lucky break that offered him such a vulnerable target near the nerve center of *RECON*.

Viktor used the local team's connections to recruit three young women to dress up like Naperville High School students and conduct surveillance on Carl's house. Viktor quickly pieced together Carl's routine and saw an opening: the Swintons went to church every Sunday. He knew this because one of the girls had opened their mailbox when it was dark and found a newsletter from the local

Episcopal church. The same girl had seen the Swintons drive away the next Sunday morning and return almost three hours later: *Sunday, church, lunch,* the girl speculated to him.

"Is that really useful?" she asked, peering up at him from the passenger seat of the car when they met a few blocks from Carl's house. She was small and defenseless, and he thought of her as he drove home, feeling the temptation mounting. *It would be so easy.* Then he shook it off. *Not important. Focus.*

Viktor entered Carl and Wendy Swinton's home in Naperville at 9:25 a.m. the following Sunday. He left his car in a nearby park, walked to the house and down the driveway, and was relieved to see that trees obscured the backyard. He scanned around as he listened for noises from inside. All clear. Through the kitchen window, he could see the security system keypad was off. There were no external cameras, the locks were ordinary and easy to pick, and moments later, he was standing in the Swinton's kitchen.

Viktor decided the light fixture above the kitchen table was just right for his purposes, so he tested the wall switches until he found the right one and turned off the power. Then he unscrewed the base of the fixture, slid it down the decorative chain and wired in a small, electronic device consisting of a circuit board, a tiny microphone, and a thin cable that served as an antenna. He reassembled the fixture, ensured the microphone was pointed through the hole, and entwined the antenna wire with the decorative chain. The setup was practically invisible, and the transmitter only needed a couple of hours of power per day to broadcast continuously. The device communicated a secure signal through a cell phone network, allowing Viktor to hear everything Carl and his wife discussed when they were nearby.

Viktor did one last check to make sure he had left no trace of his presence and noticed Carl's badge to the *RECON* building sitting in a bowl by the door. *That might come in handy,* he thought, as he pocketed it. Then he glanced out the back window and carefully exited. As he walked to the corner of the house, he almost ran into a large man coming the other way.

Both men stopped. Viktor assessed his opponent: early forties, muscular, self-confident, and completely surprised; he showed no tactical awareness. It remained to be seen if the man had any fighting skill.

The opponent spoke first. "Who are *you*?" It was a challenge but a polite one—the man didn't like what he saw but he was allowing for the possibility that Viktor was there for something other than nefarious reasons.

"I'm Dwight," Viktor replied. "Who are you?"

The man sized him up. "Bob Johanssen. I live down the block. My lawn mower won't start, so I was going to borrow Carl's. Is he home?"

Viktor had to make sure the man was not a U.S. intelligence agent of some kind. To do that, he needed to keep him talking. So, instead of answering Johanssen's question, he asked, "Do you always come to the back door?"

"Everybody comes to the Swintons' back door," the man answered. And then a thought occurred to him. "All their friends know that."

That *was* a challenge. Clearly, Viktor had made the man suspicious, but he was now certain the man was just a neighbor. "Nice to meet you, Bob," he said, and began to walk around the man.

"Hold on," Johanssen objected. "You're not going anywhere." He put his right hand up to stop Viktor and it was his last act before dying. Viktor grabbed Bob's head, his right hand cupping the man's chin with the other wrapped around the back, just above the neckline. The Russian rotated hard left, using the momentum of his body to generate an abrupt and powerful twisting motion on the man's neck. Viktor heard vertebrae snapping and before the movement was complete, he let go and Bob Johanssen fell to the ground, dead.

"Shit," Viktor muttered under his breath, annoyed at the complication. But it was a good, clean, efficient kill and if he could get rid of the man's body without being seen, the whole operation might be saved. Viktor retrieved his car and backed it down the driveway to the edge of the house. He grunted as he picked up the body and dumped it into the trunk, fairly certain there were no prying eyes to see him. With the bug installed, he'd know from the Swintons if the authorities suspected anything.

Two hours later, long before a missing person's report was filed, Bob Johanssen's body was incinerated in a mortuary on the south side of Chicago. His wife, Heather, had been at church with the Swintons; she didn't know their lawn mower wouldn't start, and no one had seen Bob walking to Carl and Wendy's house. It was as though he'd vanished into thin air.

The device Viktor had installed worked perfectly. That night, he listened to the Swintons discuss their missing neighbor. Now, he needed them to talk about the fucking videos and whether *RECON* was planning to broadcast them. His luck was returning, and he was anxious to take care of business.

Beth and Warren sat across from Hubert at the headquarters of North Shore Data Analytics. Under Hubert's leadership, NSDA had grown to more than three hundred employees, including an army of brilliant machine data scientists who built artificial intelligence systems. Hubert glanced forlornly at his desk, where printouts of Heath's screenshots lay, a little crumpled. He was keenly aware that this was the first professional favor Beth had ever requested of him, and he worked to hold back signs of anxiety after seeing the meager offering Warren brought.

Hubert wasn't sure how to play it. He desperately wanted to help, but the odds of his team tracking down a single individual based on such a tiny amount of data were...not good. He didn't want to set expectations he couldn't meet, but he also didn't want to appear less than confident to Beth, since there was at least a *small* chance they would find something.

"I'm *certain* we'll be able to find something," he blurted out, regretting the words as he spoke them.

"Really?" Warren replied, brightening noticeably. "Just on this? Big Data and AI models must have progressed a ton since the articles I read."

"That's really encouraging, Hubert," Beth said, studying her boyfriend carefully. He smiled at her but suddenly knew his false bravado was apparent to his very intuitive girlfriend. This sparked a new thought. *This isn't about impressing Beth, damn it. You're trying to solve a murder!*

"Well," she responded carefully. "Let's not get ahead of ourselves. These may be the only posts by this individual we'll ever find."

"Well, that's true too, of course," Hubert agreed, welcoming the opportunity to take the edge off his upbeat prediction. He was painfully aware that Beth's estimate of the situation was much more accurate than his. Despite more than thirty years of experience in analytics and AI, he'd made the mistake of allowing love to influence his assessment.

Warren looked a little crestfallen. "Oh, okay. So, maybe we shouldn't feel *certain,* as much as optimistic?"

Hubert nodded and glanced over at Beth to see if he had disappointed her.

She gave him a warm and supportive smile. "If anyone can do it, you can," she reassured him. "And that means if you can't find this guy, it's strictly because we don't have the data, and we'll have to keep searching."

They planned for a follow-up meeting and then Hubert stuck out his hand to Warren, who took it in his large paw and shook it vigorously. Not knowing the protocol in such situations, and not wanting to offend Beth with a show of unprofessionalism in front of a coworker, Hubert then offered his hand to Beth. She smiled affectionately, walked around his desk, hugged him, and kissed him on the lips.

"You're the best," she said. "Thank you for helping us." Hubert flushed with embarrassment. Warren grinned.

As Beth released him and turned to go, Hubert gathered his wits. "You're the best, too!" he shouted, awkwardly and too loudly, much to the amusement of his employees within earshot. They loved their boss and were thrilled to see him with such a great woman (finally). But it was still fun to laugh at his utter nerdiness, which seemed to be emphasized in contrast to Beth's sophisticated professionalism.

As they walked towards the exit, Warren could barely conceal his amusement. He glanced over at Beth, and she gave him a look that silently communicated, *I know that was cute and I'm glad you appreciated it, but if you say anything that might embarrass Hubert or me, I will make your life miserable.*

Warren understood. A few steps later, he laughed deeply and said, "Hey, I get it. I won't say a thing."

Behind them, Hubert called his team together to tackle the nearly-impossible task of finding a killer with a few shreds of information from the world's most unreliable source—the bowels of the dark web.

I wasn't happy to see Brendan Braswell standing at Rosalie's cube the next morning. Braswell was technically my boss, although when a show is as enduring and successful as *RECON*, we fall outside the normal corporate hierarchy. That galled Braswell, who was very aware of his own authority and had a huge ego. For example, if someone referred to him as a "Vice President" he'd interrupt them.

"*Executive* Vice President, actually." He and I were old rivals. He had been the executive producer of *RECON* before me, but the show had performed much better after he left. It didn't help our relationship that I made a lot more money than he did.

I could tell the conversation wasn't going well for him. His face was red with anger, because he'd wanted to wait in my office, and Rosalie refused to let him in. I shook his hand and steered him away from her cube.

"Did you just fly in from New York, Brendan? And sorry about making you wait in the hallway. Rosalie is protective of my space." I wasn't really sorry, and he obviously wasn't mollified, but he had a more important topic to discuss as he sat down at my conference table.

"Rich, I heard a rumor that you received a strange video. Perhaps more than one."

I'd had a feeling this was why he had shown up suddenly in Chicago, but it bothered me that he'd found out. We had agreed to keep the information about the videos a secret for now, and I wondered who had told him. It couldn't have been anyone on my team, but all of them had assistants and there were files on servers, emails and other communications.

I disguised my surprise. "That's true. We've received some odd videos." I gave him a brief description of them.

"What do you make of that?"

"No idea. We don't know where they're coming from, who made them, or even how they were made."

He furrowed his brow. "I'd like to see them."

"All right. How about we watch them now?"

"Good. Please ask your assistant to get us some coffee."

"Sorry, but Rosalie doesn't fetch things for me. Help yourself; it's in the breakroom."

He wasn't happy about it, but he got his own coffee, sat down at my conference table, and I queued up the videos. We spent the next few hours watching them, and I told him about our research to investigate their accuracy. He was naturally skeptical and asked me dozens of questions about their origin, how they might have shown up on my computer, and more.

Finally, he asked, "Are you going to air these, Rich?"

"I'm not sure. I keep asking *cui bono,* but I don't have any answers."

"Just be careful. This feels like an elaborate hoax. We've built *RECON*'s reputation over many years. I'd hate to see it destroyed because you were tricked into broadcasting something like this, only to find out it was all a prank."

"Don't worry. We'll do the usual due diligence before we consider airing anything about them."

But he wouldn't let it go. "I'm sorry but that's not good enough. I don't normally do this, but this is a special case. I don't want you to air any of this without running it by me. Something feels off with these videos."

I had to hide the anger I always feel when someone tries to tell me what to do. I felt that our ratings and Emmys had put us above his meddling, and I didn't want to give him control of this decision. "Brendan, we're a long way from deciding if these videos are genuine or not. There might not be a story here, but if we decide to broadcast anything about them, I'll let you know first."

He didn't like that I refused to acknowledge his authority, but we were stalemated, and he knew it.

12

TULSA VALIDATION
AND THE STARS ALIGN

May 19th: 149 Days Before Arrival

Beth, Carl, Eliza, and I flew to Tulsa to meet with the staff of the Greenwood Cultural Center. The Center is named after the Greenwood District, which is where the massacre occurred in 1921. The next day, Eliza and I would fly to Boston to meet with Dr. Chandra Ramanujan at MIT.

Julia Halliday, one of the center's historians, met us in the lobby and welcomed us into a meeting room where we gathered around the table. After introductions, I asked her to give an overview of the Tulsa Race Massacre.

She gathered her thoughts and began. "Greenwood was the most prosperous African American business district in the country, with doctors, lawyers, stockbrokers, and many other professionals. It had everything, from fine restaurants to theatres, shops—you name it. It was called the 'Black Wall Street of America.' African Americans had built an oasis for themselves in Tulsa. And then, on Monday, May 30th, 1921, a nineteen-year-old African American man named Dick Rowland was accused of assault. The alleged victim was actually a friend of his, Sarah Page, a young white woman, who operated an elevator in the Drexel Building. Rowland was a shoeshine boy, and he was in the elevator because he was only allowed to use the restroom at the top of the building—the other restrooms were off limits to 'coloreds.'"

She paused, letting that sink in. "Any physical contact between the two was almost certainly an accident. Some witnesses said Rowland tripped when he walked onto the elevator and grabbed Sarah Page's arm reflexively. The event was over in a few seconds, but a white store clerk reported Rowland for assault. Dick Rowland had never been in trouble and was well-liked by Blacks and whites. Why would he attack his friend, in broad daylight, on an elevator, on one of his two-times-a-day trips to the restroom? One of many rumors was that Dick and Sarah were dating in secret. In the 1920s, that would have been enough to cause outrage on its own.

"The police arrested Rowland, but Sarah Page refused to press charges. Under normal circumstances, the story would have ended there. However, the *Tulsa Tribune*'s headline the next day urged action. It said, 'Nab Negro for Attacking Girl in Elevator.' Allegedly, an editorial on the back page called for a lynching. I say *allegedly*, because when the newspaper microfilmed its historical issues decades ago, the back-page editorial had been cut out and there are no surviving copies."

Julia's description of the massacre matched what we'd seen in the video. "Thirty-five square blocks of African American residences and businesses were burned to the ground. Fifteen hundred homes, and hundreds of businesses owned by African Americans, were looted or destroyed. At least three hundred African Americans were murdered. Eight hundred were hospitalized, and many more suffered serious injuries. Thousands of people were missing, homeless, or held in six internment camps in Tulsa. Not one of the thousands of insurance claims filed by African Americans was ever paid. Authorities charged more than one hundred white people with crimes related to the event, but none were ever convicted. After a long legal battle, the Oklahoma Supreme Court overturned a Tulsa ordinance that prevented blacks from building homes in the city. The city responded by requiring all homes to be made from brick, while conspiring with local suppliers to prevent the sales of bricks to blacks."

The injustices Julia described were atrocious. "But that's not the end of the story," she continued, "because African Americans rebuilt Greenwood, despite having no insurance money or access to the mandated building materials. Many of them had nothing, yet they overcame the laws, the racism, and the hatred to rebuild their community. In five years, it was completely restored. That speaks to the determination, tenacity, and courage of those people. The massacre was a horrible tragedy, but they refused to be defeated."

My team had been exchanging glances as Julia spoke and she noticed the unspoken communication. "What's going on? It's like you're having a silent conversation."

Beth gave me a questioning look. I nodded, and she pointed to a large-screen television on the wall. "We have a very important video to show you. May we use that?"

"Sure, but it sounds like something our director might be interested in. I'll see if she's available while you set up."

Beth connected her laptop to the television and Julia returned a few minutes later with the Director of the Greenwood Cultural Center, Dr. Kayla Vincent. I shook her hand.

"Thank you for having us, Dr. Vincent."

"Please, call me Kayla. Thank you for coming."

I told the women the video we wanted to share was about the Tulsa Race Massacre. I clarified that I didn't know who shot the video, who sent it to us, or how it was made. I also warned them that it was extremely violent.

"It was a race massacre," Kayla remarked dryly. "They tend to be violent."

We could see the shock on Kayla's and Julia's faces as the video played. I suppose if you've devoted much of your professional life to studying and documenting a horrific event, it would be particularly upsetting to see it come to life via high-definition video.

When it was over, Kayla recovered first and looked at Beth. "As you might expect, I have a thousand questions."

"We'll do our best, but I'm sure we can't answer most of them."

Kaya had her guard up. "Can't or won't?"

"We *can't*," Beth insisted. "You now know as much about the video as we do."

Julia and Kayla told us the video lined up perfectly with their understanding of the massacre. They recognized many of the people, incidents, and locations from their research. Every scene in the film matched with historical photographs. Finally, Kayla's eyes locked onto mine. "You're going to air this, right?"

I wavered. "Maybe someday. Not yet."

She did not like that answer. "It's unacceptable for *RECON not* to air this video."

Beth jumped in. "We don't know where it came from, who shot it, or why they sent it to us. We need to know more before we put this in front of our audience. *RECON* has spent years building a reputation for—"

Kayla interrupted her. "You're missing the point entirely! As far as we can tell, this is a *perfect* depiction of the Tulsa Race Massacre. Regardless of who made it, people need to see it! And yes—it's violent, but this is how it was for blacks in the early 20th century! Did you know that a hundred years ago, the US was one of the *only countries on earth* where people were regularly lynched or burned at the stake for nothing more than the color of their skin?"

There was a part of me that knew this; I'd learned it in school. But hardly anyone talked about it now. How did this get lost in our national consciousness?

Kayla pressed on. "Whatever the motivations of the filmmaker, you have a moral obligation to share this with the world. The story of this massacre was forgotten to history until we revived it—and it's still not mentioned in many history textbooks. It wasn't required curriculum in Oklahoma until 2002. Even today, many Americans don't know about it."

Kayla's words made a huge impact on me and the rest of the team. I hadn't thought of the broader implications of the video until she showed them to me. The room was silent, but the seriousness and weight of what she'd said hung in the air.

"I'm sorry," I told her. "You're right. I've been thinking about this video in the context of another project we're working on. But the video brings to life a terrible incident, and that story needs to be told, too."

"On *RECON*?" she asked.

"On *RECON*," I confirmed.

"When?"

I looked at Beth. As our producer, she was the one who planned our episodes. We waited as she opened her laptop and logged into our network. She looked up at Kayla. "It takes a while to do it right and we have another story we're working on right now. If we move forward with that story, the Tulsa Race Massacre video will be a part of it, but I agree with Rich that what happened here in Tulsa deserves its own episode, too." She paused. "I'll commit to broadcasting an in-depth piece on the Tulsa Race Massacre within a year. It will take several months to produce the story. Rich will anchor it, and we'll work with you to get it right."

"Thank you," Kayla replied.

I shook my head. "No, Dr. Vincent. Thank *you*."

When the meeting ended, Carl and Beth headed back to Chicago. Eliza and I got a hotel in Tulsa. I read a book on my tablet while she borrowed my laptop and began watching the opening sequence of the race massacre video repeatedly. She also did some online research and took notes, but when I asked her what she was doing, she just mumbled that she was "checking something."

Early the next morning, we boarded a flight to Boston. As I dozed, Eliza kept working on her project. She nudged me awake as we began our descent into Logan International Airport.

"We're landing. Pull your seat up."

"Did you get your project done?" I asked, sleepily. She was staring out the window and seemed lost in thought. Then she turned to me.

"I checked the positions of the stars and planets on Monday, May 30th, 1921. I compared that data to the positions of the same objects in the opening sequence of the Tulsa race massacre video. Every single object in the sky that I checked—every planet, every star—was exactly where it should have been at that date and time. And I verified the positions of more than forty objects."

I was astonished. "That's incredible!"

Eliza shook her head in wonder. "What kind of filmmaker would go to that level of effort when nobody but a few academics like me would ever check, and literally *no one in the world* would care?"

I was too stunned to say anything else and after a moment, Eliza continued. "Rich, do you understand the implications of this? There's no reason to create a film with that kind of pointless accuracy. The effort to determine the exact locations of these objects, place them in a scene and have them all move perfectly in relation to each other—that would be madness." Her eyes were wide, and she spoke urgently, her voice shaking. "It's more likely that this video—"

"—is real?" I asked in disbelief.

Every video we'd received contained facts, images and obscure details that had been confirmed by the experts we'd consulted. But the positions of stars and planets at a certain point in time wasn't subject to anyone's judgement or opinion. If Eliza was right, then this video was exactly correct. What could it mean? What was I supposed to do with these videos?

I shook my head and looked at Eliza. "The videos can't be real. I mean, I know there's no other explanation, but—."

"—but they can't be," she agreed. "Traveling backwards in time is impossible..."

She paused.

"...for humans. Remember, though; the math says it's *not* impossible. Some physicists think that's just a quirk of the math. But perhaps a civilization far more advanced than ours has figured out a way to do it. And we're about to meet with one of the world's leading experts in how it might have been done."

A car took us from the airport to the MIT campus. We arrived at the Green Center for Physics and were ushered into a conference room by a graduate assistant. Waiting for us was Dr. Ramanujan, who appeared to be in his fifties. Dressed in a suit and tie, he was of medium height and build, and his eyes lit up as he smiled broadly and embraced Eliza.

"Eliza, what a pleasure to see you again!"

"How are you, Chandra?" She beamed at him.

I was immediately engaged by the man's warmth as we shook hands; he insisted I call him, "Chandra."

"'Ramanujan' is quite a mouthful," he joked.

Chandra was truly a fascinating individual. I'd read about his life to prepare for the visit. As Eliza had said, he'd grown up in desperate poverty and had to sneak into school and borrow classmates' textbooks to complete his studies. Despite the odds, he achieved perfect results on the extremely demanding admissions tests for ISI, one of the most prestigious universities in India. His scores caught the attention of the school's administration, which offered him a scholarship and helped him ease into a whole new world mostly populated by students from affluent, private-school backgrounds. He was now a highly respected scientist, and there was a lot of conjecture that his work on time travel could win him a Nobel Prize.

The graduate student connected my computer to the large television in the conference room as we sat down. I turned to Chandra. "Thanks so much for spending time with us today. I think Eliza has given you an overview of what we wanted to talk to you about."

He shook his head. "I understand you want me to evaluate some videos that may have connections to time travel. That's all I really know."

"That's right," Eliza explained. "Chandra and I agreed that in order to preserve his objectivity, I wouldn't tell him much beyond that."

"Well, let me give you this context. Strange videos keep appearing on my work computer. We have no idea who made them, why they're sending them to me, or how they get past our network security. If I delete them, they come back within a few minutes."

Chandra raised his eyebrows. "I can see why you're puzzled."

"I've received four videos. One of them looks like a movie scene of a nuclear missile hitting Chicago. It's only four minutes long and obviously not about a real event, so today, we're going to share the other three. Not only are they much longer, but they're of historical events which they depict with perfect accuracy, according to all the experts we've consulted." Eliza explained her recent finding about the astronomical accuracy of the stars and planets in the Tulsa Race Massacre video. Chandra didn't comment but he shook his head in astonishment.

I hit the play button. It took about two hours to watch the videos all the way through. The butchery and savagery of the films was appalling, but Eliza and I had seen them before. Chandra, who seemed to have a heart to match his brain, kept wiping away tears. When we finished, he asked, "Since you are showing these to me, and you told me there's a time travel connection, is your position that this is somehow actual footage from these incidents?"

I paused for a moment, surprised at how readily he considered that possibility. "Well, based on everything we've learned, we can't rule it out."

He nodded. "Go on."

I glanced back and forth between Eliza and Chandra. "I have to say that I'm surprised you two have been more open to the possibility that this is authentic footage than just about anyone else. I thought scientists were supposed to be skeptics!"

Chandra laughed. "We *are* skeptics. But a skeptic is simply someone who requires good evidence to be convinced. If you won't even consider the evidence, you're not a skeptic—you're closed-minded, which is a much different thing. Although, to be honest, I've run into many closed-minded scientists. When you work on time travel, you tend to collect critics."

"I bet," I chuckled. I felt my own reluctance to believe the videos were real take another hit. The enormity of it made me pause. "If you don't mind me asking, Chandra, what inspired you to explore time travel?"

He grinned at me. "This will sound silly for a scientist. But since I share the surname of one of history's most brilliant physicists, I studied his life, even when I was young. I became quite curious about how he could have possibly come up with such incredible visions of mathematics and physics, seemingly out of nowhere. I wondered if I could accomplish something in my life even a little bit as fantastical as he did. And then one day, it hit me: if I could solve time travel, not only would I achieve something incredible, but perhaps I could travel back in time and ask him how he did it."

I smiled at him. "Now that, Chandra, is a worthy life goal."

"Thank you," he replied. "Most young boys don't hold on to their foolish dreams through adulthood, though."

Eliza and I laughed.

"Rich," Chandra began, "I'm not a filmmaker or an investigative journalist like you. Do you really have no other theories about how these films were made? Nothing besides time travel fits the data?"

"That's right. If it's not time travel, we don't know how these were made. We cannot explain them."

Chandra shook his head in wonder.

"Chandra," Eliza asked. "If this footage is genuine—in other words, if someone or some*thing* was able to travel into the past and take video of historical events—what would be the mechanism?"

He sighed thoughtfully. "There are several theories. I'm personally working on understanding how the topography of the universe could allow information to travel backwards in time. That could, mathematically anyway, mean that matter could travel back in time, too."

"Why don't you give Rich an overview of your approach?" Eliza suggested.

Oh boy, here we go. You're talking to a guy who got stranded on the moon by his girlfriend because he couldn't answer a basic question about the speed of light.

But Chandra's explanation was straightforward, probably because he radically simplified it for my unscientific mind. I actually understood it, sort of.

"What about sending objects or people back in time?" I asked him.

Ramanujan shook his head. "That is vastly more daunting. Sending information demands a tiny fraction of the energy and complexity."

"Are there other mechanisms for traveling back in time that don't violate the laws of physics?" I asked.

"Oh yes! I'm sure Eliza's described Einstein's theories of relativity and how great speed and gravity affect a clock—not just a mechanical clock, but even your metabolism."

I recalled Eliza's explanation at dinner. "Yes!" I exclaimed, like a proud student. "As you either go faster or move closer to a large mass, time slows down."

"Exactly. Either of these might lead to actually reversing time somehow. Another approach would be to use a rotating black hole, because it drags spacetime with it. You could potentially create a closed circle in time so that if you enter at one point, you emerge at an earlier point."

"And that's the most likely mechanism?" I asked.

"Well, there are also wormholes. Einstein and Rosen originally theorized them, and Kip Thorne suggested that if you accelerated one end of a wormhole close to the speed of light, a particle—or object—entering that opening would emerge from the other end in a time prior to its entry."

"Okay." I understood little of what he was saying, but I wanted to learn as much as I could. "Are there other methods?"

"Many. One is called 'spacetime twisting of light,' or STL. Others include cosmological phenomena like massive, infinitely long, rotating cylinders or cosmic strings, left over from the Big Bang. If they crossed one another, they'd create closed time loops."

"I'm completely lost," I blurted out.

Chandra smiled, sympathetically. "Most people don't run into these ideas on a regular basis."

"So, suffice to say, there are several mechanisms for traveling back in time that do not defy the laws of physics. Is that correct?"

He paused for a moment. "Yes, but the gap between our theories and the technology required to build such a device is enormous."

Something occurred to me. "Wait! If it's possible to travel back in time, how come no people from the future are visiting us now?"

"That's a common question, and no one knows the answer with certainty. But many scientists believe that if we ever build a device for transporting information or matter backward in time, it won't be able to bring anything back to a date earlier than the moment it was originally activated."

"Got it," I said. "So, if you build a time machine on April 1, 2050, it can never transport anything—or anyone—to March 31, 2050, or earlier?"

"Exactly," Chandra answered.

"But if that's the case, is it really theoretically possible for someone to have traveled back to shoot a video of The Battle of the Little Bighorn?"

"With human technology? No."

"I agree," Eliza offered. "And this is tied to our question of what entity or intelligence shot the videos, and why. But we're moving from theory to conjecture."

"Go on," Chandra encouraged her.

"If a non-human intelligence invented time travel before any of these events, then that limitation wouldn't apply."

"Such as an extraterrestrial or interdimensional civilization," Chandra suggested.

I could hardly believe my ears. Here I sat with two brilliant physicists, and they were speculating about extraterrestrials and time travel. "Is there a scientific basis for any of this?" I asked, a little disoriented by what sounded like science fiction.

"Sure," Chandra answered. "The universe is likely teeming with life, and the Sun is a relatively young star. Other civilizations could have developed much earlier and be thousands, millions, or even billions of years ahead of humans. If they've conquered spacetime, they could travel to Earth and back—or at least share information with us—from billions of light years away using wormholes, for example. We've only been a technological civilization for one hundred and fifty years, and look how far we've come. Imagine what another billion years of technology would bring!"

I nodded. "You mentioned an 'interdimensional civilization.' I assume that's an intelligence that resides in another dimension. But I don't really know what that means."

"Think of it as a parallel universe," Chandra said. "Quite consistent with quantum theory. Their mechanism of traveling here would still be a wormhole, but it would connect two universes instead of two different points in the same universe, of course."

"Of course," I repeated, entirely baffled, wondering how I'd ever explain any of this to *RECON* viewers. "Chandra, I'm just a simple, investigative journalist. But I know that whoever is doing this is expending enormous resources. So, there has to be a motive. Why would any of these—um—'intelligences' do this?"

Chandra shook his head. "Not necessarily a lot of resources, by their definition."

"Not if it's a Type III civilization," Eliza offered.

"Exactly," he continued. "The resources available to a Type III civilization and their ability to access energy would be, pardon the term, *astronomical*. And just imagine their computing capabilities."

"Um...What's a 'Type III' civilization?"

"Oh, sorry," Chandra responded, hastily adding. "that's a civilization capable of controlling energy at the scale of a galaxy."

"Do you believe such a thing exists?"

"No one knows," he shrugged. "But it's a big universe, even if it turns out there's only one."

"So, you're saying that if a Type III civilization exists, it could, hypothetically, access wormholes, travel back and forth in time, and place videos from the past on my computer?"

"Yes, but I want to bring us back to the discussion about moving information versus objects or biological entities. Even if your videos are genuine, it doesn't mean someone is traveling through time. They may just be moving information through time. *Seeing* through time."

"That makes sense to me," Eliza agreed. "A sufficiently advanced civilization from this universe or another one could easily do this."

"For God's sake, *why*?" I asked.

"It could be their way of establishing communication with us," Eliza suggested.

"To what end? And why me? Why not go to the United States government?"

"Well," Chandra suggested, "you don't know that they *haven't* done that. The government tends to keep that kind of information classified."

"Fair enough," I conceded, but I doubted it.

"And you don't know how long this is going to go on. Maybe they have important information to share. Or a warning of some kind. Maybe their universe and ours are connected in such a way that our actions affect them somehow."

"I agree with Chandra," Eliza said. "We have no idea. We don't even know if it's extraterrestrial or interdimensional. I think it's not likely to be humans from the future. It would be risky to interfere with past events."

Chandra mulled this over. "I tend to agree, and that gives me another thought. Note that in none of the videos was there any attempt to intervene in the scenes. Whoever shot them wanted to show you something, or maybe prove something to you, but they didn't try to alter the outcome of the events. Either they chose not to interfere, or they couldn't, because they were observing and not physically there."

"Good point," Eliza agreed. "But the real mystery is why they're sending the videos to Rich. What is he supposed to do with them?"

Chandra furrowed his brow, deep in thought. "I think whatever intelligence is doing this—if it isn't a prank—is just proving its capabilities to you right now. It may have a specific objective, but it wants to demonstrate its *bona fides* first."

At 3:00 p.m., we wrapped up our visit with the brilliant Chandra Ramanujan, and I summoned our driver to take us back to the airport. Just as the car pulled away, Chandra burst through the doors waving his hands at us. I asked the driver to stop, and we jumped out of the car.

"I just had an idea!" Chandra exclaimed.

"What is it?" I asked, mystified.

"The three videos you showed me—they're all from the past, right?"

"Yes, of course."

"And I told you that the intelligence that made them might be trying to establish its *bona fides*." Chandra's face was grim. "The first video—the one you didn't show me of the missile hitting Chicago. Did you receive it before the others?"

"Yes."

"And you said you ignored it, right?"

"Right. We were mostly frustrated that we couldn't stop it from popping up on my phone and computer. Why does that matter?"

"Because the first video could be the warning!" he exclaimed. "Whatever this Intelligence is, it's proven it can see through time. Maybe the first video was a warning about something that will happen in the future. When you ignored it, the Intelligence decided to establish its credibility by demonstrating, beyond a shadow of a doubt, that it knows what it's talking about because it knows every-thing. It's *ultima veritas*!"

"*Ultima veritas*?" I asked.

"The *ultimate truth*!'" Eliza explained. "It knows everything that has ever happened and all the possibilities of what *might* happen!"

"Rich, do you have the missile video with you?" Chandra asked, excitement in his voice.

"Yes. I couldn't delete it if I tried."

"Oh, that's right; you said that. Let's watch it right now."

We followed Chandra back to the conference room. As the video played, we stared at the screen showing Chicago's magnificent skyline and, after a minute, the missile entered the frame. It streaked down, plunged into the ground, and exploded into a huge fireball. The blast wave rippled out, destroying everything in its path.

"Oh, my God!" Eliza moaned, her eyes wide. "I just didn't notice when I saw it on your phone. The screen was too small."

"What?" I demanded in disbelief. "Are you saying the Intelligence is warning us that a missile is going to destroy Chicago in the future?"

"That's not a missile, Rich," Chandra said, sadly, as Eliza nodded. "That's an asteroid. The Intelligence is trying to warn you that an *asteroid* is going to destroy Chicago."

13

RANDOM BOLTS OF LIGHTNING

It was 5:30 p.m., and Hubert Gossich sat behind his desk as his company's custom AI algorithms searched for clues to the identity of Monalisa's killer. His team had been working feverishly, excited to be solving a crime instead of the relatively mundane analysis they did for corporate clients. Unknown to Hubert, they had another objective: They wanted to make Hubert look good in his girlfriend's eyes.

"I love the guy," someone said in the breakroom, "but I'm not sure being the king of the nerds is going to help him hold on to a woman like Beth Robileski!"

So, *Catch the Killer; Keep the Girl* became the mantra—the unofficial slogan—of the dedicated geeks of North Shore Data analytics. For reasons of brevity—and to disguise the full meaning from their boss—they decided to call the project, *CTK-KTG*, or *CTK* for short.

Considering their progress so far, Hubert was discouraged. A handful of messages from the dark web wasn't much to go on, particularly since so many of them were redundant. His team broke all two hundred messages into component parts to isolate certain combinations of words, which they used to search for similar phrases across the web and dark web. And they found matches. Indeed, they found *countless* matches; nothing they tried narrowed down what was essentially a pool of hundreds of millions of people. Most of the words and phrases were just too common—they were used everywhere, by everyone, it seemed.

The username didn't help. BlackSpider150 didn't seem to mean anything. When his team searched the World Wide Web, they found exactly two uses of the term: one from a video game and one that was an image file of a black spider. On the dark web, it only appeared in the messages that Warren had brought them.

"Mr. Gossich?" An accented voice interrupted Hubert's train of thought. One of his company's maintenance technicians stood in his doorway. He was an older man, and Hubert remembered his first name. Hubert made it a point to know of all his employees no matter how senior or junior. But in this case, it didn't matter: *Stan* was stitched onto a patch sewn to his shirt.

"Yes, Stan?"

"I fix the air conditioning today," the man said, proudly, with a strong accent. "Does it work for you now?"

"Yes, it does. Thank you." Hubert smiled.

The maintenance tech grinned happily and began to turn away.

"Stan?" Hubert called after him.

"Yes, Mr. Gossich?"

"Is Stan short for Stanley?" Hubert realized he didn't know the man's full name and he needed to rectify that, given his principles around such things.

Stan hesitated for a moment, surprised by the personal question. Then he shook his head. "No, Mr. Gossich. It stands for 'Stanislav.' I immigrated from Russia in 1990. I am American citizen," he added, with pride and a note of concern, as though wondering if Hubert was about to inquire about his immigration status.

Hubert smiled to put him at ease. "That's great. I'm glad you're working at NSDA."

Stan beamed. "Thank you, Mr. Gossich. Five years in August."

"Congratulations," Hubert responded and then remembered August was more than two months away. There was an awkward silence. Stan looked like he wasn't sure if he was supposed to stay and await more questions or if he was rudely taking up the time of the firm's CEO. Hubert had no more questions, but now felt compelled to ask one because Stan was looking at him. So, he improvised. "Um...Stan, does the name *Black Spider* mean anything to you?"

To Hubert's astonishment, Stan's face lit up. "Oh yes!" he exclaimed. "The Black Spider is Lev Yashin! He's the greatest goalkeeper ever in football!"

Hubert was too stunned to react for a moment. Then he leaned forward. "Say that again."

"All Russians know of the Black Spider! They call him that because it was like he had eight arms, the way he played goalkeeper. He won the Olympics and the European Cup for the Soviets. But I consider him a Russian, since he is from Moscow." He looked surprised. "You know of Lev Yashin?"

Hubert shook his head. "No. No, I'm sorry I don't. Someone mentioned *Black Spider* to me, so I thought I'd ask."

"He was a great player. The best."

Hubert considered this new information. "You don't have to tell me if you don't want to, but may I ask how old you are?"

"Don't worry that I am too old, Mr. Gossich. I'm young at heart."

Hubert waved away his concerns. "No, no, Stan. I'm just wondering how old most fans of Lev—*Yashin*—you called him—would be today?"

"He died the year I came to the US. I'm 63 and my son is 35. He knows Lev Yashin was the Black Spider. But I don't think he is a fan, as you say. So, maybe not as young as my son, but older would probably be a fan."

"Thanks, Stan. That's very helpful."

Stan beamed. "You're welcome, Mr. Gossich. Goodnight."

Hubert turned back to his computer, googled the name "Lev Yashin," and brought up the Wikipedia entry:

Lev Ivanovich Yashin (Russian: Лев Ива́нович Я́шин, 22 October 1929 – 20 March 1990), nicknamed the "Black Spider" or the "Black Panther," was a Soviet professional footballer, considered by many as the greatest goalkeeper in the history of the sport.

Hubert scrolled down the page to Yashin's accomplishments.

Estimated to have made over 150 penalty saves during his career.

"Oh, my God!" he yelled to an empty room. "*Black Spider 150!*" Heart racing, Hubert switched over to email and wrote a note to his team.

Subject: Potential Lead on BlackSpider150

Team,

I believe it's possible that the username 'BlackSpider150' refers to a Russian soccer player named Lev Yashin. Here's the link to his Wikipedia page. *This suggests the suspect is a fan from that era; probably a Russian male between the ages of 45 and 65.*

Stan had said his son wasn't a fan, so Hubert had added ten years. But he didn't think the killer was older than sixty-five, because men commit fewer violent crimes as they age. It was logical that a fan of Russian soccer was Russian. Someone posting with a screen name based on such an obscure reference was undoubtedly an *avid* fan. Combining that information with a twenty-year age range reduced the pool of suspects from billions to millions. It would also give them clues to follow. They could search for screen names incorporating references to other famous Russian soccer players and their statistics. They had, at last, established a tendency, a mode of behavior for the killer—hopefully. If Stan was right, it was an absolute game-changer.

That reminded him. He added a note to his email.

P.S. By the way, if this is correct, you can thank Stan, our mainte-nance man, for figuring out what none of the rest of us could.

He sent the email and headed home to tell Beth the good news.

The next day, Hubert's team dug into their challenge with renewed vigor. And Stan was mystified to find himself the most popular person in the company, getting high fives, free meals, and big smiles everywhere he went.

He felt as popular as Lev Yashin!

The morning after we returned from Boston, I woke up to a text from Molly, Angela's primary caregiver: *Mr. Penton, please call or stop by when it's convenient.*

A rideshare took me up Lake Shore Drive and I gazed out on the lake. The day was cloudy, and the water was choppy due to the winds, so there was little boat traffic. We reached the facility, and I walked quickly up two flights of stairs. I stepped into Angela's room and saw her sitting on the veranda, where she seemed to be all the time now, binoculars to her eyes as Molly sat next to her.

Molly saw me, tapped Angela's shoulder and said something softly to her before stepping inside, pulling the door closed behind her. "I'm getting worried about Angela," she began.

"What's wrong with her? Has a doctor checked her out?"

"Yes, an M.D. and a psychiatrist. There's nothing *new* wrong with her physically. It's just that..." Her pause was excruciating.

"What is it?"

"She's *obsessed* with the boats on Lake Michigan," she finished.

I felt a sense of relief. "Oh, that. She's always loved boats. What's the issue?"

"Well, until now, all the boats she saw were *real*. But some of the ones she's been seeing lately don't really exist."

"Yeah, now that you mention it, I know what you mean. What do the doctors think about that?"

Molly hesitated. "Well, they're *doctors*, you know, and I'm not. And they don't seem that worried about it, Mr. Penton, although they asked me to keep an eye on it. But something is different, and I'm concerned."

My instincts told me she was on to something. "Molly, you're not going to be in any trouble with me for speculating. You spend a lot more time with Angela than any of those doctors. Or me," I added, feeling a little guilty. "Tell me what's bothering you."

Molly seemed reassured. "Well, first she described that one big ship that showed up that wasn't real."

"The *Tillbeck*?"

Molly nodded. "And then the *Deutschland*. I couldn't see that one, either. And now there's a third ship. She says all three are there right now, and she's really anxious about it. She wants them to go away. But I can't help because, well, they're not real."

"Maybe that's just the dementia progressing," I suggested.

"Maybe." Molly seemed doubtful. "But she still talks about other boats, and they're all real. It's just these three that aren't."

"Okay, Molly, I'll sit down and talk with her."

"Would you like me to join you?"

I shook my head, walked to the veranda door, and stepped out into the windy, cool air. A storm approached. Angela sat unmoving, the binoculars to her eyes.

"Hi, Angela."

She didn't respond. There were no boats, no ships—nothing on the rough water. I put a hand on Angela's shoulder, which startled her. She pulled the binoculars down and looked up at me disapprovingly, with no hint of recognition in her eyes. I felt a sharp pang of sadness. She brought the binoculars to her eyes again.

"What do you see, Angela?"

A moment passed. "They're all here now."

"The *Tillbeck* and the *Deutschland*?"

"Yes. And the..." she hesitated, as though she was having trouble seeing the name of the ship. "The *Capricorn*," she concluded, tentatively. She fell silent and continued studying the empty lake, so I pulled out my phone and googled, "SS *Capricorn*." This time, I got an interesting hit. The *Capricorn* was a freighter that had caused the U.S. Coast Guard's most serious peacetime accident. In 1980, the vessel got caught up with a Coast Guard maintenance ship, the *Blackthorn*. The *Blackthorn* was dragged underwater and twenty-three of her crew drowned.

"Is the *Capricorn* okay?" I asked, trying to connect some dots. Perhaps years ago, Angela had read about the accident, and her mind was conjuring up an image of it now. I was grasping for an explanation.

She kept staring through the binoculars as storm clouds moved over us. We were in for a squall. The wind whipped across the veranda, stirring Angela's hair and the collar of her thin robe.

"We should go inside, Angela," I said, touching her gently on the wrist of her right hand. She pushed my hand away and leaned forward a little.

"We should go," I repeated softly without touching her.

Angela lowered the binoculars from her eyes and stared across the water. Rain spattered across the deck, and tree limbs swayed with the growing wind that filled the air like a liquid. I moved in front of the chair, just to the right, where I wouldn't block her view, and knelt so we were at eye level. I called to her above the wind, "We should go inside now, Angela."

She turned, her eyes suddenly bright, wide open, and locked onto mine. Rain drops struck her face, but she didn't blink her eyes in response. It was eerie—as though she was an automaton. Then, abruptly, the hollowness melted away, replaced by recognition. It was vivid, almost tangible. I caught my breath and felt a chill in my spine.

Her eyes burned with determination. "You have to tell the story," she insisted urgently, above the driving rain, enunciating loudly and clearly in a way I hadn't heard for years. "Promise me!"

I was stunned, literally at a loss for words.

As the wind whipped up and drove the rain in sheets over us, she spoke again, almost shouting. "You have to tell the story, Rich. Promise me!"

I was confused, thrilled, mystified, and terrified, knowing I'd lose her again. My mind raced as I tried to think of something to say, so I could hold onto her.

"I—I promise."

Her eyes bored into mine.

"I promise, Angela!" I repeated loudly, stressing my sincerity even though I was completely baffled. Every investigation she and I had discussed had happened years ago. What story did she want me to tell?

My wife held my gaze for another moment and then she smiled sadly.

"Good," she said simply. She paused, her lips quivering, rain running down her face. "Heloisa will help you." She took a sharp breath, and her body trembled. I saw the light of her soul flicker in her eyes and then switch off.

I fell forward, my head pressing against her shoulder. I wrapped my arms around her and began sobbing.

Angela ignored me.

The clouds opened up fully, releasing a downpour as she put the glasses to her eyes and gazed towards the lake, now obscured by the deluge. As the storm washed over us, I clung to her thin body, cold from the rain and unresponsive to my embrace. I rocked back and forth until I heard Molly shouting my name and felt her pulling on my shoulder as I begged for Angela to come back to me, to stay with me, to take away this terrible pain.

But I couldn't let go. My wife had left me forever, again.

14

FRIENDLY FIRE

I'm not sure who was more conflicted, Eliza or me. On the one hand, we both knew there was nothing *wrong* with our relationship. When we met, Angela hadn't recognized me in years and had been fading for long before that. But Angela's—spirit?—had begun reappearing for fleeting moments. For me, each experience was thrilling, but unnerving. What if, by some miracle, she recovered? My relationship with Eliza would be over, and I hated that like I hated losing Angela.

Eliza couldn't help but withdraw a little when I told her about what happened. She'd always struggled with the idea of being in a relationship with a married man, even under these unusual circumstances. Hearing about the brief reappearances of recognition in Angela's eyes added to her anxiety. In the middle of the strangest story I'd ever investigated, and still grieving over the death of Monalisa, I felt trapped. I had no idea how to deal with this difficult and heartbreaking predicament.

Two days after the incident with Angela, I was discussing the videos with Carl in his office when I heard a *ding!* from my phone. It was a text from Eliza.

I need to see you.

I tensed up and was tempted to call her but instead, I replied:

Where would you like to meet?

Your office. Be there in 30 mins.

I sat back, sighed, and gazed out the window.

"Everything okay?" Carl asked, concern in his eyes.

"I'm not sure," I replied, as I studied the city. Chicago's history was full of joy, tragedy, triumph, and heartbreak. I wondered if it was my turn for more heartbreak. Honestly, I felt like I'd experienced my share.

I tapped on my phone. *Can't wait; see you soon!*

She didn't reply.

I forced myself to finish the conversation I was having with Carl, and then I went to see Rosalie.

"Eliza's coming over." I looked at my watch. "She'll be here soon."

"Okay, Rich. I'll call security and have them send her up." She picked up the phone as I walked to the men's room. I wanted to look as good as possible when Eliza arrived.

Four floors below, Warren had just finished watching a forty-one-minute video that had been added to Rich's computer that morning. He received notifications whenever a new file appeared and had downloaded it to his laptop. The violence was horrific. The scale of the death and destruction was far beyond what he'd seen in the other incidents, which were truly awful on their own. With a few minutes of Internet research, he identified and read a synopsis of the event. It was one of the greatest tragedies in history, he decided. It had happened only eighty years ago, and he'd never heard of it until now. Warren headed to Rich's office.

Beth was on the phone in her office listening intently. "Thank you, Hubert," she said finally. "Great work; let me know what else you find."

Hubert had given her a detailed update on his team's search for BlackSpider150. It looked increasingly like they'd be able to identify the killer, and Beth decided to update Rich on the news. She headed out her office door to the stairwell.

When I got back to my office, Warren and Beth were standing at Rosalie's cube waiting for my return. Beth seemed pleased and a little excited. Warren looked like death warmed over. Rosalie was focused on her screen, ignoring them both.

"Hey," I called out.

"Hi," Beth replied, smiling.

"You have another video," Warren blurted out.

I stopped walking, Beth stopped smiling, and Rosalie stopped typing.

"Eight forty-two this morning," Warren said. "I researched it. It's one of the worst things that's ever happened, and I've never heard of it."

Under normal circumstances, that would have sounded like hyperbole. But based on our experiences with the videos so far, we weren't skeptical.

"Rich?" A voice spoke from behind me. I turned around and saw

Eliza walking towards us. I could see on her face that she'd picked up on the tension.

"What's wrong?" she asked.

"There's another video. Warren's the only one who's seen it."

"It's one of the worst things that's ever happened," Warren repeated.

"Wow," Eliza responded. "Then we should watch it right now."

Rosalie called Carl and the two of them joined us in my office.

"I have it on my laptop," Warren said, plugging in the cable. There was little talk. Warren's comments created a sense of foreboding about the video. "Are you guys ready for this?" he asked, dread in his voice.

I nodded. "Play it."

The film began inside an airplane which, based on the look of the cockpit and the pilot, was from World War II. Then the camera moved straight through the canopy of the plane, as if it were porous, and tracked alongside. It rotated 180 degrees, and we could see a group of fighter planes carrying the distinctive roundel of the Royal Air Force—a red bullseye surrounded by concentric bands of white, blue, and yellow. Underneath their wings, they each carried eight sixty-pound rockets. We later learned these were called RP-3's, a late war innovation.

"Those are British fighter bombers from WWII called 'Typhoons,'" Warren explained.

I counted eight aircraft in the formation. Now the camera rotated downward, revealing a small city next to a large bay, where many ships were docked. I could make out several submarines and freighters, plus small boats all over the place. Towards the middle of the bay were three ocean liners. Two were very large, and the third was about half as big. The planes began descending, heading for the largest of the three ships. I could see Nazi flags flying from its masts and I glanced at Warren. "This is sad, Warren. War sucks. But it's hard to be too upset about some old war footage of British planes attacking Nazi ships."

Warren face was nearly white. "Those are Nazi ships, but they're holding thousands of concentration camp survivors. The British pilots don't know it."

I heard Beth gasp. We watched flashes of tracer rounds emerging from the leading edges of the fighters' wings as the pilots began to fire machine guns at the helpless ships. The first airplane flew over the ocean liner and launched two rockets. An enormous explosion rocked the ship, and smoke poured out of the superstructure.

"Oh, my God," I yelled. "Those poor people are being killed by friendly fire! When the hell did this happen, Warren?"

"This was May 3rd, 1945. Those three ships are the *Thielbek*, the *Deutschland*, and the *Cap Arcona*."

I was stunned. "What did you call those ships?"

Warren hesitated, trying to understand my reaction. "The *Thielbek*," he pronounced carefully. In English, it sounded like *Tillbeck*, but then he spelled it out. "*T-h-i-e-l-b-e-k*. The *Deutschland*, and the *Cap Arcona*."

"The *Deutschland* was scrapped twenty years before the war!" I protested.

"No, Rich. There were two ships called the *Deutschland*." He held up his phone to show he'd done his research.

Eliza's eyes met mine as she said what I was thinking. "Not the *Capricorn*. The *Cap Arcona*."

I nodded, and we both turned to watch the screen. The planes were focusing on the *Cap Arcona*. They launched their rockets, sometimes one at a time, sometimes in salvos, and buzzed around the ship, spraying it with machine guns. The giant vessel was already ablaze, but there were few people visible on the top decks.

"Where are the concentration camp prisoners?" I demanded of Warren.

"They're locked below." His voice conveyed the enormity of the tragedy. "The bombs are about to blow the doors open. But it doesn't matter; they're all doomed."

Suddenly, my cell phone vibrated on the table in front of me. I glanced down out of habit. The call was from Molly, Angela's caretaker. My head was spinning. The video was intense, the news of the three ships was astonishing, and now Molly was calling me, which she only did in emergencies. I reached for my phone and Warren's hand moved to his keyboard to pause the video. He tapped repeatedly, but it kept playing.

"Molly?" I answered, as Warren kept trying to pause the video.

"Mr. Penton, please come as quickly as possible," she cried rapidly, her voice shot with anxiety. "Angela's hysterical. Something is happening to those ships she sees!" In the background, I could hear Angela screaming and crying.

"It won't stop playing!" Warren said to no one in particular. I waved at him to keep the video running.

"Molly!" I yelled into the phone so she could hear me over the din coming from the video on our end and Angela's screams on hers. "Put her on speaker!"

Molly hesitated. "Okay, Mr. Penton, but please come quickly!"

I put my phone on speaker, too. Moments later, we heard Angela's tortured cries of anguish. "They're killing those poor people! Stop them! Oh God, get those planes away from there!"

On the screen, another aircraft swooped in and launched two more rockets at the stricken liner. An enormous explosion ripped through the ship. As though reporting as an eyewitness, Angela screamed in terror and horror as we watched the fireball envelop the ocean liner.

"Oh God, no, no, no, no, no! They're attacking the wrong people! Get off the ship; get away from the fire!"

A Typhoon flew low over the waves, machine guns blazing, and Angela sobbed hysterically. "They're murdering those poor people in the water!"

I heard Molly shouting, her voice shaking. "Please come quickly, Mr. Penton! The doctor will be here soon. I can't calm her down!"

"On my way!" I yelled. I gestured at Warren to stop the video.

Warren tried again but couldn't. Finally, he unplugged the HDMI cord from his laptop, but that didn't work, either. The video kept playing on the screen. "What the heck?" he yelled, helplessly.

Then the image on the screen began to ripple oddly. We watched, dumbfounded, as the scene of the battle floated straight off the monitor, which switched off. We were all so startled that we scrambled out of our chairs and jumped back from the table while the video kept playing, as though on an invisible glass panel three feet in front of the screen. *And then the image began to expand.* It stretched in all directions, a foot over the table, and formed into a three dimensional, brilliantly lit hologram of the battle—about six feet long, three feet high, and two feet across.

"What the fuck is *that*?" Carl cried, his voice on the edge of panic.

I heard the others yelling, too, but my eyes were fixated on the scene. The bottom of the hologram was the Bay of Lübeck, Germany. The ships floated there, and planes buzzed around them. We could hear the machine guns and rockets and see tiny figures jumping from the ships into the water.

"Oh my God," I heard Beth say, her voice trembling as she covered her mouth with her hands. Eliza was pale, her eyes wide, unbelieving. Warren stared at the hologram and then at me, confusion written across his face. Tears streamed down Carl's cheeks. He was shaking with fear from the specter, and grief from the destruction. Even Rosalie looked awestruck at the incredible sight. I felt my heart pounding as we watched the battle go on in three dimensions. An enormous explosion erupted from the *Cap Arcona*.

"AAAHHHHHHHH—nnoooooo....make them stop!" Angela cried in terror. She broke down sobbing. "Those poor people...those poor people..." I heard a doctor yelling in the background, and the call was cut off.

I knew I should leave and run to Angela, but it was impossible to move while the holographic battle raged in front of us. Airplanes suddenly popped into view from the top of the hologram as they dove in to attack the ships, which were now a conflagration. The rockets broke open some of the chained doors, and prisoners streamed onto the deck as the camera zoomed closer, weaving in and about the chaos. Concentration camp survivors began jumping from the decks and squeezing out of portholes to escape the rapidly spreading fires. In one particularly close shot, water splashed up toward me, and I jumped back instinctively, only to see it disappear when it reached the edge of the hologram.

The camera pulled back again, and we could see the water around the ships filled with desperate people—some swimming, others floating dead. The British pilots flew over repeatedly, in low, slow passes, strafing the prisoners, the heavy machine guns ripping them to pieces. Dead, torn up bodies were everywhere. The bay was covered with blood. Finally, the *Cap Arcona* capsized, throwing hundreds of people off its decks as its bronze propellers protruded above the water. The *Thielbek* was still ablaze as the camera moved in to follow the *Cap Arcona*'s passengers as they swam for shore. Weak from years of starvation and abuse, relentless airplane attacks, and now stranded far from shore in cold waters, many of the prisoners ran out of strength. You could see the panic in their movements as they struggled and then failed to keep their heads above the waves.

For those strong enough to go on, more hell awaited. We watched as the survivors made it to shore, dragging themselves onto the beach where they collapsed in exhaustion. The camera moved in among them, scanning around to find bands of Nazis wielding clubs, knives, and shovels, rushing towards the concentration camp prisoners. It was as though these monsters ran in from between us, invisible until they burst through the walls the hologram. And then

I realized that many of these evil people were not soldiers at all. They were old men and young boys—not a part of the military, yet full of Hitler's hatred and ready to add their own measure of cruelty to the toll extracted by World War II. They slaughtered nearly all the prisoners on the beaches, in the surf, and in the woods lining the bay, brutally beating and hacking them to death as we watched.

The audio was nearly as horrific as the imagery. We couldn't understand the words, which were in a variety of European languages, but it's apparent when people are screaming with rage or dying in pain. Hatred and terror have their own resonances. The violence, gore, and horror went on until night fell and the only signs of the ships were the funeral pyres they made in the bay. Finally, the hologram began to fade out and then disappeared entirely.

We stood there in silence, still staring at where it had floated, awestruck by what we'd just witnessed.

"Jesus Christ," Carl cried. "Jesus Christ." Beth hugged him, and he sobbed into her shoulder. Rosalie looked around, as though checking to see that we'd all witnessed the same event.

I stared at the empty table until Eliza walked over and wrapped her arms tightly around me. We held each for a long time before she pulled back and lifted my chin with her fingertips.

"Come on," she said, softly. "We have to go see Angela." I nodded, still in shock. She led me from the office as Rosalie called up a *RECON* SUV and a driver. We made the trip to Angela's memory care facility in complete silence.

By the time we arrived, I had regained my composure, but there was nothing for us to do. The resident on duty had given Angela a strong sedative, and she was in a deep sleep. Molly was distraught and told us what she could about what Angela had described. We didn't tell her we'd witnessed it ourselves. The doctor attributed Angela's visions to her worsening dementia and tried to reassure us. "She'll be okay, I think. She'll be asleep for a long time."

Eliza and I knew this wasn't about dementia, but we said nothing.

We got back in the car, and as the driver steered silently down Sheridan Road, I stared ahead, numb from the traumatizing events. I felt Eliza's hand slip into mine and I turned to her, still trying to grasp what we'd witnessed

"What was that? How is that possible?"

She shook her head. "All I can guess is that the Intelligence can gather and project true holographic imagery, and they saved it for the most important video."

"Important because of Angela's involvement?"

She thought for a few moments. "I think Angela was their insurance policy. They wanted to make sure you believed the messages, so they sent this one in a way no one else could. You not only got the video, which I'm sure experts will verify is perfectly accurate, but they projected the image into Angela's consciousness at the same time."

Eliza turned to me. "Do you have any doubt now that this is a real warning?"

I shook my head. "None whatsoever."

She smiled a little sadly. "Then I guess it worked."

When we got back to my office, Beth, Warren, Carl, and Rosalie were eager to explain what they'd learned about the incident while we were gone. At the end of the war, the Nazis were determined to kill as many Jews and other prisoners as possible before surrendering. So, in April of 1945, as the Russian army approached from the east, the Nazis emptied various concentration camps, particularly Neuengamme, the largest in northern Germany. Ragged and emaciated inmates were driven by foot or transported by railcar and barge towards the Bay of Lubeck, where the *Thielbek*, the *Deutschland* and the *Cap Arcona* offered nothing but a tragic and horrifying end to the prisoners' hellish existence.

"How many people died in this disaster?" I asked.

Beth shrugged and held up her hands. "No one knows for sure, Rich. Most experts think between 8,000 to 10,000 of the concentration camp prisoners on the *Thielbek* and the *Cap Arcona* died that day."

Warren spoke up. "There were about 350 survivors."

"Holy shit."

"It gets worse," Warren said. I motioned for him to continue. "Both the Swiss and the Swedish Red Cross had warned the British that the ships were loaded with prisoners. For some reason, the RAF never got the information."

"Jesus Christ."

"And the attack was on May 3," Carl added. "Nazi forces in Northern Germany surrendered to the allies the next day. The British Army actually arrived at the scene as the Germans were killing the last prisoners who made it to shore. That's the main reason there were *any* survivors."

I shook my head in disbelief. How could this tragedy—this senseless, awful, horrific tragedy—have escaped the attention of the public over the years? The scale of the lives lost, and the senseless cruelty of the nightmare, far exceeded the sinking of the *Titanic*.

I was now sure that an asteroid was going to hit Chicago, and that *RECON* had been chosen to warn the city and get the United States Government to stop the object. The hologram was terrifying, but the connection between Angela and the Intelligence was even stranger to me. They'd used her to convince me that the videos were authentic, and no hacker, no rival network—*no one*—could have arranged for that. I looked over at Eliza and she met my eyes.

"You have to tell the story, Rich," she said, knowingly. "You promised."

Rosalie left work early and walked into Miller's Pub. She met her contact at a table far from the door and the bar. He was a well-dressed older man who looked like any other executive working in downtown Chicago. Neither of them had ever been inside the pub, which was part of the security plan.

"New information," she began. "Too much for a text."

"Go on."

As concisely as she could, but without leaving out any important details, Rosalie summarized the events with the "CA asset," the hologram, and Rich's wife, Angela.

"That's impossible," the man replied.

"No, it's not, because I saw it myself," she snapped, annoyed. "And I don't know what to do with it. Report it!"

Neither of them spoke for a minute. "Okay," he agreed. He stood up and walked out of the bar.

15

ESCALATION

May 27th: 141 Days Before Arrival (Cont'd)

From our patio overlooking Lake Michigan, Eliza and I studied the late afternoon sky, ablaze in hues of orange and red from the setting sun. Our deck chairs were pushed close together, and we held hands. I turned to look at her. Her sharp blue eyes were thoughtful as she gazed across the lake. I could see the moment she sensed I was staring at her, breaking her train of thought. She returned my gaze, and I smiled at her.

"How did you know I needed to see you today?"

Eliza was pensive. "I don't know. I just had a sudden sense that I was supposed to be with you."

I sighed.

"What?" she insisted, her curiosity piqued.

"I thought you were coming to break up with me," I admitted.

"Because of that moment with Angela?"

"Yes."

She paused and took a deep breath. "Rich. I don't know how to express this, my love. I believe that Angela and I both have important roles to play in your life. But her time as your wife—I mean *wife* in a real sense—is over." She checked for my reaction.

"Yes." I had tears in my eyes.

She continued. "And I'm so, so sorry about that, Rich; I really am. But I also feel wildly, wonderfully, lucky. And I don't want to feel bad about it, because we aren't doing anything wrong. Being with you makes me so happy that I don't want to ruin it with guilt we don't deserve."

"I feel lucky, too. And we aren't doing anything wrong."

Eliza hesitated and then went on. "Angela is involved in this crazy, exciting, scary...*important* experience we're sharing. But her part has changed." She reached out and laid her palm against my face. "I'm not just your girlfriend anymore. I believe, in my heart, that *I've* become your wife now." She studied me, gauging my reaction.

"Yes," I whispered.

"Maybe not in the eyes of anyone else," her voice wavered. "But I *am* your wife now and nothing—nothing—could make me happier or prouder."

I put my hand over hers and pressed it tightly to my cheek. For a moment, neither of us spoke, then I leaned in conspiratorially and whispered, "I'm really glad you didn't break up with me today."

She laughed softly and I felt my chest shaking as I joined in. Then she shook her head affectionately. "You nut."

I smiled at my brilliant, beautiful, loving, and intuitive...bride. "I wish I could marry you," I told her gently. "I would if I could."

She smiled back, and through her tears, her eyes brimmed with love, compassion, and understanding. "Me too," she whispered.

Carl and Wendy Swinton sat at their dining room table. They'd had friends over that evening, including Heather Johanssen. Given her crippling grief, Bob's disappearance was nearly all they talked about. Some gossips suggested that Bob had gone missing deliberately, which Heather didn't believe, although she wanted to. If he had left on his own, the odds that something tragic had happened were much smaller.

As Carl and Wendy finished the last of a bottle of white wine, she asked him about the hunt for Monalisa's killer, a subject her gentle husband found painful and generally avoided. To her surprise, Carl smiled when she brought it up.

"Actually, we might have a break."

"Really?"

"I mean, it's a long shot, but we're making progress."

"What did you find?"

"We found a screen name that could be the murderer. Or lead us to him."

"What is it?"

"BlackSpider150. They think he took the name from a Russian goalkeeper, who blocked 150 penalty kicks."

"A Russian?" Wendy asked. "Does that mean they think the suspect is Russian?"

"Probably. It's not a sure thing. But I doubt there are many Russian soccer fanatics who aren't Russian."

"That's very exciting!" Wendy exclaimed, and then spoke calmly. "Carl, I know you don't like to talk about this, but please tell me when you learn more." She smiled at him. "I thought Monalisa was marvelous, just like you did, and I want you to catch the sonofabitch, too."

Carl grinned and assured her that he would do a better job keeping her updated.

Twenty miles away, Viktor bolted upright in his bed. He'd been listening to the whining drone of the Swintons and their guests for hours, struggling not to drift off when the name "BlackSpider150" jolted him awake, blood pumping hard as his brain switched into flight-or-fight mode. He couldn't believe what he'd heard. It wasn't possible. The Swintons had stopped talking, so he rewound the digital recorder until he found the exact spot.

BlackSpider150. They think it's a Russian goalkeeper who blocked 150 penalty kicks...I doubt there are many Russian soccer fanatics who aren't Russian.

Somehow, the *RECON* people had identified one of his screen names. "*GAV-NO!*" he yelled, driving his massive fist into the mattress. But as he thought about it, he worried a little less. Certainly, he'd been careless to use that name. Lev Yashin was world-famous. Lots of people might have recognized a reference to "The Black Spider." Once they did, it wouldn't be that difficult to associate it with the number "150." The *RECON* people must have searched the dark web for posts by the McPeek girl and found their exchange.

But Viktor had never used BlackSpider150 except to look for information on the soldiers and Indians video. If that was all they had, then he was sure they were already at a dead end. Hearing the name had been extremely startling, and it took him a few minutes to calm down. He decided not to worry too much about it. His tap of the Swinton home was working fine. If anything changed, he'd hear it from them.

Hubert and Beth were curled up on the sofa in his living room. Beth had told him about the amazing and terrifying events at *RECON* that day, so they researched the *Cap Arcona* disaster. They were disturbed by how little information they could find about such a horrible, hatred-driven historical event in the recent past.

But Hubert had something else on his mind. He'd finally heard the office secret. His entire team had convinced themselves he needed their help to keep Beth and had rallied around the slogan, "Catch the Killer, Keep the Girl!" Hubert found himself not at all offended. He decided that pursuing a noble cause like solving a murder, while simultaneously strengthening the bonds of love and galvanizing his team, was the ultimate win/win/win. Perhaps he could write a management book: *Hubert Gossich: Triple Threat.* He pictured himself on the cover, dressed in a suit, sporting his auburn afro, with a big smile stretching his freckles in every direction.

Maybe not.

His thoughts were interrupted by a question from Beth. "Any progress on finding Monalisa's killer?"

Hubert hesitated. "I think so," he answered as she snuggled closer.

"That's great! Tell me!"

"Well, you remember how our maintenance man figured out the first clue? Of course, that was really just luck."

"Nonsense," Beth objected lovingly. "How many CEOs would think to ask a maintenance technician to help figure out a mystery?"

Hubert thought back to the incident and remembered that he'd asked Stan if he knew what *Black Spider* meant strictly because he didn't know what else to say.

He decided to move on.

"Anywho, that gave us the idea of searching for online identities consisting of names and statistics of Soviet soccer players from the nineteen-seventies and eighties."

"Umm hmm," Beth murmured.

"So, we approached it from two different directions. We kept scouring the web for posts that used the same phrases as BlackSpider150, just like we had from the start. But we also compiled a list of several dozen Soviet soccer stars along with their notable stats. We fed that data into the model, which parsed and combined the terms, one player at a time."

"What do you mean, parsed and combined?"

"Well," Hubert explained. "Let's say there's a Soviet soccer player named Ivan Drago."

"You mean the Russian guy Rocky Balboa fought in *Rocky IV*?"

"Yeah, just as an example."

"Go on."

"And say Ivan Drago scored three goals in one game in 1974, and that appeared in his profile," Hubert continued.

"Okay."

"Well, we'd load up the name 'Ivan Drago,' the numbers '3' and '1974' and lots more data, like his middle name, the year he was born, and every notable statistic associated with him. The system we built assembled every possible combination of names and numbers, then looked for matching screen names across the Internet."

"And did you find anything?"

Hubert shook his head. "Not at first. So, we changed the rules."

"How?"

"We told the program to search for word parts. In other words, don't just seek matches that include complete words like 'Ivan' or 'Drago' plus separate numbers like '3' and '1974.' The system started looking for matches like 'IDrago,' or 'IvDrag.' And the numbers might be '374' or '1974-3,' for example."

Beth was listening, raptly. She curled up more tightly with her brilliant boyfriend. "And did that work?"

He nodded. "We think so."

Beth popped up on her elbow. "Oh my God. You found something. Why didn't you tell me!"

Hubert grinned. "Well, I didn't want you to get too excited! We have a long way to go, but we have a lead we think is fairly strong."

"Tell me!"

"So, one of the players we put into the database was a guy named Oleg Blokhin. He played forward for the Soviet Union in the 1970s. He was a big deal, a really prolific scorer."

"Go on!"

"One of his accomplishments was that he scored forty-two goals for the Soviet national team in his career. Since we'd rewritten the algorithm, our system found a user named OBlo42."

"Oleg Blokhin," she tried out the words, "and 'OBlo42.' That's pretty good. Were you able to get any information about him?"

Hubert smiled again, obviously pleased. "Oh yeah. Whoever OBlo42 is, he's definitely Russian. He loves Russian soccer and uses some of the same phrases as our old friend BlackSpider150."

"Oooh, that's good," Beth agreed.

"It gets better," Hubert continued. "OBlo42 has commented all over the place. He's written thousands of posts, with dozens of distinct phrases. We're checking to see where they're repeated on the Internet, regardless of the name of the poster. When we find them, and they aren't written by OBlo42, we add those names to the list of possible aliases. That gives us more screen names, even more phrases and word sequences to evaluate, and so the search expands. By this time tomorrow, the system will have analyzed billions of usernames and comments and assigned each one of them a probability of being the person we're hunting. We'll soon have a list of screen names we believe are synonymous with the killer."

"That's amazing," Beth replied, truly impressed. "Do you have a name for this special system you built?"

Hubert blushed slightly. "Um...yeah. The *technical* name the team chose for it is 'CTK-KTG.'"

Beth wrinkled her brow. "That's clunky. What does it mean?"

"Computer stuff," he replied vaguely. "We call it, 'CTK' for short."

"So now what?"

"That depends. First, using the world wide web, we'll try to identify a unique individual or a small set of suspects based on the analysis so far. If that doesn't work, we'll take those screen names over to the dark web and see if we can match any of them to a real person using information that's been stolen from banks, governments, private corporations, and God knows where else."

"What are the odds?"

"Strong enough to be optimistic," Hubert said, excitedly. "I really think we're going to get him."

Beth could hear the authentic confidence of a genius in his element now, not the bravado he'd tried to project when she and Warren visited him in his office.

She smiled at her wonderful boyfriend. Tonight, his decency and brilliance made him the most attractive man in the world. "Whether you catch him or not," she said, running her fingers through his red, curly hair, "I love you for trying."

Hubert stiffened. Beth had never told him she loved him. That thought was immediately followed by the realization that she hadn't *actually* said, *I love you* in the time-honored manner. She'd said, *I love you for trying,* which might mean she loved *that* he was trying. He had no idea how to react. Anxiety shot through him as he began to sense that *this*—this was the moment he'd ruin the relationship by saying exactly the wrong thing.

"Hubert," Beth whispered a moment later as he went rigid. He stared at her, his eyes filled with fear.

"I love *you*. And I *also* love that you're trying." She pulled him close to her and kissed him hard.

Hubert felt a wave of relief and excitement wash over him. In his mind, he loaded Beth's words into his dataset, analyzed it using his considerable processing capacity, then reran his calculations to confirm the result. He broke into a huge smile.

"I love you, *too*!"

16

DEFENDING THE INDEFENSIBLE

I knew just who to call in the United States government to share the information about the asteroid. Senator Howard Roosevelt was the chair of the Senate Intelligence Committee and a distant relative of two presidents. Roosevelt hailed from New York and managed to remain above the fray most of the time in an increasingly fractured climate. I called his cell number.

"You're about the ruin my day, aren't you, Rich?" he answered.

I couldn't help but laugh; Roosevelt often reminded me that I never called him about anything positive. I either had bad news, or I was pumping him for information.

"Well, if it's helpful, Senator, I can assure you that this call, while important, is not about you, your state, your party, or anything scandalous."

"Said the spider to the fly," he laughed. "What's on your mind?"

I chose my words carefully. "I've come into possession of some very unusual information that bodes ill for a major US city. Disastrous, even. And while I can't do anything about it myself, it seems to me that someone should. Someone such as the United States Government."

Roosevelt didn't respond for a few seconds. "We have two options at this point. You can come to see me in DC—and I don't mean to act like I'm summoning you. I just can't leave right now because the Senate is in session. Or I can set you up with temporary access to a SCIF at your local FBI office for a call."

"I don't mind coming to see you. When can you meet?"

"As soon as you get here and I'm not in a committee meeting. I'll make it a priority."

"I'll leave this afternoon. I can meet with you sometime tomorrow, if that works."

"It does. I'll have some other people with me to help answer your questions."

I knew then that he had information about the videos, the asteroid or both.

At 7:00 the next morning, I was on the treadmill in a DC hotel when Roosevelt called me. His fast action made me feel a little relieved. Maybe I'd been building this up to be more of a mystery than it was, and the government was already at work to address the threat.

"Nice of you to call so early, Senator," I panted, catching my breath. "I'm just finishing my workout."

"Good, good," Roosevelt said, distractedly. "How soon can you be at the Pentagon?"

That caught me by surprise—I was expecting to meet at the Capitol.

"About an hour?"

"Excellent. I'm here now. I'll make sure you're on the Visitor Access Roster at the Corridor 2 entrance."

It was a function of the senator's influence that such a meeting could be arranged so quickly. To attend a meeting at the Pentagon, you usually need a sponsor, visitor registration, and a background check. Even then, there's a long wait while they question you at the entrance. But when I arrived, a lieutenant colonel fetched me immediately and walked me past a long line of people waiting to get in. I checked my bag with security, passed through a metal detector, and was hand-wanded by a guard.

My escort walked me to a conference room in the outermost or "E" ring of the Pentagon. The most senior people work in that ring because it's the only one with windows that offer exterior views, although they're a strange greenish color due to a protective coating. The lieutenant colonel opened the door, announced, "Sir, Ma'am. Mr. Rich Penton," and then closed the door behind me.

Four conference tables made up a large rectangle. Besides Senator Roosevelt, there were seven people in the room, three of them in military uniforms. The others were dressed in suits, and I guessed they were from intelligence agencies. Roosevelt was robust like Teddy, but his accent was more patrician, like FDR. He was one of the few politicians I liked and admired.

"Rich!" he greeted me, shaking my hand. "It's good to see you!"

"You too, Senator," I answered warmly. "But I'm a little surprised at the reception. You must know something about what I came to discuss."

"I think so. And rather than me passing along your information, I thought I'd bring along the 'A' team so you could tell them yourself."

I gestured at the other attendees. "Am I entitled to know with whom I'm meeting?"

They introduced themselves. It was an impressive group: a three-star Air Force general, a Navy Vice Admiral, a sturdy but outranked Army Colonel, and representatives from the FBI, the CIA, and the NSA. I was disappointed that no one was in attendance from NASA or Space Force.

The Senator asked me to fill them in on what I'd alluded to during our brief phone conversation. I started with the incident on the train and the four-minute asteroid video. I described the footage of the Little Big Horn, Amelia Earhart, the Tulsa Race Massacre, and the *Cap Arcona* tragedy, although I left out the part about the hologram and the connection with Angela's visions. I gave them a detailed rundown of all our research to validate the historical accuracy of the events, but I could tell that my story didn't amaze or even surprise them.

When I finished, Senator Roosevelt spoke first. "Rich," he began, sensing my puzzlement. "The reason no one is reacting to what you're saying is that we've seen the same videos." Some of the other people were nodding slightly.

This confirmed what I'd begun to suspect. "You've seen these videos?"

"Yes. And the reason I asked you to come here is that we think whoever made those videos is plotting to harm the United States. We believe they may be trying to use you to execute that agenda."

I struggled to gather my thoughts. I had been on offense before because I thought I had an information advantage, but now I was on the defensive. One of the men in a suit spoke up. His name was Andes, and he was from the FBI.

"Mr. Penton, we aren't accusing you of anything. In fact, I won't be surprised if you tell me the videos appeared on your computer as if by magic."

I was immediately suspicious. How could they possibly know how I'd received the videos? I hadn't told them that detail. "Are you bugging *RECON*?" I demanded. "That would be a major violation of freedom of the press!"

"No!" Roosevelt exclaimed, glowering at Andes, "Nobody's bugging *RECON*. Well, no one in the U.S. Government is bugging you."

"What's *that* supposed to mean?" I asked, pushing my anger down. Roosevelt gestured towards a woman named Young. She took his cue.

"Mr. Penton, I'm going to bring you in on some highly classified information. You are forbidden from sharing it, and there will be consequences if you do." She waited for me to acknowledge her threat, but I wasn't having it. I simply waited for her to continue and after a moment, she gave up. "Okay, Mr. Penton; I'm going to keep going, but I hope you will consider very carefully how you use this information. It could be damaging to your country if it's not handled delicately. As the Senator pointed out, we received these videos months before you did. We analyzed them frame by frame, and we're just as impressed as you are with their historical accuracy and production quality. But, unlike you, we believe we know who made them and why."

She was obviously expecting me to make some comment. So, I asked, "Are you going to tell me who made them and why?"

"Yes. And then I'm going to ask you to forget about them. Pretend you've never seen them. I know you can't delete them—we can't either—but that doesn't mean you have to act on them. They were made by the Russians. We believe their purpose is to cause panic. Create chaos. Trick us into taking actions that would not only waste resources and frighten the public but also humiliate and discredit the United States Government."

I was dubious. "They went to a lot of work just to cause some panic."

"Maybe," she shrugged. "Maybe not. The Russians have gone to great lengths to meddle in our democracy. They expend enormous resources trying to influence opinions on social media. They've undermined confidence in our electoral system, and they've successfully supported candidates who are sympathetic to them."

"Okay," I answered, thinking about what she'd said. "But why do it this way? Couldn't they just hack into the Pentagon's computer systems or something?"

She shook her head. "They've already done that. We disclosed it when it happened in 2015 and again in 2020. That was embarrassing, and yet it barely made the news. Since that didn't cause any reputational harm, now they really want to humiliate us by tricking us into announcing that we know about an asteroid threat, thanks to some alien or otherwise non-human source that put warning videos on our computers. Imagine the damage that would cause. We'd evacuate Chicago unnecessarily, frighten people across the Midwest, and we'd be the laughingstock of the world. Maximum humiliation, along with corrosive effects on the nation's trust in its security apparatus, would be an enormous coup for any adversary."

"Especially the Russians," I noted.

"Especially the Russians," she agreed, and then smiled. "I appreciate you understanding the situation."

I laughed and shook my head. "Oh no, Ms. Young. I don't understand the situation at all."

"What do you mean, Rich?" Roosevelt asked; he seemed genuinely interested.

"Senator, the United States has the most advanced filmmaking experts in the world, the leading technologists, and some of the best cybersecurity experts. Are you telling me that the Russians are so far ahead of us in these areas that we can't figure out how they made the films or stop them from penetrating the Pentagon's security?"

I could see Roosevelt weighing how much to reveal. Finally, he sighed, and I felt I was going to get the full story.

"Our experts believe," he motioned to the people in the room, "and I agree with them, that the most likely explanation for the existence of these videos is that the Russians have developed some breakthrough technologies involving quantum computing that allow them to create new kinds of CGI and penetrate networks at will."

I'd read that quantum computers would someday allow hackers to get into networks that had previously been considered impenetrable. I hadn't heard anything about quantum computers enabling new kinds of CGI, but it seemed possible. "Do you have any evidence of this? I thought quantum computers were years away from outperforming current technologies."

The Navy admiral spoke up. "We thought so, too, Mr. Penton." He skipped over my question about evidence and continued. "We know the videos are startling. When I first saw them, I could hardly believe they weren't the real deal. I've never seen images so terrifying, and so persuasive, in their authenticity. But then I asked myself, *cui bono?*"

"Who benefits?"

"Yes. And what's the answer to *cui bono* here? Time-traveling aliens have taken videos of important events and put them on your computers and ours? Or the Russians, who are the world's best hackers and are quickly building best-in-class deep fake technology, want to harm us? Until we got these videos, we had no idea they had such a technological edge in quantum computing. But as focused as they are on damaging the United States, it makes sense that Russia would invent new ways to undermine our stability. Consider how the Tulsa Race Massacre video could stir up racial tensions. It's difficult to watch."

I remembered my conversation with Dr. Kayla Vincent at the Greenwood Cultural Center. "A lot more people should see that video," I countered and then continued. "What if you're wrong? What if there really is an asteroid headed towards Chicago right now, and we do nothing about it? Surely, you can't just exclude the possibility?"

"We're not 'excluding the possibility,'" the Air Force general interjected irritably. "We take our responsibilities to defend this nation seriously, so of course we've looked for this object on the remote chance these videos are actually from an intelligence none of us understands. As soon as we received the asteroid video, we shared it with senior people at NASA, JPL, the Minor Planet Center—all the experts."

"Okay, that's reassuring," I told him.

He continued. "They're searching for such an object. So far, they've found nothing. Besides, we believe we've identified almost all of the asteroids that could cause major regional damage."

My B.S. alarm went off. Eliza had given me a crash course on potentially hazardous objects or PHOs—comets or asteroids that will come within 4.6 million miles of earth. "No one saw the Chelyabinsk meteor coming in 2013. It was only nineteen meters in diameter, so it falls well below the size that would cause 'regional damage.' But it exploded over the city and 1,500 people were injured by flying glass. If one that size hit Chicago, sections of the city would be devastated. And there are thousands that size, and a lot larger, that haven't been identified. And what about asteroids that come from the other side of the Sun? You have almost no visibility to those. I appreciate the job PHO hunters are doing, but we all know a large meteor could strike earth at any time and we simply would not see it coming."

We argued like this for another hour. They were completely hardened in their views, even though they presented no evidence of Russian involvement. I'd seen groupthink and irrational commitment before. This conversation was full of red flags, but they weren't Russian. Finally, Senator Roosevelt cut off the conversation, holding up his hand.

"None of this is going to do any good, Rich. We are convinced the Russians are behind these videos and I'm asking you, as your friend, to accept that what we're telling you is the truth".

"Senator," I replied. "I need to tell you something else." I had been debating whether to describe our experiences with Angela. Given their skepticism, I felt I had no choice. But as I talked, I could see they didn't believe me. Even Roosevelt wasn't buying it. When I was done, he glanced around the room and then gave me a sympathetic look. As though I was the one who had lost my mind, not my wife.

He spoke as delicately as he could. "Well, there's a lot we don't know about Alzheimer's. Maybe it's a coincidence, or there's some universal connection we don't understand. Maybe the Russians have learned how to generate holograms, too."

I know he didn't mean to be patronizing, but it sure came across that way.

And then things got nasty when one of the FBI suits spoke up. "Mr. Penton, your earlier refusal to commit to confidentiality about this topic is not acceptable. I'm warning you that if you discuss this meeting or broadcast the videos you received, you will be arrested and prosecuted under the Espionage Act."

Through a massive effort of self-control, I didn't react. Thanks to the 1971 Supreme Court ruling in the Pentagon Papers case, it's extremely difficult to prosecute journalists for revealing information they've received lawfully, provided it's of public importance. The odds that the United States Government would pursue a *RECON* anchor over files that appeared on a computer were laughably small. And if they did, they'd lose the case, and the publicity would make the effort backfire. But I didn't want to antagonize these people, so I let his threat hang in the air.

And then the meeting was over. I was escorted to the exit, and I flew home to Chicago. I had hoped to come away from the meeting with reassurances that our government was aware of the threat and acting to mitigate it. Instead, I learned they'd accepted the Russia hypothesis and, besides passing a warning to NASA and other agencies, they planned to do nothing.

I went straight to North Pond restaurant from the airport. Eliza was waiting for me when I arrived. I told her what had happened and asked her if she had any ideas.

"Actually, I do," she answered. "There's a PHO conference in

Tucson on June 16th. I reached out to David Clancy[*], who's the CEO of Planetary Defense. I told him we were facing a dire emergency, and I needed to meet with him at the conference."

"CEO of Planetary Defense?" I asked. "Is that a real title?"

Eliza nodded. "He runs NASA's Planetary Defense Coordination office. He's in charge of detecting hazardous asteroids and comets and protecting the Earth from them."

I shook my head. "There was a time when I would have thought that was science fiction. Now, it sounds like a deadly serious job. He must be quite an impressive individual."

"He is," Eliza agreed. "He's also incredibly busy. I told him you were coming with me to the meeting in Tucson, and I think that helped sway him to make time for us."

"Count me in. We need him to stop this object."

"NASA may have to see the object before he'll approve a mission, Rich. Depending on the direction it's coming from, that might be impossible before it's too late."

I thought about that for a moment. "Do you think the asteroid is coming from behind the Sun?"

She shrugged. "I think it could be an interstellar object, like 'Oumuamua." She went on to describe that object and how it didn't arrive on the same plane as the solar system. Unlike nearly every other asteroid, 'Oumuamua "flew in from the top," to use her words.

"Since interstellar objects like that can come in at an oblique angle compared to the planetary plane, we're much less likely to spot them. Both because they're extremely rare, so we don't look for them, and because they're just harder to see."

I had another topic to discuss with her. "Do you think what they told me about Russian involvement is all bullshit?"

To my surprise, Eliza shook her head. "No. I think the Russians could be involved. I don't think they made the videos or put them on

---

[*] David Clancy is based on NASA's real Planetary Defense Officer, Lindley Johnson.

your computer, but there's a strong likelihood they know the asteroid is on its way."

"How so?"

"Several years ago, the Russians launched two satellites. One was called the *Leonid Kulik,* and the other was the *Nikolay Fedorov.*"

"Do those names mean anything?"

"Yes, they do. Kulik and Fedorov were the scientists who led a mission to investigate the Tunguska Event in 1927."

I'd read about the Tunguska Event. In 1908, a meteor around two hundred feet in diameter exploded over a remote area in Siberia. It released the force of 1,000 atomic bombs and flattened trees in an area of more than 800 square miles.

"What do these satellites have to do with the videos we received?"

"Their locations give the Russians a unique ability to see objects arriving from behind the Sun. Russia is more motivated than any other country to care about NEOs. It's eleven percent of the world's land mass—the largest country by far—and nearly twice as big as the United States."

"So, it's more likely to be hit by asteroids?"

"Not just more likely. It's been hit by asteroids quite recently. Once, just a decade ago. Counting Tunguska, it's been hit twice in a little more than a hundred years. Both were close calls, in the sense that they missed major population centers but caused enormous amounts of destruction. I believe the Russians launched *Kulik* and *Federov* to detect incoming objects because they're afraid to be hit again. It's possible they can already see the one that's on its way to Chicago. Orbital mechanics are extremely complex, so at first, they probably had just a general idea of where it would hit. But when they figured out its destination was somewhere in the United States, it became an opportunity to see enormous devastation inflicted on a strategic adversary."

"And you think the Intelligence behind the videos messed up the Russians' plans? First, by sharing the videos with Washington and, when that failed, with *RECON*?" Chandra Ramanujan had suggested that the United States Government may have been notified already and I had dismissed the idea. He had been right after all.

"Yes," she replied. "I think that could be what happened. The Intelligence tried to warn our government. They may have warned the Russians and Chinese as well—any nation that might have assets that can deflect asteroids."

I nodded. "Russia and China wouldn't necessarily tell us if they knew. And, as it stands, the American Government doesn't believe the information. They think it's a ruse by the Russians. Damn, it's a paranoid circle! So, the Intelligence reached out to me."

"Think about it, Rich. You're famous, you're credible, you have the leading news show on television, and you're motivated to pay attention and act because you're located in the target city."

"Why don't they just send a message in English?" I asked, exasperated. "Or show a video of the asteroid itself and its trajectory?"

Eliza grinned at me. "They did send a video of the asteroid, and you ignored it, remember? But now that you've asked to see its trajectory, they'll probably show it to you."

I was confused. "What's that mean?"

"Think about it. Every time you've complained about something in a video, the next one fixed that problem. With the missile video, you said that since it was from the future, you couldn't investigate it, right?"

"Right."

"So, the next video was the Battle of the Little Bighorn. It was shot close to the action, with lots of details you could verify. Based on your complaints from the first video, it had everything you asked for, but you said it was still missing something. Do you remember what it was?"

"We couldn't hear what the soldiers and Native Americans were saying."

"That's right, and so—"

"The next video was about Earhart, and we could hear everything perfectly! But what about the Tulsa Race Massacre?"

"The problem with the Earhart video is that you can't verify how she died. Sure, some interesting details matched up with Thibodeaux's research, but you don't know for sure. But the details in the Tulsa Race Massacre video could be confirmed in ways that even the Little Bighorn film couldn't—with actual photographic evidence of the event."

"What about the *Cap Arcona* video?"

Eliza waved her finger. "They began setting up *that one* a long time ago. Angela had her first visions in March, so the *Cap Arcona* hologram was always going to be the clincher. But now that you've asked for a video showing more information about the asteroid— exactly where it's coming from and what its trajectory will be—you'll probably get it!"

"But the government got the same videos," I protested. "The Intelligence was probably just sending me the ones they had, not because I was 'asking' for them!"

"How do you know? They didn't show you any of their videos, and they certainly weren't going to tell you if they had anything different. I stand by my theory. The Intelligence is listening."

17

UNVEILING

The SVR was very unhappy with Viktor for using a screen name that *RECON* could track back to him. He told them that he'd only used the name for the Little Bighorn deep fakes discussion, but that didn't mollify them. It wasn't Viktor's job to post on dark web forums. They had other experts for that work, and this was why: he was likely to make mistakes. His boss told him to remain in his hotel room for a week to let things cool down.

For the most part, Viktor did as instructed. But the tension got to him, and he eventually walked to a liquor store for vodka and, on a whim, cigarettes, which he'd given up more than ten years ago. He sat on the cold radiator housing in his room with the window open and blew smoke outdoors while he drank. He wasn't drunk—he thought of it as *prinyat na grud*. The alcohol was like a medicine to keep him calm until he could act again. In the evenings, he put on the headphones and listened to Carl and Wendy Swinton, who, he decided, were the dullest people in the world.

But not tonight. He was only half listening to the Swintons when he finally received the call from his superiors that he was cleared to go back to work. He acknowledged the message but, as he hung up, he felt waves of shock and fury. Carl had just told his wife that they'd found a screen name called, "OBlo42," and it could be the person who'd murdered Monalisa.

Beth and Hubert rarely met during the workday, but he invited her to lunch at Cindy's, on top of the Chicago Athletic Association building, which offered a great view of the lake. Beth arrived first and watched Hubert come in wearing a white collared shirt, a tailored blue suit, and snazzy Johnston & Murphy shoes. He sported new glasses he'd ordered online.

"You look fantastic," she told him as he bent over to give her a kiss.

"I should hope so," Hubert replied with a grin, his freckled face going crimson. "You picked out this entire outfit."

"And it works," she noted.

They chatted happily and shared a sense of contentment, as couples do when they are good for each other in all the right ways. Beth could tell that Hubert was in good spirits; he could barely contain his smiles as they talked.

He wants to tell me something.

Before she could ask what was on his mind, Hubert blurted out, "I think we may know who killed Monalisa!"

Beth stopped eating, her fork in midair. She felt her pulse quicken and goosebumps appeared instantly on her arms. "Who?" she asked, calmly.

Hubert paused and focused on pronouncing the name correctly. "*Viktor Stolypin Dyavol.*" He repeated it with more confidence. "Viktor Stolypin Dyavol."

Beth put down her fork, smoothed her slacks with her hands and folded her arms, settling in for an explanation. "How did you identify him?"

Hubert was surprised at her reaction. She wasn't conveying excitement. If anything, her reaction seemed...clinical. *Why is she being so matter of fact about this?* he asked himself, then realized that he was seeing her in her professional role as a producer for *RECON*. He was confident in his team's work, but he suddenly felt nervous and began to second-guess himself. Then he shrugged it off—there was nothing to do but tell her everything.

"Do you remember how BlackSpider150 led us to the screen name, OBlo42?"

"Yes."

"Well, we found four more screen names that all belonged to BlackSpider150."

Beth looked skeptical. "And you think they belong to the same person because they're all combinations of the names and statistics of famous Russian soccer players?"

Hubert smiled confidently. "No. That would be thin evidence. We found thousands of screen names that could be interpreted that way."

Beth seemed relieved. "Go on."

Hubert leaned in as though he was admitting a terrible secret. "We identified the other four by looking at stolen identities on the dark web. We're 90% confident that BlackSpider150 and OBlo42 are the same person. And we know OBlo42 is the same person as the other four screen names."

"How?"

"Because they all used the same credit card. In the first three months after Russia invaded Ukraine, hackers went after Russian banks. They stole and released the identities and account information of more than 113,000 Sberbank credit card customers. Sbrebank is majority owned by the Russian government, and Viktor Stolypin Dyavol was one of the victims."

"Hmm," Beth pondered. "The credit card data matches to five of the screen names, so you're 100% certain they're all the same person. And there's a 90% chance that this BlackSpider and Oblo42 person are the same. So that means, the overall probability that the guy who chatted with Monalisa and killed her is this *Viktor...Sto*-something..."

"Stolypin Dyavol," Hubert offered.

"...is 90%?" she finished.

Hubert shook his head. "No. It's higher. The algorithm matched BlackSpider150 *to all five* screen names to more than a 90% probability. That means the odds that BlackSpider150 is Viktor Stolypin Dyavol are approximately 99.6%."

Beth smiled at him. "'Approximately,' huh? Superb work, Hubert."

"Thanks," Hubert answered, blushing deeply. Despite his brilliance with numbers, he would have made a terrible poker player.

"So, who is he?" Beth asked. "Who is Viktor Dyavol?"

Hubert shrugged his shoulders. "We're not sure. We can tell by his credit card data that he travels all over the world. He buys airline tickets, food, hotel rooms, and tickets to soccer matches. But most of his charges are from the Moscow area."

Beth sat back, deep in thought. "Well, it's not enough to win a conviction—yet. But it's an unbelievable amount of information to get so quickly. Now it's up to *RECON* to finish the investigation, track down more information and see if we can put him in Chicago at the time of the murder."

"I wish I could help you with that," Hubert said, apologetically, "but we don't have any credit card records more recent than 2022."

Beth waved away his apology. "Don't be ridiculous. You've done an incredible job. More than anyone else could have done."

Hubert beamed and blushed.

"Do you have a photograph of this character?" Beth asked.

Hubert shook his head. "Not yet. I mean, we have a ton of possible photos, but we're not certain which one is him. We're hunting for a recent one."

Beth paused, thinking. "Okay, so as soon as you're confident you've got a photo of the right guy, say 90% sure, text it to me immediately, okay?"

"Of course."

"And text it to Rich, too" Beth added. "He'll want to know right away."

Warren was getting a cup of coffee when Jessica walked into the breakroom. They'd only spoken a few times since he'd asked her out, and today she smiled at him. He smiled back; he could hardly help it. Ever since he'd met her, he couldn't get her out of his mind.

"Good morning!" she said brightly.

"Good morning!" he replied, trying to mask his enthusiasm. For some reason, when she'd rejected him, he hadn't just headed back to bars to pick up women. Hookups were easy for him, but he was tired of them. He wanted something authentic and meaningful. After a moment of awkward silence, he started to walk out of the breakroom when she called out behind him.

"Hey Warren?"

He turned around, hearing the nervousness in her voice.

"I've been thinking about that day you asked me out."

Warren's pulse raced. He couldn't quite determine what it was about her. Certainly, he'd dated women who drew more attention. But he felt a different and deeper attraction to Jessica than any of them.

She smiled at him. "I went through a pretty ugly divorce, so I didn't want to date until I was sure I was ready. And I wasn't going to do the whole hookup scene."

"That's smart," he told her. "You shouldn't rush it."

Jessica seemed hesitant. Warren was unsure what to do in this unprecedented situation. This was the kind of problem he would have historically brought to Monalisa for her analysis and advice. A sharp pang of loss hit him. Monalisa would have gently made fun of *the big stud's* discomfort, then helped him figure out exactly how to handle it.

But Jessica took care of the next step for him. "Would you still like to go out sometime?"

Warren smiled. *I'm so glad I waited.* "How about after work tonight?" he suggested. "Maybe get some drinks and dinner?"

"That would be great! Text me around five?"

Warren grinned all the way back to his office. Much later that evening, after spending hours talking, the two of them held each other close and fell asleep under a blanket on her sofa. Warren's blissful brain didn't wake him when the cell phone notification came in.

It was dark in Rich Penton's empty office in the middle of the night, but not pitch black. Ambient light outlined the chairs, the table, and the desk. The screen on Rich's computer woke up, emitting enough light to illuminate much of the room. There was no one to see it, and no one to touch the keyboard or the mouse to keep it awake. It shone brightly for a few minutes, then the computer reentered slumber mode, and the screen winked off again.

18

PERUN'S HAMMER

When I arrived at work the next day, Hubert and Beth came to my office and described the incredibly sophisticated process NSDA had developed to identify Viktor Stolypin Dyavol. They didn't have a picture of him yet—our assassin was apparently and understandably camera shy—but Hubert was confident he'd find one soon. Learning the name of Monalisa's killer heightened my desire for revenge. All I wanted to focus on was finding him, so I was almost annoyed when I found a new video on my desktop that morning. We picked 10 a.m. for the screening. The *RECON* crew squeezed around my conference table to accommodate our guests—Hubert was already there, and I'd called Eliza, too. The file information told us the video was twenty-two minutes long.

The video opened showing an object flying through space, and I heard Eliza catch her breath the moment it came into view. She pointed at the screen in shock, her eyes wide. "That's not an asteroid! That's a...a...*spacecraft*!"

No one spoke. We stared at the screen, watching a large, cylindrical object tumbling awkwardly across a dark canopy of stars, galaxies, planets, and sometimes the Sun, as the angle of view changed. It was hard to make out. The object was dark gray with a textured, almost mesh-like surface. On one side, we could see enormous dents, as though it had been sideswiped by an asteroid at some point in its long voyage. I felt a chill as I realized we were seeing, for the first time in the history of the world, evidence of a non-human intelligence, capable of traversing the stars.

"It's artificial. Manufactured," I murmured. "But not by humans." The implications were so awesome, the information so overwhelming, that for a long time, we just watched the object. Everything about mankind's perception of itself was about to change. We could never again think of ourselves as occupying the top of the evolutionary pyramid. Another species was advanced far beyond us. Whatever civilization built this craft must have done so long ago, perhaps thousands or millions of years before mankind evolved from our primitive ancestors.

Almost reverently, Beth asked, "Eliza, what do you think that spacecraft is for?"

Eliza shook her head, mesmerized by the video. "There's no way to know. It could be a probe, a communications satellite, an occupied craft. But *somebody* made it."

This revelation was hard to process. This new variable—that the asteroid wasn't really an asteroid but was something manufactured by another intelligent species—was awe-inspiring, even though we knew this object might bring disaster to Chicago.

The Earth emerged from the dark background as the tumbling spacecraft approached. We could make out the shape of Lake Michigan, and the object seemed to be pulled towards it. We followed alongside as it entered the atmosphere. It began to glow red-hot and caught fire, but it remained intact. The speed of the fiery spacecraft was stunning. It rapidly closed the distance to Chicago, plunging out of the sky and striking just north of downtown. The explosion and fireball were enormous. Flames and a shock wave erupted from the point of impact and spread out for miles, roiling across the land, crushing buildings, cars, and people, who vaporized before our eyes.

"Oh, my God!" someone cried.

After giving us a brief tour of the carnage, the video ended. No one spoke as we gathered our thoughts and processed what we'd just witnessed. A few people stepped out. Beth and Warren brought back coffee and water from the breakroom. Carl fetched a bottle of Jameson. Alcohol of any kind was not allowed in the *RECON* offices, but most of us gratefully accepted a dollop.

I gathered my thoughts and faced the group. "Now that we know this isn't a natural object, I have to ask the question. Is this a deliberate attack?"

Eliza shook her head. "No, I don't think so. I think it's an accident. Maybe that spacecraft was sent to pass by Earth, but I doubt it was sent to hit the planet."

"How can you know that?" Carl demanded. "It hit Chicago like it was aimed at us."

"That could be a coincidence," Beth said, putting her hand on Carl's arm.

"Bullshit," Carl exploded. "That thing—"

"Looked broken!" Hubert interjected. "That looked like a dead spaceship. If it was aimed at us, if it was a weapon, it wouldn't be tumbling out of control like that. And—"

"It was dented!" Warren jumped in, nodding. "Hubert's right. Whatever that thing is, it's broken."

"How can you *know* that?" Carl repeated, unconvinced.

"Because a cylindrical shape would be ideal for either a communications beacon or an occupied vessel," Eliza answered. "The form of a spacecraft serves its function, so I assume a cylinder like that was designed to rotate smoothly along its axis. If it was meant to be occupied, that would create gravity against its walls. It's impossible to tell how big that object is, but based on the damage it caused when it hit Chicago, it's probably massive. It could have plenty of room inside to house dozens of people—aliens—creatures—whoever built it."

"Because the spinning motion would allow you to live on the interior walls?" Warren asked.

"Yes. These objects have been invented in science fiction. Arthur C. Clarke created an enormous, rotating, cylindrical spaceship for his book, *Rendezvous with Rama*. In that story, *Rama* even has a sea running around a band in the middle." Then a thoughtful look—a realization—came over her face. "Maybe that's why the Intelligence cares."

"What do you mean?" Rosalie asked.

"Maybe that's why the Intelligence cares," Eliza repeated, her eyes bright.

"I don't understand," I blurted out.

"Don't you see? This could be why they're sending the messages —the warnings."

And then it hit me. "You're saying that this spacecraft, this object, belongs to the Intelligence?"

Eliza nodded.

If that was true, then the Intelligence wasn't merely acting as a galactic Good Samaritan by warning us about the object. Eliza was suggesting that the Intelligence was taking responsibility for its failed spacecraft and was telling us it was coming so we could do something about it.

"I don't know," Carl shook his head. "How could the Intelligence see through time and send us warnings, but they couldn't see that some space rock was going to hit their ship?"

Eliza smiled at Carl. "Because the Intelligence we're dealing with today probably launched that spaceship thousands of years ago.

Maybe then, they couldn't see into the future, so they didn't see the accident coming."

"Eliza," Hubert asked, "the object is dented, but it probably doesn't have punctures in its hull, right?"

Eliza shook her head. "I don't know, but I didn't see any."

Beth looked back and forth between Hubert and Eliza. "Why does that matter?"

Hubert answered. "Because in the video we just watched, this thing didn't burn up in the atmosphere. That means the hull is probably heat—shielded. If it had been punctured, even a little bit, then Earth's atmosphere would have entered the interior of the ship. It would have burned up in the sky, instead of striking Chicago intact —like the biggest bomb in history."

"That's speculation," Eliza cautioned. "After all, we don't know what this spacecraft is made out of. We certainly couldn't construct a craft that size capable of surviving a fall through Earth's atmosphere at that velocity. Maybe nothing can stop it from destroying the city."

Rosalie slammed her hand on the table. Everyone jumped—not just due to the sound, but because we'd never seen an emotional outburst from her. "No!" she said, her face stern. "That makes no sense. If this spacecraft, satellite, probe—whatever it is—is that tough, then there would be nothing we could do about it. Why would the Intelligence send us warnings if we had no options?"

We sat in silence for a few moments. Finally, Eliza spoke up. "Maybe the best we can do is evacuate the city."

Rosalie wasn't buying it. "No. We *have* to do something. We *can* do something. I will not believe that with all our technology, we can't move this thing enough to make it miss. Chicago is *your* city, just like it's mine. Chicago is our *home,* and we have to defend it with everything we have. And that starts with you, Rich. You need to use all your influence to persuade NASA to do whatever it takes to go after this thing. Maybe Eliza's right, but we have to try. We can't give up."

Eliza turned to me. "Rich, you asked for this video, remember?

We don't know if the Intelligence heard the words coming from your mouth or your brain. But we now have the data we need to launch a deflection mission."

"Whoa, wait!" Carl protested. "What do you mean, you 'asked' for this video?"

"So, a couple of days ago," I explained, "I said we needed a video that showed the actual asteroid, in flight. If we had that, we could figure out when it would arrive, right,?" I looked at Eliza for confirmation.

"Yes. By analyzing the relative locations of the celestial objects in this video, we can determine the exact date it will hit Chicago, as well as the trajectory it will take to get here."

"How soon can you know?" Hubert asked.

She shrugged. "I'm not sure. But I'm going to call Jay McMahon and Chloe Long at the University of Colorado's ORCCA Lab. I'm hoping they can do it in less than a week."

I considered that information. "So, once we know that, we can start contacting U.S. government officials who specialize in asteroid redirection. We'll announce what we know on *RECON* and keep covering the story until we get the action we need. Eliza, will NASA listen to us about the videos, the research we've done, and maybe even what happened with Angela?"

Eliza mulled over my question. "They'll listen, but to convince them it's true, I'll need your help. We need to make one hell of a pitch at the PHO Conference in Tucson."

"How can NASA stop this object?" Beth asked.

Eliza answered. "With an ordinary asteroid, you either nuke it, or smack it really hard. In either case, the direct hit only provides part of the force that slows it down. It also damages the asteroid, so it begins ejecting material where it's struck, and that slows it down, too. But this object's different. It's not likely to create a stream of ejecta, so the kinetic force will have to be enough to slow it down."

"Why slow it down instead of turn it?" Warren asked.

"It's the same thing. We think of meteors as rocks that fall out of the sky, but they're really just asteroids that happen to reach a specific point in space at the same moment Earth does. If you slow down an asteroid—or this dead spaceship—even a little, then Earth and the object don't reach that place at the same time anymore."

"Does NASA have asteroid deflectors we could launch in time?" Hubert asked.

"I won't know about the timing until the ORCCA Lab people analyze the data. But I know we have one asteroid deflector that is completed. I'm guessing it could be launched in six months, once we got the mission approved. You have to launch it early enough to intercept the asteroid—well, object in this case—while it's still far off in space. Otherwise, there's not enough deflection to make it miss. But it's going to be difficult to persuade them to launch a mission against an object they've never seen, especially when we tell them it's alien space debris!"

Carl spoke up. "You know...um...we might cause a huge panic with this. I'd really feel bad about that. And we're all going to get fired if there really is no spaceship."

I thought that over. "I think the sooner we air the story, the less the panic. If people have months to plan, they won't panic like they will if they only have weeks." Then I grinned. "And we're probably going to get fired no matter what. The timing could work out so this show airs months before NASA confirms there's a real threat out there."

That hadn't occurred to everyone. After a moment, Carl sighed. "That's okay. If there's no threat, I'll be glad. I'd rather get fired than do nothing."

The horror we'd shared while watching the object hit Chicago was replaced by a sense of energy and excitement. When we'd first viewed the video, it seemed like a vision of our own executions. The incredible detail and accuracy of the previous videos made the destruction of Chicago seem preordained. But as we now understood it, this video was not like the others. It only showed one possible future. We had a chance to write a different ending to this story.

After months of wondering why we'd received the videos and what the hell we were supposed to do with them, it was good to have some direction. If we could prevent the destruction of our beloved Chicago, that would bring real meaning to Monalisa's otherwise-senseless death.

"What should we call this object?" Beth asked—a minor question in the scheme of things, but we needed to call it something.

"How about *Perun's Hammer*?" Warren said, after a few moments. He pronounced it "pa-ROON," like "Peru," but ending with an "n."

"Who's Perun?" I asked.

"He's a Slavic God," Hubert offered. "The highest god of the pantheon, associated with the sky, thunder, and lightning. Closest thing to a Russian God."

"And he carries a hammer," Warren added.

I saw some nods, so I said, "*Perun's Hammer* it is. We're going to tell the world all about this sonofabitch, and we're going to try to air this story before the network even knows it's coming. So, don't tell Brendan fucking Braswell about it." Everyone laughed, but I reminded them we had a leak somewhere in the organization. We'd need to take extra precautions and ensure we handled all the material about *Perun's Hammer* with extra diligence.

Rosalie was among the last to leave. I knew she always had more going on inside than she revealed.

"Rosalie?"

She stopped and faced me. "Yes?"

"Thanks for what you said. You really got us refocused on attacking this thing."

"You're welcome," she answered, but looked lost in thought.

"What's on your mind?"

She held my gaze. "Not everyone will be happy about you going public with these videos. And not just the people you met in Washington." Then she walked out.

That night, Viktor listened from the confines of his small hotel room as Carl told Wendy about the developments with the object they were now calling *Perun's Hammer*. He was as energized and excited as he'd been in ages, he told her. But he was worried about Brendan Braswell, who was coming back to Chicago again the following week. It was highly unusual for him to visit again so soon.

Their annoying chatter faded into the background as Viktor considered the ramifications of *RECON*'s decision to produce a story about the strange, cosmic object. From the start, his primary mission objective had been to prevent the videos from ever being seen publicly. His bosses had already picked up on the significance of OBlo42, and after tonight, they would know about *RECON*'s broadcast plans. He had been summoned to a west side office building the next day, to meet with his handlers. They'd told him to bring his resources, which meant weapons and various tools of the spy trade. At the very least, he was off the case. He might be fired—or worse.

For a long time, Viktor had been harboring resentment and anger at the *RECON* team. From his first interaction, they'd plagued him. After surviving years of fighting in Afghanistan and beating every opponent he'd ever faced, his career was at risk thanks to a bunch of fucking journalists. Tomorrow's meeting was going to be extremely unpleasant. But whether they took him off the assignment or not, he knew it was time to deal with *RECON* in his own, violent way.

Rosalie met her contact in person for the second time in three weeks. She hated taking risks like this, but once again, there was too much to cover by text. They sat in the bar of The Gage restaurant, and she told him about the video of the artificial object flying through space before destroying Chicago.

"Why didn't you tell me about this asset?" Rosalie asked. Her voice was low, but her tone was angry.

The man shook his head. "As far as I know, we don't have it."

She stared at him in disbelief. "Either you're lying, or they're lying to both of us."

The man's face flushed with anger. "I wouldn't lie to you. And I don't think they're lying to us. I think the subject's starting to get assets we don't have. Did you consider that before making accusations?"

Rosalie pondered that for a moment. "Okay, let's say you're right. What am I supposed to do with this? Not only does the subject believe the ET theory now, but I do, too!"

"Don't say that." The man shook his head. "We have orders, and you can't carry them out if you think we're wrong."

"I *can*," Rosalie replied. "But I *won't*."

The man sighed. "You're lucky I've known you so long, or I'd pass your comments up the chain." He took a sip of his drink.

Rosalie thought for a moment. "I think you should."

The man was startled. "What's that supposed to mean?"

"It means you should tell them I believe they're wrong. They need to abandon the original plan and take the new evidence into account." She studied him. "How long have you lived in Chicago?"

"Twenty-two years."

"Are you certain it's not at risk? After everything I've told you?"

He held her gaze and then shook his head. "No. I'm not sure. Not anymore."

"Then do the right thing. Tell them they're wrong, and we need to change our plans. Say that's my recommendation. It's up to you if you want to make it yours, too."

He sighed. "I'll share your opinion. And I'll tell them they should listen to you."

"Thank you," Rosalie replied.

19

THE DEVIL YOU KNOW

June 5th: 132 Days Before Arrival

Rosalie sat with Michael and their children after dinner. Everyone was holding a book. The kids had to read twenty pages before TV or video games, and Michael was wrapped up in a biography of some historical character. Rosalie was trying to get interested in a popular novel someone had left in the breakroom at work when her phone chirped with a notification.

Hubert had texted a photo of Viktor Stolypin Dyavol to Rich and, thanks to the app hidden on his phone, the message was copied to Rosalie in real time. Hubert offered to meet in person to provide more details, and Rich replied that he was still in the office and suggested a breakfast meeting. Rosalie had not been with Hubert and Beth when they told Rich about the Russian, but she recognized him. If Hubert's team had identified Dyavol as the killer, there was a good chance he knew and had been activated for a kill—or would act on his own; he was known to default to violence. That could mean Rich Penton was about to be eliminated.

She jumped up out of her chair. Trying to sound calm, she said, "Something came up at work. I have to go to the office." She went quickly to the front door, grabbed a small backpack from a high shelf, snapped up her car keys, and hurried outside.

"Dad, is Mom okay?" Olivia asked. Michael pondered what had just happened, then he forced a smile. "Everything's fine, sweetheart." He tried to sound reassuring. "Mom just has to run to the office. She'll be back soon." But he knew something was very wrong. The bag Rosalie had taken contained her weapons.

Viktor didn't get out of his meeting until the evening. He was surprised he'd been allowed to leave at all, based on what they'd said. He'd been taken off the assignment and was being sent home, as he had feared. His bosses pointed out numerous times that, instead of containing the problem, he'd actually made things *worse*. The Russians wanted the videos kept secret and, thanks to his failures, millions of people would be watching a broadcast about them in a month. Also, he'd been identified, which would create a huge mess for the SVR if he was arrested for the girl's murder. Viktor hadn't tasted defeat like this since Afghanistan. And all because he'd killed a girl who worked for *fucking RECON*.

He was riding in the cab back to his hotel when they pulled onto Monroe Street, just a few blocks from the *RECON* offices on Marshall. "Stop the car," he said to the driver, who glanced in the rear-view mirror and then pulled over. Viktor paid him, lifted his massive frame out of the taxicab, and began walking in the darkness towards Marshall Street. He slid a burner phone out of his coat pocket and dialed Rich Penton's office number, which he'd gathered during his research but had never used. Until now.

"Rich Penton," said the voice on the other end.

Viktor grinned and hung up. He dropped the phone onto the sidewalk, smashed it with his foot, and dropped it into a trash bin. Rich Penton was at work, quite possibly alone, at night.

His bosses had taken away all the weapons they'd issued to him, but they let him keep the knife strapped above his ankle because he had purchased it himself. Viktor knew he had one last opportunity to set things right as he reached for the security badge he'd stolen from Carl, turned in the darkness, and walked towards the *RECON* building.

Beth and Carl developed most of the script for the *Perun's Hammer* story, but I decided to write the introduction myself. As I worked late into the evening, I was focused on my writing when Hubert texted me a photo of Viktor Stolypin Dyavol. We agreed to meet for breakfast to discuss the next steps.

My office phone rang, but the caller hung up as soon as I answered. Seconds later, I was startled to hear a *ding!* and an icon appeared on my desktop. It was a video file, just like all the others, but this was the first time I'd seen one appear in real time. After I got over the surprise, I clicked on it.

The video was short, and incredibly gruesome: it showed a murder victim lying in the darkness on a sidewalk on Madison Street, which I took every day to the train. The man wasn't quite dead. There was enough ambient light to see his throat was slashed. Thick, bright red blood pumped out of the gash. The man's eyes were filled with terror, and he had his hands wrapped around his throat in a hopeless attempt to contain the bleeding. *But the worst part was that the man was me—dressed in the same clothes I was wearing right now.*

The shot pulled back as the victim died, his—my—hands falling to the sidewalk.

It was shocking to see a video of my own death. I sat dazed for a minute, before my mind worked it out. *The Intelligence is warning me that I'm about to be killed!* My mind slowly began to function again, and it occurred to me that it might be a random attack. They happen all the time. So, I decided to take a different route home: Monroe instead of Madison. I watched the video again, to see if I could find clues about the time of my upcoming... murder. But the video had changed. Now I was dying on a sidewalk on Monroe. The video reflected the new route I'd planned to take. *What the hell?*

And then I got it. I had changed the future with my decision. When I replayed the video, the Intelligence showed me the new outcome. That meant it was an assassination—and the assassin was outside, right now, preparing to kill me. It had to be Viktor Stolypin Dyavol. Fear washed over me, and I forced it away. *Maybe I can take the utility elevator down and sneak out the back door of the building.* I played the video again, and this time I saw myself dying in the alley behind our building instead of blocks away, which meant the Russian was approaching. He was almost here! I fought back the rising panic.

I didn't have all night to keep testing scenarios. Very soon, I would have to act, and so far, I'd found no way to prevent my own murder. Could the killer get inside the building? We had security guards in a couple of locations, and all the doors required badges to open, but if this was Viktor Dyavol, he was an experienced assassin and would find a way in. I felt—no, I knew—that if that if he wasn't already inside, he would be soon.

I'd been in many dangerous situations, but seeing my own murder rattled me in a way I'd never experienced. And then anger began to rise up inside of me. I welcomed it and coaxed it, feeding the fire intentionally, reminding myself that the man about to attack me had brutally killed Monalisa. My fury grew, and this pushed the fear down, away from me, rendering it useless.

I watched the video again, determined to figure out how to fight back. This time, my body was lying on the floor a few feet from where I was sitting. My assassin was going to arrive any second.

I looked around for something to use as a weapon. The pickings were slim. I had a letter opener that could be used as a dull knife, and a polished rock paperweight from Puerto Rico that Angela had given me years ago. The bell of the elevator rang out clearly from across the office floor, and my heart went into overdrive. I was out of time, and I had to act. I grabbed the letter opener, stood up from my chair, and strode out of the office, determined to fight. I headed straight towards the elevator to confront the killer when something struck me with incredible force, launching me off my feet and headlong into a wall. I bounced off it and sprawled onto the floor face first. I twisted my body around awkwardly and looked up to see a huge, blonde, muscular man approaching.

It was Viktor Stolypin Dyavol. He was a little older than in the picture, but there was no mistaking that chiseled face. He seemed massive and invincible. He'd hit me so hard I was barely conscious, and he glared at me with hatred and contempt burning in his eyes. I tried to get off the ground, but I was weak from the blow and striking the wall. Besides, I couldn't take my eyes off Dyavol. He didn't say a word as he bent down, pulled up his pant leg, and drew a long, black knife from a sheath strapped to his calf.

When he spoke, his voice was low and menacing. "I'm going to kill you. But first, I want to hear you beg and scream." He moved towards me, and I pushed myself backward, desperately trying to get to my feet. Even at my best, I'd have no chance, but in my current state, I knew I wouldn't be able to put up much resistance. *Damn it! I don't want to die without a fight!*

Out of the darkness, a long, low, blur shot from the hallway to my left and hit the assassin in the legs. He slammed to the floor, the knife flying several feet away, bouncing along the tile, and I saw that Warren—the former defensive end—had tackled the Russian like he had many an opposing quarterback.

The two big men tumbled, struggling, and then Warren jumped to his feet, assuming what I thought must be a jujitsu position. I tried to stand again, and just managed it by leaning against the wall. I wanted to help. I *had* to help. As big and athletic as Warren was, he was no match for a man like Dyavol. They were about the same height, but the Russian carried another twenty pounds of muscle.

"Is this the guy that killed Monalisa?" Warren hissed with a rage I'd never heard.

"That's him," I answered weakly. I felt my head pounding and dropped to my knees. I was sure I had a concussion, and I was dizzy. Through the haze, I could see the fury in Warren's eyes. Monalisa had been his best friend, and I knew he felt protective of her. But no one could expect him to win a fight against Viktor Dyavol.

Warren glared at the giant Russian. His eyes teared up with anger and he pursed his lips. "You're an... ASSHOLE!" he yelled. It came out like a young boy using the one word he's not supposed to say.

This did not have the intended effect. Whatever respect Warren had gained by tackling Dyavol evaporated, and the Russian's face eased into a contemptuous grin. Confidently and smoothly, he stepped forward and unleashed a roundhouse right, big enough to separate Warren's head from his body. Surprising me and astonishing Dyavol, Warren effortlessly dodged it and delivered a lightning jab that caught the assassin right in the center of his arrogant face. His nose broke loudly, and blood sprayed from it, covering his face and shirt.

It was the kind of punch that would have floored most men. Dyavol's head, supported by his thick neck, barely flicked back. But the look on his face was one of pure shock. He wiped his sleeve across his bloody nose and stepped back to reassess.

"Stay out of his reach, Warren!" I yelled, trying to stand up. The Russian advanced again, more cautiously this time. Warren threw another punch, and Dyavol snapped his head back in time to avoid it. Warren's fist blurred through empty air, and he was almost thrown off balance but managed to pull back before Dyavol could grab his arm.

Dyavol threw a short jab, and Warren tilted his head out of the way. As the Russian dodged back, Warren used an undercut to catch him with a wicked punch in the gut. Dyavol grunted a little. Warren pulled his fist back and muttered under his breath. "Dang," he complained, massaging his hand. He called over to me, as though keeping me updated on the fight, even though I was watching it in real time. "This guy's hard as a rock, Rich!"

I wasn't sure who had gotten the worst of it—the Russian, who'd received the blow in his solar plexus, or Warren, who acted like he'd almost broken his hand. But he quickly lashed out again with a right jab that caught Dyavol on the side of his face; the assassin responded with another roundhouse punch that would have been devastating if it had connected, but Warren dodged back, and it missed him by a foot.

The two fighters squared up. Dyavol reminded me of the Terminator. Huge, emotionless, machine-like—although, to be fair, his blood-spattered face and crooked nose took the edge off the effect. They circled, and I pulled myself up, still holding onto the wall. I wanted to vomit, and my head was spinning, but I tried to think of how I could help. Warren was muscular, game, and using all his training, but now that Dyavol had taken his measure, I was certain the Russian would quickly overwhelm my defender.

But someone forgot to tell Warren that he couldn't win. He wasn't intimidated at all. I knew he was a good man, but I guess I'd never really understood that part of his virtue was that he would do anything necessary to protect a friend or avenge one.

As I watched through a cloudy veil, I saw Dyavol leap forward, trying to wrap up the younger man. Warren spun around, elbowed the Russian in the gut, and wiggled out of his grasp. I had to admire what a great athlete Warren was; he must have devoted the same discipline to jujitsu that he had to football. He had a lot of practice grappling with huge, tough men.

Dyavol pulled his right fist back but then tried to surprise Warren with a ferocious, left jab. Warren saw it coming, nodded his head out of the way, and delivered a right hook into the side of Dyavol's head, followed by left jab right into his broken nose. Dyavol grunted in pain, and Warren leaped up and launched a wicked kick into the middle of the Russian's chest. The blow was so powerful that Dyavol flew backward, crashing through the wall of the cube behind him. He scrambled back to his feet, but he was obviously hurting.

I was dazed and my vision was blurry, but it occurred to me, almost as an abstract thought, that the Russian—a highly trained, professional, state-sponsored, assassin—was getting his ass kicked by our Eagle Scout.

Dyavol was wary now. I doubt he'd ever faced anyone who could beat him in hand-to-hand combat, and Warren's goodness and apparent innocence had confused him. How could this man, with all the characteristics of a nice guy, be so damn tough? The Russian moved to his right, and Warren turned to face him. Dyavol whipped a vicious right fist through the air. Warren stopped it with a stiff, open left hand and launched a monstrous upper cut that caught the Russian under the jaw, spinning him around, and dropping him to the floor.

Dyavol lay still for a moment, and for a fleeting second, I thought the fight was over. Warren dropped his fists and watched as the Russian got on his hands and knees. Suddenly, the assassin darted forward, stretched out, and grabbed something.

I tried to yell a warning, but all I choked out was, "*Warren!*" He looked over at me, and I pointed at Dyavol, but I'd made a terrible mistake by distracting him. By the time Warren's eyes followed mine, the assassin was already throwing the knife he'd dropped earlier. Warren brought his hands up to protect himself, but the knife flew between them, burying itself to the hilt just below his ribcage.

"No!" I yelled and stumbled forward as Warren screamed in pain. The perennial excitement and enthusiasm that shone in his eyes switched off. He stared as though focusing on something far away and wrapped his hands around the hilt of the knife, trying to remove it. He fell to his knees, and Dyavol walked over, ignoring me, and jerked the knife from Warren's body. He stood over the younger man like a winning prize fighter relishing his victory.

Desperate fury washed over me. I didn't care about my life or the danger or anything but keeping the knife away from Warren. I lunged forward and wrapped my body around the killer's arm before he could bring the blade to Warren's throat. I pulled it down, away from my friend, whose eyes followed our movements, even though he was in bad shape and helpless. He fell backwards and landed awkwardly, his knees bent beneath him.

Dyavol was so strong, he lifted my whole body off the ground, trying to push me off his arm. I felt his left fist beating the back of my head and knew I was about to lose consciousness. My vision dimmed, my body went limp, and I let go, sliding to the floor, only just managing to catch myself before I fell. I stumbled over to the low wall of a cubicle and spun around to face my demise. The assassin moved towards me. I tried to get away, but I had no strength. His eyes blazed with triumph, and I felt sad that I would die—but worse that he would kill Warren when he was done with me, assuming my friend was still alive.

Something caught Dyavol's eyes, and he looked past me to his right, down the hallway. Then he yanked me to my feet by my neck, spun me around, pulled my body to him, and placed the edge of the knife against my throat. Standing in front of us was Rosalie. She was a good forty feet away, pointing a gun right at us. My guess was that she had tried to sneak up on us but had to reveal herself too soon when she saw him about to finish me off.

"Don't come closer," Dyavol warned. "Or I will kill him."

"If you do, I'll kill *you*," she answered calmly.

Forty feet is a long shot with a handgun, and Dyavol was holding me in a position that made him a small target, especially in the dim light. Even in the moment, I wondered what the hell Rosalie was doing there. How did she know about Dyavol? Why was she holding a gun like it was second nature?

"Shoot him!" I yelled. "Warren needs help right now or he'll die!"

Dyavol tightened his forearm around my neck to silence me. I could hardly breathe and began to feel lightheaded.

"How about this, Viktor Dyavol," Rosalie said, her voice calm and steady. She took slow steps towards us, closing the distance as much as she dared. "Why don't you drop your knife, and I'll put down my gun, and we'll settle this one-on-one?"

I shook my head, pushing hard where his forearm crossed my neck. I was desperate for air. Using all my strength, I managed to loosen his grip just slightly so I could breathe again. "No!" I rasped. "He'll kill you!"

"Shut up, asshole," the Russian growled, tightening his grip around my neck again. "And don't you come any closer," he warned Rosalie.

Rosalie didn't take her eyes off him, but she stopped advancing about twenty feet from us. "He's right, Rich," she said. "Shut up. I've got this."

I could sense what the Russian was thinking. This woman was no match for him. He was more than twice her size.

"You're the one with the gun," he told her. "You go first."

To my shock, Rosalie slung a bag off her shoulder, released the hammer of the gun, and pushed it deep inside. I felt Dyavol's chest growling with satisfaction. She held the bag at arm's length and then lowered it, holding it by the strap. "Now let him go. And put your knife on the ground. Unless you're afraid of a girl," she taunted.

Dyavol tossed me aside, and I tumbled against another low cubicle wall. I was getting tired of being thrown around by this man, but all I could think about was Warren and Rosalie.

"Check on Warren!" Rosalie ordered without taking her eyes off Dyavol. "Plug the wound and stay out of the way."

I wanted to attack Dyavol, but I was still gasping for air. He and Rosalie seemed to be at a standoff, at least for the moment. I glanced over at Warren and could see a lot of blood around his body. He wasn't moving at all. Then I caught just a slight motion in his chest, and knew he was breathing. Still, he wasn't going to live long without proper medical care—not that any of us were likely to live long. I scrambled over to him, bunched up his shirt, and pressed it against the wound. He moaned a little, and his chest heaved with irregular, tortured breaths.

"R....R...Rich," he choked out the words. "Help her...kill him." Tears formed in his eyes. "He k-killed Monalisa...he...*killed* her."

"Stay with him!" Rosalie called. "I've got this under control."

Dyavol smiled. He wasn't just confident, his words dripped with hubris. "I'll put the knife down when you let go of that bag."

Rosalie complied, and the Russian dropped the knife. It clattered on the floor next to him. Rage welled up inside me again. This man had killed Monalisa, probably Warren, and now he was going to kill Rosalie and me, too. I couldn't do anything else for Warren, so I struggled back to my feet, powered by nothing more than hatred.

Suddenly, catching both me and Dyavol by surprise, Rosalie sprang forward with unbelievable quickness, covering the space between them in what seemed like a fraction of a second. The assassin gauged her speed and let loose an enormous right cross, timed to deliver a crushing blow to her rib cage when she reached him.

But he was too slow, and Rosalie anticipated his move. She

feinted to her left as she closed the distance, forcing him to change the trajectory of his fist as he tried to follow her movement. When she reached him, she slid under his fist and wrapped both hands around his left arm at the elbow. I thought she was trying to pull him off balance, but her hands merely slid down along the length of his forearm. It looked like she had lost her grip on him, but Dyavol let out a terrible scream and blood spurted from his arm. Then I understood—Rosalie held a blade inside her hand. When she grabbed his arm, she'd plunged it deep into his skin and pulled it all the way down to his wrist. She must have palmed the blade when she returned her gun to her bag. The movement was so quick and subtle, I knew she must have practiced it many times.

Who is this woman?

Rosalie used her momentum and the assassin's now lifeless left arm to pull herself up behind him, spinning him 180 degrees so he was facing her as she let go. Then she pivoted back around. She must have sliced through connecting tissue because his left arm dangled uselessly. I couldn't believe how much blood poured from it. However, Rosalie had lost her grip on the blade when it slid into his wrist—I could see it embedded just above his hand.

Rosalie was entirely untouched. Dyavol was shaky, backing up several steps as he regained control of himself. He rocked back and forth, obviously in agony, his gaze piercing her with hatred, then moving back and forth between two of us. When I started to move toward him, he reached down with his right hand, yanked the blade from his wrist, and held it up in a warning. Rosalie's purse lay just behind Dyavol, and I lunged for it. He gave it a massive kick, and it sailed into a maze of cubes. Then he turned to kick me, and I just managed to scramble out of the way.

"You're bleeding out, Dyavol," Rosalie warned. "Give up or you'll bleed to death. Or I'll kill you."

Without taking his eyes off her, the Russian put the blade between his teeth and then reached down with his right arm, unbuckled his belt, whipped it from around his waist, and wrapped it around his left arm at the elbow, using it like a tourniquet. Then he grabbed the blade and began advancing towards Rosalie, occasionally waving it at me to keep me at bay as well.

I moved in closer. He was still dangerous, but he'd lost a lot of blood and was weakening quickly.

Dyavol tried to get a hand on Rosalie, but she was faster than he was, and time was on her side, at least when it came to the fight between them. We were going to lose Warren if this didn't end soon.

Rosalie flicked her eyes at me and then back at the assassin. She had circled in such a way that Dyavol's back faced me. Mustering all my strength, I launched forward, fell to my hands and knees behind him, and rolled under his legs.

The Russian cried out in fury as he fell awkwardly onto his back, and Rosalie's blade went flying off towards the elevator. He was big; even the weight of his hips and legs smashed me to the floor.

Rosalie leapt over both of us and crisscrossed her knees around the assassin's massive neck. He reached up with his working arm and tried to pry her loose.

"Grab his arm!" she ordered. I struggled out from under him and, for the second time in the fight, wrapped myself around the Russian's right arm and held on, using the weight of my body to pin it to the floor.

"You can't break his neck. He's too strong!" I called out.

"His windpipe isn't," she countered, calmly.

The giant struggled, with me holding down his arm and Rosalie pinning his neck to the floor. He used his massive legs to lift his torso up again and again. I heard him gasping for air, but Rosalie had his throat clenched tightly between her knees and he was bleeding profusely.

He writhed on the floor, trying to get back the use of his arm, but by applying all my remaining strength, I was able to keep it under control. After a minute that seemed like hours, I felt his body twitch a few final times and then go still as he died on the floor of the *RECON* offices.

I let go of his arm and rolled away, exhausted. Rosalie jumped up and ran over to where Dyavol had put down his knife earlier. She raced back, slid to her knees next to the body, and jammed the blade through his chest into his heart. His body didn't react at all, and only a small amount of blood emerged from the new wound.

"You should always double check," she said matter-of-factly, like she was reminding me to make sure my garage door was closed. Then she rushed over to Warren, snapping up her bag along the way. She sliced off some of his shirt, made a crude compress, and held it there with one hand as she fished out her cell phone and dialed a number with the other. She yelled instructions into the phone, then stretched Warren into a more comfortable position, pulling his knees out from under him and laying him flat on the floor.

"Stop the bleeding as much as possible and keep him awake if you can," she ordered before disappearing towards the elevator while I sat with Warren. His eyes were barely open, and his breathing was ragged and tortured.

"It's okay, buddy," I reassured him. "Help is on the way. You're going to make it." There was no sign that he heard me, and I had no idea if what I was saying was true. He was in bad shape, and I was sure that only his fitness and youth were keeping him alive.

A few minutes later, as it seemed Warren would stop breathing any second, I heard the elevator bell and Rosalie came running over. An older man in a suit held the doors open for paramedics pushing a gurney. They rushed to Warren's side, gently slid him onto the gurney, and rolled him to the elevator as they hooked him up to saline.

The older man walked over and looked at Rosalie and the lifeless body of Viktor Stolypin Dyavol before his eyes settled on me.

"You okay?" he asked.

"Yes. Thanks to him," I nodded towards the elevator. "And

Rosalie. That reminds me," I turned to her. "Who the hell are you?" Then I scrutinized the man in a suit. "And who the hell are you, too, for that matter?"

Neither of them answered. I pointed at the huge body of the dead man; his blood pooled on the floor around him. "I know that's Viktor Dyavol. He's the one who killed Monalisa."

Rosalie walked over to the Russian's body, pushed his massive right shoulder up from the carpet, and tore his shirt open to expose his back. We could see the recent scars where someone had dug multiple sharp objects—like fingernails—deep into his back.

"Good riddance," I said. "But you still haven't told me who you are."

Her eyes went to the man in a suit, like she wanted his advice. He just shrugged. I sensed they were colleagues, but he obviously wasn't her boss.

"I'm Rosalie Carter," she answered, finally. "CIA SAC, on temporary assignment to the FBI right now."

I'd worked around intelligence agencies long enough to know what this meant. The Special Activities Center is considered the special forces division of the CIA. The elite agents who work in this unit are specially trained for a variety of assignments, including undercover and lethal tactics.

"That explains why our background check came back the way it did," I surmised.

She cracked a wry smile. "Did you really believe I used to be a schoolteacher?"

"The kids would behave," I noted as exhaustion swept over me. I sat down on the floor as more people in suits streamed in. FBI and CIA, I assumed, but at the moment, I didn't care. All I could think about was Warren. He'd saved my life tonight as much as Rosalie had, and now he was on the verge of death.

I knew there was more to the story than what Rosalie was telling me, but my mind was shutting down as the adrenaline worked its way out of my bloodstream.

Rosalie walked over and knelt by me, putting an arm on my shoulder. "It's okay, Rich. Everything else can wait. Let's get you to a hospital."

"Okay," I mumbled weakly. "Take me to the hospital where they took Warren."

Rosalie helped me up and then held me up as we walked to the elevator.

20

LIFE, JOY, AND AN ONGOING THREAT

June 9th: 128 Days Before Arrival

Warren was alive! He'd been through four hours of surgery to repair a punctured lung, tissue damage to his diaphragm, and a gash in the right atrium of his heart. His wounds were serious but not permanent. However, if the knife had penetrated his heart just a little deeper, he would have been Viktor Stolypin Dyavol's second *RECON* victim.

I'd awakened in a hospital bed. As soon as I arrived, a doctor admitted me to the ER for concussion protocol. Overnight, I'd suffered from dizziness, vomiting, ringing in my ears, and a wicked headache. They didn't want to let me out of bed to visit Warren in the ICU, but I told the nurse I was going anyway. After a brief argument, she reluctantly fetched a wheelchair and rolled me to his room.

Warren was unconscious, with tubes and wires hooked up to him everywhere, but he was breathing regularly and had much of his color back. A doctor came in a few minutes later and was about to order me back to my room when he recognized me—occasionally my celebrity comes in handy—and let me stay. I explained that Warren and I were friends and had been involved in the same incident.

"Must have been some fight," he announced, looking from Warren to me. "You look terrible, and we had a very close call with this one. Somebody really did a number on you two."

"Yeah, well, you should see the other guy."

As a precaution, they kept me in the hospital for one more day. I was sore and dizzy, but I insisted on staying with Warren, understandably annoying the healthcare professionals. Eliza joined me, and we whispered back and forth as I answered all her questions about the incident, including Rosalie's true identity. At one point, she stood up, walked over to Warren, who was still unconscious, and kissed him on the cheek. Then she took his face gently in her hands. "Thank you for saving Rich's life."

The next day, I was released and went to the office. Out of curiosity, I watched the file that had kept changing the night Dyavol showed up. It was a clear and full video of our fight, a chilling and vivid reminder that the only reason I was alive was because Warren and Rosalie had showed up when they did.

As I watched, I thought about something Eliza had explained to me. Physicists and philosophers debate whether we really have free will. Many physicists believe we don't. They think all moments in time, from the beginning to the end of the universe, already exist, and we are simply moving through the *frames of reference* that make up our lives. Some claim that's what Albert Einstein meant when he said, "For those of us who believe in physics, the distinction between past, present, and future is only a stubbornly persistent illusion."

But I believe in free will. I know the future is malleable, because I'd seen different versions of it the night of the fight. That gave me hope that Chicago wasn't really doomed. The videos we'd seen of *Perun's Hammer* destroying Chicago were like the ones I'd watched of Viktor Dyavol killing me. They were *a* future, not necessarily *the* future. Perhaps this was the lesson from the Intelligence—this was *ultima veritas*: Our fate is in our hands.

I looked up when Rosalie came in my office and closed the door. "We have to talk," she announced.

"Yes, we do," I replied. "I know this will make you uncomfortable, but I want to say thank you for saving my life. If it weren't for you and Warren, I'd be dead now. There's no doubt in my mind. I've seen the movies." I realized she didn't know about the videos of my murder, so I played the file and described the earlier versions.

After she got over her amazement, she frowned. "Actually, that means the Intelligence saved your life by sending you those videos. And Warren, of course. I was just there at the end to—"

"Now, stop that," I interjected. "The Intelligence warned me Viktor was coming and bought me a few seconds to step out of my office. You and Warren both get the credit for stopping him. So please, let me say thanks, because I will be forever grateful." It was almost comical how uncomfortable she looked.

Finally, she gave me a tiny nod. It was apparent she wanted to move on as quickly as possible because she changed the subject. "Why do you think the Intelligence could warn you that Dyavol was about to assassinate you but didn't show you that Warren and I were on our way to help?"

"The Intelligence did show that – both of you are in this version of the video. Remember that the future was changing quickly at that point—Warren had just seen the video about Dyavol arriving, and you were on your way here. The Intelligence updated the video as the future changed but when I heard the elevator bell, I walked out of my office without having a chance to watch the latest version."

"That makes sense," Rosalie nodded. "And that was the right choice, because if you'd been sitting in your office when he reached you, he might have killed you before Warren could arrive on the scene."

"I've been thinking about how you arrived just in time that night," I continued, "and God knows I'm grateful, but given your timing, I assume you've tapped my phone?"

She sat down in one of my conference table chairs and held my gaze. "Not your conversations. Just your emails and text messages. I felt I had to, in order to protect you."

I nodded. "I'm glad you did, or I'd be dead. Now that Viktor's gone, can you stop? It's a little uncomfortable to have a federal agent —even you—monitoring my communications."

She shook her head. "Not yet. The Russians don't want *RECON* warning people of the threat posed by *Perun's Hammer*. And they definitely don't want you to be successful in deflecting it, if you can, or evacuating Chicago, if you can't. They're still furious over the assistance we provided Ukraine during the war, so seeing Chicago destroyed would be extremely satisfying to them. The Kremlin views this, literally, as a once in a millennium opportunity."

"How could they stop us now? Too many people know. They'd have to murder the entire *RECON* team."

Rosalie smiled sadly. "They want to see millions of American killed by this object. Do you really think they'd hesitate to assassinate you and everyone on your team?"

I pondered that horror for a moment. "No. I guess not. Does that mean you're going to arrange for protection for all of us?"

"It's already in place. You've got me, and I've had agents assigned to protect Beth, Carl and other key *RECON* personnel. They operate nearby, but mostly in the background. We're adding new security protocols to *RECON*'s offices, and twenty-four-hour protection around the building. You and your team need to stop taking public transportation for now. Hired security professionals or agents will drive you to and from work. You're as secure as we can make you, but I need to keep tabs on you until this over. Now, I have to know everyone who has the information about what happened that night."

I told Rosalie that Eliza knew, and that I would fill in any gaps for Warren when he regained consciousness.

She nodded. "Eliza won't talk, and we'll have to bring Warren into the loop. He's figured out I'm not just your assistant anyway. But everyone else thinks that someone intending to assassinate you broke into the *RECON* offices two nights ago, and Warren killed him in a fight that nearly cost him his life. We need to leave me out of it and make sure Warren does, too."

"I can't let that stand," I protested. "People should know what you did to save my life, not to mention kill the man who murdered Monalisa."

"No!" Rosalie insisted. "I have more work to do here. You have to produce and air one of the most important stories in history, or people are going to die. Everyone here needs to believe I'm just your assistant."

I took in what she said. "That reminds me. I assume you were sent in undercover here because of the videos. But how did you know we'd need your help? And since you're still here, does that mean the CIA disagrees with the military and intelligence community about the videos? Does the agency think they came from Russia?"

She hesitated. "I was sent here to make sure you *didn't* broadcast anything about *Perun's Hammer*. We thought the Russians were behind all of this and identified *RECON* as the most likely non-government organization that might start receiving the videos. The CIA went through the network's CEO to 'retire' your previous assistant and have me replace her."

I was stunned. "Our CEO did that?"

"He's a patriot who did the right thing. Or, at least what we thought was the right thing at the time. But what I witnessed here changed my mind, and I've shared that information up the chain of command. I told them about Angela and her visions. I told them about the hologram we watched in your office. No one has the technology to do that, not even the best Russian hackers."

I was surprised. "And they believed you and changed their minds just like that?"

Rosalie shook her head. "Not everyone. But enough to make sure I stay here to support you while you produce and broadcast the segment. And Howard Roosevelt's defending you, too. He prevented you from being arrested and charged with espionage."

"That was an empty threat. I came by those videos honestly, and they're in the public interest."

"Doesn't matter. There's been a war going on between branches of the government. It came to a head a couple of weeks ago, when the FBI persuaded a federal judge to issue an arrest warrant for you."

"Holy shit. What happened?"

"Senator Roosevelt found out and threatened to go to the President. Thanks to his pressure, the FBI asked the judge to have the warrant recalled. Roosevelt decided you might be right after all."

Well, how about that? A politician who has my back. And then a question popped into my head. "What changed his mind?"

Rosalie flashed a sly smile. "I may have gone a little outside the lines of authority in providing him information. Roosevelt said he won't compromise me, but the Bureau is suspicious. I'll have to watch my step for a while."

I realized then that Rosalie hadn't just saved my life, she'd stopped me from going to jail, which might end up saving the city of Chicago. I wondered if anyone would ever understand her incredible contributions. Certainly, she was never going to tell anyone.

"You're a hero, Rosalie. Maybe for millions of people, and no one will ever know."

For the only time in my entire relationship with Rosalie, she blushed and, unsurprisingly, changed the subject. "I can only push back on the Pentagon, and much of the intelligence community, for so long, even with Roosevelt's help. It would really boost the credibility of the videos if we could see the object with earth- and space-based telescopes. You and Eliza need to push to make that happen as soon as possible. And you need to broadcast the story soon, to get public opinion behind you."

"I agree. But I want to ask you about something else. What do you know about the disappearance of Carl's neighbor, Bob Johanssen?"

She hesitated for a moment. "I'm pretty sure Dyavol killed Johanssen. He knew a lot about what was happening at *RECON*. However, I know he didn't bug our offices because I've had them swept weekly for months now."

The thought of FBI security people coming in at night to sweep our offices bothered me, but I let it go as Rosalie continued.

"That means they were getting their information from some-where else, and the most likely source would be someone on your team. I don't believe any of them would turn on you, and we've been watching them for a while now."

"Damn it," I blurted out. "I trust these people implicitly. You didn't need to surveil—"

"I don't trust *anyone*," she interrupted. "Goes with the job. Anyway, they're all clean, but I think Dyavol bugged the home of one of them. Beth's got Hubert, and he's diligent about security at both of their homes. Same with Warren. It wasn't you. You live in a secure building with lots of surveillance cameras, plus I'm looking after you, so Carl's the most accessible, and Johanssen was his neighbor. Also, the Swintons hardly ever turn on their security system."

"Why am I not surprised you know that?"

She ignored my question. "I want to send an FBI team to search his house. We need to find out if it's bugged."

"That's up to him," I shrugged. "But since you're trying to remain undercover, how are you going to ask him? Wait, you *are* going to ask him first, right?"

"Yes," she answered. "Well, yes and no. Someone's going to ask him first. It won't be me. Remember; I'm just your assistant."

She got up to go, but I had one more question. "Rosalie, are you the one who gave Monalisa access to Clearview?" That was the facial recognition program Monalisa had used to identify individuals in the Little Bighorn video.

She held my gaze. "I told her my brother was in the FBI and had access. I wanted her to have all the information. We could tell it wasn't normal CGI. I thought maybe she could figure out how it was made, and the Clearview analysis might help." I could see pain in her eyes. "I'll always wonder if that contributed to her decision to meet with Dyavol. And her death."

I shook my head. "No, it didn't. Monalisa was going to meet with Dyavol with or without the Clearview analysis. You're not responsible for her death. Viktor Dyavol was, and you killed him. You did right by Monalisa."

She nodded, almost imperceptibly. "Keep me involved in everything, please. And remember, for now, I'm just your assistant. I had nothing to do with killing Dyavol. I was never here that night."

I hated it, but I knew it was necessary, and I agreed.

Warren was sitting up in his hospital bed while a nurse checked his vital signs when I walked in. "Am I interrupting?"

"Hi, Rich!" Warren waved excitedly, even though he had an IV attached to the back of his hand. "Come on in!"

I embraced him as well as I could and then sat and waited until the nurse finished and left the room. Warren appeared weak but healthy, all things considered.

He looked me up and down. "I'm really glad you're still alive."

"You too. But I'm only alive thanks to you."

He blushed. "I was happy to help. But man, he was a really tough dude, wasn't he?"

I laughed. "Yes, but you were kicking his ass until he found that knife."

Warren shook his head. "I don't know. I was afraid he'd get those big mitts on me, and I wouldn't be able to get away." Then he got serious. "The last thing I remember was Rosalie walking in with a gun. Did she kill him?"

"Yes."

"What happened?"

I told him everything and asked him not to share it for now. "But don't worry, everyone knows you're a hero!"

He shook his head. "Nah. Rosalie's the hero. She's the one who killed him."

"Warren, if you hadn't shown up when you did, I would have been dead long before Rosalie got there. You saved my life as much as she did."

We chatted for a bit. Everything seemed a little brighter now. Viktor Dyavol was dead, Warren was on the road to recovery, I was confident I could expedite the broadcast, and I was hopeful that telescopes could see the object in time to mount a deflection mission.

But when I walked into the condo that evening, Eliza met me at the door, her face covered with concern.

"What's the matter?" I asked, alarmed.

"I just heard from the ORCCA Lab."

"Bad news?"

"Very. Based on the data in the video we received, *Perun's Hammer* will hit Chicago on October 15th. That's just over four months from now."

"Damn it! Is there even time to launch a deflection mission?"

Eliza sighed. "I don't know. There are a lot of variables. How long will it take to assemble the launch vehicle? What's the mass of the object? How far out do we need to hit it to deflect it by enough to miss Earth? But I know one thing for sure. If we don't get the mission approved soon, there'll be no chance at all. When we're in Tucson, you and I might have to persuade David Clancy—NASA's planetary defense officer—to launch the mission before NASA ever detects *Perun's Hammer*."

Rich's team threw themselves into producing the feature on *Perun's Hammer*. Once they finished the outline of the story, Beth and Carl went into overdrive planning the broadcast. They identified the expert they planned to use for the *Cap Arcona* incident. Dr. Stefan Foreman had written an historical account of the disaster called *Hitler's Ship of Terror*. Rich spent an hour on the phone with Foreman and sent the video for his analysis before the professor would agree to participate.

They also decided on a title for the feature, *Perun's Hammer: An Existential Threat to Chicago*. Everything was on track for the show to air the last Sunday in August. As the team raced through the last weeks of production, nervousness was replaced by excitement. Finally, they could tell the most amazing story they'd ever produced, and maybe—just maybe—change the future.

21

THE TUCSON REVEAL

On the day we were scheduled to fly to Tucson, an FBI agent dropped Eliza and me off at the General Aviation terminal at O'Hare, where the network's aircraft were kept. We were on time but wound up waiting in the lobby for more than half an hour before the Chief Pilot walked in from the hanger. He looked deeply concerned. "Mr. Penton," he nodded.

I introduced Eliza but could tell the pilot was preoccupied with something. "What's wrong?" I asked him.

"Would you mind coming into the hangar to look at something?" We followed him into the cavernous building and up to the Gulfstream G280 we were to fly to Tucson. Mechanics were working on the aircraft as the pilot led us to a utility cart near the root of the right wing.

"See that?" He pointed to a black bag on the cart. It had a rough texture and bulged with about a quart of some liquid. A thin cord about a foot long was attached to the end of the bag and terminated in a small, black, metal hook.

"What's this?" I asked him.

"I found this bag in the fuel filler neck when I did my walka-round this morning. I almost missed it. You could barely see the end of the hook hanging on the edge of the fueling port. The bag itself was stuffed inside where you couldn't see it at all." He picked up a wrench and smacked the bag, which split open. It was much more fragile than it appeared. A thick, black liquid oozed out.

"What the hell is that?" I asked.

The pilot shook his head. "I'm not sure, but I bet when it's mixed with avgas, it burns or explodes."

"Sabotage," Eliza said, softly. "That bag wouldn't last the trip, but it would last long enough to get us off the ground." She touched my arm. "Someone's trying to kill you, Rich."

"That's what I decided," the pilot agreed. "I talked to the facility manager, and they experienced a very unusual power outage in the hangar last night. The electricity went out, but only in this building."

"Isn't there a backup generator?" I asked.

"Yep, and guess what? That failed, too. The place was dark for forty minutes."

"Is the aircraft safe to fly?" Eliza asked.

"I'll know soon. I've got mechanics checking out every system, and sampling or replacing every fluid on the aircraft. Then we'll run it up, check the gauges, and I'll do another walkaround." His eyes met mine. "Mr. Penton, I can make sure this aircraft is safe to fly. But Ms. Sage is right. Someone's trying to kill you. Are you sure you want to make this trip without taking some security along?"

I could see the concern in Eliza's eyes, but we both knew what was at stake, and she shook her head. "We don't have a choice. This meeting is too important."

"I agree. But I have an idea that might help."

An hour later, we were in the air. Even though the Chief Pilot reassured us that everything was okay, it was hard not to react to every little bump and sound. I used the Jet ConneX phone to call Rosalie and told her what happened.

"Damn it," she exclaimed, "I thought the trip to the airport would be where you were vulnerable!"

"Didn't occur to me, either. It would be great if you could arrange for an FBI agent or local law enforcement to meet us in Tucson and take us to the conference."

"I've done that. Your limos in Arizona are armored SUVs, driven by federal agents."

I laughed. "Of course you did. Wait, did you say, 'limos,' plural? Do we need more than one?"

"You're stopping in Flagstaff on the way. Eliza will give you the details."

When the call ended, I frowned at Eliza. "Why are we stopping in Flagstaff?"

"You'll see," she answered, mysteriously. "I know how you love surprises."

When we landed in Flagstaff, a black SUV met us on the tarmac. The driver headed east on I-40 until we entered the high desert landscape of northern Arizona. Bristly junipers and sage shrubs dotted the landscape. Thirty minutes later, we took an off ramp and headed south for several miles, along a narrow, two-lane road with no shoulders. A sign with a graphic of a fireball flying through space pointed us to the left for *Meteor Crater*. The driver followed the sign, drove up onto a plateau, and we parked in a lot full of RVs and cars with plates from various states.

We were met by a tour guide wearing a badge identifying him as *Alan*. Alan beamed and waved as he stepped towards us, zeroing in on Eliza.

"Ms. Sage?" he asked.

"Hi, Alan. This is Rich Penton."

He shook my hand with genuine, if overwrought, zeal. "Nice to meet you, Rich! I've never watched your show, but my parents never miss it."

"Nice to meet you too, Alan," I answered dryly, as Eliza smothered a chuckle.

Alan told us that Meteor Crater was created 50,000 years ago, when an asteroid about 60 meters in diameter hit the Earth at 26,000 miles an hour. "That's fifteen times the speed of a bullet!" He pointed to the ground. "This isn't a hill we're standing on. This is the wall of ejecta the meteor displaced when it hit."

Something didn't compute in my brain. We were about one hundred and fifty feet above the desert floor around us. What kind of meteor could have ejected enough material to create a whole plateau? Alan led us into the visitors' center, up two flights of stairs, and pushed through a door to some exterior decks and a pathway. The view opened up and I stopped in my tracks. In front of us lay a canyon thirteen football fields in diameter and six in depth. Eliza and Alan let me stand there for a moment as my mind made sense of the sight.

"Please tell me whatever created this was a lot bigger than *Perun's Hammer*," I said softly to Eliza.

"Based on the last video," she whispered back, "*Perun's Hammer* is much larger. It's probably hollow, but no one knows its mass."

It's not possible to describe Meteor Crater in a way that conveys its magnificence—and terror, if you happen to be expecting a similarly devastating object to arrive soon in your neck of the woods. I turned to Alan. "How powerful was the blast when the asteroid hit?"

"About ten megatons."

"How does that compare to an atomic bomb?"

"The bomb that exploded over Hiroshima was about fifteen kilotons. That means this impact was equivalent to about six hundred and sixty Hiroshima bombs. Or five times the power of all the bombs dropped in World War II."

Eliza studied my reaction. I murmured, "If your goal was to give me an idea of what *Perun's Hammer* could do to Chicago, mission accomplished."

Alan overheard me. "What's '*Perun's Hammer?*' Did an asteroid hit the Chicago area, too? I never heard that before."

I shook my head. "No. But it might soon." Our tour guide probably thought I'd lost my mind, but I was worried about losing my city.

Two hours later, we landed in Tucson. The University of Arizona has been a leading institution for astrophysics for decades, and most of the world's top theorists and practitioners in identifying, cataloguing, evaluating, and deflecting NEOs were attending the conference held at a nearby resort.

Rosalie had reserved a meeting room where we were joined by three people. Ryan Manion was a Senior Research Scientist at JPL. Shawna Adams was a Professor of Astronomy at the University of Arizona, and worked with data from *NEO Surveyor*, a space-based satellite that had some unique capabilities for detecting NEOs. The third individual was David Clancy, the Planetary Defense Officer for NASA, and the *de facto* global CEO of asteroid hunting. Clancy handled himself with the kind of calmness and competence you'd expect from a person with such incredibly important responsibilities.

As the person connecting all of us, Eliza kicked off the conversation. "What we're going to share with you today is the most startling, mysterious, and profound series of events I've ever encountered." That got the attention of the other scientists. Eliza was well-known, highly credible, and not prone to hyperbole. She gave them an overview of our experiences with the videos. They'd seen the first one thanks to the DoD, but they didn't know there were others.

While Eliza did the play-by-play, I provided the color commentary. The scientists were polite, but skeptical. Due to Eliza's standing in the physics community, and my decades-long reputation with *RECON*, they hung in there, trying to take us seriously despite their understandable doubts. *Wait until they hear the 'asteroid' is a spaceship we've named* Perun's Hammer.

"I assume you're telling us this because you want us to launch a pre-emptive strike to deflect an asteroid we haven't yet detected ourselves?" Adams asked.

"Correct."

She looked over at Clancy. "You're the one who would have to approve such a mission."

Clancy didn't react, and I couldn't read him. He simply said, "Let's watch the videos."

We started with the Battle of the Little Bighorn video, followed by the films of the other historical events, describing the many inexplicable accuracies along the way.

When we had answered their questions, Clancy asked, "Why does this 'Intelligence' care about what happens to Earth? It's hard to imagine even an advanced civilization would track every rock in the universe and warn planets with space programs every time they're about to get smacked."

"That's an extremely insightful question," Eliza responded. "And one we hadn't been able to answer until we received the last video."

"There's another one?" Clancy asked.

"Yes, but this one is very different."

"Different how?"

"You'll see."

I started playing the video that began with *Perun's Hammer* in space.

"That's a spacecraft!" Manion exclaimed in shock. The three astrophysicists watched intently as *Perun's Hammer* flew through space and then struck Chicago. We played the video twice more as they analyzed it carefully. I described our theory that the stricken craft belonged to the Intelligence, which is why they were warning us of its approach.

It was a lot to take in. As astrophysicists, they'd dedicated their lives to studying the cosmos. Seeing the first images in the history of mankind of a spacecraft from another civilization had a profound effect on them, even if they weren't sure if they believed it. We had decided in advance not to stretch their credulity any further by telling them about our experiences with Angela and the hologram.

Manion was the first to speak after a long silence. "The issue is, we have exactly one deflection asset we could launch within the next six months."

"We don't have six months," Eliza told them, somberly. "ORCCA figured out the timing based on the relative positions of celestial objects. *Perun's Hammer* hits Chicago on October 15th, four months from now."

"Well," Clancy said, "I suppose a highly expedited mission might be launched in a few months. But as Ryan pointed out, we won't have any additional deflectors for a long time." He glanced back and forth at Eliza and me. "You two are highly credible, and the story you've shared is amazing and, honestly, persuasive because of who you are—not because of the videos, which someone could have faked, given enough time and resources. You've admitted that our own intelligence agencies think it's a Russian hoax to humiliate us. But if we use our one deflector chasing this thing—*Perun's Hammer*, you called it—?"

"That's what we're calling it."

"—and you're wrong, then we'll be defenseless if there's a real threat before we can deploy new ones. That takes several years, assuming we get the funding approved. Which won't be easy if it turns out we wasted the one we had on a wild goose chase." Clancy furrowed his brow as though something had just occurred to him.

227

"Do you know about the *Kulik* and *Fedorov* satellites the Russians launched a few years ago?"

"Yes," I told him, as Eliza nodded.

He continued. "If this dead spacecraft is coming from behind the Sun or perpendicular to the planetary plane, there's a very good chance the Russians will see it before we do. In past years, I would have been certain that Roscosmos would warn us if they saw an object bound for the U.S." He shook his head. "But they're encrypting data from *Federov* and won't tell us anything about the mission. Since they invaded Ukraine, there's no telling what they'd do with that kind of information."

We hadn't yet told them about Viktor Dyavol, but it was pertinent to the discussion, so I gave them a quick summary of Russia's attempts to stop the broadcast. I could see growing acceptance in David Clancy's eyes, but he had truly awesome responsibilities. We were asking him to spend a billion dollars to launch a single-use asset to deflect *alien space debris* that no astronomer had seen—and our evidence was a wild story, supported by mysterious videos.

"I have to admit," Clancy said with a wry smile, "This is the most unusual decision I've ever had to make."

"*NEO Surveyor* would see this object before terrestrial telescopes," Adams suggested.

Manion agreed. "It can see a lot closer to the Sun than anything terrestrial."

Eliza nodded her head in approval. "*NEO Surveyor* sees in infrared."

"Yes," Adams confirmed. "Plus, it's space-based, so it can observe every hour of every day, not just at night. It's very good at spotting objects coming around the Sun—like *Perun's Hammer* does in your video—that aren't visible for days or weeks from any other telescope."

"Could *NEO Surveyor* see *Perun's Hammer* in time to justify a mission to deflect it?" Eliza asked.

"I don't know." Shawna answered. "According to your numbers, how far away will *Perun's Hammer* be from Earth when it rounds the Sun?"

"Its path is about one hundred ninety-five million kilometers," Eliza said. "It came in at a steep angle to the Sun, and it's decelerating. It's following an elongated hyperbolic arc that will push it farther from the Sun than the Earth, then bring it back towards us. The bottom line is, the ORCCA Lab estimates it will take about sixty days to reach Earth once it rounds the Sun."

Adams thought about it. "Given the color and texture of the object, it's going to be a challenge to pick it up. I think *NEO Surveyor* could do it, but that assumes the mission is approved."

All eyes turned to David Clancy. Despite the weight of the decision and the extremely unusual circumstances, he didn't exhibit any anxiety. I guess when you're the CEO of Planetary Defense, you know how to make tough decisions. "Shawna," he asked, "Do you think you can have *NEO Surveyor* pointed in that direction about a week before ORCCA thinks this thing will come around the Sun? Say, early August?"

"If you make the request, David, I doubt anyone's going to push back."

"Good," Clancy replied. "Consider the request made. Rich, Eliza, we have some work to do. *NEO Surveyor* has to spot this object to ensure it's real before we launch a deflection mission. I hope you can understand that."

"I do, David," I replied, "but you never answered the question about the timing. With sixty days' notice, could you launch a mission and hit this object far enough out to stop it?"

Clancy shook his head, slowly. "Not even close. Even if we started prepping the mission right now, hitting the object that close to Earth might not deflect it enough to miss the planet."

"Then it's hopeless?" I blurted out, confused.

Clancy shook his head, and I could see that something had just occurred to Eliza.

"It's not an asteroid," she said slowly. "It's a spacecraft. So that means you think you can *destroy* it, not *deflect* it."

David Clancy grinned. "Well, I wouldn't say I'm confident, but this isn't a giant rock. If we hit it hard enough, it should shatter into pieces. At least if they build theirs like we build ours."

"Then this isn't a deflection mission," Adams concluded. "It's a destruction mission."

Clancy laughed. "How about we call it a 'search and destroy mission?'"

"That takes weeks off the timeline," Eliza exclaimed. "How far out will you want to hit it?"

Clancy pondered for a moment. "I don't know for sure, but as far as possible. Maybe ten million kilometers or so, which would take about nineteen days, if ORCCA's estimates are correct. But let me be clear: We face two decisions. Decision A is the preparation phase. We have to make that one within the next week or so, because it will take about three months to put the hardware together and plan the mission—and that's an absolute minimum amount of time. Decision B is the launch phase. We can't just leave the rocket sitting on the launch pad for weeks, so Decision B includes moving it in place, fueling it, and doing final checks. You can add that week to the nineteen days."

Eliza nodded. "So, Decision B has to happen by September 19th."

"Yes," Clancy concurred. "But here's the difference: Decision A is a two-way door. It's expensive to assemble the deflector spacecraft and put the rocket on the pad, but if we don't launch it, we can use it in the future. Decision B is a one-way door. If we launch the asset, we can't get it back. That means Decision B is orders of magnitude more serious, because it's much costlier and, if you're wrong, Earth will waste the only planetary defense weapon we have and will be unprotected for years."

He waited for that to sink in. "I will let you know about Decision A within a week. But I will not approve Decision B unless *NEO Surveyor* confirms this object—*Perun's Hammer*—really exists."

I didn't like it, but I understood. Decision B hinged on *NEO Surveyor*.

Clancy pointed at Eliza and me. "Honestly, I'm worried you two have been taken in by some sophisticated prank."

Eliza held Clancy's gaze. "I used to worry about that, too, David, but no more. I'm convinced this is real."

He smiled and I could tell he trusted her, which was helpful, but still had his own reservations, which I understood.

After another twenty minutes of conversation, we wrapped up. Eliza and I left encouraged that they'd taken us seriously, meaning there was a decent chance David Clancy would make Decision A in our favor. Then it was up to *NEO Surveyor* to spot *Perun's Hammer* in time.

A little while after our flight took off from Tucson, I saw Meteor Crater clearly visible in the desert below. Eliza placed her hand on my arm. "David will approve the pre-launch work. We just need for *NEO Surveyor* to see *Perun's Hammer* with enough time to justify the launch. I don't know if ground telescopes could do it, but I think *NEO Surveyor* can."

It didn't occur to us that the Russians had figured this out, too.

22

TELL THE STORY

Rich, Eliza, and the *RECON* team felt the clock running down as they waited to hear back from NASA. There was precious little time to assemble the components of the mission in order to make the launch date. After numerous Zoom calls, frantic emails, and text message exchanges, David Clancy called Rich and, in his calm way, confirmed that he'd signed off on Decision A. In six weeks, *NEO Surveyor* would begin the work necessary for him to approve Decision B.

NEO Surveyor was the successor to *NEOWISE*, the first satellite in history dedicated to searching for near-Earth objects. But while *NEOWISE* was repurposed for the task, *NEO Surveyor* was built from the ground up for its mission. The satellite used state-of-the-art infrared detectors that gave it much greater sensitivity than its predecessor, enabling it to spot smaller objects from a greater distance. In addition, it had a much wider field of view.

However, *Perun's Hammer* had several characteristics and unknowns that could pose difficult challenges even for the advanced capabilities of *NEO Surveyor*, whose infrared detectors were designed to detect heat sources. Based on the videos from the Intelligence, the object's surface was a rough, dark texture, meaning it wouldn't reflect very much light and, thus, not much heat. Additionally, *Perun's Hammer* might be made of some kind of metallic material with low thermal conductivity, which could further reduce heat emissions. It was quite possible that any infrared signal the object did emit was very faint indeed.

There were other issues. *Perun's Hammer* was moving at a high rate of speed, meaning as *NEO Surveyor* scanned the sky, the object might move through its field of view quickly, making it hard to pick up. Plus, it was rotating, meaning any infrared signals it produced would fluctuate, making them even more difficult to detect and characterize. Still, *NEO Surveyor* was the best tool anywhere for finding hard-to-spot NEOs, and Shawna Adams' team was preparing it to hunt for *Perun's Hammer*.

The *RECON* team planned to broadcast their incredible story on July 7th, about a month before *Perun's Hammer* would round the Sun. That would leave six weeks for *NEO Surveyor* to spot it and for David Clancy to approve Decision B. At that point, *RECON* would have the support of NASA, JPL, and the entire NEO community. Even astronomers who didn't believe that *Perun's Hammer* was an alien spacecraft would support the mission, because the evidence of an approaching, devastating object would be right there in the keen eye of a highly specialized, infrared, space-based telescope.

Braswell arrived at our offices as planned, one week prior to the broadcast. He showed up first thing in the morning, but I kept working as though he wasn't there. He ignored me, too, until 3 p.m., when he showed up at my office, walked in uninvited, and sat across from me.

"You can't air the videos, Rich. I'm killing that story, and I'm not willing to discuss it."

I was enraged. "Bullshit, Braswell. You can't exercise that kind of editorial control over *RECON*!"

"It's for your own good." He shook his head, sadly. "I know you've been under a lot of stress with your wife." Then he added, "I'm sure seeing a hologram float out of your television while she narrated the scene was quite traumatic."

"How in the hell did you know about *that?*" I demanded.

He smiled, knowingly. "I have my sources, too, Rich. Even for nonsense tales like this hologram story."

I could hardly believe it. The only people who knew about our experiences with Angela and the hologram were Eliza, Rosalie, Carl, Beth, and Warren. We had all agreed not to talk about it, or even write about it. I knew none of them would backchannel information to Braswell, yet he'd found out anyway. But how?

"Angela's involvement isn't the point, Brendan," I argued. "We have excellent evidence that an object is on its way that could destroy Chicago. Millions of people could die. We can't just withhold this information from the public. We have to tell what we know, and let people decide for themselves!"

Braswell shook his head. "Not just an 'object,' Rich. An alien spacecraft, right? You're seriously proposing to broadcast a story claiming that some non-human intelligence that can see through time has chosen *you* to warn the world that their derelict spacecraft is out of control and will destroy Chicago a few months from now?" He paused to let that sink in. "I don't mean to question your sanity, but do you see how that sounds like a god complex?"

I lost my temper. "I don't care how crazy it sounds. Not only is it true, but we've got the evidence to prove it! And you can take your god complex and stick it up your ass!"

Braswell was getting angry, too. "Rich, I'm not going to let you squander *RECON*'s reputation—which is a valuable asset this network has developed over decades—on a story that is patently nonsensical!"

My arguments went nowhere. Finally, he stood up and walked towards my door before turning around to face me. "This is my decision and it's final, Penton." His voice was low and nasty. "And since I know just how much you hate being told what to do, I'll be here on Sunday to make sure you don't bring up this topic during the show. I'll be in the production booth. If I hear one word about an asteroid, *Perun's Hammer*, or any other bullshit, I'll pull the plug on you live. You need to get it through your head that you've been duped. If you're not going to protect the reputation of this show, I'll do it myself." He walked out, leaving me furious and feeling helpless.

A few minutes later, Rosalie came in, closed the door, and sat down. "I heard everything."

"What am I going to do now, Rosalie?"

She thought for a moment. "Why would it be easier to get David Clancy to believe you than Brendan Braswell?"

"Brendan and I have been rivals for years. And David Clancy is one hell of a lot smarter than that asshat."

"Well, you're going to have to do the show anyway."

"I agree, but what about the leak? Braswell already knows about the show. If we try to broadcast this episode, he's going to show up and shut us down."

"Let me take care of that," Rosalie answered.

"That sounds ominous."

She smiled. "It's not. Just trust me."

I didn't know what else to do, so I called the team together, explained what had happened with Braswell and swore them to silence again. I refused to believe that any of them were leaking information to him, and I reinforced again that they needed to handle information about *Perun's Hammer* with the greatest care.

It seemed like no matter how hard we tried, no matter how hard we worked, no matter how much energy we poured into the fight to save Chicago from *Perun's Hammer*, there was always another seemingly insurmountable obstacle in front of us. Rosalie's confidence in her ability to "take care" of Braswell helped a bit, though, and I knew the team was pouring everything they had into producing a story that would get the world's attention. And we were blessed to be able to rely on the incredible capabilities of NASA and its brand new, state-of-the-art, near-Earth object-detecting satellite.

And then, on June 28th, *NEO Surveyor* blew up.

That morning, with no warning, Russia issued a NOTAM—notice to aviators—instructing them to keep out of the airspace above Kosmodrom Plesetsk, located about five hundred miles northeast of Moscow. *NEO Surveyor* was defenseless against the Nudol anti-satellite weapon the Russians launched. The satellite instantly and silently disintegrated into thousands of small pieces in the vacuum of space.

Russia had timed the launch so the missile struck *NEO Surveyor* right as an old Russian communications satellite passed behind it. They claimed they'd been aiming at their own satellite and had hit *NEO Surveyor* by accident, but nobody believed them, and no one accepted the formal apology extended by the Russian government. The loss of capability to the community of scientists responsible for protecting the Earth from hazardous objects was enormous. The potential consequences to the city of Chicago were disastrous.

David Clancy sat in his office and put his phone back in the cradle. He'd spent the last hour talking with Rich Penton about the implications of the loss of *NEO Surveyor*. He knew Rich and Eliza were absolutely convinced of the reality of the threat posed by *Perun's Hammer*, as they called it. It hadn't yet been given an official name since its existence hadn't been confirmed. The evidence they'd shared was extremely compelling, but also very strange. *Would this hold up in a court of law?* he asked himself. He doubted it.

He had no idea what he should do. On one hand, it seemed insane to launch a deflector against an alleged abandoned alien space-craft they'd never seen. When he thought of it that way, he sank into doubt. But on the other hand, the Russians did have eyes on the skies behind the Sun, and it was incredibly suspicious that they'd taken such an enormous risk by destroying *NEO Surveyor*. They were going to face massive consequences. Several nations were already threatening sanctions.

Why would Russia take such an extreme action if Perun's Hammer *was just a hoax?* he wondered. He was lost in thought when the idea hit him like a lightning bolt. He snapped up the receiver of his desk phone and dialed quickly.

"Hello Linda, this is David Clancy." Linda Wu was the adminis-trator at NOAA, the National Oceanic and Atmospheric Administration. They didn't know each other well but shared a mutual respect. "I have a funny question for a guy who spends all his time looking into space, but where's the *Okeanos Explorer* right now?" He listened for a minute. "And in an emergency, how long would it take to get it halfway around the world for a special mission?" He took notes as Wu talked. "Well Linda, if you have some time right now, I'm going to blow your mind with a tale that seems absolutely incredible. I need the *Okeanos Explorer* to help us decide if we're going to launch a one-shot rocket that cost about a billion dollars."

They talked for more than two hours. During the conversation, Clancy sent Wu links to the files Eliza and Rich had shared. By the time he hung up, Clancy had enrolled NOAA into his plan and had been invited to oversee it.

When I heard that *NEO Surveyor* had been destroyed, I was distraught and furious. We'd worked so hard to research the videos, decipher the meaning, and put together a plan to save Chicago. And paid a hell of a price—in blood. We'd put our hearts and souls into producing what we believed would be a compelling *RECON* segment and managed to convince David Clancy and others that they should at least investigate the threat. Of course, they had their own problems. Losing *NEO Surveyor* was a huge setback for dedicated scientists around the world.

When Eliza and I went to dinner at North Pond that night, she persuaded me that things might not be as bad as they seemed. "David's brilliant. You should have more confidence in him. He's not the world's only Planetary Defense Officer for nothing."

July 7: 100 Days Before Arrival
The Day of the RECON Broadcast about Perun's Hammer

Brendan Braswell made good on his threat and flew in to monitor the broadcast. He worked in his office most of the day and was preparing to head to the set when he heard someone open his door. He looked up and was surprised to see Rosalie walk in. She closed the door behind her and walked towards his desk.

"What do you want?" he demanded, coldly. Very aware of corporate hierarchies, Braswell never liked Rosalie. She obviously didn't understand that a *secretary* should treat an Executive Vice President with proper deference. He was appalled when, instead of answering his question, she sat down in the chair in front of him.

"Who the hell do you think you are?" he demanded. "Get out of my office!"

His words made no impact on Rosalie. Unbelievably, she just stared at him and after several moments of this, something in Braswell's lizard brain began to make him afraid.

Then she spoke. "Was it money, or do they have something on you?"

Braswell felt fear begin to overtake him and he stood up, trying to assert his authority. "I don't know what you're talking about!" he yelled. "Get the FUCK out of my office, you bitch!"

Rosalie didn't move. "Sit down, Braswell. And stop yelling, or I'll have you removed right now. Two agents are waiting in the next office, and they're going to take you out of here when I'm done. But I want to ask you some questions first."

Braswell's face flushed, and he was sweating; he fell into his chair. When he spoke, his voice was filled with fear. "I want my lawyer. I know my rights."

Rosalie barely shook her head. "We're not handling this through the justice system, Braswell. This is a national security issue and you're a spy."

"I'm not a spy," Braswell protested. "They just wanted me to kill the broadcast. It's stupid anyway; I would have killed it even if they hadn't paid me!"

"But they did pay you. So, it doesn't matter if Rich is right about the object. You're a traitor to your country, and we take a very dim view of that."

"I'm not a traitor! I did the right thing for *RECON* and for Chicago!"

"You did this for yourself. I'm asking you again. Do they have something on you?"

He shook his head.

"So, it was just the money."

He didn't react.

"How much money did it take for you to sell out an entire city?"

"I didn't sell out *anyone*," he snapped. "There's no alien spaceship. It's all *bullshit*!"

"And what about Rich and Eliza's flight to Tucson? That wasn't public knowledge. Someone tipped off the Russians, and it nearly cost them their lives."

Braswell's eyes were bright, his words rushed. "I didn't know they would try to kill them. I thought maybe they'd—"

"Sweet talk them?" Rosalie interrupted. "You're not very bright, but even you know better than that."

"I want my lawyer," Braswell repeated. "I want my lawyer right now!" He began to panic, and he stood up, his eyes wild. "I have to get out of here!"

He rushed past Rosalie, as though trying to escape, but then his office door burst open, and two agents dressed like EMTs barged in pushing a gurney. They closed the door behind them. "You can't make me get on that thing!" Braswell yelled.

One of the men stepped forward and shot Braswell with a Taser. His body quivered for a moment before he crumpled onto the floor. The other agent knelt down and used a syringe to inject Propofol into the stricken executive. In less than a minute, Braswell was unconscious.

Rosalie ordered, "Now, get him out of here like he's had a heart attack."

The men loaded Braswell's limp body onto the gurney, rigged up something that looked like an IV drip, and placed an oxygen mask over his face. One of them said, "Go!" and they opened the door into the hallway and ran out, yelling for people to get out of the way as they rushed him towards the elevator.

Ten minutes later, Rosalie walked into the production booth. It was dark. A dozen technicians sat at panels and looked onto the set where Rich sat on a stool, an audio engineer hovering over him, making last second adjustments.

"Where's Braswell?" Carl asked, in a frightened whisper. "I'm terrified he's going to show up any minute and shut us down!"

Rosalie leaned against the wall next to him and crossed her arms. "He had a heart attack. They just took him to the hospital." Everyone in the booth stopped what they were doing and turned to stare at her. Rich caught the movement from the set and put a hand to his ear to indicate he wanted to know what was going on. It took a moment for Carl to recover. Then he pressed a button and spoke into a mic. "Uh, Rich. Brendan Braswell just had a heart attack."

Rich's eyes widened at the news. "Is he going to make it?"

Carl turned to Rosalie. "Rich wants to know if Braswell's going to make it."

"I think so. But he's going to have some hard days ahead of him."

When the house lights came down, Rich was sitting alone in the darkness. Then a technician brought up the opening video sequence. As it faded out, the stage lights came up, revealing Rich against a dark background. Visible on the monitor, a production editor had imposed a graphic: Perun's Hammer: *An Existential Threat to Chicago.*

"Good evening, and welcome to a special edition of *RECON.* I'm Rich Penton. Tonight, we'll spend the entire hour exploring the biggest mystery I've come across in my forty years as a journalist. You'll see the evidence, and you'll hear from experts, who will weigh in with their analysis of several videos we've received that should have been impossible for anyone to make. These videos seem to be a dire warning, from an intelligence we can't identify. As you'll see, they indicate that an object no astronomer, no one at NASA, or any other agency has yet detected, is at this moment streaking through space towards Chicago. If it's not stopped, or if Chicago is not evacuated, hundreds of thousands, or even millions of people could die."

Rich began with an excerpt from the first video, including the moment *Perun's Hammer* exploded in Chicago, but the team had decided to withhold the nature of the object until late in the show. Then, he showed a collage of the historical videos, identifying the scenes and describing how they kept showing up, no matter how *RECON* tried to stop them.

"We've explored the possibility that this is a hoax. For months, we've researched every detail of the strange scenes in these videos, and we can find no evidence they're created with CGI—not even the most advanced artificial intelligence systems, or anything currently in development. The stories they tell are extremely, and often painfully, historically accurate, to a degree that astonished the researchers who reviewed them for us."

Rich reported that an FBI expert had used facial recognition software to match dozens of people in the videos, including Amelia Earhart, Fred Noonan, Custer, several of his officers, and even more people from the Tulsa Race Massacre video. Then he wrapped up the first part of the segment. "So, if this a hoax, *RECON* can find no evidence of it. We don't know who sent us this warning. There are many in the United States government who believe this is nothing more than trickery from the Russians, who have proven to be capable hackers. But we disagree. We think the evidence is overwhelming. There is a non-human intelligence warning us of a devastating event about to be visited on Chicago.

"For a long time, we were mystified. Who is responsible for the videos? How did they send them to me? How were they made? Are they real, or brilliant reproductions of the scenes they portray? We finally determined that the first video was a *message*—an interstellar object is on its way to destroy Chicago. The rest were merely evidence to prove the credibility of the Intelligence sending that warning. But the most surprising part of the mystery wasn't revealed until the last video we received. More on that when we return after this break."

Brendan Braswell recovered consciousness. He was slumped over a table, and when he tried to sit up, a handcuff on his left wrist banged against the gray steel arm of his chair. He was in a small room, behind a heavy metal door. The only furniture was the table and two chairs. A large, mirrored window covered most of one wall. An older, well-dressed man sat across from him.

"Who the hell are you?" Braswell demanded.

The man smiled. "I have a lot of questions for you, Mr. Braswell. If you answer all of them honestly and thoroughly, there's a chance you'll see the outdoors again in your lifetime." He let that hang in the air. "Lie to me, and no one will ever see you again."

"I want to see my attorney," Braswell pleaded. "I have rights."

The man shook his head, slowly. "You have no rights and no attorney. I told you the terms and they're not negotiable. Now, are you ready to answer some questions?"

Fear like he'd never experienced washed over Brendan Braswell. He began talking and didn't stop for hours.

23

THE REST OF THE STORY

After the commercial break, Rich described the Tunguska Event and the Chelyabinsk meteor and shared video and facts about Meteor Crater in Arizona, including what a similar impact would do to the area around Chicago. He showed a graphic illustrating how the *Kulik* and *Fedorov* satellites had a unique ability to detect interstellar objects and described the destruction of *NEO Surveyor* just as it was about to search for *Perun's Hammer*.

The next section was a deep dive into the historical videos, including excerpts from interviews with the experts. Then came the biggest news of all: The object was not an asteroid, but a damaged spacecraft from a non-human civilization. They ran the video of the object flying through space and crashing into Chicago, along with scenes of the damage. Rich also shared *RECON*'s theory that explained why the Intelligence was trying to help.

Rich wrapped up the show with a live discussion with Chandra Ramanujan, first asking him how such startling imagery could have been produced from scenes that transpired decades ago. Chandra went through the same time travel explanations he'd given Rich earlier, using the simplest language possible. He noted that passing information through time was different and vastly simpler than *traveling* through time.

"Chandra," Rich asked, "do you believe we've heard the last from whatever intelligence is behind these videos?"

The physicist shook his head. "I think that may depend on what we do next. Given the efforts this intelligence has apparently made to deliver this warning, I doubt it will accept, 'no thanks, we'll just ignore the threat and go on like it doesn't exist' as an answer. But I want to mention one more hypothesis, Rich."

"Go on."

"Clearly, the video of Chicago's destruction, if it's not a hoax, is a vision of the future. Perhaps it's real imagery, brought back in time to the present day. Or perhaps the 'Intelligence' is simply projecting what will happen if this object lands in Chicago. Even the imagery of historical events might have been captured without the Intelligence traveling, or even looking, into the past."

"I'm surprised to hear you say that Dr. Ramanujan," Rich replied. "Given that you've devoted your life to that exact goal. How can you explain the videos if there's no time travel involved?"

"Perhaps whoever shot these videos has been here all along."

That possibility, seemingly obvious once mentioned, had never occurred to anyone on the *RECON* team. They cut to a commercial break, and Rich prepared for the closing monologue. In the production booth, Carl was beaming. Beth gave him a thumbs up, and even Rosalie smiled when he caught her eye.

An assistant producer counted down the time. "We're back in 20...10...5, 4, 3, 2, 1."

"Welcome back to *RECON*," Rich began. "What we've shown you tonight seems to defy explanation. You might even think it defies science. And yet, those of us at *RECON*, and many of the experts we've spoken to, believe there's nothing unscientific about anything we've experienced. It's simply that there is a great deal of science we do not yet understand. Before we started researching this story, I thought time travel was nothing more than science fiction fantasy. What I've learned since is that traveling in time at different rates than we experience in our daily lives is not only possible, but it happens all the time. Space stations and astronauts travel forward in time by tiny amounts. GPS satellites have mechanisms to counter the effects of time displacement, or they'd be off by miles after just a single day. You could even say that traveling *forward* in time, by enough to matter and measure, is ordinary."

"Traveling backwards in time is a more difficult problem, but it's not something that's been proven impossible, either. Learning this, thanks to Dr. Ramanujan and other physicists, made us more open to the possibility that this footage is real. And Dr. Ramanujan's newest hypothesis introduces the possibility that the videos were made with no time travel at all. In any case, as we continued our research and uncovered enormous amounts of evidence that the videos were authentic—and absolutely *none* that they weren't—we all wondered, *why?*

"We struggled with this question for months, then realized we'd had the answer all along. In fact, it was in the first video we received. We believe *RECON* was chosen to share these videos with the world because we are at imminent risk of an object destroying Chicago, the home of *RECON*, and the city from which I'm talking to you right now. Analysis of the impact video shows the object will arrive on October 15th, three months and one week from today, unless NASA decides to launch a mission to destroy it and is successful. That technology is real and has been tested successfully quite recently."

"But there's a problem. The United States' own intelligence agencies, the Department of Defense, and many elected politicians, believe this is all a ruse. They say the Russians have fabricated the videos to embarrass us and persuade us to expend resources to address a threat that doesn't exist. The American people need to hold our politicians and bureaucrats accountable and demand immediate action to use our asteroid killing resources to confront the threat. To address the doubts anyone has about the videos, and to ensure they are vetted by the best scientists around the world, we're making all of the footage available online. We'll also post a great deal of the material we gathered during our investigation but couldn't fit into this one-hour time slot."

The *RECON* team ended the show with a graphic listing the steps residents of Chicago should take, along with other advice designed to prevent mass hysteria: *Don't panic. Prepare to evacuate in the weeks leading up to October 15th. Remember that the rest of the country is not at risk. There is no need to stock up on supplies.*

Finally, Rich gave his signature sign-off, wondering if it would be for the last time. "From the City of Big Shoulders to our friends around the world, thank you for watching *RECON*. We'll be watching out for you." The theme music started, the studio lights came up, and the credits scrolled across the studio monitors.

"Cut!" Carl called out. The ON AIR light went out, and the production booth and set exploded in applause.

I stood up as everyone cheered. The camera operators came over to shake my hand, Carl and Beth hugged me and, much to my surprise, Rosalie did, too. Warren, who had gotten back on his feet just in time to attend the live broadcast, was reading excerpts of online chatter to everyone. The message was certainly getting around. Social media and headlines around the world were already telling the story of *RECON*'s *Perun's Hammer*. Finally, I made my way back to my office, and Rosalie followed me in, closed the door, and sat across from me. She waited several seconds before speaking.

"Brendan Braswell was paid by the SVR to kill the story," she said, simply.

My mouth dropped open, and I stared at her.

She continued. "You're the one who put me on to him, Rich."

"How did I do that?"

She smiled. "Because of what you said about your people. You told me none of them would have violated the team's confidence. As you know, I don't trust anyone. But you do, and you've known these people for a long time. So, I began to think about how else Brendan could have known about Angela's involvement. If your team didn't tell him about her visions, then he must have learned another way."

"That makes sense," I agreed. "How did you find out it was the Russians who told him?"

"We found a bug in Carl's house. Then we found Dyavol's car. It was behind a hotel in Ravenswood. Dyavol had a room there, with a receiver connected to a digital recorder he was using to listen in on Carl and his wife. Carl told her about Angela, the hologram, and the investigation, and Dyavol heard everything. The SVR must have prepped Braswell."

I thought about that for a minute. "How did you know it was Braswell?"

"Rich, do you remember when I asked you why Brendan was harder to sell on this story than David Clancy?"

"I remember."

"You attributed that to David being a lot smarter than Braswell. While that's true, Braswell is a network executive, and this story is huge. I could imagine he'd want you to soften the story, maybe tell it as a theory rather than a certainty, but to kill it? That didn't make sense to me."

I shook my head. "Damn. That's insightful. I should have seen through that. Even if we're wrong, the ratings are going through the roof."

"Yes. So, I had Braswell's phone bugged with an app that would copy me on all his text messages and emails. He's a terrible spy. We nailed him in three days."

"That's the same way you bugged me."

"Yes, but I was almost too late. He's the one who gave the Russians the information about your flight to Tucson."

A cold fury come over me. Brendan Braswell had facilitated an attempt on my life—Eliza's, too. This was a lot of information, and my head was spinning. "What happens to him now?"

"He's in custody. The heart attack story was a ruse to get him out of the building. I'm sure by now he's broken, and he's telling us everything."

"And after that?"

She shrugged. "We want to turn him. Use him as a double agent. See if we can follow the thread back to the SVR agents he's been working with. He doesn't know that yet, by the way. He thinks he's in some Chicago version of Guantanamo."

"You're going to *release him*?"

"Maybe. But don't worry. He'll get what's coming to him."

"I don't see how, if you don't prosecute him."

Rosalie smiled. "Trust me, Rich. You're good at that, remember?"

I shook my head and grinned as she got up and left my office. While we'd been talking, my phone had been buzzing with voice-mails, and I returned a few calls. Half an hour later, I grabbed my briefcase, stepped into the hallway and locked the door behind me. As I walked by Rosalie's desk, I glanced over, and something made me stop short.

All of Rosalie's personal belongings were gone. She had never kept much in her cube—a few knickknacks, a sweater, and her ever-present water bottle. I checked her desk drawers. They were empty except for company documents, folders, and office supplies. I felt a deep sadness that I hadn't been able to say goodbye properly, but I knew sentimentality wasn't part of her makeup. I wondered if I'd ever see her again. Then I noticed a sticky note on one of her computer monitors. Written in Rosalie's familiar hand, it said:

I'll go into battle with you anytime. Well done.
-R

My eyes misted up as I plucked the note off the monitor and slipped it carefully into a folio. I'd frame it and display it with my Emmys, even though only a few people would ever know the back story. Then I made my way towards the elevator, our condo, and into Eliza's arms.

We'd had two goals for our broadcast. One was to put pressure on the United States Government to take the threat seriously and do something about it. The second was to persuade the people of Chicago to evacuate in an orderly fashion in the weeks leading up to October 15th. Even if NASA went through with the mission to destroy *Perun's Hammer*, it could fail. If that happened, the object would reach Chicago only three days later, thanks to its incredible velocity. Trying to evacuate then would be chaos.

But for the *RECON* team, *Perun's Hammer* caused chaos long before it got anywhere close to Chicago. Our offices were inundated with calls from other national networks, news programs from more than a hundred countries, bloggers, conspiracy theorists, and private citizens. Demands for me to do interviews in every time zone kept me working sixteen-hour days. As difficult as it was, I was thrilled. We'd dreamed of alerting the world to the imminent threat of an object hitting Chicago with only the videos, the experts, and our own story-telling skills to make the case.

Almost immediately, major networks began airing interviews

with astrophysicists involved in planetary defense. Most of these scientists weren't sure what to think of our story, and if it weren't for the reputations of Eliza and *RECON*, many of them probably would have been more vocal in their skepticism. But the scientific community took full advantage of the opportunity to educate the public about NEOs, and at the very least, we'd succeeded in raising the awareness and concern about potential disasters from near-Earth objects. I had a feeling funding for these programs was going to *skyrocket* over the next several years.

The reaction of the scientific community, along with the incredible ratings, must have been the reason we weren't fired. I kept expecting to get that phone call, but it never came. Of course, with Brendan out of the picture for the time being, I reported directly to the network's CEO, and he and I had been friends for many years. I wondered what would happen if Braswell came back.

Oddly, David Clancy was nowhere to be found. My calls to him went to voice mail, and he appeared on none of the television programs, despite his position as Planetary Defense Officer. I felt certain he was trying to figure out what to do, but I wished I knew what it was.

Perun's Hammer became a cultural phenomenon. Most organized religions were extremely helpful. Protestants, Muslims, Jews, Catholics, Buddhists, and others rallied around the cause, helping to prepare their followers for the possibility that they would need to evacuate the city. The Vatican, which employs professional astronomers, also came out in support of our message.

But a small number of extremists claimed we were representing the devil's vision of the future and preached that mankind, or at least Chicago, could be spared only if people prayed hard and gave often. Most of these radicals were unaffiliated with any major religion and instead formed their own bizarre cult with the slogan, *Jesus is Greater Than Perun*, although they understood neither.

A growing number of people began wearing t-shirts and hats

imprinted with the words, *Jesus > Perun*. They'd worked themselves into increasingly extreme views, with the prevailing belief that a global complot was planning to transform Chicago into a haven where cannibalistic pedophiles could move in and do whatever horrible things cannibalistic pedophiles do. As the primary messenger about *Perun's Hammer*, I'd been tagged as the leader of the cabal and received countless threats on my life.

The constant strain put the whole *RECON* team on edge. When Carl and Beth started snapping at each other about some minor issue, I knew we needed a break. So, at the end of another long Monday, I called both of them and Warren into my office. Warren still moved pretty stiffly, but he was clearly on the road to recovery.

When we sat down at the table, it was as though the weight of the world was on our shoulders. I could see the anxiety in their eyes as I said, "I want to thank all of you for the fantastic job you've done over the last few months. This is the best research, writing, and shooting I've ever been a part of. And that's the best damn story I've ever anchored. I was as optimistic as anyone at first, and when the story broke, it seemed like we were going to change history in a few short weeks. I still think we can, but it was never going to happen that quickly or easily."

The words helped a little; they needed to hear that they had done good work, regardless of the outcome. "But I also know that, at the rate we're going, we'll burn ourselves out soon. So, I want all of you to take Thursday and Friday off. In fact, consider it an order."

Warren spoke up. "I just got back. I appreciate your offer, but—"

"Of all people, Warren, you deserve the time off. Of course, I'm a little biased about that." Warren blushed, Beth laughed, and Carl patted him on the back.

"And don't use your vacation time. As far as *RECON* is concerned, you're working from home but you're unreachable, unavailable, and entirely unproductive. On Friday, Eliza and I want to take you and your significant others out to our favorite restaurant. This is a tough challenge, and we may not win. But let's recharge our batteries and see if we can get ready for another round when we're rested. Sound good?" We spent a few more minutes together, and I felt the tension ease a little bit. As they left my office, I saw Carl and Beth chat quietly and hug, which I took as a sign they'd patched up their disagreement.

The problem was that we were running out of time. With *NEO Surveyor* gone, NASA's Planetary Defense Coordination Office had to rely on terrestrial telescopes to spot *Perun's Hammer*, which wouldn't emerge from behind the Sun for more than three weeks. But it could be weeks after that before ground telescopes spotted the object, and there was a significant risk that wouldn't happen before the launch deadline.

Due to threats from the *Jesus > Perun* crowd, I wasn't taking the train, so I rode home that evening in the back of an SUV, driven by an armed guard. As I watched the city go by, I became increasingly discouraged that we hadn't been able to generate enough pressure to persuade NASA to commit to the mission or get civil defense authorities to announce an evacuation of Chicago.

I got home before Eliza did, took a glass out of the cupboard and tossed in a few ice cubes. Swinging by our liquor cabinet, I grabbed a bottle of bourbon before heading out to the veranda and stretching out on a deck chair. I had downed half a glass when I heard the door open, and Eliza came out to join me.

"Hi," I said, feeling the welcome, warm buzz of alcohol.

Eliza must have seen the anxiety on my face. "How are you?" I could hear the concern in her voice.

"Terrific. I'm in the process of failing to save Chicago, and millions of people might die as a result." I held up my glass in a toast. "But hey, everyone fails at something."

To her credit, Eliza didn't argue. She knew I didn't need her encouragement. I just needed *her*. She sat down on the chair next to me and motioned towards the bourbon. "Are you going to leave any of that for me?"

"Yeah, but you'd better hurry. There's only three more bottles in the liquor cabinet, and I'm drinking all of them tonight."

She put her hand on my shoulder. "I love you for risking everything on this." When she smiled, a little happiness penetrated the haze that had gathered around my brain.

"Thank you," I said, gratefully. "You're the best woman I've ever known."

She laughed softly. "That's the liquor talking. Speaking of which..." She grabbed the glass out of my hand and downed it.

"Hey, lady," I said, in mock outrage. "Get your own drink!"

"I think I will. With ice." A minute later, we were both reclining in our favorite chairs, holding hands. But when I started again on how disappointed and depressed I was about the response to the *Perun's Hammer* story, Eliza put down her glass, stood up and offered me her hand.

"Come on, Mr. Penton. The fight isn't over, and I don't like hearing you talk that way. I think what you need is a good romp in bed. And I *know* I need one."

I looked up at her. "Are you propositioning me, Madam?"

She nodded.

"Then I accept," I said, as she helped me get out of the chair.

An hour later, as we lay in each other's arms, the whole world seemed a little brighter. I enjoyed the best sleep I'd had in weeks and woke up to a beautiful morning. I made coffee as the sun rose above Lake Michigan, and Eliza joined me a few minutes later.

I turned on the morning news and did a double take. The scrolling chyron at the bottom of the frame announced: *Russia*

Admits Responsibility for "Perun's Hammer" Videos. The Russian ambassador to the United States "confessed" to making the videos, penetrating both our computer network and the Pentagon's, and then apologized for the actions of the director of the SVR, who'd just been sacked. I was astounded at how far Russia was willing to go in order to see Chicago destroyed. Everything the ambassador was saying would be proven a lie in a few months. But the immediate problem was that millions of people would believe the Russians. How many Chicago residents would choose not to evacuate as a result? Even more important, what would David Clancy think?

Adding to the frustration, when I got to the office, I learned that Brendan Braswell had recovered from his "heart attack" and was back at work. Fortunately for him, he stayed in our New York offices. I left him alone, betting that Rosalie was right about him getting what was due to him.

24

WARNING OR ATTACK?

August 7th: 69 Days Before Arrival

We rented the front room at North Pond Restaurant for our team dinner. Warren and Jessica arrived first. Jessica was lovely, and Warren looked like the Hollywood heartthrob he might have been. The Swintons were next, with Wendy absolutely adorable in her flower-print summer dress. Carl wore a worn-out sports coat over a rumpled polo shirt.

"He won't let me iron a thing," Wendy explained, exasperated. "He says he's just going to wrinkle it anyway."

Beth and Hubert arrived last, illuminated in the blissful glow of two people madly in love. We learned why when Beth held out her left hand and flashed a large, beautiful, diamond engagement ring. They announced a Spring wedding as they held each other tightly and smiled as we toasted them. We applauded wildly, but I'm sure I wasn't the only one who wondered if there'd be a Chicago to get married in by then.

After cocktails, we sat down and ordered a variety of great appetizers, bottles of fantastic wine, and savory entrees. Carl and

Wendy Swinton told us the murder of their friend Bob Johanssen had been solved. The FBI had found hair and fabric samples in the trunk of an abandoned rental car behind a boutique hotel on the North side of Chicago. Fingerprints from the car matched those found on a listening device the FBI had removed from their kitchen. The FBI believed the person who rented the car had planted the device in their house and had killed Bob in an accidental run in. They hadn't found Bob's body, unfortunately, but it was enough evidence for the coroner to rule him deceased and the cause of death homicide.

For the next few hours, we celebrated what we'd accomplished so far, even though there was more to do. It was about 9:20 p.m. when the *maître d'* tapped me on the shoulder and told me I had a phone call. As I got up, I glanced around the room. Everyone was engaged in conversation, including Eliza, who was having an incomprehensible discussion with Hubert about some concept from philosophy or physics (same thing anymore, Eliza said). The team was relaxed and happy.

It occurred to me that I hadn't gotten this sort of phone call at a restaurant in years. Cell phones had made them unnecessary. But when I got to the *maître d's* stand, he handed me the receiver of an actual, plugged-into-the-wall phone, and walked off as I put it to my ear.

"Yes?" I said, a little cautiously.

"Look out the front door," a familiar voice instructed.

I peered through the glass. Standing sixty feet away was Rosalie. I hung up the phone, pushed open the doors, and walked towards her. As I got close, she led me farther into the darkness.

"I'm surprised but delighted to see you," I said.

She smiled, bemused. "I just flew in from DC and stopped here on my way home. I wanted to share some information."

"Okay. What is it?"

She hesitated, weighing her words carefully. "You remember that we—the intelligence agencies—received some of the videos before you did?"

"I do."

"Yesterday, intelligence people who live in Chicago began to get a new type of video. Others may get them, too. They're hard to watch, but if you think about it, they're really helpful. Stay focused, don't get distracted."

"What do you mean, 'a new type of video?'"

"I can't tell you. I shouldn't even be telling you this much, and we're not one hundred percent certain the problem is going to be as big as it seems. The bandwidth required to deliver these videos to everyone in Chicago isn't available, so we're not sure they'll get distributed."

"*Everyone in Chicago* is going to get a video? For God's sake, what are you talking about?" After a few moments, it became clear she wasn't going to continue. I sighed. "Okay. Thanks, I guess. Now, I have a question for you. Are the intelligence agencies buying the Russians' lies that they made the videos?"

"The Russians made this a lot harder. They confirmed what some senior people already believed. Besides, we're not astrophysicists. But David Clancy believes in you and Eliza and he's doing some...innovative work to see if you're right."

"What's David doing? I can't reach him."

"I can't tell you that either. But he'll know soon."

"He'll know *what* soon?" It was maddening.

Rosalie wasn't willing to reveal much more. "Something that can't be refuted, if he's right, and it has nothing to do with telescopes or near-Earth objects."

"How can what he's doing have nothing to do with telescopes?"

She didn't answer.

"Well, thanks for doing what you can. It seems like most scientists don't believe us. And with the Russians' claims, a lot of other people think we're wrong, too."

She shook her head. "You and I know you're not wrong. I was there when the videos arrived, and I witnessed Angela's reaction over the phone. I saw the hologram, and I believe you about the videos of your own murder. But if I hadn't been involved in all of this? I might be one of the doubters."

"Damn," I lamented. "I just feel like I missed something. Like there's more I could have done to make the case."

"I understand. I came here tonight to give you a little encouragement, because there are many of us—including some very senior people—who want you to keep going."

"Thanks Rosalie. We're pushing as hard as we can. But since you're here, tell me why Brendan Braswell is back at work. He's a traitor and you caught him dead to rights."

"Brendan's story isn't over. Remember, I asked you to trust me on that?"

"Okay. I don't understand, but I do trust you. In the meantime, I have to figure out how to get NASA to launch the mission, and I need to get civil authorities to evacuate Chicago. And I'm all out of ideas."

She smiled at me. "You're *Rich Penton*. You'll think of something."

I just shook my head at that. It was quiet for a moment, then Rosalie said, "You'd better go back inside. They're going to miss you soon."

"I wish you could come inside and say 'hi'. Everyone would love to see you."

She grinned wryly, as though she found my sentimentalism innocent and naïve, but in a good way. "Thanks. But I have to go."

"Okay, but one more thing. How did you know I was here? I thought you stopped tracking me."

Rosalie smiled slyly. "I removed all the electronic trackers. But I always know where you are."

I broke into a startled laugh. "Well...thank you for everything. We couldn't win this fight without you."

"My whole life's been about fighting. *Semper Fi.*" That was news to me, but not surprising. Rosalie Carter was a warrior; I'd seen that myself. It made sense that she'd served in the Marines.

"Goodbye, Rich." Rosalie turned and began to walk away from the restaurant. Then, as if on impulse, she turned around to face me, but kept walking, now backwards. "Rich!" she called out. "The only reason I'm here and able to fight is because someone paid for a surgery to repair a heart valve when I was a baby living in a homeless shelter in New York."

I drew in my breath sharply. "You're *Heloisa!*" I couldn't believe it.

Rosalie smiled broadly, enjoying the realization that spread across my face.

"Oh my God!" I asked, incredulous. "You're the girl Angela loved so much!"

She grinned. "That's why I volunteered for this job. You and Angela paid it forward. I figured it was time to pay it back." She winked at me and flashed a huge smile.

"Wait!" I called after her. "I want to know the rest of your story!" But she turned away and disappeared into the night.

I had assumed that Angela was imagining the girl she knew as Heloisa was visiting her regularly. But Rosalie—no doubt the name her adoptive parents had given her—must have been going to see my wife at the memory care facility. Angela's ongoing reassurances that "Heloisa" would help me weren't a product of her deteriorating mind; they were factual statements. I walked slowly back to the restaurant and sat down next to Eliza.

She smiled sweetly at me, obviously a little buzzed. "You okay? You were gone a long time."

I grinned and nodded. "I ran into an old friend. I'll tell you about it later. But right now, let's have some fun." The people at the table had become family to me. Beth, Carl, Warren, and especially my beloved Eliza. All of them happy and intoxicated by friendship, love, and a little wine. And sitting in a doomed city. I didn't know what to do, but I knew I'd persist. From what Rosalie had said, the Intelligence was persisting, too.

Warren and Jessica stayed at the restaurant after everyone else had left. The bar was still open, there was live music, and they basked in the afterglow of a wonderful evening. When it was closing time, the bartender asked Warren if he could settle-up with cash. North Pond's credit card processing system was down. He paid the bill, and the two of them stepped into a cool Chicago night. Warren pulled out his phone to summon a rideshare as they walked, but it timed out.

"What's wrong?" Jessica asked.

"Not sure. The app's not working."

Jessica couldn't connect either and, when Warren opened his web browser, he received an error message: *Cannot open the page because you are not connected to the Internet.* They reached North Stockton Drive where a car with a rideshare sticker was parked at the curb. The driver looked mystified as he stared at his phone.

Warren called to him. "Are you taking rides?"

"No. Both of my phones quit working, and I can't take electronic payments."

"I'll pay you fifty bucks in cash to drop this young lady off in Rogers Park and then take me to 20 East Marshall."

"No way!" Jessica objected. "If there's something going on, I want to be in on it."

Warren smiled. It was exciting to have her with him. He turned back to the driver. "Fifty bucks to take us to 20 East Marshall."

"It's your money," the driver replied with a shrug. "That's about twice what it's worth."

"It's late, and you're our only option," Warren pointed out.

Jessica feigned disgust. "You guys are negotiating wrong."

The driver laughed. "Hop in." As they drove to the *RECON* building, Warren studied his phone. He still had no cell phone signal at all. The driver said he had the same problems.

"Did your service go out all at once or gradually?" Warren asked.

"Gradually, I guess. About four hours ago, GPS stopped working. Then the Internet slowed down and quit. I could make calls for a while, but not in the last half hour."

When they got to the building, the security guard told them his computer wouldn't connect to the Internet and the badge scanners were down. They read the bar code but failed to match to an identity.

"The actual scanning is done by the devices," Warren explained, "but they're not connecting to the database in the cloud. When did the computer and badge scanners quit?"

"Couple of hours ago. I called it in right away. I tried to call back about an hour later and couldn't get through."

"What about your cell phone?"

"Nope. Went down about 45 minutes ago."

"Damn," Warren lamented. "We seem to be cut off from the world."

The guard reached into a cabinet under the security desk and grabbed something stuffed way in the back. "Maybe you can use this," he offered, holding out an old radio. It had a long, collapsible, chrome antenna and an old-fashioned dial. A red needle moved across a metal plate with FM, AM, and shortwave radio frequencies on it.

"Wow," Warren exclaimed. "I haven't seen one of these in years. I'll take it. Thanks." The guard smiled, and Warren and Jessica rode the elevator to the 43rd floor.

"I've never been up here this late," Jessica remarked.

"You're lucky," Warren sighed. "I've spent a lot of all-nighters here, thanks to software updates, patches, break-fixes, and cyber-attacks." He grinned. "And the occasional fight to the death with a gigantic Russian assassin."

She groaned.

"Too soon?"

The elevator doors opened. "Fortunately, everything's in the cloud these days." A thoughtful look crossed his face. "Satellites!"

Jessica waited for him to continue, then understanding dawned. "Are you saying it's the satellites that are down, instead of the Internet?"

"I'm not sure yet." He handed her the radio. "Here, plug this in and find WGN, okay?"

Confirming that his work computer couldn't connect to the Internet, he opened a utility closet and grabbed a box. He pulled out a dozen Motorola walkie talkies and began charging them.

Jessica grinned. "Nice work. You have a ham radio tucked away somewhere, too?"

He reached even farther into the closet, pulled out a larger box, and slid it next to the desk. Jessica raised her eyebrows in a question.

"One ham radio, as requested."

Jessica laughed. "Oh my God, you really ARE a nerd, aren't you?"

Warren nodded, unabashed. "This unit can run on batteries. I bought it years ago, in case there was a long power outage, and we needed to know what was going on in the world."

"Your nerdiness might come in handy. If the Internet doesn't come back online soon, this ham radio will be the only way to talk to people across the country—or around the world."

"That's the idea, although I hope it doesn't come to that." He set the radio and some other instruments in metal boxes on a table and connected them to a computer.

"Are you going to talk to someone now?"

Warren shook his head "I have to set up the antenna on the roof first, so I can turn it with this rotor control."

"On the roof?" Jessica asked, alarmed. "You're not ready to climb around up there!"

"There's no one else to do it—"

"Oh, shut up, Warren," she said, affectionately. "I grew up on a farm and helped my dad fix everything that broke. Just tell me what to do."

Warren argued, but to no avail. "Okay, okay," he surrendered. "But let's at least turn on the AM/FM radio to see if we still need the ham."

Jessica turned up the volume on the security guard's radio, and a WGN news announcer was on the air. ".... limited to Chicago or not at this time. Cell phones aren't working, so we have to wait for reporters to return to the station to give us updates. We've checked with our television affiliate, WGN-TV. They're reporting that they can't connect to satellites and, as a result, are unable to transmit via satellite or cable, but they are still broadcasting over the airwaves..."

"Over the air!" Warren exclaimed. He reached back into the closet for a coaxial cable, which he screwed into the back of the television. He switched the input to "Antenna" and found WGN; a moment later, the news station came on. At the bottom of the screen, the scrolling chyron said: *Widespread Internet Outage Continues.* The anchor reported that the station had lost contact with most news organizations around the world. Before all the long-distance landlines stopped working, WGN was able to confirm that the outages included at least portions of many states from coast to coast, including New York and California.

It took Jessica about half an hour to assemble the ham radio antenna. After she'd finished, she walked into the security office smiling. "Easy stuff for a farm girl," she boasted.

She pointed to the big radio on the desk. "Let's see if we can raise anyone on the ham." Warren switched on the power supply, turned the rotor controller, and within a few minutes, he was talking to someone in London. The Internet was down there. Hiroshima, Japan was also down. As was Sydney, Australia; Lagos, Nigeria; Dawson City, Yukon Territory; the Marshall Islands, and on and on.

Finally, Warren switched off the radio. "There's nothing we can do. It's global, which means it's going to last awhile. How about we go to 47? Braswell's got a comfortable couch in his office. Ready to get some sleep?"

"Yes, for sure," she replied, her voice tapering off. "But not right away. It's been a while since you were injured..." She winked at him. "I'll be gentle." Warren smiled happily, and the two of them spent a fitful night on the too-narrow-for-sleeping but just-right-for-canoodling sofa.

At 6 a.m., Warren made coffee while Jessica freshened up, and they met in his office. "Oh man," Jessica joked. "We're gonna get caught wearing our date night clothes the morning after." He laughed.

The whole *RECON* team came in early, but Beth was the first one to arrive, and she wanted to talk to Warren right away. Her cell phone wasn't working, the trains weren't running, many FM and AM stations were off the air, and satellite radio was, of course, down entirely. Warren and Jessica met with her in her office. He summed up what they'd learned, including the apparently global nature of the problem, and told her about the walkie talkies and the ham radio.

"The trains aren't running for safety reasons," he explained. "A lot of communication between them and METRA or CTA is dependent on the Internet, as well as GPS. That's one way they prevent accidents."

"I thought GPS signals went directly from satellites to our devices."

Warren wondered how much to explain. He knew he tended to get too technical.

Beth appraised him. "You have a theory about this, don't you?"

"Yes, but just about what's wrong—technically—not how it happened. I don't think the Internet itself is down. I think satellites are down. But the net effect is the same."

"Why not the Internet?" Beth asked.

"I can't imagine how it *could* be. There are so many different ways computers are networked together that a widespread outage while the power is still on is nearly impossible. This situation is consistent with satellites going down. Performance would degrade, certain services would go offline, and eventually much of the Internet would stop working, including most television broadcasting. The systems are so integrated, the Internet can't really function without the data and connectivity of satellites."

"Why are the phones down?" Beth asked.

Warren thought out loud. "All interlinking offices are timed by satellite, using BITS clocking, based on a stratum clock. If clocking is lost, all connecting systems, like DS1, DS3, and OC48, cease to—"

"In English," Beth interrupted.

"Sorry. Basically, telecommunication networks depend on satellites, too."

"Which satellites do you think are down?"

He shrugged. "It could be all of them."

"How could they all be down at the same time?"

"A massive solar storm could do it. There was one in 1859 called the Carrington Event, that wreaked havoc with *telegraph systems*— and telegraph signals ran through thick, well-insulated electrical cables located near the ground. That meant they were protected by Earth's atmosphere, and yet the solar radiation was so powerful that telegraph operators with their hands on their keys actually got shocked. Now, imagine what something like the Carrington Event could do to satellites in space, which have no atmospheric protection. A similar event happened in 2012, but Earth was lucky enough to be out of the target zone of the coronal mass ejection. We missed it by nine days. If we'd been hit, it could have wiped out most of our satellites."

Jessica couldn't restrain herself. "Man, you really *are* the package. Looks *and* brains. How in the world do you know all this stuff?"

Warren blushed, and Beth squelched a smile.

"My job is keeping *RECON* connected," he said. "I have to know the risks."

Beth continued. "And you think that's what happened? A solar flare wiped out our satellites?"

"Maybe, but I'm not sure. There could be other causes. It might be military action by Russia or China, although I don't think they could take out so many satellites at once. The military protects our space-based assets very carefully. Besides, ham operators all over the world are reporting the Internet is down, including people I've talked to in China and Russia. But it could be something else," he said, cautiously.

Beth's face darkened with understanding. "A warning? From the Intelligence?"

"That, too, I suppose. And I hope so. Because the other possibility is that it's an attack."

25

WHEN DEATH GETS PERSONAL

The global collapse of the Internet caused equal parts confusion, frustration, and panic. For people of my generation, it was like being thrust thirty years into the past, but even stranger. For one thing, telephones didn't work. Local retail stores couldn't take credit cards, and ATMs were offline, which caused a major problem since many people no longer had paper checks. There was simultaneously an immediate cash shortage, along with frantic crowds rushing out to hoard toilet paper, gasoline, food, and water. Crime spiked as people panicked, so governments around the world called out their militaries, and most cities put curfews in place.

News outlets scrambled to find ham operators to get information about what was happening in the rest of the world. The once-ubiquitous portable radio was a relative rarity now, but people dug them out of closets, attics, and storage units. Within a couple of days, almost everyone had figured out how to wire an antenna of some kind to their televisions. The Russians' claims that they had created the mysterious videos backfired. Most people blamed them for the Internet outage, too.

On the second evening of the crisis, the President addressed the nation via radio and broadcast television. Warren was right. The world's satellites had simply stopped transmitting data—every one of them had failed, as far as anyone could tell. The President said that he'd been able to talk to his counterparts in Russia and China, since the secure lines still worked. They'd reassured him—and he them—that they were all facing the same challenge. He stressed that the world's leading experts were working on the problem, and prepared Americans for the possibility that it could be some time before the situation could be remedied.

Conspiracy theorists tried to exploit the situation, but their influence was dramatically limited by the sudden disappearance of the Internet. Warren's walkie talkies turned out to be very useful. They wouldn't reach as far as Carl's house in Naperville, but they connected those of us downtown with reliable—but not secure—communication. Warren warned us that the radios required licenses he'd let expire years ago, but we decided the FCC had more pressing issues than tracking down rogue walkie-talkie users.

Warren stayed in the office 24x7, configuring our systems to work on local computers as well as possible, so we could still operate. I was worried about his health, but he reassured me he was fine. The building had a gym with showers, so he could camp out nearly indefinitely. Jessica shuttled clothes and other necessities to him.

For three days, the President told Americans that the government was working on the problem while admitting they hadn't identified the cause yet. He would not give any projected date the satellites would come back online, and people became increasingly anxious, as they had no way to check on loved ones unless they lived nearby.

On the fourth night, I was fast asleep when the crackling of the walkie talkie woke me up.

"Rich, come in."

I glanced at the clock to see it was 2:37 a.m.

"Rich, come in."

I switched on the lamp and picked up the radio.

"This is Rich."

"Satellites are back online," Warren said.

I found my phone. "I don't have a signal."

"Give it a little while. My GPS unit just started working. Mobile networks will take longer to reset."

"Want me to come in?"

"Nope. I have a ton of work to do. Just wanted you to know that the satellites are coming back up."

"I really appreciate it. See you in the morn—well, later this morning."

"Goodnight."

Eliza had awakened enough to figure out what was going on. "Great news," she yawned. We talked for a minute, then drifted back to sleep.

As Internet functionality was restored, Warren spent hours reconfiguring systems. His cell phone registered a signal at 3:44 a.m. He switched his television back to satellite, and at 5:11 a.m., it came to life. The news stations didn't know what to make of the incident. He sympathized with them; neither did he.

He was finishing his work when his phone vibrated. A video file had been added. He hesitated a moment, then clicked on the file to play it. He watched the forty second video, and his face turned ashen. "Holy crap," he stammered, his voice shaking. "Holy crap, holy crap, holy crap." He put his head down on his desk as his heart raced, and he fought back panic.

A security agent escorted me from our apartment door to a waiting SUV. I was on my way to work when Warren texted me: *Let me know when you get here.* I called him when I arrived and a few minutes later, he walked into my office.

"Well, I'm glad that's over," I told him. "How are the sys—" His face was white, and he was shaking. "For God's sake, Warren, what's wrong?"

He pulled out his phone, started a video, and handed it to me. Warren and Jessica were standing by Adler Planetarium, staring across Lake Michigan. An object brighter than the Sun appeared in the sky. Warren pointed and shouted in terror as Jessica screamed and wrapped her arms around him, their faces contorted in horror. The object streaked down from the sky and hit Chicago about five miles northwest of them. The explosion was enormous and in seconds, flames lit up their bodies like small suns. They were incinerated, and the shock wave blew away the ash. The video ended.

"Oh, my God!" My hands trembled as I handed the phone back. I was stunned and I shook my head. Warren stared at me blankly, his face wrapped in pain. What I'd seen on the video didn't make sense. Warren and Jessica were too smart not to leave the city, if they knew *Perun's Hammer* was about to destroy it.

"Is this what you were planning to do?" I asked, dubiously. "Watch *Perun's Hammer* from the lakefront?"

"Not really. Well, sort of. If NASA destroys it, we might stay, just to see some small meteors from the debris. But, we won't stay if NASA fails!"

I thought about my experiences with the Intelligence. "I think this is a video of something that will never happen, Warren. Like the videos of my murder, it's just one future, and if you leave Chicago, it's not *the* future. Once you plan to leave, I bet that decision will be reflected in your video—or it will be gone."

"Does this mean we can't stop *Perun's Hammer*, Rich?"

"No, I don't think so. I believe there are many possible futures, and the Intelligence shows us the most probable version at any point in time. So, this just means we haven't done what it takes to stop the object *yet*."

"So, why did I get this video? Again, we won't stay in Chicago if *Perun's Hammer* isn't destroyed."

It was a good point. Then I remembered what Rosalie had told me outside the restaurant.

"Maybe..." I began, working out an idea. "Maybe these videos are different. Perhaps the Intelligence is going to use videos like this to get people to evacuate the city. Remember that Chandra Ramanujan predicted they wouldn't just accept our inaction? Well, he was right. They're going to terrify the people of Chicago into leaving the city."

Warren shook his head skeptically. "*Everyone* in Chicago? Do you know the kind of bandwidth it would take to—" He paused. "This is why the satellites were down! The Intelligence needed to configure them—how, I'm not sure—to deliver the videos!"

I felt a buzz in my pocket as my phone vibrated. I fished it out to see the message that a new video had been added. For the second time in a few months, I watched my own death in high definition. I saw a searing flash followed by a shock wave, then I was simply gone. And I realized that I hadn't made plans to leave yet, either.

The following week must have been among the most frightening in the history of Chicago. The Intelligence slowly and relentlessly rolled out what came to be called, "Personal Death Videos,"—PDVs for short—to the phones, computers, and tablets of anyone who hadn't planned an exit strategy for the day *Perun's Hammer* hit.

I wasn't sure why the Intelligence didn't download everyone's videos all at once. If it was a tactic designed to drive maximum terror, it was working. People were on edge. If they hadn't received their PDVs, they might come at any moment. Plus, there was the constant chance that someone nearby would get theirs and break down in grief. It happened everywhere—on trains, in grocery stores, at work. Authorities cautioned against watching the PDVs, but most people couldn't resist. Interestingly, if you decided to leave the area, you could delete your PDV. If you were doubtful or determined to stay, you couldn't—the same video came back in minutes. The Intelligence was single handedly causing a large-scale evacuation of Chicago. Corporations were transferring headquarters and personnel to other cities. Flights into the city were cancelled by the thousands.

On the third day of this nightmare, Eliza and I got on a video call with Chandra Ramanujan. I told him how terrible things were in Chicago. "I know we can change the future, but since the Intelligence is still showing us images of the destruction, and the date is getting very close, do the videos show the most likely outcome? That we won't be able to stop *Perun's Hammer*?"

"Probably," he admitted. "But that doesn't mean you should give up. There could be other futures, with similar probabilities."

"If they're so powerful, why don't they just destroy the damn spacecraft?" I demanded.

Chandra shook his head. "I don't know for sure, but remember, the Intelligence may be many light years away. We have no evidence they've traveled here, just that they can move information through time and space. This is probably all they can do."

What he said made sense, but it was discouraging to think that the best-case scenario might be the destruction of my beloved Chicago, albeit with minimal loss of life.

September 2nd: 43 Days Before Arrival

My phone rang just after midnight. I woke up with a start and reached for it with a sense of foreboding. No normal person calls you in the middle of the night with good news.

David Clancy is no normal person.

"Rich? It's David." There was a lot of background noise. It sounded like he was at the beach, as I could hear waves and seagulls.

I was instantly wide awake. "What can I do for you, David?"

"Nothing. But I'm going to do something for you and the city of Chicago. I'm immediately authorizing the launch of the search and destroy mission. We're taking your videos as gospel, and we're working out the trajectories so we can hit *Perun's Hammer* ten million kilometers from earth. We're going to do our best to destroy that spacecraft."

I was stunned and thrilled. Eliza was awake now too, so I put Clancy on speakerphone. "David Clancy's going after *Perun's Hammer!*" I yelled. "David, Eliza is here, too."

"Hi, Eliza," David chuckled. He was obviously in a good mood.

"Hello, David." Her eyes were bright with excitement. "Does this mean you were able to spot *Perun's Hammer* even without *NEO Surveyor?*"

"Nope. We still haven't seen it."

I was amazed. "Then what changed your mind?"

He laughed heartily. "Not what. *Who!*"

"Uh, okay. *Who* changed your mind?"

"Amelia Earhart!"

I was confused. "You mean the video convinced you?"

I didn't learn it until later, but David Clancy was standing on the stern of the ship NOAAS *Okeanos Explorer*. A crane held a cable, from which dangled the front landing gear of a small aircraft.

"No. We just found her Lockheed Electra. It was exactly where the video showed it sinking. It's two and a quarter miles west of Nikumaroro Island."

"Oh, my God, you're a genius! Why didn't I think of that?"

He laughed again. He *was* in a good mood. "I had to be sure. But I figured if the Electra was where the Intelligence showed it to be, the rest of the videos must be real, too. You, Eliza, and Amelia Earhart make a compelling team."

I was bursting with excitement. "Let me know how I can help you! If you need publicity, news coverage—anything. You name it."

"No thanks. I'll be too busy coordinating the mission. Based on our data, we barely have time to finalize the planning and reach *Perun's Hammer*—I'm making that the official name, by the way—before it's too late."

"Thank you, David! On behalf of the entire city of Chicago, thank you! And please send me the exact position where you found the Electra. Marc Thibodeaux will want to know. It's been a lifelong goal for him to discover it."

"Don't worry about that. I brought Marc with me."

It was my turn to laugh. We said goodbye, and Eliza and I jumped out of bed, hugging and crying, finally optimistic about the future of Chicago. With David Clancy's support and the launch of the search and destroy mission, our hometown finally had a chance to escape disaster.

But *Perun's Hammer* held more surprises for us to discover, and it would save one of them for its encounter with David Clancy's deflector spacecraft.

26

PERUN'S UNCERTAINTY PRINCIPLE

September 23rd: 22 Days Before Arrival

NASA named the *Perun's Hammer* mission *SLEDGE*—ostensibly because it stood for *Special Launch to Eliminate Derelict Giant Exocraft*. But in the spirit of many previous scientific missions and experiments, the name was a double entendre. A *hammer* packed a lot of power, but a *sledgehammer* packed a lot more, and NASA intended to blow *Perun's Hammer* to smithereens.

SLEDGE launched from Vandenberg Space Force Base near Santa Barbara, CA. Essentially identical to the *DART* mission in 2022, which was the world's first attempt to deflect an asteroid, it succeeded far beyond its mission goals.

The launch vehicle was a SpaceX Falcon 9. Two and a half minutes before liftoff, the Launch Director verified, "Go for launch." A few seconds before launch, the engines ignited and at precisely 9:09 p.m. Pacific Time, the rocket's nine Merlin 1D+ engines began lifting the spacecraft and assembly off the launchpad.

At 1:12 into the mission, the rocket achieved Max Q – or peak mechanical stress. At 2:33, the first stage cut off and separated seconds later, beginning its descent back to earth, where it would land so it could be used on future missions. The second stage, powered by a Merlin-Vacuum engine, ignited for about five minutes and executed a small dogleg maneuver to position the craft towards its target. While this was happening, the fairing covering the deflector deployed, revealing the part of the craft that would eventually impact *Perun's Hammer*.

After coasting for twenty minutes, the second stage reignited for one minute until it achieved escape velocity. Twenty-six minutes later, frangible bolts fired, the pyrotechnics silent in the vacuum of space, and *SLEDGE* was released on its way to intercept *Perun's Hammer* in nineteen days. Until then, the people of Earth, and especially the citizens of Chicago and northern Illinois, would be praying that the spacecraft would not only hit its target, but destroy it.

I watched the launch at the *RECON* offices. We jumped up and down, cheering and yelling, as the magnificent spacecraft rose from its fiery berth and then streaked into the night sky. It was a glorious sight. *Thank you, David. And thank you, too, Amelia.* I had a feeling that, somewhere, she knew her tragic ending would now help save countless lives. Her death, like Monalisa's, would serve a purpose.

Hopefully.

I shook my head. I was making the same mistake as everyone else. Since NASA's *DART* mission had exceeded expectations, I assumed *SLEDGE* would, too. But David Clancy had spent an hour on the phone with me explaining the risks. First, there were the ordinary risks, like equipment failures. But *SLEDGE* also faced unprecedented challenges. For one thing, *Perun's Hammer* was much faster than the object *DART* had impacted, making it a harder-to-hit target. And *SLEDGE* was a deflector device, designed to strike a rocky object.

Perun's Hammer was a spacecraft, and no one knew what materials its builders had used to construct it.

"We don't know for certain what will happen, assuming we hit it. We can't build a spacecraft strong enough to withstand the force of a blow from *SLEDGE,* but that doesn't mean some other intelligence can't. There's a possibility *SLEDGE* will bounce right off it," Clancy said.

"But wouldn't that force redirect it?"

"Yes, but we don't know by how much. According to our estimates, any significant transfer of energy from *SLEDGE* to *Perun's Hammer* that doesn't blow it up, should push it far enough off course to miss Earth. But if it's extremely massive—not hollow, like we believe—we might do more harm than good. Push it into New York City instead of Chicago, for example."

"Oh shit. Please tell me that's a very remote possibility."

"Of course it is, or I wouldn't have approved the mission. But there are many unknowns that make a positive outcome less than certain."

Authorities had finally issued a mandatory, general evacuation order for an area extending one hundred miles west and fifty miles north and south of the city. Most people were leaving in an orderly fashion, but some decided to stay behind, either out of absolute faith in NASA, or because *Jesus > Perun.*

A skeleton crew at *RECON* would stick around until October 12th, the day *SLEDGE* was scheduled to hit *Perun's Hammer.* But should there be any doubt about the outcome, we all had plans on how we'd leave. Since a failed mission meant the alien object would destroy the city three days later, staying under those circumstances was suicide.

Government agencies announced that if *SLEDGE* failed, all personnel—law enforcement, fire and rescue departments, civil defense workers, medical personnel, and the National Guard— would pull out on October 14th. On the same date, the military would enforce a strict no-fly zone over the area, and private boats would be allowed to operate only if they were engaged in evacuation activities. The network wanted me to depart immediately, but Warren was planning to stay until the 14th to back up and secure our systems. I wasn't going to leave without him, so I called a friend of mine and asked him to be ready to transport us on his yacht to Holland, MI. He assured me he'd be there, and he had friends who could help us if something went wrong.

Four days before *SLEDGE* was scheduled to reach *Perun's Hammer*, the alien spaceship was finally spotted by a terrestrial observer. He notified the International Asteroid Warning Network. Other astronomers confirmed the sighting and calculated where its trajectory ended: right in the heart of Chicago. The Intelligence had been right, all along. If David Clancy had waited until then to approve the mission, there simply wouldn't have been enough time to intercept the object.

I visited Angela just before the memory care unit evacuated to Minneapolis. She was on her deck overlooking the lake, but her binoculars were in her lap, and she seemed sad. Molly told me that Angela hadn't been talking much lately, and rarely looked for ships anymore. I sat down next to her, but she didn't notice. She sighed, tapped her fingers on the arm of her chair, then saw me.

"How did *you* get in here?" she demanded.

"Hi Angela, I'm a friend. I wanted to stop by and say 'hello'." This appeared to mollify her. "It's a beautiful day," I said, trying to make conversation.

"Mmm," she agreed.

There was another long silence as she gazed out on the lake. "My husband told the story."

"Did you see that on television?"

She seemed confused, as though trying to recall how she knew. "N-no... I just know he did. He promised me, and he never breaks a promise. Not to me." Something startled her. She gasped and reached for her binoculars, pointing them high up into the sky, east of Chicago. There was nothing there, but I studied her movements as she appeared to track something falling from the sky.

"Oh my," she said, breathlessly. "Such a huge fireball!"

I knew better than to disregard Angela's visions. I wanted to know what she was seeing, but I couldn't push her. She'd tell me in her own time. Or not at all. Finally, she put the binoculars back into her lap and resumed staring across the water.

"What did you see, Angela?" I asked, gently.

After a long pause, she said, very softly, "A fireball."

"Did it hit Chicago?"

She didn't reply.

"Is Chicago okay?"

She pointed to the skyline in the distance. "It's fine," she answered, confused. "It's right there. Can't you see it?" The vision of the fireball was lost in her memory.

For another hour, my wife and I sat next to each other, but we were strangers. The love I still felt for her wasn't returned in even the smallest of ways. Finally, I got up to leave, put my hand on her bony shoulder, and told her goodbye. She was startled for a moment, then turned to me and smiled. I caught my breath when she addressed me by name.

"Rich, do you remember the cascarones we bought in Carnival in Mexico?"

I searched desperately for recognition in her eyes, but there was none. *How can she see me, and say my name, but not know who I am?* I recovered from the shock and thought of the question she'd asked me. Cascarones are hollowed-out, painted, and decorated chicken eggs—the Mexican version of Easter eggs. We'd bought several filled with confetti at Carnival one year and wound up playing "dodge the Cascaron" in our hotel room. We made quite a mess.

"Yes, Angela. I remember the cascarones."

"My husband and I thought they were very fun," she recalled, with a note of sadness.

I wasn't her husband anymore. Instead, I was a stranger, to whom she was telling a story involving her husband and a vacation from long ago.

"What made you think of cascarones?"

She paused and tilted her head. Ignoring my question, she said fondly, "They were so pretty." Then she added, earnestly, "But quite fragile."

SLEDGE reached *Perun's Hammer* right on schedule. It made its final approach on October 12th, the two spacecraft moving towards each other with a combined closing speed of 36.6 kilometers per second—a blazing 81,872 miles per hour.

Like its predecessor, *DART, SLEDGE* carried an observational satellite in a spring-loaded box. *SLEDGE*'s version was called *LICIA2*. There was a very good chance that *LICIA2* would be destroyed by debris when *Perun's Hammer* shattered, but scientists hoped it would provide detailed imagery of the impact first.

SLEDGE was scheduled to intercept the alien spacecraft at 2:02 p.m., Chicago time. Most of the *RECON* staff had already left the city. The remaining group gathered in our largest conference room.* On the screen, we watched Mission Control, located at the Johns

---

* Large portions of this section are adapted from the actual *DART* event. Many thanks to the great people who worked on that mission; their brilliance and dialogue is far better than any the author could have imagined on his own.

Hopkins Applied Physics Laboratory (APL), the same group that had managed the *DART* mission. *SLEDGE*, nearly identical to its predecessor, was about the size of a vending machine. On either side of the box, roll-out solar arrays protruded about twenty-eight feet on extendable arms, providing the electricity needed to power the spacecraft's electronics.

As we watched, Dr. Melinda Munoz, the APL Mission Systems Engineer, announced that the sixth and final trajectory correction maneuver had been completed successfully. We were entering what APL called the *terminal phase*.

Terminal for Perun's Hammer, *I hope.*

The television screen was almost entirely black, but in the middle was a small, round dot that slowly changed intensity. Eliza nudged me and pointed excitedly. "That's *Perun's Hammer*!"

Even though we'd seen it up close, thanks to the Intelligence, this was different. Now, we were watching it through a camera on a manmade spacecraft. Humanity was defending itself from an imminent threat from outer space for the first time in history.

"Team, it's one hour to impact," Munoz said. She sat behind a large monitor at a console and conveyed a very high level of competence. "We'll now do our first status poll as scheduled. Image quality?"

A voice answered: "High resolution on the object, with consistent brightness and a stable track."

"Acknowledged," Munoz replied. "SMART Nav?"

"SMART Nav projects a miss distance of thirty meters. We expect a maneuver when we transition in about ten minutes."

I leaned over to Eliza. "They're going to miss by thirty meters?"

She shook her head. "No, it means the maximum miss from the target point is thirty meters. Given the size of *Perun's Hammer*, that's a bullseye, and *SLEDGE* will deliver its full impact on target."

"Guidance, navigation, and control?" Munoz asked.

A male voice replied, "GNC is nominal."

"All right, let's see...autonomy?"

"Autonomy is nominal. Heaters are cycling."

"DSM?"

"DSM looks good."

"Ground system?"

"Ground system is nominal, with a clear vision of *Perun's Hammer*."

"Confirmed. One more poll after this. In the meantime, we're planning to transition in fifteen minutes to locking, so standby."

Eliza nodded approvingly so I asked her, "What are they transitioning to?"

"Target lock. That's when the optical targeting system has enough data to take over all tracking of the spacecraft, to guide it into *Perun's Hammer*. Once it's locked onto the object, *SLEDGE* is going to nail *Hammer*—hopefully." She smiled, nervously.

Minutes later, APL announced it had achieved target lock. Eliza was probably the only one in the room who knew what that meant, but when she jumped up and started clapping, the excited but anxious crowd of *RECON* employees quickly joined her.

At thirty minutes before impact, Melinda Munoz took the second and final status poll. Now the screen was split into two windows. On the right side, the camera on *SLEDGE's* nose showed the fast-approaching *Perun's Hammer*. On the left was the view from *LICIA2*, which had moved perpendicularly so it could see the length of *Perun's Hammer*. The derelict, alien spacecraft appeared identical to the way it did in the video from the Intelligence: Smooth, cylindrical, a very dark gray, with dents on one side that we could see every few minutes as it tumbled awkwardly through space.

Melinda Munoz began speaking again. "We are now two and a half minutes from impact and SMART Nav has stopped maneuvering the spacecraft. *SLEDGE* is now coasting towards *Perun's Hammer*."

I'm sure there was a lot of tension in mission control, but it was almost unbearable in our conference room. I was certain that, all over the world, people were glued to their screens. I thought about the years of dedicated work by astronomers, engineers, and astrophysicists, who had developed the technology that enabled this incredible mission.

On the right side of the split screen, we could see *Perun's Hammer* growing in size. The object began to fill the screen, while the side view from *LICIA2* showed it still tumbling along. A male voice came from APL. "Control system is settling down. Angular rates look really good. Our projected miss distance is twenty-one meters."

And then the entire right side of the screen was filled by *Perun's Hammer*, and the last image was half spacecraft and half red pixels— meaning *SLEDGE* had struck its target right in the middle of a frame. Everyone in the room stood and cheered. After all the tension, it was impossible not to react to a direct hit. But it was still muted. No one was ready to break into an unrestrained celebration until we were certain *Perun's Hammer* had been destroyed.

I turned my attention to the view from *LICIA2*. From that perspective, *Perun's Hammer* hadn't changed at all. At first, I thought the signal was delayed, but as the alien spacecraft kept tumbling on and on exactly as before, the professional chatter from Mission Control died down to an ominous silence. In the *RECON* conference room, we stared at the object as though willing it to shatter.

Perun's Hammer hadn't broken apart. I couldn't even see any cracks. No telltale debris or liquids spewed from it. It was as though the whole mission had never happened. Eliza's face was covered in disbelief.

"Wait—" I yelled, confused. "We *missed* it? How can that be? *SLEDGE* ran right into it!"

She shook her head. "I...I don't know what happened. We hit it. We *hit* it. But there's no sign of any damage." She stopped to think.

"I have to call ORCCA and find out if we changed its trajectory." She started to leave, then stopped and turned to me.

"*SLEDGE* is gone. *Gone.* We don't have any other options. Unless we slowed it down or knocked it off course, *Perun's Hammer* is going to destroy Chicago in three days."

27

SELF PRESERVATION

"It passed *through Perun's Hammer*?" I exclaimed in shock. It was 5:15 a.m. and I was in my office with Eliza, Carl, Beth, and Warren. We'd been up all night. David Clancy was on speaker phone, still at APL, as they waded through the imagery downloaded from a wide assortment of terrestrial and space-based instruments. But only *LICIA2* had a close enough view to show what had happened.

"Yes," Clancy said. "We thought there was more than a 93% chance *SLEDGE* would destroy the spacecraft, and the rest of the risk assumed the shell might be so hard we couldn't penetrate it. It never occurred to any of us that we'd shoot right through it."

No one spoke for a minute as we processed this information. Finally, Eliza asked, "So that means *SLEDGE* is still out there? Is it communicating?"

"It's still out there, but it's not communicating," Clancy replied. "But even slight contact would rip off its antenna, so that doesn't mean anything. In the imagery from *LICIA2*, we can see *SLEDGE* pass neatly through the center of the object and fly out the other side. It barely slowed down, which means it didn't transfer any energy to *Perun's Hammer*. It's early, but we haven't yet detected any change in the object's trajectory."

"David," I asked, "does the fragile structure of *Perun's Hammer* mean it won't make such a devastating impact when it hits us?" That didn't square with the videos from the Intelligence, but now we had new information.

"I don't know if it's fragile. It's constructed from something we don't understand. We've consulted with the best materials engineers in the world, and their best guess is that *Perun's Hammer* is made from a *non-Newtonian solid*. We don't have those on Earth yet, but we might in another decade or two. The best analogy would be *non-Newtonian fluids*, which we've already engineered."

"Non-Newtonian? What's that mean?"

"Non-Newtonian fluids disobey Newton's viscosity law. For all other liquids, stress doesn't affect their viscosity. Throwing a rock into a swimming pool doesn't make the water thicker or thinner, it just flows around the rock. But non-Newtonian fluids become thicker under stress, and this can happen instantly. There are types of body armor that are filled with non-Newtonian fluids. They're soft and pliable until they're struck. Then they turn rock hard so quickly, they can stop a bullet."

"How does this relate to what happened with *SLEDGE*?"

"If it's a non-Newtonian solid, it works in reverse. It's strong, rigid, and durable most of the time, but if it's struck by a high speed planetesimal, an asteroid, or—to put a point on it—*SLEDGE*, it liquifies or separates, allowing the object to pass through, hardening again afterwards. Instead of trying to design a craft so strong that it can resist any impact, which could be impossible, the Intelligence likely used a material that allows very high-speed objects to pass right through it. The engineers we consulted came up with several alternatives for the nature of the non-Newtonian material, but they think the most likely answers are that the craft is constructed from a phase-shifting or metastable material that can make a solid-liquid transition. Or it's made of nanobots with selective permeability."

Eliza considered that for a moment. "If it's nanobots, they could soften selectively on a molecular level in the area of impact. Their response would be instantaneous, even anticipatory. A craft like that would be more durable in the long run. If you're planning to leave it in space for thousands of years, then impacts become more likely. With a non-Newtonian solid, you'd have virtually no long-term damage from asteroid or planetesimal strikes."

"That's our best guess right now," Clancy replied. "The problem is that the same material may be totally impervious to other forces, including atmospheric pressure. It may have allowed *SLEDGE* to pass right through it as though it wasn't even there, and still survive a fall through the atmosphere and destroy Chicago."

"Did *SLEDGE* leave any punctures?" Eliza asked.

"Yes, it did. Big holes. The non-Newtonian material opened up quite a bit from where *SLEDGE* entered and exited the object. And you're thinking along the same lines we are. We're hopeful that, even though we didn't destroy *Perun's Hammer*, maybe the punctures *SLEDGE* left will allow air and heat to enter the object when it comes into our atmosphere. That might burn it up, or break it apart, before it reaches Chicago. The problem is that those holes are, well, healing."

"What do you mean, *healing*?" I asked, incredulous.

"They're slowly closing up again. Which is what you'd expect a non-Newtonian structure to do after it's punctured. Nanobots, for example, would instantly begin repairing the shell. We're not sure how fast, but ground-based observers think the holes are getting smaller."

"That sounds like some kind of miracle material," I told him, not quite believing what I was hearing.

"It's not unprecedented. The U.S. military has been using self-sealing fuel tanks in aircraft since World War II. Machine gun bullets pass through them and the tanks stop leaking almost instantly. Like non-Newtonian solids, it's just a material sciences problem, and nanobots are lot more advanced than the material in aviation gas tanks. You have to remember that even though this object is probably extremely old, the civilization that made it was technologically advanced far beyond us at the time it was launched."

Something didn't add up for me. "Here's what I don't understand. I get the idea of building *Perun's Hammer* out of non-Newtonian material, but wouldn't the people—well, passengers—get killed by objects flying through the ship?"

"I think our assumptions about that were wrong, Rich. My best guess is that it was some sort of communications buoy, and the shape wasn't to create a gravity field inside, but to enable 360-degree broadcasting and reception."

"If it's made of this exotic material, then how did it get dented?" I asked.

"Somewhere in its travels," Clancy explained, "which, keep in mind, could have started millions of years ago, it must have been smacked by something really big. Chances are that object hit it at a relatively slow speed, just a glancing blow, which knocked it off course and towards Earth. That object—probably an asteroid—put permanent dents in *Perun's Hammer*. But now we can make an educated guess as to why there aren't any holes or tears from that collision. They healed up over time."

"Wait a minute," Warren interjected. "If this was a communications buoy, maybe the Intelligence is still using it. Maybe it's a vital link in the network used to send us the videos. I mean all of them. The ones from the future, the ones from the past, and the PDVs!"

"What makes you think that?" I asked.

Warren continued. "I have friends who were going to stay in Chicago. But after *SLEDGE's*...uh...problems, some of them decided to evacuate, too. But here's the thing. They still had their PDVs, even though they had driven to St. Louis. So, I asked them to delete their videos, and they didn't come back. It's like the PDVs don't work at all anymore."

"Did you hear that, David?" I asked.

"I did and that is extremely interesting. Who said that, by the way?"

"That was Warren, our technology guru."

"That's very helpful, Warren," Clancy said. "Are you saying the PDVs stopped disappearing abruptly? Around the time *SLEDGE* passed through *Perun's Hammer*?"

"I think so!" Warren exclaimed. "The timing seems about right for that to be the case."

"That's bad news," Eliza said. "If it was an essential component in their communications network and *SLEDGE* disabled it, then they can no longer show us what's going to happen. Now we don't know if *Perun's Hammer* is going to destroy Chicago or not."

I was confused. "If *SLEDGE* didn't cause any permanent damage, how could it be knocked out of commission?"

"I think it needs a complete hull to operate," Warren said. "Maybe if the spacecraft has holes in it, it's like opening a circuit. It stops *Perun's Hammer* from communicating."

David Clancy cut in. "Or it could be that the object switches into a 'limp' mode that diverts all its energy into the repair process until it's completed. Warren, can you call several of your friends who are still planning to risk it by staying in Chicago? As many as you can find, and ask them to delete their PDVs?"

"Sure," Warren answered.

"How does this help us?" I asked David.

"Well, all I can say is that I hope those PDVs stay deleted. Because if they do, it means there's a chance that Warren's right and the Intelligence isn't showing us new images of the future because they can't. Or that Chicago will survive *Perun's Hammer*. If they *do* come back, it means the Intelligence can see the future, and Chicago isn't in it."

Warren started making calls and over the next couple of hours, the answers came in. Deleted PDVs weren't coming back. Warren tried to explain to his friends that this might be simply because *Perun's Hammer* had been taken offline, but most of them insisted it meant that *SLEDGE* had done its job.

Overall, though, this gave us hope. We did *not* have confirmation that *Perun's Hammer* would spare Chicago. But we also did not have confirmation that it would destroy the city. Chicago still had a chance—or, at least, we weren't sure that it didn't.

When *SLEDGE* failed to shatter *Perun's Hammer*, most of the people who remained in Chicago decided to leave—all at the same time. City agencies were quickly overwhelmed by the sheer volume of traffic. To expedite the mass exodus, the city changed all the major roads to one way—out of the city.

I sent everyone to safety, including Beth, Carl, and the rest of the *RECON* team. Warren told me that Jessica had driven to Holland, Michigan and would meet us there when we arrived. Eliza and a group of scientists had been staying at Northwestern University, making observations and setting up experiments in preparation for the arrival of the alien spacecraft. They flew to Boulder, Colorado where they'd watch *Perun's Hammer* do—well, whatever it was going to do.

About noon the day before *Perun's Hammer* arrived, I called Warren from my office. He was wrapping up, and we planned to meet in the lobby to walk to the Chicago Yacht Club, a few blocks due east of us. My friend had anchored his boat a couple of hundred yards offshore and would briefly dock when we arrived. He didn't want to risk being hijacked by some desperate straggler while he waited. However, things had grown less chaotic. Authorities reported that the congestion had largely dissipated, and they predicted that everyone who wanted to leave could do so. Some people had cut it dangerously close, considering the expected impact zone.

I finished packing up my briefcase and walked over to the windows of my office one last time. I studied the city. It was hard to believe it could all be wiped out tomorrow. Sadness, frustration, and anger overtook me. The universe was so large, and in that context, Chicago was miniscule. I'd learned that more than 6,000 meteors hit Earth annually, and about one per year blows up in the air with the power of an atomic bomb. However, most of these objects land in the ocean. After all, the Earth is 75% water. If that broken craft landed in, say, the Pacific, the damage would be minor or nonexistent. Why Chicago?

I turned from the window, walked out of my office lost in thought, and headed to the elevator. Warren was waiting in the lobby, carrying a duffel bag. He smiled when I got off the elevator, and I frowned back at him. How could he possibly be so upbeat when our city was about to be destroyed?

"Hey, Rich!" he called, waving to me even though we were the only people in the building.

"What are you so happy about?"

He grinned, broadly. "I think that old, alien spaceship is going to burn up in the atmosphere."

"Really, why?" I led Warren out the back door. We made our way to the sidewalk and began walking briskly towards the harbor. We didn't really need to hurry, but now that we were leaving, I wanted to get out quickly.

Warren continued. "I think *Perun's Hammer* is just a giant

antenna. Maybe not for radio waves or any other technology we know about yet. But I don't think there's anything important inside of it. In fact, I don't think there's any structure to it except the shell. I checked in again with some of my friends, and none of their deleted PDVs have come back, even for people who are still planning to stay in Chicago. So, it probably still has holes in it."

I shrugged. "Maybe it's not working because *SLEDGE* knocked something loose on the inside. The self-healing shell might have made the structure of the object as strong as ever by now, but there's something else broken."

Warren shook his head. "I don't think so. If *SLEDGE* had struck anything, it would have either slowed down or been redirected when it exited *Perun's Hammer*. But that didn't happen."

The streets of downtown Chicago were emptying out. We made our way south to Monroe, then crossed a nearly traffic-free Michigan Avenue. As we walked past Crown Fountain, I could see a crowd gathered below Nichols Bridgeway on the south side of the road. They were holding signs and chanting: *Jesus > Perun* protesters. I guided Warren north, towards Lurie Garden. That took us around the protesters, and the foliage would provide some cover.

We were walking by Cloud Gate, the giant, mirrored sculpture popularly called, "The Bean," when I saw a woman wearing a *Jesus > Perun* t-shirt coming towards us. She stopped and stared at me, her eyes growing wide with hatred. Then she screamed and waved at the other protesters a block ahead of us. *"It's Rich Penton! It's Rich Penton!"*

It dawned on me that I'd been so preoccupied when I left my office that I'd forgotten put on the sunglasses, Cubs hat, and face-mask I'd planned to wear. She had recognized me from half a block away. Warren and I stopped, dumbfounded, as the protesters dropped their banners and flags and began running towards us.

"Oh, shit!" I cried. "We have to get out of here!" We began running back towards the *RECON* building. We had no choice—

there were dozens of protesters between us and the Chicago Yacht Club, and there was no way we could escape all of them. Warren had no difficulty separating himself from the charging crowd, but I'm no slowpoke either, and we managed to widen the distance between us and most of the protesters. We crossed Michigan Avenue at a full sprint with the mob still comfortably behind us when we reached the *RECON* building.

At the entrance, I bent over, hands on my knees, breathing hard as Warren scrambled to pull his ID badge from around his neck. I heard the locking mechanism release and stood upright to find myself eye to eye with a *Perun's Hammer* protester. He must have come around the corner of the building on his way to join the others and walked right into us. He was halfway through a massive swing with a baseball bat, aimed where my head had been moments earlier. When I stood up, it was too late for him to change the trajectory.

The aluminum bat struck my left knee with such force that it buckled backwards. I felt ligaments tearing. I cried out and fell onto my destroyed knee as he screamed, "Go back to hell, Satan!" and wound up to hit me again. Warren spun around, ripped the bat from the man's hands and struck him across the chest so hard I could hear ribs cracking. The attacker shrieked in pain and fell onto the side-walk, moaning.

"Oh, crap," Warren said, urgently. He pulled me from the side-walk and wrapped my left arm over his shoulder. "We have to get inside."

The protesters were closing in as Warren practically carried me through the door. He made sure it was locked behind us and we struggled to the elevator. With no one in the building, one of the cars opened immediately. He helped me hobble inside and eased me into a sitting position with my back against the wall. As the doors slid shut, I could see the protesters outside, trying to smash the front door open with signs, sticks and bats.

"Can they get in?" I gasped, grimacing as the pain began to push past the adrenaline.

Warren was still catching his breath. I watched the floor numbers count off, trying to concentrate on anything but the pain. "Maybe," he replied. "But I can shut down the elevator power, so they'll have to climb forty-six stories to get to us. And I can lock down the interior doors." He thought for a moment. "I think I can make sure they can't reach us."

The elevator door opened, and Warren helped me to my feet, supporting me on one side as I hobbled towards my office. The pain was excruciating. "Warren... I'm not going anywhere with this knee and that mob outside. And there aren't any cops or ambulances and Chicago's a no-fly zone."

Warren unlocked the door with my badge and half carried me inside, where he eased me onto the floor next to my desk. I laid down with a groan. Sharp pains shot out of my knee and, when I tried to bend it seeking relief, I almost passed out from the agony.

Warren shuffled through my drawers. "Do you have any painkillers?"

I forced myself to focus. "Just some Advil. Top right drawer."

He retrieved it, grabbed a half-full bottle of water from my desk and fed me four of the pills. Then he took a pair of scissors from my desk and cut my slacks off above the knee.

"Oh, man." His face was painted with concern. "He really did a number on you. It's swollen to twice its normal size. You're going to need major surgery." I stole a look down at my purple knee and felt sick to my stomach. I dropped my head back on the floor as Warren jumped up.

"I'll be back with some ice. Then I have to lock down the doors, in case those protesters make it up here." Minutes later, he wrapped a towel with ice around my knee and raced away again. The pain was so intense that I just laid on the floor and sobbed.

What seemed like a long time later, Warren returned. I came out of my stupor as he knelt by me and reassured me that we were safe. "I shut off the elevators and turned off the lights in the stairwells. They don't know what floor we're on, and if they try to break in anywhere, it'll be on forty-three, because that's what the lobby sign says. Years ago, we installed doors designed to keep out active shooters. Those protesters aren't getting in here without explosives, and I doubt many of them are going to climb up more than forty flights of stairs to try."

What he was saying barely penetrated through the fog, but I got enough of it to understand that we were probably safe from the protesters. But of course, we had much bigger problems. "Warren," I grimaced through the pain. "You have to leave. *Perun's Hammer* is going to destroy this place tomorrow. Use the back door or the VIP entrance but *get out of here*."

He kept talking, as though he hadn't heard me. "I rifled through about a hundred desks until I found a bottle of Percocet. It says to take one pill but, in your condition, I think you should take two."

"Give me three," I groaned.

"You sure?"

I nodded. Warren spilled the pills into my shaking palm, and I managed to get them into my mouth as he helped me take a swig of water to wash them down.

"Listen to me," I tried again. "There's no point in both of us dying here. Get out, *please*. Thank you for saving my life again, but now you *have* to save your own. My phone is in my pocket. Call my friend and have him meet you on the Chicago River. Leave now and find Jessica. Call Eliza and tell her what happened. Tell her I love her —I love her more than anything. I'll call her when I'm not in so much pain. I don't want her to hear me this way."

"I'll call her right now," he assured me. "And Jessica."

I was in agony as Warren pulled my phone from my pocket and left to make the calls. He returned with more ice for the towel and some coats he'd scrounged from around the office. He gently cushioned my head and then sat down next to me. It bothered me that he wasn't leaving.

"Warren...thanks for everything but it's time for you to go."

"I will," he reassured me. "I'll just wait a few minutes, okay? Now, get some sleep. Sleep, Rich."

The Percocet was working on my pain, and I let consciousness slip away from me as Warren sat next to me on the floor of my office.

28

HAMMER TIME

Day of Arrival

It was dark when I awoke, and I was confused about where I was. When I tried to sit up, the searing pain in my knee made me catch my breath, and it all came back to me. I laid back down, hearing my own anguish vocalized as a half-cry, half moan. I saw nothing but the distant reflections of city lights in my windows and the glow of the night lighting coming through my office door. The building *felt* empty, and a terrible wave of loneliness swept over me.

I heard a rustling sound coming from inside my office and I froze. Did one of the protesters make it into the building?

A voice called out. "You okay?"

"Warren?"

"Yeah."

"What the hell are you doing here? You should have left hours ago!"

"I couldn't leave."

I missed his meaning. "Are the protesters still outside the building?"

"I don't know. I haven't looked for a while."

And then I knew Warren hadn't stayed because he *couldn't* leave, but because he *wouldn't*.

"Damn it, Warren. Thank you. You're a good man. But you have to go."

We argued, keeping our voices low for some reason, but it was no use. Since I was stuck here, Warren wasn't going anywhere. Hours ago, he'd called my friend with the boat to tell him neither of us were coming.

"I wish you'd left," I told him. "But as long as you're here, can you get me more Percocet?"

The morning sun rose across the lake and cast crimson light through the windows of my office. Warren had found more coats to make a bed for me, but I was achy and stiff from the uncomfortable night on the floor. I lay there miserable for a few minutes before Warren walked in with coffee, plastic-wrapped cinnamon rolls from a vending machine, and crutches he'd found in a closet. He helped me to the men's room and back, and I collapsed in my office chair with my broken knee propped up.

The Percocet kept the pain down to the point where I didn't have to focus on it constantly, but I needed surgery soon—or would if we somehow survived *Perun's Hammer*. When Warren checked the security cameras, he saw a growing number of protesters outside the building. With law enforcement evacuated, there was nothing we could do about it.

He sat across from me while we ate our breakfast. As I sipped my coffee, I thought back to the discussion we were having before we were spotted by the protestors. "You said that *Perun's Hammer* is just a shell. But I don't know, Warren. In the video the

Intelligence sent us, it did a lot of damage for something that's hollow."

"Well, it's *huge*," he countered. "Like seven hundred feet long and three hundred feet around. If it survives the fall through the atmosphere, and all that pressure builds up inside of it, of course it's going to do a lot of damage when it hits."

I pondered that for a moment. "You heard what David said about the material it's made from. He called it a non-Newtonian solid? And you think that those two punctures by *SLEDGE* are enough to make it vulnerable? That doesn't seem like a very durable communications buoy for an advanced civilization."

"Oh, I don't think it would be offline forever, if it wasn't about to land right here. I think it's self-healing, but I bet it takes a while. After all, that thing has been in space for who knows how long—a million years? It might take months for those punctures from *SLEDGE* to fully heal, but for a million-year asset, that's high service level performance."

"And until then, you think it's vulnerable?"

"Not to space rocks. If David's right, it could get hit by those over and over again and repair itself. But I think it's vulnerable to burning up in an atmosphere like Earth's, if those holes *SLEDGE* made are still open. It'll be facing a ton of atmospheric pressure and friction soon, and that will ignite it inside and out. It may be heat shielded on the exterior, but it won't be on the interior." He grinned at me. "In our atmosphere, *Perun's Hammer* is as fragile as a cascaron."

My coffee cup was halfway to my lips, but I froze, holding it there, stunned. "What did you just say?"

"I said in our atmosphere, it's as fragile as a cascaron. You know what that is?"

I didn't answer.

"What, Rich?"

"It's really strange. I haven't heard that word in years, but in my last conversation with Angela, she mentioned some cascarones we bought years ago in Mexico. And how fragile they were."

He shrugged his big shoulders and smiled. "Wow. Maybe that's a sign."

"You said that was just part of your theory. What's the rest?"

"Well, there's a reason we call the Intelligence 'the Intelligence.' Eliza even calls it *ultima veritas,* because it knows everything."

"Sure. *They* know what's going to happen. But if you're right, they can't show us anymore, because we disabled the communications beacon they were using to send us messages."

"Okay, Rich, but the Intelligence knew the only thing we could do was send an impactor like *SLEDGE* to punch holes in *Perun's Hammer.* And they must have known that would be enough to make sure their old spacecraft didn't destroy Chicago. Otherwise, why would they have even tried to warn us?"

Maybe the whole point was to get us to evacuate Chicago because that's all we could do, I thought. "That makes sense," I said instead. "But since we've lost the ability to receive signals from the Intelligence, there's no way for us to know for sure until *Perun's Hammer* shows up"

When we were done eating, Warren stepped out to call Jessica and I dialed Eliza's number.

"Hi." Her voice trembled. She'd been crying.

"Hello."

"Rich, it's not too late."

She sounded scared and on the verge of panic. I'd never heard her this way.

"Please find a way to get out. Get out...please. I can't lose you, especially not like this." She was overwhelmed with despair. Before I could answer, she continued, the words spilling out. "You saved millions of lives, Rich. It's not fair that you can't get away. But I've called everyone—Chicago police, the National Guard, private helicopter services—and none of them will fly in to save you! The city's shut off!"

"It's okay," I tried to soothe her. "I just can't—"

"And you're hurt. My god, Warren told me what that man did to you. How bad is the pain?"

"It's not too bad," I lied. "But we're trapped in the building by *Jesus > Perun* protesters."

"No, no no. This can't be happening. Rich, don't leave me, please. Please don't leave me." She broke into sobs, and my heart broke into pieces. I talked to Eliza for a long, long time. We reminisced about some of our favorite times together, talked about how much we loved each other, and I told her how important it would be to move on when I was gone. That made her cry again, so I changed the subject to Warren's theory, and she acted a little brave and tried to sound hopeful.

But I knew Eliza didn't believe any more than I did that Warren and I would be alive tomorrow.

It was less than two hours before the arrival of *Perun's Hammer* when we heard people testing the stairwell doors. The protesters must have made their way into the building, and at least a few had climbed up to try to get into our offices. They failed, but we'd been hoping to sneak down to the basement, and now we were stuck on the 47th floor of the *RECON* tower—not ideal, considering the building was likely to be destroyed soon.

Twenty minutes before impact, Warren rolled my chair over to the windows facing Lake Michigan. "We're going to stay several feet back to avoid flying glass. And here, wear these." He handed me sunglasses. "They'll protect your eyes from the brightness of the object—and any debris if the windows shatter." All of this sounded like the least of our worries. Then Warren dragged my conference table over and flipped it on its side in front of us. He planned to pull me down behind it in case the windows blew out. He fetched my crutches and leaned them against the table in front of me.

Eliza had shown me where *Perun's Hammer* would travel across the sky, so we pointed our chairs in that direction and waited. Warren walked to the window. "There's lots of protesters still in the streets. And I can see people on some of the buildings."

"Crazy bastards."

"The protesters, or the people on the buildings?"

"All of 'em."

Warren came back around the overturned table and sat down next to me. I checked my watch, and the seconds ticked away. It seemed to take forever for the fateful moment to arrive, but finally Warren pointed and yelled, "There it is!"

We saw an enormous, yellow ball streaking towards us from slightly south of due east. It was very high in the sky, and it was extraordinarily bright—much brighter than the Sun. Even with sunglasses, you could hardly look directly at it.

"It's still in one piece!" I yelled. It was terrifying. The object was so large that it made an enormous fireball, just as Angela had described during our last visit. It only took seconds to shoot across the sky towards us, but the terror and accompanying adrenaline rush seemed to slow down time. I felt like I was watching a movie frame by frame, as the giant, burning object came closer, bringing what seemed like certain doom to the great city of Chicago. I was paralyzed with fear, convinced we were living the last seconds of our lives. I only hoped when the end came, it would be swift and painless.

Thanks to the videos we'd received from the Intelligence, we knew that if the object's non-Newtonian structure held together, the enormous pressure inside *Perun's Hammer* would turn it into the largest bomb in the history of the world when it exploded on impact. As we learned later, the holes *SLEDGE* punched into *Perun's*

Hammer hadn't yet fully closed. The gases venting from its punctures ignited into two massive jets of flame as atmospheric friction superheated the object. This steadily released the built-up pressure into the sky, instead of as an explosion on the ground. The intense heat consumed all of the air inside of *Perun's Hammer*, creating a powerful vacuum.

Instead of exploding, the spacecraft *imploded*. Having lost its aerodynamic shape, the wrecked spacecraft faced much more wind resistance and rapidly lost velocity and altitude. It finally ended its journey—one that began millions of miles away and a long time ago —not in the city of Chicago, but about three miles offshore, in Lake Michigan.

It hit with tremendous force. Post-event analysis estimated that more than a hundred million pounds of material, still moving at twenty-two thousand miles an hour even as it slowed due to atmospheric friction, knifed through the water and cut deep into the lakebed. The lake is only about two hundred and fifty feet deep in the area east of Chicago, and the impact accordioned the remains of *Perun's Hammer*, compressing it laterally to the bottom almost instantly after smashing through the water at a terrific speed. The impact created a massive hole in the water. Satellites directly overhead could see the bottom of the lake for several seconds.

The force was transmitted in all directions as an earthquake that registered 5.5 on the Richter scale in Chicago. We were knocked around as the building swayed. For a moment, we were more worried about a structural collapse than direct damage from *Perun's Hammer*. Thousands of windows across the city broke. Car and burglar alarms went off and architectural elements fell off a few buildings while the contents of houses, apartments, and businesses were shaken into disarray. Fortunately, our windows held, although two of them cracked, the sound like gunshots.

The gigantic spacecraft displaced more than 1.6 billion gallons of water in a fraction of a second, launching enormous waves in every direction. These were highly asymmetrical—the wall of water was much bigger in the direction *Perun's Hammer* was traveling than behind it.

Warren jumped up and I grabbed my crutches and hobbled around the table to the window, and we watched, slack jawed, as a ninety-foot wall of water raced towards Chicago. Since Lake Michigan is very shallow compared to an ocean, the wave only moved at about forty miles an hour; much slower than a Tsunami. I froze in terror as I watched it roll relentlessly towards us, like an unstoppable force. It covered the distance to the city in four and a half minutes, fortunately losing energy along the way. Still, it hit the shore as a 40-foot tidal wave.

It quickly swallowed Navy pier, destroying the Grand Ballroom, its belvedere towers, and the Festival Hall; tearing down the Ferris wheel, smashing windows and flattening structures all the way until it reached Gateway Park. It picked up a few small cruise ships still docked along the pier and swept them into the city, where they tumbled into the streets and smashed into buildings.

We were awestruck as the gigantic wave enveloped The Art Institute, the water curling around the front of the building until the historic, stone lions at the entrance were submerged. We watched in horror as a large crowd of *Perun's Hammer* protesters, who had been staring at the object's impact in the lake, suddenly turned and fled towards the city as the wall of water approached. The wave swept over them and roared on. I saw The Bean tumbling over and over, until it floated off and was finally deposited in front of Remington's Restaurant, on Michigan Avenue. The water rushed underneath us and turned Marshall and other streets into swirling whitewater rapids, flowing away from the lake. Downtown Chicago is graced with numerous rivers and canals which run many feet below the streets of the city. These arteries swallowed most of the water and directed the flows along their lengths, preventing the worst flooding from extending further west.

We didn't witness it, but south of us, the wave crashed through the glass walls of the Shedd Oceanarium, releasing thousands of non-native species into Lake Michigan, most doomed to die in the fresh water. Adler Planetarium was nearly destroyed, and the rising waters drenched the Field Museum before racing across Lake Shore Drive, drowning Buckingham Fountain, and then disappearing from our view as it washed around Soldier Field.

Chicago's South Side was hit by a deluge that smashed through the windows of the Museum of Science and Industry, flooding its lower levels, temporarily refloating the museum's prized World War II German submarine, the *U-505*. Cities like Gary, Indiana and Muskegon, Ludington and Holland, Michigan suffered minor water damage. The Wisconsin shores saw swells of several feet, although many communities were elevated enough to see only minor damage.

When it was all over, more than 1,800 people died from *Perun's Hammer's* violent demise in Lake Michigan. Ironically, these were mostly *Jesus > Perun* protesters, caught in the streets when the wave struck. In a further irony, the presence of protesters outside the doors of *RECON* saved our lives. We would have drowned in the basement, because the first two floors of the building were flooded.

Property damage added up to more than eight billion dollars—analogous to a mild hurricane. But compared to the utter destruction of Chicago and most of northern Illinois, the damage caused by the giant, alien craft striking earth seemed very minor.

As we looked out the windows of my office, watching the water running through the streets of the city, my racing heart begin to slow down. Our city had only been wounded, not wiped off the map. Neither of us spoke until the water stopped rising and slowly began to recede.

I looked over at Warren. "Holy shit, we're still alive," I said, in disbelief.

His face was covered with a huge smile. "Of course we are! The Intelligence knows what it's doing. It's *ultima veritas*!"

EPILOGUE

My phone chimed and I pulled it from my jacket to see a text message from Warren. It was a video he'd taken with Jessica. They were vacationing in France. I pulled out my ear buds and hit the play button. Both of them wore sunglasses and hung onto each other unsteadily as Warren held the phone up high to take a video selfie. In the background, I could see a gigantic, gray industrial structure shaped oddly like a really squat, super heavy-duty Eiffel Tower.

"Hey, Rich," Warren began, slurring a little. They were giggling and struggling to hold it together. I suspect champagne was involved. "This is the Creusot steam hammer in France," he explained, loudly. "It was built in 1877, and it's still the largest hammer in the world. Well, it is now that we killed *Perun's Hammer*!" The two of them broke into uncontrolled laughter, so pleased with themselves that they were practically falling down. The image swung around crazily as Warren tried to hold onto Jessica, then the video ended. I chuckled so heartily that passengers near me glanced over curiously.

I got off at the Washington/Wells train stop. I was still limping a little, but my knee was rapidly healing from the surgery. A crazy-looking guy, who had obviously been waiting for me, walked confidently in my direction. "We tried to tell you!" he yelled smugly. "Jesus is greater than Perun!"

I grinned at him. "So is David Clancy." He opened his mouth to argue, but I brushed by him, and soon I was outside the *RECON* offices. I stopped at the corner in front of our building and admired the new street signs. We were no longer located at 20 E. Marshall Street—and not because we'd moved. Our new address was 20 E. Rich Penton Street, thank you very much. One of Chicago's more prominent roads had been named after me for my contributions in saving the city when it was threatened by *Perun's Hammer.*

But I liked the sign for the cross street even more. For nearly two hundred years, Chicago's most famous boulevard was Michigan Avenue. No more. Now it was David Clancy Avenue, and no one was more thrilled about that than me. I was happy to take a back street to the man who had *really* saved the city.

I went through security, rode the elevator up to the 46th floor, and basked in the energy of the newsroom. It buzzed with excitement as *RECON* employees put together stories from around the world. I found Beth in her office, and we visited for a little while as she updated me on several of our active investigations. Then the talk switched to her upcoming wedding, and she asked me to officiate the ceremony.

"Don't get a big head about it," Beth teased. "You're cheaper than hiring a minister *and* a rabbi." I laughed, took the elevator up a floor, and stopped to check in with my new assistant, Ethan, who was extremely competent and, as far as I could tell, unaffiliated with federal law enforcement. Then I walked into my office, went to the windows, and took in the magnificence of the City of Big Shoulders for a few minutes.

I sat down at my desk to check my email. There was an urgent announcement from our CEO. Brendan Braswell had somehow fallen out of a window in his twenty-second story Manhattan condo. Police were tentatively calling it a suicide, but it occurred to me that people who fell out of favor with the SVR often fell out of windows, too. Rosalie had been right, again. As far as I was concerned, Brendan had gotten exactly what he deserved.

I shook my head at the news, then caught up on a few emails, reviewed scripts for upcoming features, and hosted a meeting with Beth and Carl. We talked about Brendan for a while and then worked on our upcoming, in-depth feature on the Tulsa Race Massacre. I made a few calls, and Eliza arrived so we could go to lunch.

As I was picking up my wallet and sunglasses from my desk, my computer emitted a *Ding!* It stopped me in my tracks and Eliza drew in her breath. "Did you hear that?" I asked her.

She nodded. "It could be a regular file transfer from someone in the office."

I shook my head. "I don't think so. The only person close enough is Ethan." I turned towards the door and called out, "Ethan, did you just transfer a file to my computer?"

"A file to your computer?"

"Yes."

"No."

My eyes met Eliza's. She turned up her palms in a question.

"Close the door, please."

She pushed it shut and pulled a chair next to mine. I had to move several application windows out of the way to see my desktop and there it was—a video file, just like all the others. I moved the cursor over the icon and double clicked it.

The file played but there was no video, just audio. The voice was of a young woman—her voice was a little raspy, like she smoked too much, but she sounded happy, at peace, in a good place. It was a voice from what seemed like a different lifetime. A voice I hadn't heard in more than six months.

"Hey, Rich!" the woman said. "Nice job, especially for an old man! And tell the *big stud* I'm abso-frickin'-lutely thrilled for him!" She laughed and laughed, like a little girl.

Then the recording came to an end and the file disappeared.

Angela was on her balcony at the memory care facility, staring blankly at Lake Michigan. Molly sat to one side, making sure not to block her view. It was a sunny day and Molly studied her patient. Angela was emaciated now. Despite the staff's best attempts, most of the time she refused to eat anything. Her eyes seemed duller, she didn't speak often, and even the lake seemed to hold little interest to her anymore.

Molly was startled as Angela suddenly perked up. She leaned forward, her brow furrowed as she peered intently into the distance. Then she reached down clumsily, grabbing her binoculars by the strap. They spun around as Angela lifted them and it took her several seconds to straighten them out and bring them to her eyes.

Molly followed the direction Angela was peering and saw nothing. "What do you see, Angela?"

It was a few moments before Angela spoke. "Oh my...it's coming out of the water!"

Molly looked again at the empty lake in front of the facility.

"Angela," she said, gently, "There's nothing happening on the water at all." For a moment, she wondered what Angela was talking about but decided it must be the alien spacecraft. "And the...object... was destroyed when it landed in the lake."

After a long pause, Angela lowered the binoculars and looked knowingly at Molly. "It knows how to heal itself, dear." She leaned closer and whispered, "It's healing now."

THANKS & FREE OFFER

Thank you for joining me in this adventure. If you enjoyed the story, **please leave a review on Amazon**. Reviews are invaluable to authors and help other readers discover great novels to enjoy.

FREE OFFER

Want to Explore Deeper Into the Tech of *Perūn's Hammer*?
The book left you curious – and maybe a little mystified:

- How did the Intelligence create those impossible videos?
- What was Perūn's Hammer made from that let it survive re-entry into Earth's atmosphere?
- Is instant communication across space even theoretically possible?

Author Ian Heller pulls back the curtain in **Perūn's Hammer Declassified**, an exclusive Bonus Tech Brief that reveals fascinating, behind-the-scenes insights about the technology driving the story.

This seven-page deep dive answers your burning questions, explores the real-world science behind the fiction, and even provides hints about the sequel, **Perūn Rises**.

 **Free Download:** Visit ianheller.com and claim your copy today. Join the conversation, and learn what's fact, what's fiction, and what's frighteningly close to reality.

INVITE IAN TO YOUR BOOK CLUB

As a special offer to you as a reader of *Perun's Hammer*, Ian will be happy to visit your book club either by Zoom or in person.

Please contact Ian directly to schedule an appearance at your book club: ian.heller@yahoo.com

ACKNOWLEDGMENTS

I wrote *Perun's Hammer* thanks to the help and support of many individuals without whom the book simply would not have been possible.

First and foremost, I need to thank my wife of thirty-five years, Penny Heller. Penny not only spent countless evenings and weekend days without my company as I wrote but also read drafts along the way and offered many useful insights and valuable suggestions that made the book better.

My sister, Rosalind Fassett, was the most important creative muse for me as I wrote. She was grieving the loss of her husband of 40+ years, Bob, when I asked her to help me with the book and her talent for reviewing, critiquing and improving the manuscript made it immeasurably better. She turned her grief into a focus on helping me write a better story and I was honored to have her brilliant analysis and suggestions as I developed the manuscript.

My son, Austin, designed the cover, utilizing his amazing talent to help create a beautiful book. He also read the manuscript, giving me ideas that made it better.

My friend, John Pendleton, read the manuscript several times and offered not only helpful insights into the story, but some key phrases that I wove into the narrative that will stand out to the reader. The line, "This conversation was full of red flags, but they weren't Russian," is my favorite, but there are several others.

My brother, Clive, read every version of the manuscript and always offered his support, insights and encouragement. My friends,

Dale Berkbigler and Lauriann Blakeman, were similarly eager to read revised editions. The excitement these three motorcycle-riding buddies shared encouraged me to keep writing and revising to make the book as good as it could be.

Steve Tomczyk is a scientist and dear and generous friend who read the manuscript twice, offering great insights as a lover of science fiction.

I worked with several editors and experts along the way. Chloe Long, an Astrodynamics Ph.D. candidate at the University of Colorado, provided consulting on various highly technical topics. My former high school English teacher, Nancy Gill, provided expert editing on grammar. Kristen Hamilton edited an earlier version of the manuscript and Kendra Harpster at Kevin Anderson & Associates provided key insights that drove extensive revisions that made the book shorter, better and much faster moving. Eva Fox Mate did the final editing, and my friend and colleague Julie Cameron provided encouragement and support for the final manuscript. These individuals collectively made *Perun's Hammer* a much better book.

So many people read drafts and provided feedback that I hardly know where to begin acknowledging them since I know I'll inadvertently leave out key contributors. With apologies to anyone I've forgotten, I'd like to thank Steven Diaz (who provided input into how telecommunications networks operate that wound up in the narrative), Scott Boyd, Gary Slack; Sheryl Roche; Stephanie Suggs; my mom, Margaret Maxwell; my sisters, Jennifer Stohler and Yvonne Thiede; Cindy O'Keeffe; Keith Shandalow; Paul Salazar; Rick Meyers; Fidencio Montalvo; Mike Otte; Micah Armijo; Debbie Mohney; Dave Eskes; Bond Lengsfield; Geoff Gray; Mike Martz; Jim Hicklin; Tammy Tomczyk; Trish Lilly; Beth Heller; Anna Messmer; Bob Miller; Christine Burrell; Jere Brown; Kelly Stohler; Austin Garrison; Phil Clark; Nancy Markisohn and Julia Klein.

Julie Cameron recommended I work with Polly Letofsky and the team at My Word Publishing, who provided fantastic assistance in publishing and promoting the book. I strongly recommend them to any author seeking to self-publish effectively.

I very much appreciate Ric Gillespie for allowing me to base the fictional Marc Thibodeaux and the SARTA organization on him and his very real and amazing group, TIGHAR. Thanks also to Lindley Johnson of NASA for inspiring the character David Clancy as his fictional counterpart; brilliant as David is, he's a pale copy of the original.

As I conducted research for the manuscript, I read dozens of books on physics and other branches of science. These often covered highly complex topics, and I worked hard to use the concepts accurately in the book. I hope the reader will take any inaccuracies in stride and chalk them up to creative license or perhaps an occasional misunderstanding of some of the deeper ideas.

I also relied on dozens of sources including books, articles and videos to understand the historical incidents described in the book. In all cases, I attempted to describe the events accurately; of course, I had to make a few changes or assumptions here and there to fit the plot. But the reader can be confident that these tragic events largely unfolded as described and hold lessons for today that I hope their recounting in *Perun's Hammer* will help to reinforce. The demise of Amelia Earhart is more speculative, of course, but I'm convinced that Ric Gillespie's analysis is the most likely of those I've studied.

Thank you for reading *Perun's Hammer*. I hope you liked it enough to read the sequel I'm working on now.

Ian Heller
Longmont, Colorado
February 2025

ABOUT THE AUTHOR

Ian Heller lives in Longmont, Colorado, with his wife, Penny, and their three dogs. An avid motorcyclist and photographer, he's also a proud father to Austin and Blaine. Ian has founded two startups and held senior executive roles at five major corporations. He earned a B.A. in History from Roosevelt University and an MBA from Northwestern University's Kellogg School of Management.

www.ingramcontent.com/pod-product-compliance
Lightning Source LLC
Chambersburg PA
CBHW030930260626
47169CB00002B/432